THE TALLONS

BOOKS BY WILLIAM MARCH

COMPANY K
COME IN AT THE DOOR

THE

Tallons

BY

WILLIAM MARCH

The University of Alabama Press
Tuscaloosa

THE LIBRARY
OF ALABAMA
CLASSICS

The University of Alabama Press
Tuscaloosa, Alabama 35487-0380
uapress.ua.edu

Originally published 1936 by Random House

Inquiries about reproducing material from this work should be addressed to
the University of Alabama Press.

Manufactured in the United States of America
Cover design: Emma Sovich

∞

The paper on which this book is printed meets the minimum requirements of
American National Standard for Information Sciences—Permanence of Paper
for Printed Library Materials, ANSI Z39.48-1984.

Library of Congress Cataloging-in-Publication Data

March, William, 1893–1954.
The Tallons / William March.
pages cm — (Library of Alabama Classics series)
ISBN 978-0-8173-5810-5 (pbk. : alk. paper) — ISBN 978-0-8173-8825-6 (electronic)
1. Brothers—Fiction. 2. Alabama—Social life and customs—Fiction. I. Title.
PS3505.A53157T35 2014
813'.52—dc23
2014024835

TO
EDWARD GLOVER

*as a slight recompense for the gray
hairs I have put in his head.*

CHAPTER I

AFTER the Hodge brothers had bought timber rights to the land owned by the farmers of Pearl County and had built their sawmill, they had laid out a village and had erected a series of inexpensive frame dwellings for the use of their workmen. At first Hodgetown had been hideous with its copings and fluted woodwork and its canary-colored paint, but years of weather had toned it down, and the slow growth of transplanted trees had shaded it in time and softened its harshness. The streets of the new town had been named personally by Mrs. Thompson Hodge, in honor of what she, at least, believed to be the names of individual Indian tribes and the houses that lined them, ornate or simple to accord with the relative importance of their occupants, were grouped together with a military exactness of distinction.

Calumet Avenue, a short street which ran diagonal to the rest of the town, was considered the fashionable section, and on it lived Russell Hodge, the president of the corporation, in a white house with gray trimmings. Across the street from him, on the less desirable lot, lived his brother, Thompson, in a gray house with white trimmings. The fact that these houses were not painted yellow and were slightly at variance with the general pattern of the place, gave the occupants a certain distinction, as if they were not to be regulated by the ordinary rules demanded of their employees, which was precisely the impression the Hodge wives sought to create.

Flanking the homes of the two Hodge brothers lived T. L. Dolan, manager of the commissary, and Regis Batty, foreman of the planer mill; then, in the following order, came the residences of Sam Newsom, woods superintendent, and Horace Atherton who ran the lath mill on a commission basis. Wampum Street lay to the rear of Calumet Avenue, away from the more exclusive district, and it was here that Neil Bickerstaff and his family lived in a somewhat battered, two-storey house. Due to a rise in the ground, the Bickerstaff house was set a little higher than its neighbors, and from its rear windows the log-pond could be seen, with purple logs lying like defeated giants inert in the stagnant, oil-streaked water.

Neil Bickerstaff had come to Pearl County only a short time before to take a job as millwright for the Hodge brothers. He was a heavy-set man with a quantity of dark-red, tightly curling hair. He scrubbed his face and hands with a soap made to remove stains, but his thick nails were perpetually soiled and there were generally smudged traces of grease behind the lobes of his ears and about his eyes and nostrils. He seemed at first sight like an actor whose business it was to black-up for comedy, but one too careless or too harried to remove the stains his profession left upon him after his audience had gone away. For a few weeks Neil boarded at the hotel the company had built for its unsettled employees, and then, in the early spring when the weather was warmer, he moved his wife and family from their old home in Georgia.

There were six of the Bickerstaff children, but Myrtle was the eldest of the lot, and at twenty she was a slow, strongly built girl with jutting, prominent breasts and faint growths of black hair on her forearms and legs. At first she was homesick, being alien in Pearl County, and she cried a great deal for the friends she had left behind her in Georgia; but gradually she began to meet both the farming people of the county and the mill people of Hodgetown, and she became more reconciled to the new place. The first eligible young man she met was Andrew Tallon, and this was the way it came about:

8

Mrs. Ed Wrenn, the wife of one of the Pearl County farmers, was planning a dance at her place near Green Point, and some days prior she saw Myrtle at the regular weekly prayer meeting in the Hodgetown church. As a rule, Mrs. Wrenn didn't like the new people the sawmill had brought into the county. The saw-mill with its noise and its energy meant change and a passing of the security she had come to feel was necessary for her, but she was sorry for this handsome girl who sat sullenly through the services, apparently acquainted with nobody as yet. At the end of the meeting Mrs. Wrenn came up to her and touched her arm.

"You're Neil Bickerstaff's daughter, ain't you?"

"Yes, ma'am," answered Myrtle in her small voice, her words spoken with hardly any movement of her lips.

"I'm Mrs. Addie Wrenn—Ed Wrenn's wife. Mr. Wrenn and I are having a dance at our place next Saturday week in honor of our daughter Agnes, who'll be back home then on a visit. We'd be mighty glad to have you come, too, and meet some of the young folks of the county, if you feel like you want to."

Myrtle stood up in her pew, a defensive look on her face.

"I know how hard it is," continued Mrs. Wrenn. "I know how hard it is to be in a strange place amongst strangers and all; but I'm not one to withhold the right hand of fellowship, so you just come along and meet some people, and the first thing you know your new friends will take the place of the old ones left behind."

Myrtle spoke gravely: "I'll be mighty glad to come."

"All right, that's fine. That's settled," said Addie Wrenn. "We'll be expecting you."

She was a small, wasp-like woman with sandy hair which was turning gray. She wore high, starched collars about her neck even in summer, and there were circular, gold earrings in her ears. Her mouth was lipless. It was merely a small, compressed dash against her face, and wavering wrinkles radiated from it like the spidery heat marks around a child's drawing of the sun.

9

"Mr. Wrenn and I will be glad to give you the welcome of our house," she concluded with nicety; "of that you may be well assured." Myrtle lowered her eyes, the anticipation in her face expiring.

"I guess I can't come, after all," she mumbled ungraciously. Then, in explanation of her sudden change: "I don't know anybody to bring me. We only been here ten days."

"Oh," said Mrs. Wrenn lightly. "Oh, is *that* all that's keeping you away? Well! . . . Well, now, we'll fix that up pretty quick! I'll bet there's a dozen young fellows nearabout who'd jump at the chance to take a pretty girl like you, if they were just *acquainted* with you." She laughed the frail, tinkling laugh that one would expect from a marble angel guarding a frosty grave and looked about her efficiently. She saw Andrew Tallon standing at the steps of the church, talking with his sister, Susan, and her sweetheart, Carl Graffenreid.

"Andrew!" she called. "You, Andrew! Come here a minute. I got somebody I want you to meet."

"No," said Myrtle. "No. I can't be *asking* a man to take me. Whatever would he think?"

"Oh, shucks!" said Mrs. Wrenn. "Just leave that part of it to me. Why, I've known Andrew all his life. I was in the room when he was born, as a matter of fact. His mother and me were girls together. He'll be glad to take you, if I ask him to, even if he don't go out much in society."

Andrew came over, his head lowered, slightly embarrassed. He was a powerfully built man with thick shoulders that tapered to compressed flanks. Between his thighs and his knees the line of his legs flared out, and curved again, less strongly, at his calves. His hair was light brown and it grew close and kinked against his skull; his eyes were small and light blue, and except for his mouth, with its triangular cleft which sprang angrily from lip to nose, he would have been considered a handsome man. He had just turned twenty-six the month before and he had reached the full measure of his vigor. His body as he walked bulged out so strongly that even the cheap, ill-fitting suit he wore could not entirely hide its magnificence.

Myrtle stared at him, her glance fixed on his torn mouth, as if disbelieving the evidence of her eyes, her own mouth slightly opened in awe. Then she turned and would not look up again until the sound of his steps, the faint creaking of his heavy shoes, ceased, and she heard Addie Wrenn introducing them. She held out her hand, her eyes still fixed on the strip of church carpet, and felt it taken by another hand. She looked up at last and stared into Andrew's face, at his angrily cleft lip and the flash of white bone beneath it. She felt that she was being discourteous, that she should look instead at the blank wall behind him, but she was powerless to draw her eyes away.

"I particularly wanted you young people to meet each other," said Mrs. Wrenn, "because I'm having a party and a dance next Saturday week. I just asked Miss Myrtle to come, and I was intending to ask you and your brother, Jim, too, the first chance I got."

Andrew said: "Yes, ma'am; Jim and I will be very glad to come. I'll tell him when I see him tomorrow morning at breakfast."

His voice was shocking. It was grunting and tortured and so blurred that his words were scarcely distinguishable as speech. Only those who had known him for a long time and were used to him were able to understand him at all.

Myrtle stepped backward when she heard it and pulled her hand away in sudden confusion, as if her thoughts had somehow been caught and exposed to everybody's eyes. Andrew's face and neck turned red slowly. He closed his eyes. He raised his hand and covered his mouth for the first time in his life with the shamed, defensive gesture that was later to become habitual with him.

"I hope Miss Myrtle will give me the pleasure of her company, if she's not going to the dance with somebody else."

"I'll be glad to go with you, if you're sure it's not putting you out in any way."

"Well, that's all fixed," said Addie cheerfully.

She called to Susan and Carl. They came over and joined the group, and Mrs. Wrenn introduced Myrtle to them. She explained about the party again and asked them to come, too, if they thought they could spare the time from their sweethearting. She put her hand on Carl's shoulder, shaking him.

"I do declare, Carl! You ought to be ashamed to take little Suse off there to Oklahoma, away off amongst those cruel, bloodthirsty Indians."

Susan said: "I'm coming over to see you just as soon as Agnes gets back home, Miss Addie. You can tell me then how to manage a husband. I'll need some advice, if Carl don't manage to back out on me before I get him before the preacher." She moved with her fiancé toward the door, with Andrew walking slowly behind them, his head lowered like a lumbering sentinel stationed by nature to guard the happiness of more fortunate men. When they had disappeared, Addie Wrenn turned apologetically to Myrtle, for she felt a little perturbed at the unconventionality of her conduct, particularly in a house of worship, and she was anxious to justify herself.

"I know just what you're thinking, and I can't blame you: You want to know something about Andrew Tallon and his people before you go out with him. I keep forgetting that no matter how well I know him, he's a stranger to *you*. . . . Well, put your mind at rest, for I can promise you he's as substantial and as upright a young man as there is in the whole county."

"He scared me a little," said Myrtle. She laughed nervously and shuddered. "He scared me at first, particularly when he begun to talk."

"He's harmless! He's harmless! I do declare," said Mrs. Wrenn. "But I'll tell you something about him and his family, in case your mother asks you to tell her how it happened when you get home, and criticizes me. Well, to begin with, old Lemuel Tallon, the father of the family, was born right here in this county, but he's been dead for about ten years now, and his wife followed him to the grave not long afterwards. I want you to know the whole truth, so I must confess that Lem was a violent man, especially when he was drinking. It wasn't that he was selfish or cruel to his family; he was just coarse and he didn't have any finer feelings." She sighed, lifted her eyes to the ceiling and touched her circular earrings, as if to verify that they had not been stolen. "I, personally, wouldn't have lived two minutes with a man like Lem Tallon," she said.

The janitress of the church was collecting hymn books from the pews and stacking them behind the church organ in warped, unstable piles. Mrs. Wrenn drew her body inward to let the cleaning woman pass and moved into the aisle. "I remember Lemuel Tallon well," she continued, "and the way he used to drive down the dirt roads we had in them days with a jug of corn whisky beside him. He used to beat his mules with a rawhide whip when he was drunk and sing sentimental songs at the top of his lungs until he woke up half the county."

"I could hardly understand anything Andrew said to me. I couldn't make out what he was talking about," said Myrtle slowly. "I just had to guess."

But Mrs. Wrenn was not to be diverted from the biographical details which she felt to be necessary as a matter of fairness to Myrtle and her mother.

"But no matter how his father behaved himself, Andrew's

steady and reliable enough, and you'll be perfectly safe with him."
She paused and swung her earrings thoughtfully as she and Myrtle
moved down the aisle toward the vestibule, a few steps ahead
of the disgruntled janitress. "Andrew's reliable enough, but I
wouldn't say the same thing for Jim Tallon, his brother, though!"
she went on. . . . "Then there was another brother whose name
was Bradford, but he got killed in the war. Susan Tallon you've
just met. Carl is going West with her after they marry. The other
sister married a man named Asa Cleaver and lives right here in
the county. Her name is Effie." The two women reached the
church steps, where Ed Wrenn waited impatiently for his wife.
Addie laughed her tinkling, icy laugh and again she shook her
sandy, gray-streaked head, the agitated earrings swinging in
restricted circles to the rhythm of her frigid mirth. "Well, I've
done my duty, and you know as much about Andrew Tallon and
his family now as anybody in the county. . . . I hope you have
a nice time at the party. We'll do our best to make you feel at
home and we'll look forward to seeing you."

Myrtle said: "I don't care anything about his family and neither
will Mamma; and so far as Andrew's concerned, I'm not scared
of him or any other man."

"He's very big and powerful," said Miss Addie. "I'd hate to
trust my daughter out with a man as big as Andrew unless I
knew he was trustworthy."

"I don't care how big they are," said Myrtle. "I can manage
to whittle them down to my size." She laughed contemptuously
and smoothed her hair.

Mrs. Wrenn said: "Well, that's one way of looking at it, I
guess!"

Andrew went to the hitching rack, more than a block from
the church, where he had left his carriage, while Susan and Carl
waited for him at the church steps. Babe, the old mare, hearing

14

his footfall, lifted her tethered head, half turned and whinnied. He spoke to her coaxingly in his pig-like voice; and Babe pointed her graying ears in the direction of the sound with an eager semblance of inappropriate youth. She held her head upright and her hide twitched with pleasure for a moment; then she blew upward against her teeth, her back sagged down and she slumped again into senility. Andrew untied the old mare and sat in the buggy, the reins held loosely in his hands, and old Babe jogged contentedly back to the church, her disconsolate bowels making the bumping noise of echoes reverberating in a cave.

Carl said: "Well, old Babe made it after all. She ran that block in ten minutes flat! I don't know whether Susan and me can stand that breathless ride back to the farm, because it makes us dizzy to see trees and telephone poles whizzing by like a solid fence."

"Wait until you and Suse are as old in proportion as Babe and see how good you are then."

"Babe must be going on twenty by now," said Susan. "I remember the morning Papa brought her home as a present for Brad's birthday. It's one of the earliest things I can remember."

"I doubt if you really remember it," said Andrew. "You just remember hearing Bradford or Jim talking about it before you."

Old Babe pulled stiffly out of the street and into the Reedyville Highway. Carl said: "Quit talking to your sister, Andy, and keep a tight grip on them lines!" He lit a cigarette and flipped the match into the underbrush. "You better keep your mind on what you're doing. It won't do to let a high-stepping, nervous mare like Babe have her head."

The old mare, as if hearing the words and reacting to them, snorted, shook her mane wildly and put on a sudden burst of speed that jerked Carl and Susan backward against the seat. For a minute or two Babe's hooves clattered smartly against the cement highway, then, imperceptibly, she slowed down to her customary stiff walk, sneezed twice and broke wind sedately.

"Now, Babe! Now, Babe!" said Andrew. "Don't let Carl sweet-talk you into something you can't do."

"I thought she was real pretty, didn't you, Carl?" asked Susan.

"Who? Who are you talking about?"

"I'm talking about that Bickerstaff girl. I haven't come across a girl as pretty as her in I don't know when."

"Sure," said Carl. "I guess she's pretty enough, but I'll bet it's going to take a lot of work before a man gets her broke to a cook-stove."

"What do you think, Andrew?"

"She'll do," he mumbled. "I guess she'll do."

"What did you say?" asked Susan. "What did you say, Andrew?"

"Nothing."

"Then quit mumbling to yourself," said Susan gaily. "Quit mumbling and sit up straight in your seat or you'll get curvature of the spine like old Mrs. Barrascale." She turned to Carl and they talked endlessly of Oklahoma and the life they expected to lead there together.

When they reached the Tallon homestead at last, Susan and Carl got out, while Andrew drove through the grove of oaks that circled the house until he came to the barn. He went to the old mare's head and took the bit from her teeth. He led her to the trough and stood with his hand resting against her ageing withers while she drank discreetly. He thought: "Suse can't possibly remember Brad's birthday party. She was too young. She couldn't have been more than three years old then."

He, himself, remembered the occasion very well, and the scene returned to him at this moment with a trance-like vividness of detail. . . . Bradford had been very proud of his pony, but later in the morning he had permitted his two younger brothers to ride also. He remembered Jim clinging to the sides of the colt

16

with his thin legs until she bolted at last in fright and threw him in to the pigpen. But Jim had insisted, despite his mother's protests, and despite the laughter of the birthday guests, on riding again, and that time he had remained seated. Jim had been the hero of the day; indeed, he had almost taken the birthday away from Bradford completely and made it his own. . . .

Effie, the eldest of the Tallon children, had married Asa Cleaver that year. She and Asa had just settled down to housekeeping in their new home, but they had come over for Bradford's birthday and for the celebration later. When the entire family had assembled, and the colt had been inspected and admired, the guests had gone back to the house. Effie had baked a birthday cake and had brought it over. It sat in the center of the dining-room table, the candles lighted, but looking out of place and somewhat silly in the afternoon glare. He remembered, too, his father, genial with corn whisky, laughing and telling jokes, one arm resting around Bradford and the other encircling Jim's slender waist.

"These are my two boys," old Lemuel Tallon had k pt saying to the guests who dropped in, "but I don't believe ere a man ever had sorrier ones!" He laughed proudly, his whole body shaking. "Lord God almighty. What a sorry passel of chillun I raised!" . . .

And so Andrew stood beside the open door of the barn, unhitching old Babe with soft, preoccupied fingers. So many things had happened since those days: Effie had grown children of her own now, and even Susan, the baby of the family, would soon marry Carl Graffenreid and move West to Oklahoma with him; and all that remained of loud-mouthed, good-natured Brad Tallon was a citation in flaming colors signed by a French general whose name could not be read.

Andrew led the mare into her stall and she turned around clumsily and stretched her neck over the gate. As he fixed her late supper, she kept whinnying and stretching out her neck to sniff his shirt. Being blind, she was frightened of unfamiliar things that menaced her, and she wanted unending assurance that her remembered world had not been taken from her with her sight; being old, she knew at last the necessity for affection. He finished at length and dumped the softened and salted mash into the mare's feed-box and she began to eat slowly. He laughed his cloudy, gasping laugh, stroked the old mare's withers and spoke with his mouth close to her twitching hide.

"Her name is Myrtle Bickerstaff and I just met her tonight. She was standing by the church steps talking to Addie Wrenn and her husband when we passed, but of course you couldn't see her," he said softly. "Naturally, you can't have any idea what she looks like." He walked to the door of the barn and breathed deeply, his small eyes bright and far away. . . . "All right, then," he said. "All right, I'll tell you what she looks like in just a few words: She's the most beautiful thing that ever walked on this earth! You can take my word for it, because it's true!" He bent closer to the old mare and whispered, but his breath tickled her ear and she jerked her head up sharply, the softened mash from her lips powdered his coat.

CHAPTER II

ANDREW awoke early the next morning. He washed and dressed slowly, and since he had plenty of time he sat on the side of his bed and cleaned his nails with his pocket-knife, pushing back the cuticle with the dull side of the blade. At six o'clock he went into Jim's room and shook his brother. "Jim!" he said. "Jim! You've got to get up and go to work. Are you going to sleep-in all morning?"

Jim threw back the sheets in which his body was tangled, sat on the side of his bed and yawned. He had been out late the night before and he was tired and inclined to be sullen. "All right! All right! Don't worry about me. I'll get to work in plenty time."

He got out of bed and began putting on his clothes. He went to the washstand and filled the bowl with water, rubbing his face and his neck vigorously; he stuck his whole head into the bowl, the water sloshing over the sides and onto the floor.

Susan called out from below: "Jim! . . . Jim! You and Andrew come get your breakfast. Everything will be cold."

Jim resembled his mother's side of the family. His eyes were dark and they moved with restless and calculated languor. He was not so tall as his brother, nor was his body cast in so powerful a mould, and yet there was a kinship which identified them at once as being of the same blood. The water refreshed Jim. He looked at Andrew and grinned. He took a towel from the rack and rubbed his face and head.

Andrew said: "You ought to quit running around with girls so much at night. First thing you know the Hodges will be looking for another saw-filer."

"Let 'em look till they get a bellyful of looking," said Jim good-naturedly. "They won't find as good a man as me, no matter how much they look." He smiled and yawned twice.

"Jim!" called Susan from the foot of the stairs. "For pity sake come on before breakfast gets cold."

Jim whistled a tune between his teeth, his lips drawn back tightly like the lips of a little boy concentrated on a difficult task. He spread his legs wide and bent downward before the low glass. He picked up his comb and parted his black hair, smoothing the sides evenly with his palms.

"Go on down, Andy, and keep Susan quiet till I get there."

But Andrew, standing by the window, gazed at his brother with an admiration which he made no effort to conceal. He shook his head and waited patiently until Jim had his hair fixed precisely to his taste of the moment.

They entered the kitchen together and sat at the table Susan had laid for them. Jim yawned again and made a faint, belching noise behind his hand.

"What's on the bill-of-fare this morning, Mrs. Graffenreid?"

"I've got eggs and fried grits, and it looks like you and Andrew might at least get here in time to eat it while it's hot."

Jim stretched his eyes and pursed his lips in imitation of Miss Sarah Tarleton. "What a pity! What a pity!" he said.

He took a match from the box on the mantel, draped his handkerchief over it like a small tent and stuck it into his ear, moving it from side to side carefully, his face screwed up as if the sun shone in his eyes.

"I do wish you wouldn't belch and clean your ears at the table, Jim. You've got worse manners than a corn-field nigger. Lord knows I've pleaded with you often enough and so did poor Mamma before she died."

Jim turned to his brother. "Did you ever stop and think what a dainty little thing Mrs. Graffenreid is?"

"Why don't you go ahead and scratch your behind, too?" asked Susan. "You've done just about everything else."

"I would," said Jim pleasantly, "only it don't happen to itch right now."

Susan came to the table and poured coffee into the cups. As she went back to the stove Jim gave her a resounding slap on her rump. Susan turned quickly and tried to pour hot coffee on his hand, but Jim laughed and sprang away from her, the table between them.

"God help old Carl, marrying a hyena like you! I'm glad it's him and not me."

Suse began to laugh too. She put the pot back on the stove. "Come on, Jim. Sit down and eat your breakfast. I don't aim to harm you any this time."

"Is that the way you and May MacLean carry on when you're out together?" continued Susan. "I'm just asking for information."

Andrew looked at the clock. "It's almost six-thirty," he said gravely. "You'd better hurry, if you're going to make Hodgetown by seven."

Jim lifted his coffee cup and drank. "They'll wait for me," he said. "They wouldn't think of starting the mill up unless I was there to give them the word."

"I never heard such conceit in all my life," said Susan. "I really never did, for a fact."

When Jim had ridden off on his bicycle and Susan was tidying up her kitchen, Andrew went outside and sat on the steps. It was late February and already the first colors of spring were hovering like mist about the bare trunks of trees. It was mild and very clear in this, the early light of morning, and the placid sky rested blue and undisturbed. Beside the creek a clump of willows stood out, breathless and withdrawn, wrapped in a haze of color which was faintly brown, with indwelling green in it. Green was beginning to show in the meadows to the east as well, under the death of last year's grass, and soon small, pink flowers would be there too.

Andrew stretched himself, flinging out his arms. The chill of morning was beginning to disappear under the power of the mounting sun, and a slight, almost imperceptible smoke rose upward from the land. A feeling of happiness flowed through him. He sat again on the steps, his elbows braced against his knees, his face resting in his cupped palms. He sighed and relaxed and stared dreamily beyond the fields and the renewing willows. He felt against his cheeks the wind that blew from the creek, a wind that lifted his hair and brought to his senses a delicate odor of spiced decay.

He was thinking again of Myrtle Bickerstaff and was weighing his chances with her. He raised his hand and touched his mutilated mouth. He thought: "It shocked her at first when she saw it, and she didn't even make much effort to hide how she felt." He shook his head doubtfully, but he was not really discouraged. His affliction was merely something which existed, and about which little could now be done; he, himself, was neither bitter nor self-conscious about it. He would make it up to Myrtle in other ways, and soon, no doubt, she would take him for granted as did Susan, Jim or the other people he knew. . . .

Susan came to the back door to shake her broom. She was a plump girl with wide, gray eyes and hair that was almost flaxen. Her face was broad, coarse and good-natured.

"What in the world are you doing out here alone? What are you staring up at those clouds for, like you never saw one in your life before?"

Andrew got up quickly and stood against the door, his hands lifting and fumbling his coat in confusion.

"If I didn't know you so well," began Susan; "if I didn't know so well that you haven't got a pinch of romance in you, I'd say you were acting like a man in love."

22

"Maybe I am in love," said Andrew. "How do you know I'm not? How do you know what's going on inside me?"

Susan laughed and beat her broom derisively against the steps. "Who is she? I can't think who she could be to save my life, Andy."

Andrew raised his hands and leaned backwards against the wall, his fingers locked behind his head. He sighed contentedly, but he did not answer.

"Is it that girl visiting the Outerbridges? I've heard all the Pearl County boys are crazy about her."

Andrew shook his head. He walked down the steps and stood in the yard, his face lifted to the warm sunlight. Suddenly he took off his coat and tossed it to Susan. He rolled up his sleeves with unexpected activity.

"I'm going to start my ploughing right now. I've been sitting around doing nothing long enough."

He started toward the barn, but when he had reached the fence that surrounded the house, he did not stop to open the gate, for he felt very young and very gay, and he knew there was nothing that he could not accomplish. He retreated a few yards, ran forward and cleared the high fence at a leap.

Susan stood gasping at him. "Heavens and earth! Why I didn't know it was in you, Andy!"

"Would you like to see me do it again, Mrs. Graffenreid?"

"It's simply not in you. You couldn't do it another time if you was going to be shot."

Again Andrew retreated a few yards, and again he ran forward and jumped, but this time his shoe caught clumsily against the top strand of the wire and he sprawled full length in the yard.

Susan sat down and swayed from side to side, her broom held tightly against her breast. She laughed until she was weak. "Wait a minute!" she said. "Wait a minute and I'll come down and open the gate for you!"

Andrew got up and began brushing his clothes. He said good-naturedly: "Well, it takes a pretty good man to do it even *once*." He walked sheepishly through the gate while Susan beat her broom and laughed shrilly.

He ploughed steadily all that day, watching the red soil up-turned before his advancing tread and falling sidewise evenly. At four o'clock he put his team up and came back to the house, and Susan heated water for him, which he carried to his room. He bathed himself carefully all over, as if his flesh, with love, had taken on a new importance for him, for already he was thinking of Myrtle Bickerstaff as his wife, and he was painting in his mind's eye the happiness of a life spent with her. A sense of the fullness of living washed through him strongly. Quietly his lips began to move, to shape the words that he must one day say to her.

Susan came to the door before he had finished, and knocked.

"Is it that Bickerstaff girl?"

"Yes," said Andrew.

"She's pretty," shouted Susan. "You could sure do worse. You've got my best wishes."

When Susan had gone, Andrew changed to his Sunday suit, but before he had finished dressing Jim came back from the mill and Andrew could hear him moving about downstairs and talk-ing to Carl. They were at supper when Andrew entered the dining room. He felt clumsy and self-conscious, and he hoped that he would escape attention. He lowered his chin, drew back his chair and sat down in complete silence.

Jim dropped his knife and fork. He stared and shook his head, unable to believe the evidence of his eyes.

"How were all the folks in Hollywood when you left, Mr. Menjou?"

"Let him alone," said Susan. "I think he looks nice."

Jim turned to Carl. "He's got his hair greased down and there's talcum powder on him by God! Take a good look at him, Carl. . . . You may never see such a sight inside the Tallon family again."

Andrew said: "I used some of your toilet water, too, and I've got on your best socks, but I couldn't get into your underdrawers; they wouldn't meet around me."

"What's her name?" asked Jim. He laughed and tossed back the wing of black hair that fell across his forehead. "I think the family ought to know her name in case of accidents."

"It's Myrtle Bickerstaff," said Susan. "He met her last night at prayer meeting and she's very pretty and sweet. Now you leave him alone."

Jim looked surprised. "I've never met Myrtle, but I've heard a lot about her from her old man. He talks about her all the time. I know Neil Bickerstaff pretty well and I see him every day of my life."

"It wouldn't do you any harm if you went to prayer meeting yourself every once in a while instead of roistering all night," said Susan.

"Neil told me a good joke on his old lady the other day," said Jim. He wiped his lips and smiled knowingly in anticipation of his story.

"It seems that when they moved to Hodgetown, Mrs. Bickerstaff forgot to get anything for supper the first night, so she sent Neil to the commissary at the last minute, being busy herself getting the furniture straight. Neil saw a smoked tongue on the counter and he figured that would be just the thing, so he bought it and took it home. . . . But when his old lady got a look at that tongue she covered it up again quick and shivered, like she was taken sick at her stomach all of a sudden. 'Why, Neil Bickerstaff!' she said. 'Do you think for one minute I'd eat anything that came out of a dirty old cow's mouth? . . . You

25

take that tongue back to the store this minute and get a dozen eggs instead!' "

The three men laughed together, but Susan shook her head, puzzled. "All right, maybe I'm just dumb. I'll admit I'm dumb, if you want me to, but I don't see anything to laugh at. . . . Neil's wife did right, if you ask me."

"It's the first time I ever heard that story told on Neil Bickerstaff and his wife," said Carl. "I've heard it told on others, but not them."

"Of course you haven't," said Jim quickly, "of course not; you see, this here is the very first time I ever *told* it that way!"

CHAPTER III

ANDREW closed the door behind him and stood on the brick walk which led from the porch to the gate. It was still early and twilight had not gone away completely, but in the sky, riding low over the tops of trees, there was a thin moon, and one star, blue and unwavering, beneath it. Before him the oaks, with outlines blurred by the encroaching dusk, grouped themselves in circles and melting half circles of shadow, wavered and grouped themselves again in other and stranger patterns. Their new leaves were still faintly luminous from beneath, as if the earth gave them back, in this first, uncertain hour of darkness, some mystical gleam of its own.

Andrew moved down the walk. There was no reason why he should not call on Myrtle if he wanted to; they were strangers in the community, and it was only natural and neighborly that he call on her. If she had a date, he would talk to Neil and her mother for awhile and then leave; but he was pretty certain that he would find her at home and that she would see him, since she knew so few people as yet.

He closed the gate, inflated his chest and walked in the direction of Hodgetown. To the left and the right of the road as far as his eyes could see there stretched acres of knee-high stumps, like huge, disintegrating toadstools, between which sweet-myrtles and second-growth pines had sprung up in unhindered profusion. When Andrew reached the place where the highway bent to the north, beyond the McRae farm, and he saw the glare of the Hodgetown slab-pit ahead, red and high against the sky, he turned from the road and walked leisurely through the cut-over

27

land, for he was, in his eagerness, too early, and he wanted to time his arrival at the Bickerstaff house as perfectly as possible.

The myrtles and the plumed young pines which brushed against his knees seemed, in the dim afterglow of light, green and very fresh against the hacked desolation which they sought to hide. He stopped after a time, looked about him idly in the deepening dusk, and sat at last upon a rotting stump. When he and Jim had been boys, the land that he was now surveying had belonged to his father, and it had been covered completely with a virgin forest of trees. That was before the Hodge brothers had built their sawmill or had bought this strip of land from Lemuel Tallon. . . .

As Andrew sat upon the decaying stump, crushing the aromatic myrtle leaves in his hands, he remembered a time, years before, when he and Jim had taken the dogs and gone rabbit hunting through this same strip. That was the afternoon his father had concluded the sale of the timber to the Hodge brothers.

The boys had returned home near sunset, and since they were tired and very hot they had gone down to the branch to swim before supper. They had come out of the pool refreshed and in high spirits, and had run a foot-race from the sandy beach to the house. When they drew near it they heard their father and their brother, Bradford, singing drunken songs and laughing in celebration of the sale of the timber.

The two boys stopped and looked at each other. Jim nodded after a moment and they stepped more cautiously, as if even the sound of their bare feet brushing against grass might betray them, but they could not have said, even to each other, what it was they feared. They circled the oak trees and approached the house from the front. On tiptoe they went upon the porch and stood screened by vines. They knelt side by side with their heads close together and peered through the window.

They saw Russell and Thompson Hodge seated in rocking-chairs. They were not twins but they dressed and looked almost exactly alike. Each wore a gold signet ring on his little finger and each had a heavy, gold chain with a Masonic emblem hanging above his pot-like belly. They were short, stocky men, shrewd traders, but jovial and very kindly in their personal relations with the people about them.

There was much talk back and forth between Lemuel Tallon and the two Hodge brothers as to which side had got the better of the trade. In the center of the room was a table with a glazed jug of aged, home-made whisky, and several empty glasses. Russell Hodge was holding Susan, the baby of the Tallon family, in his lap. She was laughing and clapping her hands and trying to plait his moustache.

"I'll bet you're going to be a little beauty when you grow up, Susan," said Thompson Hodge. "I'll bet you won't sit in Russell's lap in a few years from now."

"I will, too," said Susan quickly. "I will, too, if Mr. Russell asks me like a gentleman."

Lemuel Tallon roared with laughter, and so did the Hodge brothers.

"Mamma!" called Bradford. "Did you hear what Suse just said to Mr. Thompson Hodge?"

Mrs. Tallon came in from the dining room, where she was setting the table for supper.

"No, and I'm glad I didn't, because I know it must have been something mighty saucy." She turned warningly to Susan and shook her head in vague disapproval.

"You better be a good girl, now, or I'll send you straight to bed without a bite of supper."

She was a small, worried woman with piled masses of straight hair which fell a little sidewise on her head, as if too heavy for her delicate neck. The faint trace of Spanish blood in her family had come strongly to the surface in her. Her skin was dark and her eyes, against the background of her thin, sensitive face, seemed enormous and unfathomably dark. They were tasseled with lashes so long and so silken that they defeated their own purpose and passed beyond the limits of beauty into grotesqueness.

"Why I haven't done anything," said Susan, her face bland in its innocence. "I haven't done anything at all to demean myself."

"Oh, leave her alone, Ma," said Brad. He got up from his chair and walked toward his mother, staggering a little in his tipsiness.

Mrs. Tallon retreated behind the table, a dishcloth raised in her hand as if it were a weapon.

"Now, you leave me alone, Bradford!" she said. "I haven't got any time to be fooling with you."

She broke away from him and tried to run to the shelter of her kitchen, but Bradford picked her up in his arms, lifted her in the air and held her suspended helplessly. He stood with his legs spread wide, laughing loudly and hugging his mother to his body. She looked very small against the bulk of her son. The pins in her hair loosened under the vigor of Bradford's affection and her piled pompadour tilted loosely toward her shoulders.

Bradford walked to Susan, his mother still held tightly in his arms.

"I'll tell you what, Suse! Let's you and me change things around for once. . . . Ma's been picking on us two long enough just because we're little and can't help ourselves. Now I'll tell you what let's do: Let's give *Ma* a spanking and put *her* to bed without any supper!"

Mrs. Tallon said: "You put me down, Bradford! You put me down this minute!"

Susan's mouth opened with delight. "O-o-o-o!" she said in a long, terrified gasp. "O-o-o-o, Brad!"

Lemuel Tallon stretched himself out in his chair helplessly, his legs straight and stiff before him. He held his sides with his reddened hands until he was weak with laughter.

"What chillun I raised!" he gasped proudly. "What chillun! What chillun! . . . Folks all said when Bradford was just a puppy that we ought to drown him in the branch. Said we'd be better off if we done that!"

Mrs. Tallon began to laugh too. "Put me down, Bradford," she said pleadingly. Then, more softly: "I got to see about getting supper ready for the Hodge brothers."

Bradford lowered his mother to the floor and kissed her on her lips with a force that bent her head backwards. When he released her, she began to scold him and to hit at him with her dishcloth, half playfully, half in earnest.

She went back to the kitchen and bent above her stove. She straightened up and began fixing her hair.

"He hurt my neck a little," she said. "He hurt my neck when he hugged me so hard."

To her surprise she discovered that she was trembling. She sat on the wood box and wiped tears from her eyes. "He's a good boy, though," she thought; "and there's not a bit of meanness in Brad anywhere."

She sat on the box for a long time, hearing the noise in the room adjoining, before she went on with her preparations for supper. She had been married to Lemuel for many years and she had borne him, in all, six children; but never so long as she lived would she be able to understand or to feel at ease with either her husband or his reddened, playful children.

Andrew and Jim had remained watching, making no sound, until Andrew laughed his foolish, gasping laugh, got up from his knees and moved to the door. Jim too got up.

"What are you going to do?"

"I'm going indoors."

There was a worried look on Jim's face. He started to speak but changed his mind, realizing that he was powerless to stop his brother. He turned and followed Andrew into the room. When they entered, Jim stood just inside the door looking about him gravely, but Andrew walked straight to his father's chair and leaned against it. He laughed with delight, his mouth opened and his deformed lip stretched wide.

Lemuel Tallon pretended not to see his son. He got up heavily from his chair and walked to where Jim was standing, putting his arms about him. He gave him a playful push forward.

"Go shake hands with Mr. Russell and Mr. Thompson Hodge; I was just telling them about you, son."

"Well, you look like a mighty fine boy," said Russell Hodge. "How old are you?"

"I'm ten."

"That's fine. That's fine. I wish I had a fine boy at home like you."

"My brother Andrew is eleven."

He turned to look for Andrew, but Andrew had moved again, following his father like a shadow. He stood again beside his father, twitching his foot and grinning widely.

Lemuel Tallon said: "This is my other son. He's the afflicted one."

Mrs. Tallon came up timidly. "Go outside and play, Andy! You too, Jim!" she whispered. "Go outside with your brother and play until I get supper ready."

Jim went out of the room at once, but Andrew stood grinning before the Hodges, his irregular, half-formed teeth gleaming bone-like under the cleft in his lip.

"Shake hands with Mr. Russell and Mr. Thompson!" said Lemuel sharply. "Where are your manners at, son?"

Andrew laughed nervously, but he did not move.

"Andrew!" said Mrs. Tallon. "Go outside with Jim."

But Andrew could not draw his eyes from his father's face. He knew what awaited him, but he seemed powerless to move. and he stood in patience, waiting for his father to humiliate him before these strangers.

"Let the boy stay, Reina, if he wants to," said Lemuel at last. "I want him to sing a song for the Hodges."

"Now, Lem," began Mrs. Tallon, but she stopped, knowing her helplessness.

"Come on, son," said Lemuel. "Sing a song for our company."

"Don't know any song to sing except old ones."

"Make him recite the Twenty-third Psalm," said Bradford. "Professor Drewery made his whole class learn it by heart not so long ago, and I heard Andy speaking it to Mamma."

Lemuel Tallon began to laugh and slap the side of his chair. "That's right," he said. "That's a good one; I remember that one myself from the time I was a boy."

And so Andrew stood in the center of the room, lifted his head and began to speak slowly:

"The Lord is my shepherd; I shall not want.
He maketh me to lie down in green pastures: he leadeth me beside the still waters.
He restoreth my soul: he leadeth me in the paths of righteousness for his name's sake."

His breath moving against his shattered palate made a hollow, unreal sound and came distorted and blurred through his mutilated mouth. His face was shamed and there was a sick look in his eyes.

"Yea, though I walk through the valley of the shadow of death, I will fear no evil: for thou art with me; thy rod and thy staff they comfort me.
Thou preparest a table before me in the presence of mine enemies: thou anointest my head with oil; my cup runneth over."

At the end of each stanza Lemuel Tallon and Bradford would slap their legs and laugh drunkenly, or join in the last line, but Mrs. Tallon stood alone by the door, her hands wrapped in her apron, and shook her head. Her lips kept forming the words, "No! . . . No!" but she remained silent.

"Surely goodness and mercy shall follow me all the days of my life: and I will dwell in the house of the Lord for ever."

The psalm was finished, and at its last word Mrs. Tallon came up quickly, standing between her son and his father.

"I know the Hodge brothers want to freshen up before supper." She gave Andrew a shove which his father did not see. "Run down and draw a bucket of water," she said softly.

But Andrew stood as if he had not heard her, as if something within him held him fixed.

"Do what your ma tells you, Andrew!" said Lemuel.

Andrew turned and ran out of the room. When he reached the porch he took the bucket and walked toward the well. Jim was standing behind the wing of the kitchen waiting for him. He was still crying a little.

"Jim!" said Andrew. "What's the matter?"

Jim came toward his brother. His tears broke out again and he trembled with rage. "If he makes you do that again I'm going to kill him! . . . I'm going to kill him, by God!"

Andrew swung the cedar bucket from side to side and grinned foolishly. He said: "Papa don't mean any harm. He wouldn't have done it if he hadn't been drinking too much."

He walked to the well, Jim close behind him.

"Why don't you keep out of his way, you damned fool!" demanded Jim angrily. "Why don't you keep out of his sight, you damned fool, you!"

"I don't know."

34

They reached the well and Andrew lowered the bucket with a splash and turned the crank which would wind it up again.

"I'll kill him!" said Jim passionately, his thin nostrils quivering. . . . "Him and Bradford, too!"

"I don't mind so much," said Andrew placatingly. "I don't care what he makes me do." He leaned against the well, his face still sick and white. He laughed in spite of himself.

"I guess I do sound right funny to other people."

Then some obscure impulse which he did not understand made him put down the bucket and look at his brother as if he had not seen him before. He drew his breath in with a slow sound. There was a feeling of warm blood about his breast and in his face.

He said: "I don't care very much what other people do or how much they laugh at me so long as you and Ma don't ever do it."

The brothers gazed at each other across the well. Their mouths were half opened and their eyes stretched wide as if they were bewitched. They shook their heads after a moment to break the spell which lay over them.

Mrs. Tallon came on to the porch.

"Andrew!" she called. "Hurry up with that bucket of water, son!"

CHAPTER IV

ANDREW knocked at the Bickerstaff door and waited. At last the door opened and one of the younger of Neil's children gaped at him solemnly. Before him was a tiny hall laid with linoleum and a hat-rack covered with flung coats and littered with school books; beyond that he could see the dining room. Supper was over, as he had hoped it would be, and the table cleared, but there clung to the hall a faint smell of beef stew and the resinous tang of boiled carrots. He came into the hall and put his hand on the little girl's head: "I come to see your sister, Miss Myrtle. Is she at home?"

At the sound of his gasping voice the children grouped about the table in the dining room, under the unshaded light which hung above it, came to the hall door and stared openly. Andrew began to laugh. "I'll bet you can't talk the way I do. It may be funny, but I'll bet you couldn't do it to save your life."

"No, sir," said the little girl.

"I could," said George; "only it ain't manners."

"Go on and try. I don't believe you."

"Ho hon unt hie. Hi hont uhleeve hoo," repeated George.

"You're away off," said Andrew. He bent forward and slapped his thigh. "You're nowhere near right!"

Almost at once there drifted an irascible voice from the rear: "Who is it, Hildy? What does the man want this time?" At the sound of their mother's voice, the children retreated at once to the dining room and then one by one they sidled helter-skelter, like fiddler-crabs through a red curtain that led to some recess in the rear, their slates and their books gathered to their thin chests.

Mrs. Bickerstaff came into the hall, smoothing down her hair, a wet checked apron about her waist. She was a big woman like her daughter, and the lines of her face were set unalterably in sorrow, as if she bore on her shoulders burdens too heavy for any mortal to assume.

When Andrew had explained who he was, and the reason for his visit, she became more cordial, and she smiled sadly. She shoved her staring daughter behind her.

"I didn't expect you so soon, Mr. Tallon, but come into the parlor anyway and sit down. Myrtle told me this morning all about the invitation, and I know just who you are." She stood before her guest in the bright light of the hall, a discontented look on her face, sighing slightly at intervals.

"You must excuse the way I look. If I'd knowed who it was, I wouldn't have come out to meet company looking the way I do; of that you may be sure. I thought it was a man from the mill come to see Neil about something."

"I expect they keep your husband pretty busy at the mill, don't they? I expect they send for him every time anything goes wrong."

Mrs. Bickerstaff inclined her head slightly. She had not understood all this long speech, but she had inferred its meaning.

"At all hours of the day or night," she said, the pouches under her eyes quivering a little. "I don't see how they expect me to get any rest. . . . I, for one, wish we'd never moved here from Georgia."

There was a short silence and Andrew looked about the room. Against the window was a flower stand with pots in which begonias and maidenhair ferns were growing; beyond that was a lamp with a red shade shaped like the half of an egg, from whose sides a fringe of green bead work hung down.

"At all hours of the day and night," repeated Mrs. Bickerstaff.

"I can't get much sleep when men from the mill come hammering on the door all night looking for Neil. I got my rights as a wife, like everybody else I guess."

"Yes, ma'am," said Andrew mildly. "I guess it must be pretty hard on you, like you say."

Neil Bickerstaff entered. He had put on his coat for the occasion of meeting his daughter's first suitor in the new town, and he had brushed down his red, tightly curling hair. He brought with him into the parlor a smell of tobacco and creosote, and the sweetish odor of fresh sweat modified a little with soap. He had been eating bread and molasses in the kitchen when Andrew arrived, and there still clung to his upper lip small crumbs of his wife's hot biscuits.

Neil said: "I know your brother, Jim, real well. I got a work office right underneath his filing loft and I see him often."

"Yes, sir. Jim said he knew you well."

"I guess Jim would ruther work at the mill for the Hodge brothers than to farm like you," continued Neil critically.

"Yes, sir, he would. Mr. Russell Hodge took a liking for Jim when he was just a boy. He said he wanted to bring Jim up to be an all round sawmill man."

"He done it at that, I expect," said Neil heartily. "I guess he done what he started out to do, all right." He looked at Andrew slyly and winked. "Jim's mighty good company, I'll say that for him. I never met a fellow in all my life who knowed so many good stories or who could tell 'em so well. Jim's good company!"

When Myrtle came down at last, her parents got up and shook hands with Andrew, their arduous duty performed. They bade him good night, glancing with polite speculation at this powerful, mutilated young man who had come to court their daughter.

Andrew said, after a long wait: "I hope I haven't put you out by coming to see you unexpectedly, but I thought you might be a little lonesome and that I'd come by for a little while and cheer you up."

"That was mighty nice of you, I'm sure."

"If I'm putting you out, just say so, and I'll come back another time."

Myrtle looked at him steadily with her brilliant eyes. She shook her head. "I'm not put out in any way."

Hers was the high-colored, vigorous beauty of country belles. Her eyes were like jet, both in their color and in their uncompromising hardness, but her mouth was soft, humid and voluptuously slack. A line of silken down, hardly perceptible except in some lights, and at unexpected angles, cast a faint, perpetual shadow on her lips and accentuated the flare of her nostrils. Her coloring was dark and her hips were beautifully rounded and cushioned.

For a time Andrew talked steadily, telling her stories about the people of the county, the people she would meet later on at Addie Wrenn's party; and Myrtle listened mostly in silence, erect and stiff in her chair, her eyes fixed on her folded hands. She was not accustomed to him yet, and she understood little of what he said. When later on he suggested that they go to the drug store and have a dish of ice cream, or a hot chocolate, Myrtle got up with relief, glad of the opportunity of getting away.

Mrs. Bickerstaff called out from the dining room, where she was helping the younger children with their lessons: "Don't be out too late, daughter; and button your coat tight around your neck. The spring air is the worst of all for catching cold in."

The faint, February breeze brought to their nostrils the musty smell of the log-pond, a penetrant smell of tanned leather blended with vanilla, and blended again, but more delicately, with snuff. They turned out of Wampum Street into Hiawatha Street, where the commissary, the drug store and the post office were situated.

Far away they could hear the dull beat of water flowing over a dam and breaking with a hiss on pilings below.

"It goes on like that all the time," said Myrtle. "It's enough to drive you crazy."

Andrew pressed her arm and drew it through his own.

"When I was a little boy, before Hodgetown was built, there wasn't any dam or log-pond either. It was only a little branch called Wrenn's Creek. Jim and me and the Cornells boys used to go fishing there when we were little."

Myrtle was silent, digesting this information. "Oh," she said at last. "Oh!" Then a moment later: "I doubt if there's a fish in it now, though."

Andrew said: "Maybe not right in the mill-pond, on account of the oil and grease, but there are plenty left in the creek."

When they entered the drug store, Andrew saw his brother and his sweetheart, May MacLean, seated with friends at the big table in the center of the room. Jim got up and came to meet them. He laughed and looked straight into Myrtle's unfriendly eyes.

"May and I were just talking about you two. I told her Andrew had a date and I bet he'd bring his new girl here the first thing, but she said he wouldn't."

He took Myrtle's hand. "Andrew said you were pretty. Well, I can't dispute what he says this time."

"This is Jim, my brother."

"I figured it was Jim from what Papa said."

Later, when they were all grouped about the large, circular table, Willie Oakshot continued the ghost story which had been interrupted toward its end. Myrtle ate her ice cream with small, dainty dips of her spoon, looking up only occasionally, for she was not at ease with these people who mentioned happenings in which she had not taken part and discussed people of whom she had not even heard. She gazed steadily at her saucer and made no effort to be agreeable, or to take part in the talk.

"I'll tell you a *true* ghost story," said Jim. "It's something that happened to Herb Outerbridge, myself and a fellow named Swallow who used to be a timekeeper at the mill. . . . We had all three gone to a dance at a place near Morgantown and it was late before the dance broke up."

"I'll bet you'd all had too much to drink, too," said May Mac-Lean. "You're leaving out that part of it on purpose."

"Well, we'd had our share. I thought you'd know that without my telling it. Anyway, we'd gone out in this fellow Swallow's car, but on the way home we found out we didn't have any gas left, and it looked like we'd have to walk back to town. So we trudged along for awhile, not saying much to each other, and then Herb called our attention to a horse and cart driving ahead of us in the road. The wagon wasn't more than two hundred yards off, but when we yelled to the driver to give us a lift, he didn't pay any attention to us; he just sat there on the seat holding the reins in his hands like he was dead."

"We hurried down the road after the wagon, as we didn't want to walk home, and when we got closer this fellow Swallow said, 'What's that lying in the bottom of the wagon?' and Herb said it looked to him like a woman who was either drunk or sick. I broke away from the others and caught up with the driver first. I took hold of the bridle and the horse stopped, but the driver still sat there huddled on the seat with his hat pulled down, and he would not look at me or answer my questions. I shouted at him, thinking he was drunk too, or asleep, maybe, but he didn't answer. . . . By this time Herb and the fellow named Swallow reached the wagon and we all knew by that time that there was something funny about the whole thing."

The light, bantering manner with which Jim had begun his

story was gone. His face was serious now and pale. He licked his lips to relieve their dryness and his eyelids were twitching nervously. His audience had leaned forward, infected with his own excitement, to catch every word.

"This fellow Swallow went to the wagon and pulled back the sacking that covered the body. 'Oh, my God!' he screamed. . . . 'Oh, my God! It's a half-grown girl and somebody has hacked her to pieces with a hatchet!' Herb and I both saw the same: there lay a fourteen- or fifteen-year-old girl, all covered with her own blood." Jim's voice broke and he swallowed nervously. "That wasn't the worst, although it was bad enough, because after the girl had been cut up, somebody had tried to put her back together again. The murderer had sewn her arms on where her legs ought to be and her legs where her arms rightly belonged."

Jim's nostrils quivered and his voice was thin and unreal. "The driver of the wagon turned around then and laughed. . . . That's all any of us remember. When we came to, the wagon and the driver had gone."

There was a long silence. Over the radio, turned low so that conversation would not be interfered with, came the voice of a lush tenor singing a love song, and at the counter the soda clerk served his customers with a tinkling of glass.

Willie Oakshot put his elbows on the table. He shrugged his shoulders and smiled widely, as if to deny that the story had affected him. His front teeth had been bridged in by a dentist unskilled in his craft, and who had calculated badly, for the milky, faintly blue teeth did not quite meet their gums.

"Did you ever check up on the story?" asked Willie. "Did you ever find out any more about it?"

"Yes," said Jim. "Old Sarah Tarleton told us later that a murder had happened about fifty years ago near the place where we were. She remembered it well. She said the murderer was a blind man and that he had killed his half-grown niece who lived with him and took care of him, cut her up the best he could and then buried a part of the body in the barn, a part in the corn field and a part under the front steps."

"What made him do it?" asked Ellen Waters. "Did Miss Sarah say?"

Jim said: "Nobody ever knew exactly why he did it. She was the only person who tried to help him get about and she did everything for him. She sacrificed her whole life for him, or leastways as long as she lived. Most people thought he was just jealous of her good eyesight. Anyway, Miss Sarah did remember that later on the folks found out about it and lynched the man."

"If he was a blind man," said Willie, "maybe that's why he can't get the body back together again correctly. Maybe that's why he can never lay the curse that's on him." He got up and took Ellen Waters' arm. "Come on, Ellen," he said. "Let's be getting on home."

Myrtle finished the last spoonful of her ice cream, leaned back in her chair and wiped her lips with a paper napkin. She had heard little of what Jim had said; her mind was occupied with other matters. She thought: "He's showing off. If there's anybody in the world I can't stand, it's a man who shows off to a crowd."

"Now, Jim," said May MacLean, "just how much of that story is true and how much did you make up?"

Jim turned to her patiently. "Why, it's all true, May! What in the world made you ask a thing like that?"

"Now, Jim," said May. "Now, Jim; I know you too well."

Jim began to laugh too, his head thrown back, the wing of black hair falling into his eyes. "Anyway, some of it's true," he said, "or at least some of it *could* be true, if it had happened."

"The only thing is that it didn't!" insisted May. She gazed at him admiringly, her chin resting on her locked hands. "I declare, I don't see how you can think up things like that so quick."

"Not a word of it was true," said Jim finally. "I just made it up as I went along, for a joke."

CHAPTER V

KATE BICKERSTAFF
was awake in bed beside her husband. Neil lay sprawled on his back, his red, curling hair matted against the pillow, his oil-stained hands spread out with knuckles white at the joints, as if he sought in sleep to stretch an octave impossible for his stiff fingers. Kate turned on her elbow and looked in his face, listening for his breath, but it was even and soft and so inaudible that no sound reached her. There was only the rise and fall of his chest and a faint puffing of his lips as if, in his dreams, he blew gently against butterflies. She felt all at once a sense of sadness, a depression which she could not dispel.

"Neil!" she said sharply. . . . "Neil!"

His calm, regular breathing stopped; his hands shut spasmodically and pulled inward against his chest. He rubbed one hand with the palm of the other, as if somebody had rapped his knuckles. Abruptly he sat up, fully awake to his surroundings.

Kate said querulously: "How do you expect anybody to get their sleep when you keep grunting and puffing and carrying on like you do?"

Neil yawned and tried to answer at the same time, but his words were lost; they were so indistinct, so muffled with drowsiness.

"I don't see how you can sleep that way when Myrtle is out with that young man. It's almost eleven o'clock and she ain't in yet. There's no telling what's happened to her."

Neil yawned again and shifted his position, easing his weight on to his shoulders. He drew his wife's face against his chest,

45

her cheek resting uncomfortably there, the top of her head cupped nicely, as if by long habit, under the pink curve of his raised chin. He stroked his wife's face with his forefinger, outlining with a dainty and unexpected gentleness the quivering, pouched flesh beneath her eyes.

"Myrtle can take care of herself, I guess."

Kate said: "I don't like this town, Neil, and I don't trust the people in it. It's not like Georgia."

Neil smoothed her hair soothingly, fearful that this old subject was to be opened inappropriately when he wanted only to sleep; but his wife continued to talk in a petulant, uninflected voice, her words blurred against his breast.

The baby, asleep in his crib, woke without warning and began to cry. Kate pulled away from her husband, taking her arms from around his corpulent body.

"Drat that child!" she said crossly. "I'll be glad when the children are growed up and gone."

She got out of bed and picked up her son. She sat with him in a chair and offered her big, distended breast to his hungry mouth. She rocked back and forth, gently humming a song. She glanced at Neil when the baby had been fed and quieted, but she saw that he, too, had gone to sleep again. She stood above the crib, covering the baby carefully. She decided that she would not get back into bed, but would wait up for her daughter.

It was chilly in the room, so she put a coat over her nightgown and slipped her feet into felt slippers. She pulled a chair to the window and sat there disconsolate and neglected. Myrtle was twenty years old already, and it was time that she married. If she wasn't careful and didn't pay more attention to the boys, the next thing she knew she'd end up an old maid like her father's two sisters back in Georgia. Andrew Tallon was an upright, honest man, of that she was certain, and he'd make Myrtle a good husband. Good, steady men were scarce enough at best

46

these days. Of course, Andrew wasn't exactly handsome on account of his lip, but a woman could get used to that very easily if he treated her well. Anyway, in this world of reality, a girl must take what was offered her and make the best of it. She glanced at her own red, substantial husband, warm and relaxed in sleep, and sighed contentedly, resigning all women to their harsh fates.

She was still thinking these thoughts when she heard Myrtle open the front door and walk on tiptoe up the stairs. Her daughter was a difficult girl and it was almost impossible for Kate to understand her at times, so she waited a moment, giving her time to get into her room and undress before she followed her. Myrtle was brushing her hair when her mother's face appeared in the mirror next to her own. She turned and dropped the brush with a clatter.

Kate spoke in a whisper, her finger against her lips: "Sh-h-h! Do you want to wake up the whole house?"

"I told you I wouldn't like him any better than the others and I didn't, Mamma. I'm not going to see him another time."

"Why, I thought he was a real nice young fellow. Your Papa and I both remarked it after you'd gone out."

Myrtle sat on the bed beside her mother and continued to brush her hair, her full, beautiful mouth half opened and sullen. The slab-pit was visible before them, through the shut window, and its light cast a constant glare on the western sky and reflected itself, magnified a little, distorted a little, in the black, tideless waters of the pond.

"After we left the drug store, he asked me to go walking down to the slab-pit. I did it because I didn't know what else to say. He kept me there for an hour or nearabout, but I got cold finally. I couldn't hear all he was saying on account of the noise the dam makes. I guess I couldn't have understood it anyway, he talks so funny."

"Mr. Tallon is to be pitied for his misfortune, daughter. You haven't got any call to hold that against him."

"I don't hold anything against him," said Myrtle irritably. "He may be the best man in the world, but just the same I can't understand what he's saying more than half the time."

"Why, I understood every word he said, and so did your father. You will too before long."

"I won't either," said Myrtle, "because I don't expect to see him again, at least not after Wrenn's party."

Her mother repeated very patiently: "Now, Myrtle! Now, Myrtle! I wish you'd behave like other girls."

Myrtle got up from the bed suddenly. She reached in her dress and pulled out a piece of paper. "Oh, yes, I forgot. He asked me to read this after I got home and was in bed."

Mrs. Bickerstaff took the folded paper from her daughter, straightened it out and read the poem which Andrew had written:

Know this, ye people of Pearl County, and remember,
For I was once as sad as a spray of gray sparrows,
Sparrows that sway upon weeds and make a thin noise in the rain:
I was sad, oh ye people. I was heavy with time and I said:
"The wind blows against everlasting things: it will find me small with death: I shall be very trivial with death." . . .
Then who hath wrought a change in me that my mouth moves now with the miracle of sound?
Who is it? Who hath done this thing for me?
It is my beloved and her hand alone hath done it.

My beloved is clearer than sparks curving upward from the slab-pit: she is like ripe sandpears that lie stored in barns:
She is like butterflies that rise upward and weave together,
She is sweeter than the shavings of seasoned pine even:

48

She is a bird that circles above water; my beloved flies beautifully above water.
I am the water over which she flies,
I am the air through which she moves,
I am the food she takes out of the water.

My beloved is like the meadowland beyond Black Creek:
She will set me a table of food in her season and call me sweet names, saying:
"I have rest for you: I will quiet the cymbals in you: I will drain you of your woe."
Know this, ye people, and bear witness
That I am Andrew, the witless one, and yet
I have grasped the final release of love
In my clumsy and spilling arms.

Mrs. Bickerstaff read the poem again, but out loud and more slowly this time, her lips moving as if she chewed food. When she had finished she spoke, giving her judgment.

"It's the intention, not the deed that counts, daughter. I for one think it's real sweet, and besides that, poems ain't supposed to make real sense."

She closed her eyes and leaned against the foot of the bed. Nobody had ever written her a poem, not even a bad one; in fact she had never before known a man who had done such a thing, or who would admit it if he had, but she had often read of such things. She got up from the bed, her plait of graying hair harsh and oily in the lamplight. She bent above her daughter tenderly, as if already she had lost her, as if already she was a bride.

"There's another thing," said Myrtle, "and it's just this: I never did like a man who was tight with money and that's the way he is. Before we left the drug store he offered to buy me a box of candy. There were a lot of boxes in the show-case, each costing a dollar, but one had the tissue paper torn a little and one of the corners was broken some. Andrew picked out that box and said with everybody listening that he'd buy it if the clerk would sell it for seventy-five cents." She puffed out her lips and shivered with distaste. "They agreed finally on eighty cents while I stood there so ashamed I wished the floor would open up and swallow me."

"Now, daughter," said Kate lightly. "I wouldn't pay too much attention to that. I always admired a man who knowed the value of money. I'd say that was a recommendation in his favor, if you asked me."

Later, when she was in bed with her husband, scraps of Andrew's poem kept floating through her mind. She pressed against her husband's warm, hairy body, her arms holding him clasped. Neil woke at last. He said patiently: "For God sake, Katie, let me get some sleep. There's a time and place for everything, but I got to work tomorrow."

Kate ran her fingers through his thick hair, twisting the curls into rings for her fingers. She pressed her lips against her husband's cheek and made the small, inviting noises of love, but Neil turned on his side, the quilt raised upward in a mound to shape his buttocks, sighed twice and was asleep again.

Mrs. Bickerstaff took away her arms and dusted them with disgust. She rolled over and lay on her edge of the bed, as far from her husband as she could get.

"Men are all alike!" she whispered bitterly to herself. "All they want from a woman is one thing!"

She smiled into the darkness, contemptuous of her husband, remote from the clamoring beastliness of men, taking a dejected pleasure in the knowledge that no matter what other woman might do, she, at least, would never consent to be a man's plaything.

CHAPTER VI

MYRTLE sat on the back steps peeling potatoes for supper, while to the left her mother was washing the soiled diapers of her baby. Kate was not entirely satisfied with her daughter's account of the evening before; she felt that there must be many details of interest which Myrtle had omitted. She questioned her hopefully, although she had little faith that Myrtle would tell her what she wanted to know. Kate had long understood the character of her daughter and had accepted it. She expected few confidences, for Myrtle had that terrifying calmness of unimaginative people who are often not even interested in the essential facts of their own lives, seeing all emotions, all events in the same colors, with accent nowhere. But to her surprise, Myrtle began to talk.

She had met Andrew's brother and his sweetheart, a girl named May MacLean, and she described them to her mother as best she could. She didn't like Jim. He was too good-looking, she considered, for a man; besides that, the girls in the drug store all made a great fuss over him. He was very conceited, too, and you could see that he thought every girl he met was in love with him. She was kinder to May. May was a short girl with sandy-colored hair and her eyes were a washed-out blue, but she was friendly enough and seemed sweet, although what Jim Tallon saw in her to admire, she couldn't say. Andrew had told her that when May was a little girl her arm had been scalded while her father was dressing hogs. The scar had grown out so that it was hardly noticeable now, but May was sensitive about it and she always wore long sleeves in her dresses, summer and winter.

Mrs. Bickerstaff took the diapers one by one between her thumb and forefinger, lifting them with dainty disgust from the tin boiler, where they had been soaking, to the tub of bluing water before her. She did not interrupt her daughter, for it was rare to find Myrtle in a talkative mood and she meant to learn all that she could while the humor lasted.

Myrtle said: "I don't want you to think I'm being hard on Andrew, Mamma. I haven't got anything against him, when you come right down to it. I'm just not interested in him and I don't see any sense in fooling with him."

Mrs. Bickerstaff lifted the clean diapers from the rinsing water and fastened them on the line with clothes-pins. She finished and emptied her tubs in the yard, jumping back briskly so that her feet might not get wet. She hung up the boiler and the granite tub and wiped her hands and neck with her apron. She nodded her head thoughtfully, her mind made up. Since things were as they were, it seemed to her that the sensible thing for Myrtle to do was to go on keeping company with Andrew, for the time being at any rate. If she didn't really like him, she could easily be his friend. A girl should always have some reliable man handy to take her places and be attentive to her, otherwise how could she expect to meet other young men whom she liked better?

Kate Bickerstaff paused in her long speech and looked suspiciously at her daughter.

"Did you meet any boys in the drug store last night that you liked better than Andrew?"

"I only met three or four and I didn't like any of them." She shook her head stubbornly, remembering the occasion.

"Jim Tallon was telling a story about something or other and all the girls kept leaning over him and hanging on his words. I expect he thought I'd do the same thing. Well, if he did, he sure got fooled for once in his life."

Kate Bickerstaff said: "I'm going to invite Andrew over for

Sunday dinner. I don't see what harm it'll do. Just be nice to him and let things take their course." She walked into her kitchen with a positive stride. She would take her daughter's affairs into her own hands, since Myrtle was obviously incapable of handling them herself. It was fortunate for Myrtle that she had a mother like herself, one experienced in people and the ways of the world.

Mrs. Bickerstaff made her resolve on the same afternoon that Susan Tallon entertained a few friends who had come to help with the finishing touches on her trousseau. They were done with their sewing and were eating the refreshments which Susan had fixed. Miss Sarah Tarleton put down her plate.

"I knew there was somebody missing. It's Andrew. I haven't seen him about the place since I came over this afternoon."

Susan said: "I guess I ought not to tell this on Andrew. He'd wring my neck if he thought we were talking about him, but Andrew's got him a girl at last, and he's gone to Reedyville to look for a second-hand car to ride her about in."

Effie Cleaver spoke in surprise: "*Andrew* out sweethearting? Heavens and earth! I never heard of such a thing!" She was a huge, shapeless woman. Her teeth were bad, black and decayed, and her neck and cheeks were sprayed with brown moles no larger than bird shot. When she had been a young, slim girl, the moles had been considered beautiful; now they seemed silly and somewhat affected, as if she strove unsuccessfully to ape her betters.

"Rafe Hall went to Reedyville to help pick it out," said Susan, "and all I can say is this: Lord help that second-hand dealer if Rafe and Andrew start jewing him down at the same time."

"She's pretty," said May MacLean, "but she's not very friendly, and she don't talk much. Maybe she's not used to us yet."

The ladies discussed Andrew and his love affair for an hour or more, remembering by turns all that they had heard or surmised concerning the Bickerstaffs. They were still talking when he returned, driving the automobile he had bought. They became

53

silent when he came on the porch among them, examining him with speculative and interested glances to mark what changes love had already wrought in his flesh.

May MacLean said: "I want to congratulate you on your good taste, Andy. You picked the best-looking girl in the county when you did make up your mind to pick one."

When he was inside the house, Andrew went to his room and changed to the working clothes he wore about the farm. It would not be dark for several hours yet, and there was much work to be done; but he felt languid and at ease, and he lay down on his bed. From where he lay he could see the countryside, across the fields, beyond the branch, as far as Gentry's Ford, where the Cornells' cattle came at dusk to drink. . . .

Against one side of the wall, above the pine desk which Bradford had made, was a shelf containing his books. There were not many of them, but he had read them all over and over, a little ashamed to be so preoccupied with such womanish things. There was a set of Shakespeare, bound in red leather which had cracked badly, and a set of Edgar Allan Poe which had come to his father as a premium with a magazine subscription; two volumes by Dr. Stanley telling of his explorations in Africa. There was, also, a volume of poems by Blake and one by Browning, prizes which he had won while a pupil at Professor Drewery's school.

Andrew got up from the bed and stood critically before his small library. Below him he could hear the noise the women made as they talked. They were discussing him, he knew, and the automobile that he had bought, and the thought pleased him somehow. It was sweet flattery to be thus the topic of talk as a man who loved and who was, no doubt, loved in turn. . . . At last he selected for his purpose the Bible which had belonged to his mother and which she had given him before her death, as if she had known that he, being the afflicted child, would stand more in need of comfort than the others, must learn more truly the resignation which she had learned. He stood by the open window and read words that he knew by heart. He read slowly, turning the thin India paper with infinite care.

He felt very young and very tender. He lay once more on his bed, stretched widely on his back. He took his pillow into his arms and held it close to his body, staring upward at the sky. He let the insistent thing that was coming into his mind shape itself wordlessly, turning it and twisting it about his happiness. Later, when the depth of his feeling had found its own words and he had corrected and revised those words as best he could, he would copy his poem into the ledger which he kept locked in his desk away from all eyes. After a time he got up, sat at his desk and began to write in his microscopic, rounded hand:

My beloved is more yielding than feathers:
She is smoother than anything spun; she is softer than anything woven.
Her hair is like wood from a far land and there are golden lights in her hair.
Her eyes are golden and mottled with brown; her body is all shades of gold and brown.

In the sight of my beloved, I am like iron that the smith has heated at his furnace: iron whose surface gives heat.
I am a bar that is rigid and will not bend.
I know this thing. I know it; and yet I am also as water that flows inward,
And my breast is a cage in which birds fly.
I hold my hands against my breast and close my eyes crying:
"Her loveliness is too great, oh ye people, and I faint before it! . . .
Her beauty is too sudden for me!"

Susan's party was breaking up and he could hear the women laughing and calling to each other. He pressed his hands against his cheeks, his eyes closed, groping for words to write, words which he knew must always be foolish when spoken by his gasping mouth.

CHAPTER VII

On Saturday Andrew received a note from Myrtle asking him to dinner. He was up early the next morning, before Susan and Jim were stirring, and went to the pool to bathe, the soft-eyed, mongrel hound, Tobey, close at his heels.

Years before, when Lemuel Tallon had first married, he had widened and deepened the creek where it passed through his land and had dammed it with cypress pilings and bags of earth. To the left of the old pilings, a bar of white sand had formed. On three sides bay trees and sweet-gums grew close to the pool, screening it from the Cornells' land and from Thompson's Lane. Tobey lay folded on the triangle of his haunches and stared with incredulity while Andrew undressed and stood in the sharp air, for, although the sun was well up now, the chill of early morning had not yet entirely gone away. There was an early mist hanging above the water and long streamers of mist moved among the trees and the wet underbrush, lifting a little and fumbling like the blind hands of ghosts. A frog croaked steadily and two birds, lost in the trees somewhere, quarreled shrilly.

Andrew ran forward, lifted his arms and dived into the water. He came to the surface in a long half curve, where it was shallow, where the bar of sand lay. There was no sound now except the sucking of the creek against the old dam and the kissing noise of the water made as it touched and withdrew from his wallowing flesh. The hound watched him from the bank, stretched on his grave haunches in the dew, his forefeet straight before him, his tentative nose reaching forward uneasily and twitching.

Andrew called the dog, snapping his fingers, but the hound only yawned with his entire length, flattened more closely and beat his whip-like tail against the sand. His body trembled quickly and he rolled his eyes upward. Andrew came to him and took him by the loose flesh of his neck, and the hound, unprotesting, still patient and imploring, dug his feet into the earth and resisted with all his strength, his tongue lolling apologetically for the necessity of refusing his master's wish.

Andrew laughed his cracked, cloudy laugh. He released his grip on the hound's neck and Tobey settled again on the sand, shivered, lifted his neck and yawned twice again with jaws completely opened, the small, pink cavern of his throat pushed suddenly forward. Andrew soaped his wet body. Then he dived once more into the pool and came to the surface shaking his head. The soap bubbles floated on the dark water in lace-like designs and spread outward like a fine canopy made patiently by delicate hands.

There was a shrill yapping and down the slope of land that led to the pool Andrew saw Sambo, the black, half-grown spaniel running, falling forward in his haste, his forelegs crumpling beneath him clumsily. Andrew whistled and the dog came straight toward him, making a hysterical, quick sound. When he reached the pool he jumped into the water and swam toward Andrew, his legs working furiously. Andrew stood waist deep in the water and held the spaniel to his breast, while the dog squirmed in his arms and barked.

Tobey, the hound, had come to the edge of the pool. He touched the water with one of his paws, shrank back with distaste and set up a disconsolate baying, until, at last, he walked into the pool and swam toward his master. He shoved the spaniel away with his shoulders, his teeth bared. Andrew lay on his back and shouted with laughter, beating the water with his arms until the intricate. rainbow designs of the soap, broken and drifting together again, exploded with small puffs and floated slowly over the dam.

Susan was busy with breakfast when he got back to the house and Jim was sitting in the kitchen. He lifted his face from the paper that he was reading and Andrew saw that his lip was swollen and that one of his eyes was black and almost closed.

Susan said: "It's no use saying anything more to him. I've already said everything that anybody could say. Sometimes I'm glad poor Mamma never lived to see the way Jim carries on."

"What happened to you, Jim?"

Jim twisted in his chair and threw down the paper like a little boy amazed at the denseness of his elders. "There's nothing to it," he said. "I took May to a dance in Reedyville last night. There was a fellow who kept looking at her and I didn't like it. He talked like a Yankee and he was too damned cocky and dressed up for my taste."

Susan said: "Move your elbows, Jim, if you want me to give you your breakfast."

"So I went over to where this fellow was and invited him outside. He came quick enough. I found out later he sells feed. He comes from Chicago, or leastways that's where he was born, but he's traveling out of Mobile now. He's going to look me up, he says, the next time he makes a trip through this county."

Susan spoke: "You ought to be ashamed to throw Tobey in the branch, Andy! You know how he hates cold water." She went through the door with two plates of food for the dogs.

"What happened after you invited this fellow out of the dance hall?"

"Oh, we all went to Moore's Livery Stable. There were six or eight of us fellows, but Herb Outerbridge was the only one I knew. We knocked each other about a little. His nose was bleeding and my lip was cut, so a few minutes later a fellow from the Reedyville Bank who was refereeing said he thought that we'd both had satisfaction. Then the drummer offered to shake hands. His name is Tom Ostermann. He said he hadn't meant any harm by looking at May; he was just lonesome and he wished he had somebody to dance with him too. I said I guess I was just jealous of him and afraid that he could take May away from me if he tried. Everybody laughed at that and we all had a drink around."

"Tobey is shaking to pieces with cold," said Susan. "If you ever throw him in the branch again I'll run you off the place."

"Tom invited me up to his room at the Magnolia Hotel. After we'd washed the blood off and had another drink, we both sat down on the bed and laughed until we were weak."

Susan began scraping the plates. "Folks don't fight with their friends. If they're your friends, you don't want to do anything that will cause them pain. You have only affection for them."

Jim's good humor was completely restored. The food and the hot coffee had made him feel better.

"Listen to Suse, won't you? She's getting more like old Sarah Tarleton every day, isn't she?"

By timing himself, Andrew arrived in Hodgetown and parked his car in front of the Bickerstaff gate exactly at noon. Neil met him and opened the door. His red face was shining with cleanliness and his stiff curls were wet and close to his head, looking almost black. His wife was close behind him. Kate smiled sadly.

"Come in, Mr. Tallon," she said. "It's all ready on the table and waiting."

When dinner was over, Andrew and Myrtle sat in the porch swing. Below them in the beds that surrounded the porch, vines planted for shade were just coming up, the thick, pale shoots, with the seed bean worn like a shrunken cap, lifting above the earth.

"That's as fine a meal as I've had for a long time. I don't see how any many could kick about your cooking."

"It's mighty nice of you to say so," replied Myrtle; "but I don't

60

take any credit because cooking and keeping house comes easy to me, and Mamma taught me how to do it real good."

Mrs. Bickerstaff came to join them and sat in the rocking-chair which she always used. She began at once to talk.

"It's hard to pick up and leave your old home and your friends. Don't you find that to be the truth, Mr. Tallon?"

"I don't know. I've never been anywhere."

"I'm not saying that there's not just as good people in Alabama as there are back in Georgia," continued Mrs. Bickerstaff. "I'm only saying that if there are, I haven't met up with them yet." She lifted her broad face, sunk in sorrow, the discolored pouches under her eyes like small sacks, half slack with stagnant water.

"Neil just went down to the planer mill. He went through the back yard, as he didn't want to disturb nobody. It was something about a fan belt." She cleared her throat and rocked in silence for a moment.

"It does look like the Hodge brothers could let a man get his rest on a Sunday, at least, don't it?"

Andrew said: "If you ladies haven't got anything better to do, let's all take a ride somewhere."

"You two go," said Kate. She looked at her daughter significantly. "I can't get away from the children."

After Myrtle had gone into the house to put on her hat and to prepare for the ride, Mrs. Bickerstaff spoke in a whisper: "I wouldn't be put off by the way Myrtle acts, because she's a funny girl in some ways. She never did take much stock in men company, but I believe to my soul she likes you better than she has any of the others."

Andrew tried to speak, but she stopped him.

"Oh, other fellows have courted Myrtle right and left back in Georgia, you can be sure of that; among the nicest young fellows in town, too, but she wouldn't have anything to do with any of them."

She had made her point; she had finished. She straightened the folds of her dress, touching her hair to see that the pins were firmly in place. "I'd better go now and see what the children are up to," she said.

They drove down the Reedyville road, but branched off when they reached the Barrascale farm and took the dirt road that led to Pearl River. Andrew shut off his engine and they got out and walked through a stretch of gall-berries, the new leaves, smokily green, like fine jade, brushing their legs. They walked in silence, not knowing what to say to each other, following the path that led gradually downward to the river. When they were tired they sat down beside the path. Before them was a graybeard-tree, a tree with streamers like those of willows, but finer, more attenuated, and of a soft and ancient silver. The streamers of the tree lifted upward and curved away from the trunk, spilling downward in lines like fountain water fixed forever in the air of spring.

Andrew stretched out and lay with his head in Myrtle's lap. He touched her cheek with his hand and smiled upward at her. His small, blue eyes were soft, his body relaxed and at peace.

"If you're going to act like that, Andrew, we might as well go back home."

"What have you got against me?"

"What makes you think I got anything against you?"

"Is it my lip? Is it the way I look?"

"I didn't say it was that. You said it yourself, not me."

"Then why don't you like me a little?"

Myrtle spoke suddenly: "All right, I'll tell you the God's truth. I'll tell you just what I think of you: When I first met you that night at prayer meeting and saw your mouth I felt sort of sick at my stomach, I guess, but I'm getting so I don't pay any attention to it. I can understand better what you say, too. I wouldn't have gone out with you the first time except that Mamma persuaded me. She wants me to marry and I don't blame her for that, with all the other children coming on, but as far as I'm concerned, I'd just as soon die an old maid as not."

Myrtle laughed her rare laugh. "All right. I told you the truth, like you wanted, and I hope I haven't hurt your feelings. If I have, I can't help it. I guess there's something the matter with me, but I never could learn how to lie or pretend like other people. Mamma can do it all right, but I can't."

Andrew said: "You haven't told me anything that I didn't know, and you haven't hurt my feelings. I'm only asking that you try to like me a little if you can."

As if her confession had relieved her mind, Myrtle felt more friendly toward him. She smoothed back his hair, stroking his cheeks with her fingers. It was the first time that she had voluntarily touched him.

"I never said I wouldn't try to like you, did I? I wouldn't be out with you now if I didn't like you a little."

She moved his head and got up, brushing her skirt briskly, and walked down the path toward the river.

Andrew said: "That's the first love-vine I've seen this year." He tore the golden, parasitic threads from the bushes where they grew and which they would suck dry and destroy in time.

"Back home the boys and girls used to name the first piece of love-vine they saw in the spring and make a wish with it," said Myrtle. "I didn't know it grew in Alabama too."

Andrew separated the long, clinging cords which he had gathered, whose ends, even now lifted upward as if seeking in the insubstantial air a new substance for their grasping. He kept half of the strands for himself and gave the other half to Myrtle. He looked about him for a moment, calculated, closed his eyes and threw the vine over his shoulder.

"You mustn't look back to see if it caught," warned Myrtle. "If you look back the spell won't work."

"I'm coming back here next week and see if it grew," said Andrew. He fixed the spot in his mind. "If it grows, I'll know for certain that you're going to love me."

Myrtle laughed. "Why, I never heard anything so conceited. That's the way with men: they think every girl is crazy about them." She paused a moment and then continued slowly: "You're even worse than your brother Jim!"

Andrew said: "Jim's not conceited when you get to know him. That's just his way at first." He noticed then that Myrtle still held her portion of the vine in her hand. "You haven't named yours yet," he said. "Go ahead and throw it, but if you want to make sure it's going to live, you better name it Andrew Tallon."

Myrtle closed her eyes, repeated the formula and threw the vine behind her.

"Who did you name it for?" he begged. "Come on, tell me, Myrtle!"

Myrtle would not answer. She walked away down the path, her rounded hips swinging. In a moment they passed out of the trees into a patch of grass land, to the place where the land dipped downward. Before them was the black water of Pearl River fringed with new green. Beyond that, and against the fore-shortened horizon, were piled eternal clouds which towered upward and broke toward their summits under winds which did not touch the earth.

"Who did you name it for, darling? Come on, tell me!"

"I named it for Jim, if you must know."

Andrew looked at her in surprise.

"You are the strangest girl I ever met. I can't figure you out, no matter how hard I try."

"I don't see anything so funny about that," said Myrtle defensively. "We were talking about Jim the minute before and his was the first name that came into my mind. . . . It might have been anybody else just as well."

CHAPTER VIII

ADDIE WRENN'S party
for her daughter had already begun, but Myrtle, sitting with Andrew outside in the parked car, had become self-conscious at the
last minute and did not want to go in. She trembled and held her
arms tightly across her breasts. Inside the house there was the
sound of quick, released merriment. There was the noise of chairs
being scraped across bare boards and the sound of furniture being
moved as the place was cleared for dancing. The moon was up and
it flooded the ploughed fields and woods with shy radiance.

Occasionally a furtive figure would emerge into the circle of
light cast by the windows of the house and stand behind a
japonica bush, a flask of corn whisky raised to his lips, escaped
for a moment from the watchful eye of Mrs. Wrenn, who did
not permit drinking on her premises; or a couple would walk
out, their arms about each other, unconscious that they were observed.

Myrtle spoke: "Did you go back like you said and see whether
or not the love-vine grew?"

"Neither piece caught hold," said Andrew. "They both shriveled up and died. The sun must have been too hot for them."

Myrtle said primly, her tiny voice faint but very clear: "Well, I
hope I never get to be superstitious like a nigger, is all I can say."

Then Andrew saw his brother Jim come out of the house with
Willie Oakshot and the two Cornells boys. When he called out,
Jim left his friends and came to the parked car. He took Myrtle's
hand and held it, looking mockingly into her face. His eyes were
narrowed humorously and his lips fixed in a smile which was
half friendly, half contemptuous.

"I hear you think I'm conceited."

He turned to Andrew. "We'd about given you two up. We'd decided you'd ruther sit at home in the swing and hold hands." He stood with his foot on the running-board of the car, his dark eyes rolling a little. His face was slightly flushed and his breath was strong with the whisky that he had been drinking. He laughed gaily and swayed his shoulders, swaggering a little.

Then Myrtle too became gay, her uncertainty gone.

"Let's go inside and dance," she said. "We're late enough for the party as it is."

She opened the door of the car and got out. Her eyes sparkled and she waltzed coquettishly, her arms held outward toward some imaginary partner. When she felt Andrew's arm about her waist, she stopped. She pulled away from him, her animation gone.

"Don't!" she protested. "You'll muss up my dress."

For a moment Andrew's arm remained in the air circling the place where Myrtle had just stood. His arms fell to his sides. He looked quickly at his brother who stood by the car smoking a cigarette, grinned and lowered his head shamefacedly.

They entered the house just before the dancing commenced, at the moment when Addie Wrenn was officially welcoming her guests. She stood in the center of the room, her daughter beside her.

"Well, this is nice," she said. "We're mighty glad to have you with us, Myrtle."

She smiled, the thread-like lines about her lips deepening, her sandy hair, streaked through with gray, drawn tightly away from her skull and piled upward against a comb such as a Spanish dancer might affect. "I want you to know my daughter Agnes," she continued. "She's come all the way from Memphis just to spend her birthday at home."

Agnes was a younger replica of her mother, but even more prim, more tight-lipped. She was traffic manager for a hardwood lumber

66

company and she had succeeded in life. She wore rimless nose-glasses, secured to her ear with a gold chain, and her face had that smooth and yet puckered look of women who have remained virginal too long.

Jim said: "Well, Agnes, how's everything in the hardware business?"

"*Hardwood*," corrected Agnes. She added seriously: "We're doing well, everything considered. It hasn't been such a bad year, except for exports, but there's simply no market for ash squares anywhere."

"You must meet some of the young men, Myrtle," said Mrs. Wrenn. "I don't blame Andrew for not wanting to introduce you around, but we're not a-going to let him keep you all to himself."

Agnes was still speaking, her thin voice cutting across the thinner voice of her mother: "Business to Antwerp and Barcelona has fallen away to nothing. You can say it just doesn't exist any more. If London didn't hold up so well, I'd advise closing up the export department entirely until world conditions improve."

"I'm glad I had this party after all," said Mrs. Wrenn to her guests. "Agnes was against it, thinking it would be too much trouble for me and her papa, but I said I couldn't let the two anniversaries go by ere another year without a party of some sort to celebrate." She smoothed her sandy hair contentedly. "You see we're celebrating *two* occasions tonight instead of one, because as it happens Agnes was born on the same day I married."

Jim laughed deeply, his head thrown back, the wing of hair falling almost to his eyes.

"Good Lord!" he said with humorous concern. "I'll bet the neighbors talked!"

Agnes spoke quickly: "Mamma means that I was born on the third *anniversary* of her wedding day."

67

Myrtle laughed with the others, but she had not really understood what was said, for she had not been listening. She had been looking at Jim and thinking how much finer he was than these people about him. To herself she said: "Jim's the sweetest-looking man I ever seen, in or outside of the movies." The music started and she turned to him expectantly, but Jim took her hand and placed it in his brother's.

"Go on and have your dance. I won't interfere with your sweethearting. . . . But don't think you can get shut of me so easy, because I'll be back again for my dance before you meet too many other fellows."

May MacLean was standing by the door and he walked to her.

When he had gone, Myrtle turned her head, following his figure, as if already there were an understanding between them. She was so preoccupied that for a few minutes she did not know that Andrew had put his arms about her and that they were dancing together. After that she passed from partner to partner. She felt a new power which she had not known before, a certainty that she was admired, that there was nothing she could not have. She threw off her sullen reticence and began talking volubly to her partners, touching with an air of proprietorship their coat lapels, leaning backward from their embrace, her hips thrown forward, and examining them with amused and sensuous eyes, as she had seen women on the screen admire their lovers. She was dancing with Willie Oakshot, close to the alcove, before she had a chance to speak to Jim again. He was standing by the door with his back to the wall.

She paused before him, her feet still moving to the music, and spoke provocatively: "Well, I see you haven't come back for that dance you were talking so big about. It's a shame to let me sit on the bench all night waiting for you."

"I saw you sitting there," said Jim. "I didn't mean to treat you so bad."

68

He touched Willie Oakshot's arm: "I'll take her off your hands, Willie. There's no sense in your being stuck with her all night."

Myrtle said: "Well, I like that, I must say."

"Willie can do me a favor next time," said Jim.

Myrtle walked away, toward the porch, knowing that Jim was close behind her, so sure of herself at this moment that she did not bother to turn or even to speak. She was excited with the new rôle that she was playing. She walked through the yard and the parked automobiles, leaned at last against the picket fence and fluffed her hair out at the sides.

Jim said: "I hope you didn't get me out here to take advantage of me. My reputation is all I got left."

Myrtle turned and faced him. This, she thought, was like a situation from a moving picture, and Jim's talk and her own was the brilliant dialogue of drawing-room comedy.

"Can't I get shut of you any way I try? Can't I get a breath of fresh air by myself?"

"I don't know. Women are something I don't know much about. I never expect to, either."

"I'm glad you admit there's something you don't know."

"I read a book on how to make love once, but I didn't get any farther than the fifth chapter, which treated on the art of kissing, but I learned to do that pretty well."

"I'll take your word for that," said Myrtle laughingly. "I don't want a demonstration, thank you."

"If I'd read the whole book to the end, there's no telling what I might have learned."

"Who did you practice on? May MacLean?"

"I didn't have a girl at the time," said Jim, "so I learned on myself. I practiced in the looking-glass with the book open beside me, until I got it just right."

They both began to laugh excitedly. Jim put his arms about her

69

and pulled her body close to his own. She looked into his excited, yellow-irised eyes.

"This is the way you do it," said Jim. "This is what I learned in Chapter Five."

Afterwards he opened the gate and they walked across the road and into the pine thicket where they would be screened from the house and secure against interruption.

Myrtle was silent on the drive home. All the animation had gone out of her and she sat with her coat collar turned up, her hands unclasped in her lap. They reached the Bickerstaff gate, and Andrew parked his car under the trees. Myrtle started to get out, but he put his hand on her arm.

"Don't go in yet awhile. It's not very late."

Myrtle sat passive, her eyes vague and unsettled, as if she debated with herself. She said finally: "I'm cold!" opened the door of the automobile and stood outside on the plot of grass. "Good night," she said, "and thanks for taking me. I had a nice time."

Andrew, too, got out and stood beside her under the chinaberry tree. Something told him that she would not want him to touch her, that she would not welcome his advances, but he could not resist his desire. He put his arms about her, holding her close to him, and declared his love. Words rushed out of him at last, words which formed no coherent sentence, but which, in their formlessness, told all the things he had thought for the past days but had not dared to express.

Myrtle stood against his body like an empty sack, as unresistant as cloth and as unresponsive, while he touched her cheeks and her hair and whispered to her in his broken, gasping voice, his breath beating against her ear. She pulled away, at length no longer able to hide her distaste, turned and entered the house. She got into bed hastily, knowing that her mother would be awake and that she would come up to talk. In the darkness she thought again of the

70

scene with Jim. He seemed very strange and very remarkable to her, and she repeated his remembered words over and over to herself, as if they held some meaning not found in the words of the ordinary people she had known in her lifetime. She thought of answers that she might have made, how she might have impressed him more. She closed her eyes and pressed her cheek against her pillow hugging it in her pleasure, for on the whole she was not dissatisfied with herself.

The door opened cautiously and Mrs. Bickerstaff stood in the room. Her face was covered with mutton suet, which she rubbed into her skin with the hardened tips of her fingers. She had been nursing her baby when Myrtle came home and her nightgown even now was wet with milk from her dripping breasts.

"Poor child," said Mrs. Bickerstaff tenderly. "She's all tired out and gone to sleep already."

She closed the door behind her carefully and went back to her bed.

CHAPTER IX

ANDREW sat on the side of his brother's bed taking off his shoes. He shook out his socks and rubbed the naked soles of his feet.

Jim said: "Christ almighty, a person would think you were crazy about the girl!"

"She's so pretty and so sweet, Jim!"

"I've seen prettier." Jim yawned and crushed out his cigarette. "Come on, blow out that lamp and go to bed. I've got to get up early tomorrow, Sunday or no Sunday, and so have you."

"She's so . . ."

"I know. I know," said Jim. "I know all about that. But go to bed, for Christ sake, and sleep it off." He felt irritable all of a sudden. He was ashamed of what he had done, and for a moment he wanted to tell Andrew about Myrtle and himself, but he decided against it.

"You better get over it," said Jim. "What do you want to marry her for? Don't tie yourself up to that sort of woman for life. It's not worth it."

Andrew smiled vaguely, his mind far away. "What have you got against Myrtle? She likes you. She said she did on the way home. She said she had been wrong about you and that she'd apologize for saying you were conceited."

"I know," said Jim. "I know."

When the lights were out and the brothers were in their beds, Andrew spoke through the open door between the rooms. "I haven't got a chance with her, I guess."

Instantly Jim was alert. "Why not? She ought to be damned glad to get you, if you ask me."

But Andrew shook his head in doubt and sighed softly under his breath. He could not explain to his brother what he meant, but he raised his fingers in the dark and touched his mutilated mouth. He spoke after a long time. "She don't want me even to touch her. When I try to make love to her, she won't listen."

"You treat her too good," said Jim.

His lips pulled down in a knowing smile and he winked, as if he were satisfied with himself. He stared at the faintly luminous sky, visible through the window, his head resting in the cup of his locked fingers; but almost at once the sense of shame came back intensified. Why had he done it? Why couldn't he at least have left his brother's girl alone? She meant nothing to him; in fact, she wasn't even the type that he liked. He had always fallen in love with softer and more gentle women, like May MacLean or Sarah Cornells. Andrew's words kept coming back to him and he felt a pity for his brother which Andrew did not feel for himself. . . . Poor Andrew, cursed that way! He had had so little in life, had had to bear so much. . . .

His vague feelings of remorse turned then to a minor fury. He couldn't have done a thing of that sort. It wasn't like him to betray his own brother that way. A man would have to be a swine to do such a thing! . . . Obviously it was Myrtle's fault and she had planned the whole thing and had led him on. Otherwise, why had she given up so easily? Why hadn't she resisted him more? She had deliberately tricked him for some purpose which he could not, as yet, fathom. . . . Anyway, he wouldn't marry her, no matter what happened. He'd be good-God-damned if he'd do that! He began to feel better and his fists unclenched.

If Myrtle was that sort of woman, he had done Andrew a service, for it was certainly better to find out what she was in time. It was better for Andrew to know the truth, even if it did hurt him

73

a little at first, than for him to go ahead and marry a woman like that. It was better to see the truth, as he himself was seeing it so certainly now.

Jim smiled knowingly and lifted his fingers to his throat, as if he spread and adjusted an invisible necktie to a more seductive knot.

Although it was a Sunday morning and Mrs. Bickerstaff did not as a rule believe in unnecessary work on that day, it was obvious that the vines around the porch needed attention. The young stalks had lengthened and turned darker, and already there were thin tendrils lifting in the air and bending backward of their own weight. And so it was that she crouched before the beds on her haunches, as big and as rounded as bicycle wheels, while Myrtle stood above her and fastened the twine to the lattice-work over her head. They had been talking of the Wrenns' party of the night before, and Myrtle had told her mother what she cared to tell her, but they were not the things Mrs. Bickerstaff wanted to hear.

"What about Andrew? How did you two get along?"

"Can't you leave me alone, Mamma? Can't you tend to your business and let me tend to mine?"

Mrs. Bickerstaff spoke, her words blurred with the wooden pegs she held in her mouth. "I'm sorry if I said anything to make you mad, daughter, but I'm only thinking of your own good."

"If you want to do something for my good so bad, you can leave me alone."

"You'll regret it, daughter, mark my words. You'll be sorry some day you didn't listen to me when you had the chance."

Myrtle threw down the ball of twine angrily and sat on the steps. "Why couldn't it have been Jim Tallon I met first? Why wasn't it Jim who fell in love with me?"

"Oh!" said Mrs. Bickerstaff. "Oh! So that's the way the old

74

sow's rooting." She sat by her daughter, and after much coaxing Myrtle began to talk again. She felt that she had made a very slight impression only, now that she thought the matter over more calmly. There was something about Jim that she couldn't understand, some strange quality that eluded her.

"He goes with half a dozen girls off and on," she said, "but he's said to be engaged to marry May MacLean."

Mrs. Bickerstaff turned these new developments over in her mind. Her eyes lowered thoughtfully and her arms folded in her lap, her face so expressionless, so stone-like that she resembled a badly chiseled Buddha whose temple had been taken unexpectedly from over her head. After a time she nodded shrewdly, her mind made up.

"I wouldn't give up Andrew right away, if I was you." She stroked her lips meditatively. "I'd hold on to him a little longer and see what happens."

"I don't see what good that will do."

Mrs. Bickerstaff was surprised at her daughter's lack of intelligence and she expressed herself fully. It would do all the good in the world. How otherwise, since Jim, as she herself had admitted, was not enough interested in her, was she to see him? Going with Andrew would give her a chance to mingle freely with the Tallons, and before she knew it Jim would be in love with her too, if she just let things take their course. After that Myrtle could break off the affair with Andrew and go on with Jim.

"Poor Andrew," said Kate. "Poor boy. My hearts bleeds for him. He's going to suffer if he loves you like you say."

"I feel sorry for him too," said Myrtle. "But Andrew knows where he stands with me. I haven't led him on."

Kate said: "I've never met Jim and I'll hold off judging between them until I do, but just the same I still believe Andrew would make the best husband."

Andrew went about that Sunday thinking of Myrtle. In the afternoon he called Tobey, the mongrel hound, and took a walk through the woods, white with dogwood in blossom. Later he stopped at the Cornells' place and sat for a time talking to Sam and Harvey, the unmarried sons. It was almost dusk when he returned home and sat on the porch, tired from his long walk. Tobey pressed against him and sniffed his leg.

"What's all this I hear about you and Neil Bickerstaff's daughter?" asked Carl. "It looks like you're going to beat Jim to the barn yet."

"I will if she'll just have me."

"She'll have you," said Jim, "and jump at the chance."

He leaned back against the post and looked at his brother through narrowed eyes, and it seemed to him that he was seeing Andrew for the first time. He knew then that he had never thought of Andrew as a man like himself who might fall in love with a girl, marry and have a life of his own, and the idea was a little strange to him. Again he had that sense of shame, that feeling of bafflement over the inconsistency of his own conduct. Andrew could take his happiness and his good wishes along with it, for he would not see Myrtle again, no matter what happened. He'd done enough damage already. He got up and walked among the oak trees. He raised his right hand and his lips moved soundlessly:

"I swear to God I'll never see her again! I swear it! If I touch her again may I rot forever in hell!"

Myrtle came into the parlor, dressed in her best. There were two circular spots of rouge on her face and a fat, rather silly curl, twisted by her mother's earnest finger, rested against her cheek.

"Jim said to give you his best regards. He said he knew you'd laughed about that joke you two played on each other at the party, but he didn't have any hard feelings because he knew

76

you weren't any more serious than he was. He said to tell you he'd forgotten all about it."

"What joke is Jim talking about?"

"He wouldn't say. He said you'd know what he meant."

Myrtle sat forward in her chair. She asked many questions about Jim. She wanted to know everything about him: the dishes that he particularly relished, whether he liked light-headed or dark-headed girls the best; whether he liked them quiet or talkative. . . .

And so it was that Andrew was permitted to hope. He called on Myrtle regularly for the next few weeks. They went everywhere together. Occasionally they even drove over to Reedyville on a Saturday night to take in the movies. The whole county knew of the courtship by now and laughed at it, but they predicted that Andrew's persistence would triumph in the end.

"I presume he really loves her," said Miss Sarah Tarleton in her precise, school-teacher voice. "When a gentleman as careful as Andrew spends all his money on a young lady, even buying an automobile with his savings, he's bound to love her."

But Myrtle was disappointed during this period, for her mother's plan did not seem to work out in practice. It was true that she saw Jim often enough, but she never saw him alone, and at last even a person as unimaginative as herself had to understand that he was deliberately avoiding her. She talked this over with her mother and they were both puzzled. There was nothing very definite to say about Jim's attitude one way or the other. He was merely bantering and evasive.

CHAPTER X

THE dinner hour was announced in Hodgetown by the blowing of whistles. Most of the workmen went at once to their dinners and their families, hurrying away from the plant almost before the whistles had ceased to sound or the machinery to move. There was often sawdust on their shoulders and the brims of their hats, and as they hurried down the long gangways and up the wooden stairs that led into Hiawatha Street, they would shake it off with a forward tilt of their whole bodies, or a jerking backward of their heads. Their eyes were set straight before them, thinking of food, and at every house a man dropped out of the line, scraped his feet on the identically made wooden walk that led from each front gate to each front door, and entered his house silently.

A few of the workmen who lived too far away brought their dinners in pails and ate it at the mill, among them being Jim Tallon. Neil Bickerstaff brought his dinner for a different reason. As millwright he liked to make an inspection of machinery while the mill was shut down, or if there were small repairs to be made, to do them when the other men were away. Often Jim would bring his lunch into the millwright's office, where there was a table, and the men would eat together.

Jim said: "Susan wouldn't change if you set a stick of dynamite off under her. I know just what there'll be today without even looking: There'll be two apples on top and there'll be four sandwiches—two fried egg with sliced onion and two fried bacon with tomatoes. What do you bet I'm wrong?"

Neil said: "I'll bet the extra cup of coffee."

Jim unwrapped the parcel and Neil peered over his shoulder. "Baked ham, by God!" His full, drooping chins were trembling with triumph. He slapped the table with his fist and tears of mirth came into his eyes. He leaned forward and put his head on the table, his red, incongruous curls shining in the sunlight.

"Baked ham, by God!"

"All right," said Jim. "You win the coffee."

Neil's lunch was more varied. He said: "Try this piece of chocolate cake, Jim. The old woman made it for Sunday dinner and this hunk was left over. . . . Katie's got her faults, but when it comes to either plain or fancy cooking, I don't place her below the best."

"Did you say cooking?" asked Jim innocently.

For an instant Neil's face was vacant, his mouth slightly opened. He began to laugh again, his head thrown back, choking on the food in his mouth.

"That's what I said, Jim! That's what I said and that's as far as I'm prepared to commit myself!"

Jim took the piece of cake and chewed it slowly. He nodded and took another bite. He said: "I never ate better cake in my life. Tell your old lady if she ever wants to run off with me that a postal card addressed to R.F.D. 1 will always find me waiting and willing."

That night at supper Neil told his wife what Jim had said and she beamed throughout her body. "Well, I'm glad *somebody* appreciates tasty food; there's few enough that do!"

She was obviously pleased and she settled back in her chair. Then she turned suspiciously to survey her children. Since the barriers of discipline were down in this, her melting moment of pleasure, she felt that somebody must of necessity take advantage of her. She leaned forward ponderously and rapped the knuckles of the child nearest her.

"George!" she said. "George! . . . Don't you know by now

that a boy only ten years old can't get more than *one* sweet-potato in his mouth at a time?"

"Do you and Jim Tallon eat dinner together every day?" asked Myrtle.

"Most every day, but some days we miss."

Myrtle and her mother looked at each other, the same thought in both their minds.

"It does look like you'd have mentioned an important thing like that before, Neil!"

"Well, it's no secret as far as I'm concerned. It's just never come up before." Neil glanced at his wife and his daughter, his face puzzled. He knew there was something he was missing, but he could not decide what it was. He said: "If you want to know what I think, I think you're both crazy."

Kate rose briskly from the table. "As it happens, we ain't particularly interested in *what* you think!"

When the table was cleared, Neil read his paper and smoked his pipe while the younger children gathered about under the lamp, their school books before them, staring stupidly at the printed pages. Examinations were coming on and their lips moved conscientiously, as if to shape in memory on their mouths the learning which would forever leave their brains virginal. At last things were put in readiness for the morning and Mrs. Bickerstaff joined Myrtle on the porch.

It was a hot night for April and there was little air stirring. In the pine grove at the end of the street a bird began to sing, stopped quickly, as if listening to his own voice, and then began again, abandoning himself utterly to song. There were at first only low, reiterated notes lifted without effort; then his song became more triumphant, louder and more liquid, until it reached a trill which ended abruptly and sank into nothingness, the vibrancy of the dying sound trembling for an instant against the darkness like a drifting feather.

"I declare," said Kate, "but that bird sounds real sweet."

She sat in the swing beside her daughter, propelling it with her foot, and the strained chains which supported it creaked backward and forward on two notes in two separate keys. She let the swing come to rest, turned her head and looked at Myrtle. She cleared her throat and spat over the rail, among the lusty vines. In the silence that followed another bird began to sing, but farther away, and so faint, so ghost-like that his voice was only a thrown echo of the first bird's song.

"I'll never forget the summer I met Neil. My father didn't want me to go out with boys from the mill and he thought Neil was common, but we managed to court almost every night. Well, I never heard so many singing birds as there were that summer; they don't sing the way they used to when I was a girl. There was one mocking bird that used to come and sing in the china-berry sapling by our front gate. It looked like he started just when Neil got there and he kept up a racket the whole time. . . . Well, sir, I promised Papa I'd make my company go home at ten o'clock, so Neil would have to go out and shake the tree when it got late to make that dratted bird stop singing. We were afraid he'd make so much fuss that he'd wake up Papa."

Mrs. Bickerstaff heaved upward with her whole, solidly stuffed body and laughed in deprecation of her sentimental days. "There was a catchword between me and Neil for a long time. Every time one of us said, 'Go shake the tree!' we knew what the other one meant and both bust out laughing."

"Mamma," began Myrtle slowly, "I've been thinking about Papa having to eat a cold meal every day. I don't think it's right for him to do that. I think we ought to cook him something hot and take it to him. A man that works hard for his family all day ought to have something hot in his stomach. It would be very good for him."

Kate regarded her daughter in silence before she smiled, her lips pursed forward, the lavender pouches vibrating beneath her shrewd eyes.

"Do you want me to go shake the tree?" she asked.

Myrtle got up. "I won't stay here to have everything I say twisted." She walked into the house, banging the screen door behind her, and walked up the stairs, her feet clattering angrily. She closed the door to her room and sat by the window thinking, deeply concerned with her plans. The bird was singing again, his gray breast lifted and trembling, from the live oak that grew in the Macbeth yard, a long, passionate sound so quivering and so fluted that his throat seemed filled with a colored fluid over which the notes rippled before release.

Birds were singing all over Pearl County that night, discovering their powers again after a season of silence. They circled the land with their song from the plum thicket behind Tarleton's store, the crêpe-myrtle bushes about the Wrenns' homestead, the oaks that grew about the Tallon place, calling to each other across the land in slow bursts of flooding sound, listening and being answered.

Andrew sat at his table copying the poem he had written into the ledger that lay open before him. When he heard Susan's step in the hall outside, he covered his work with his arms.

"Don't disturb yourself," said Susan gaily. "I just came in to turn your bed down for you." She laughed, her hands on her hips. "Don't worry, you couldn't pay me to read all that stuff you write to Myrtle."

She wrapped her hands in her work apron in a manner which she had learned from her mother. She felt mature and very tender, now that her marriage was so close.

She said: "You got it bad, Andy! You surely have got a bad case; but keep after her. Keep after her and you'll get her."

Andrew said: "I can't say that I'm making much headway."

When Susan had gone away, Andrew blew out his lamp and sat by the open window listening to the birds. From the beds blooming with spiced pinks beneath his window, a pungent smell rose upward and penetrated the room.

CHAPTER XI

M YRTLE walked down
Wampum Street a little self-consciously, a little ashamed of the
burden she carried, but when she had passed the commissary and
the drug store, where the loafers hung out, she felt more at ease.
She stopped at the wooden stairway that led downward to the
cut. A switch engine was pulling a string of freight cars, and she
sat down, waiting for the train to pass. She had fixed her hair a
new way that morning and her face was rouged and her lips
made up heavily.

Again she rehearsed the scene which she had planned for herself, her father and Jim. She would speak to Jim politely, with
impersonal kindness, but that was all. She wouldn't let him think
for a minute that she cared anything about him one way or the
other, certainly not after the indifferent way he had treated her
since the Wrenns' party. If he wanted to remedy his rudeness of
the past weeks she'd listen, that being only fair; but she wasn't
going to demean herself in any way. . . .

When the train passed she got up, touched her hair again and
grasped her basket firmly. She took the long way to the mill,
past the planer and through the yards, where boards were season-
ing in the sun. The big whistle was just blowing as she entered
her father's office, and she knew that she had timed things perfectly.

Her father's face was full of soap. He thrust his head deeply
into the basin, wetting his inappropriate, Cupid-like curls and
making blowing noises with his mouth. He groped for a wad of
clean cotton waste and wiped his hands and his neck.

84

"Where's Jim?" asked Myrtle suspiciously. "I thought you said he came down and ate with you!"

"Some days he don't come; but I guess he'll be along directly if he hasn't a special job of work to do."

The door opened and Jim entered. When he say Myrtle the smile died on his lips. He stood in the doorway, his hand still on the knob, as if he might reconsider and withdraw at any moment.

"Come on in, Jim!" shouted Neil. "You and Myrtle know each other by this time, I reckon."

Jim put his lunch on the table, knowing that he had gone too far to retreat.

"I didn't know you had company. I wouldn't have come down if I'd known that."

"I don't know what's got into the old woman and Myrtle," said Neil; "but they made their minds up all of a sudden that I ought to have a hot meal in the middle of the day. All I can say is, I ain't used to so much attention."

Jim glanced at Myrtle curiously. He thought: "What's her idea in coming here to make trouble for me? She needn't think she can hold that thing at Wrenns' over my head. It's been more than a month already and nothing has happened."

He pulled up a chair to the table, smiled and sat down.

"Maybe they're fattening you up to butcher when cold weather comes."

All at once Neil had a picture of his red and disemboweled body hanging head downward from a hook in a butcher shop. He lowered his head like a great dog and shook the water out of his hair. He laughed deeply.

"Well, there's many a choice cut left on me yet, even if I am a little tough."

The men began to eat and Myrtle stood behind them. She was animated and she addressed all her remarks to Jim, but since Jim answered only when he must, and then only in monosyllables, the things she had rehearsed so carefully, and with such different answers from him, fell flat. But she was not discouraged.

"Who is she, Jim?" she demanded. "Who's the lady? Is it still May MacLean?"

Jim said: "I don't know what you're driving at."

"You're not eating anything at all. When a workingman don't eat, he's pretty sure to be in love."

"She's got you there," said Neil. "You ain't hardly had a mouthful, for a fact."

Jim raised his thin, nervous hands and looked at them. "Well, I'll have to admit that you hit it right this time."

Myrtle smiled steadily, her face fixed as if it would never be altered. "You haven't told us yet who the fortunate young lady is?"

"You guessed that, too," said Jim. "It's May."

Myrtle laughed cheerfully. "Well, everybody to his own taste!" But her gaiety was false and it sounded false even to herself. She was disturbed at the course the conversation had taken. She could not remember how things had gone wrong, but she knew that they had and that she had somehow prejudiced her case.

Jim got up, wiping his mouth on the back of his hand, and turned toward the door. "I got a little extra work to do today, so I'd better rush." He picked up his lunch, which had remained unopened, and tossed it carelessly into the littered corner. He paused at the door, turned and smiled the smile which he knew to be irresistible with women.

"Thanks for the dinner. Andrew said you were a good cook."

"Wait awhile!" said Neil. "Don't hurry off!"

Jim shook his head. When he was gone, Neil turned to his daughter. "I don't know what you and the old woman will figure up next, but I'm not going to have anything to do with this."

The next day Jim did not come down from his loft. He sat

alone on his greasy bench and ate the lunch that Susan had fixed for him. Below he could hear Myrtle's small, clear voice and the blurred rumble of Neil's conversation which almost blotted it out. He tiptoed to the stairs to listen and stood looking down like a little boy spying on the activities of his elders. Before he could retreat, Myrtle saw him. He turned back to the security of his loft. He sat on the work bench and cursed himself for his lack of dignity, feeling absurd and inept. He went angrily to his saws and began to work.

For a whole week Myrtle brought her father hot food at noon, but she did not see Jim again. On the Monday of the next week she abandoned her last reserve. She put down her father's dinner, walked past him and began climbing the stairs that led to Jim's loft. She had prepared a special dish for Jim that morning and even now she rehearsed her speech of presentation. Jim heard her coming up the stairs. He got up, too carefully unaware of her approach, and when she entered the loft he was working on his saws. The noise of the files made a rasping sound and sparks like blazing frost crystals leaped under the emery wheels and died the instant before they touched the oil-soaked floor.

He knew that she had stopped behind him and was looking at him, but he would neither turn nor look up, keeping his eyes steadily on his work. He did not even turn when she came so close to him that he could smell the perfume she wore and feel her breath on his neck.

"I fixed you a dish of fried chicken. Andrew said you liked it with tomato gravy."

"Andrew was wrong as usual. I don't want it, thank you."

"Oh," said Myrtle. "Tell me what dishes you do like and I'll fix them for you some time. It won't be any trouble."

Jim got up and stood before her. He caught her wrists with his nervous fingers. "I want to ask a favor of you: don't come here any more!"

"Why, what's wrong with that?"

"Don't come here any more," repeated Jim.

He talked mysteriously for a time, starting long sentences which he never quite completed. It wasn't that he didn't want to see Myrtle again; it was not that at all, and it had nothing to do with his personal feelings. After what had happened between them at the Wrenns' party she must know how he really felt; but there were other circumstances at work, other factors to be considered, and they prevented many things. He could not discuss these matters at the moment, but possibly she would know in time.

Myrtle who had understood nothing of what he had said, or of the things at which he hinted, nodded her head in sympathy. "I understand, Jim!" she said gently. "I won't come to the mill any more if it makes things harder for you."

When she had gone, Jim sat on his work bench and ate the food she had left. His feelings were diverse and complex, as if many emotions and many impulses mixed together and swam like confused fish seeking freedom from the small tank of his mind, but bumping inevitably against the unseen glass that bound them. When he remembered Myrtle's serious, unimaginative compliance and her whispered voice agreeing to all that he said, he wanted to laugh, because he himself had not understood what he meant, and had not been in earnest. He felt a quick sense of satisfaction because of his control over her, his ability to bind people to him. It seemed that he had some strange gift denied to others which enabled him to get what he wanted and to render nothing in return. . . .

He stretched his legs straight before him and rested his head against the oil-soaked wall, mystified agreeably at the destructive forces of his being. He must be careful in the future not to abuse his gift, since his abilities gave him so uniquely the power to hurt others who came in contact with his charm. He got up at last and went back to his saws.

He said: "It wouldn't have been so bad, and I wouldn't regret it so much, if she hadn't been a virgin."

CHAPTER XII

Susan TALLON and Carl Graffenreid were married in May. Effie Cleaver came the morning before the ceremony, and with the assistance of Edna, her adolescent daughter, she decorated the house with vines and cut flowers. Andrew moved the furniture from the downstairs rooms and stored it in the barn. He had built an altar in the back hall and Edna banked it with potted ferns and draped it with a white, long-fringed shawl borrowed from May MacLean for the occasion.

Edna was Effie's second daughter and she was plain and lanky like the other Cleaver children. Her hair grew back on her head, beyond the rounded shelf of her bulging brow, in the manner of early Flemish saints, and the strip of flesh between forehead and hair-line was like a fillet of colorless ribbon bound tight against her skull. Her face was long and shallow, with little apparent bone structure to keep it in place. It was as ungraceful and asymmetrical as the timid first egg that a pullet lays.

In the afternoon Miss Sarah Tarleton arrived to put the finishing touches on things. Bessie, her niece, came with her. Bessie was almost a member of the Tallon family, and they accepted her as such, for she had been engaged to Bradford and she had not married since his death. She lived in New York, but she came occasionally to see her father and her aunt. It was not entirely clear what she did in New York, but it was known that she had got her name into the Reedyville papers once or twice in connection with strikers and labor troubles. The people of the county laughed at her behind her back, but they treated her with respect openly, since they feared her merciless, flailing tongue.

She came onto the porch where Edna was. She held a bucket

of soapy water in one hand, a scrubbing-brush in the other. She smiled and rolled up her sleeves.

"Aunt Sarah said I was too clumsy to fix flowers and ran me away from the altar; so I thought I'd scrub the front gallery. That hasn't occurred to any of them so far."

Edna said: "Wait a minute and I'll help you." She had never met Bessie before that afternoon, but she had heard about her and she admired her greatly. She thought Bessie might be a sympathetic audience and she wanted to talk to her, to tell her her secret thoughts.

Bessie said: "I wish my friends could see me now on hands and knees scouring for a bourgeois wedding. . . . Boy! Would that give 'em a good laugh!"

"It must be wonderful living in New York, where everybody is intelligent."

"Don't be too optimistic," said Bessie. She laughed with derision. "Intelligent, indeed! Why, the man I work for might just as well be little Willie Oakshot: the only difference is that my boss has got better bridge-work."

"There's practically *nobody* in this place with any intelligence."

Bessie wrung out her rag and laughed quietly. "Except *you,* of course, and possibly me, in a pinch!"

"There's nobody except me!" said Edna passionately. "I'm the only one!" Then she added seriously: "Of course I count you as being a New Yorker."

Bessie looked at her quizzically; but before she could speak, Edna put down the soapy rag she held and began to talk rapidly. She touched on her individual solutions of the economic troubles of the world and hinted at the way governments should be run. She spoke widely of injustice and discriminations. She knelt on the damp sacking and talked for a long time, her face lifted like a martyr whose convictions made her impervious to fire or the claws of lions. Bessie glanced at her doubtfully.

"Where did you read all that old stuff? Who's been putting those ideas in your head? . . . Anyway, you didn't get it down any too well!"

Edna's eagerness vanished. She stared at Bessie disdainfully. She spoke more cautiously. She had thought, although it seemed falsely, that Bessie, since she lived in New York, a place well known for its enlightenment, would be more in sympathy with her views, more advanced, possibly, than the ordinary people of Pearl County. She hadn't meant to be offensive, and she apologized. Perhaps it would be better, after all, if they just talked from now on about Susan's trousseau. She got up and moved her bucket, her long, thin body bent forward under its weight.

Bessie said: "Wait a minute. Don't be so fast. . . . Do you mean to tell me that you thought all those things out for yourself, and didn't get it out of a book?"

"Why not?" asked Edna. "It's just plain common sense."

"There are a lot of people with those general ideas," said Bessie. "Didn't you know that?"

Edna said: "No. I thought I was the very first."

"How old are you, Edna?"

"I'm fourteen."

"Are you still going to school?"

"I got expelled," said Edna. "They expelled me in the sixth grade. I said I wouldn't answer another question the teacher asked me until they let nigger children come and study in the same school too."

"After we get Susan married," said Bessie, "you come to see me. I'll tell you a lot you need to know and I'll give you some books to read."

Edna said: "I'm game to go burn the planer mill down right now, if you are, Bessie."

"Let's not do it right this minute," said Bessie. "We'd miss the wedding." She threw her head back suddenly and laughed.

"Nothing can ever surprise me now," she said. "I'll never be surprised again as long as I live. . . . Imagine finding you at last in Pearl County, and in the *Cleaver* family, of all the unlikely places in this world!"

By late afternoon everything was in readiness and the women, surveying their work with strained, critical eyes, were not dissatisfied.

Edna said: "One of these days things are going to change for the better. I for one don't care how the change comes."

"Addie Wrenn's pink begonias show off real well," said Effie, "but be careful with them, Miss Sarah, and don't dare to break even one leaf. You know how mean Miss Addie is about her things."

"When my dear mother was married, there wasn't a decent road in the county," said Miss Sarah, her old eyes gentle and reminiscent. "It had rained hard the night before—it was some sort of cloud-burst—and the preacher couldn't get through." She laughed, her palms pressed against her withered cheeks. "It certainly created a most embarrassing situation, as you can easily surmise, because Papa had to spend the night under the same roof with his bride before they were actually married. Mamma often spoke about it. That was eighty years ago. She said she didn't know what people thought of her."

Bessie turned from Miss Sarah, smiled grimly and pulled her hat down with her rough, mannish hands. "Come to see me tomorrow, Edna; we'll take the world apart and then put it back more the way we think it *ought* to be. We got a lot to talk about together."

Susan came into the room and looked around her happily. She went to Effie and embraced her. They both cried. "It's sweet," said Susan. "It's really sweet, and no girl could ask better. Carl and I will always thank our friends for being so nice."

At six o'clock Andrew went for Myrtle. She had bought a new dress for the occasion and she felt that she was looking her best. She had rouged her face and her lips heavily and had darkened her eyes with blue salve. She stood beside Andrew in the crowded room, waiting for the ceremony to begin.

Effie Cleaver stood by the door, still crying at intervals. Her cheeks were brick-red with excitement and the archipelago of dark moles gave the impression that someone had dotted her face and neck with a leaky pen; but in spite of the routine tears, which convention, she felt, demanded of her as an elder sister, since their mother was no longer alive to mourn her daughter's happiness, she was interested only slightly in Susan's marriage. Her chief concern was for the success of Diana, her second daughter, who was making her first appearance before the public of Pearl County in the rôle of flower girl to her aunt. She glanced nervously through the cracked door at her daughter, dressed in pink muslin and sprigged with rosebuds, whose hair, limp naturally, like the hair of all her father's people, had been curled painstakingly that afternoon and was bound now with narrow ribbon. Diana was her favorite of all the children she had borne, and she made no secret of her preference. In choosing such an unusual name for her at baptism, a name outside any family connection or connotation, she had been guided solely by a story which, she maintained unshakably, had been read to her out of the Bible many years ago by a Sunday-school teacher whom she had greatly admired.

"I named her after Saint Diana of Ephesus, who is a holy woman mentioned in the Scriptures," she would say to those who questioned her. "Saint Diana was a delicate, scrawny child, as I remember the story now, because her mother didn't have any milk for her when she was born, being frightened during pregnancy by a big, one-horned goat that butted her while she was making potato soup in a black pot. But the woman had a dream one night, and an angel appeared before her and told her to

94

gather certain herbs and press out their juices and feed *that* to the baby. Well, sir, she done what the angel said, and the result was that the baby grew to be stronger than anybody else in the country of Ephesus, and she was as sweet and womanly as she was strong."

When Miss Sarah Tarleton and other authorities on the Scriptures were sceptical about this story, never having come across it themselves in their Bible reading, Effie was merely patient and a little patronizing, pointing out triumphantly the fact that even if nobody, including herself, could *now* locate the exact passage, it did not necessarily mean it was not there.

"Saint Diana done many worthy things during her lifetime and she worked some miracles to boot," she would add stubbornly; "but her chief claim to holiness was the time she swam across the River Jordan carrying Christ and eight of his heaviest disciples on her back at one time when they were fleeing from the arrows of the Philistines."

Effie went back to the bedroom for a whispered consultation with her daughter, re-curling her thin, relaxing hair on her forefinger and giving her final words of advice; but at last everything was in readiness and Willie Oakshot began to sing, his voice rising rich and beautiful and without effort. Then, somehow, Carl Graffenreid was standing at the altar, waiting for his bride. She entered on Jim's arm, her eyes downcast with guilt, as if marriage was a stealthy and shameful thing; and to placate the people about her, she must show at this moment no pleasure in its implications.

But Myrtle, watching with Andrew, was conscious of nobody except Jim. She had not seen him since the day she had gone to his loft, but she had written him. In her first letter she had reaffirmed her willingness to trust him, to wait until the time came when he was free to talk unconditionally to her, but since he did not answer, she wrote him again, this time more definitely.

Jim answered at once under her insistence, although she could make little of his reply. It was all about himself and Andrew. Jim felt that he had done both his brother and Myrtle a wrong and he hoped that they would forgive him. He went on for several pages about Andrew's barren life and the way he had suffered. He was sure that Myrtle would come to love his brother in time; at any rate, he was willing to step aside, asking nothing for himself, and he would not interfere again with their happiness.

Myrtle had read the letter over and over. She wanted to show it to her mother, to ask her advice, but she decided against it, since Jim's letter, with its references to the party at the Wrenns' was too compromising. Finally she wrote him a note asking him to meet her in the oak grove after the wedding, hoping to get something more definite from him then. Before she realized it the ceremony was ended, and Susan Tallon had become Mrs. Carl Graffenreid.

"Come on!" said Andrew. "Let's go speak to Carl and Suse!" He moved toward the altar where the bride still stood, but Myrtle turned instead and slipped through the door stealthily. When she came to the clump of oak trees she stopped and waited. She heard at last the creaking of the iron chains that weighted the gate and saw Jim against the light of the thin moon. He looked about, but he did not see her standing among the trees. When she called, he came at once. She was surprised at his manner. She had expected him to be serious and rather intense, judging from the tone of his letter, but he was gay instead. His eyes were excited and he laughed quickly. He had been drinking too much.

"A pretty girl like you ought not to be out here hiding."

Myrtle's eyes moved languorously, and in the moonlight her reddened lips and cheeks, against the whiteness of her skin, seemed smeared with tar.

"Anyhow, I didn't hide so well I couldn't be found."

Jim laughed again. He started to speak, but changed his mind.

96

There was an uncomfortable silence. Myrtle looked toward the house and said with elaborate carelessness:

"You boys are going to miss Suse when she goes to Oklahoma. You won't have anybody to keep house for you."

"Oh, you and Andrew will be getting married before long, I imagine," said Jim. He added quickly: "I hope you don't aim to move me off the place when you do."

A frown came on Myrtle's stolid face and she made a gesture of denial with her hands. She began to talk quickly, her voice a little frightened, a little pleading. She had never promised to marry Andrew and there was no understanding between them. They were just friends, and Andrew understood that perfectly. Jim leaned against a tree smoking a cigarette, but he did not interrupt her.

"What are you so worried about Andrew for? I don't see that what you and I do is any of his business. . . . Why don't you come to see me yourself? If everybody left me alone like you do, folks would think I had the whooping cough."

"Andrew thinks a lot of you, Myrtle."

"Just the same, I'm not pledged to him."

Jim threw away his cigarette. His voice became hard. "If you throw Andrew over now, it's going to just about kill him."

"It seems to me like it's pretty late for you to start worrying about Andrew. You might have thought of that before."

"I'm going back indoors," said Jim coldly. "There's a lot of people I want to speak to."

Myrtle moved toward him. An emotion blended of her passion and her despair came over her. She said over and over:

"I never cared anything about Andrew and he knows it. I never encouraged him any. If you want to know the God's truth I'll tell you why I kept going with him: I did it only because I wanted to keep on seeing you!"

"I pity Andrew if he's really intending to marry you."

"It's not my fault that I can't like Andrew, is it? You got no right to hold that against me, Jim!"

Jim said: "Why don't you scour that stuff off your face? You look like a nigger wench on pay-night."

He turned, adjusted his coat collar and walked away.

"I'll tell Andrew where you are. He'll be worrying."

When Andrew joined her a few minutes later she asked him to take her home. He protested amiably. The fun was just beginning and there was no sense in leaving so early; but Myrtle could not be budged, and in the end Andrew, uncomprehending but devoted, did what she wanted.

He said on the drive home: "Well, Suse and Carl are married at last. I hope she'll be happy with him in Oklahoma, and I expect she will."

"If she's happy with a man, she'll be the first one."

"You haven't got a very good opinion of men, have you, sweetheart?"

She began to cry. "No," she said; "nor of women, either."

"What in the world is the matter?"

She shook her head and would not answer.

"Have I done anything to make you mad with me?"

"Let me alone! Why can't people just mind their own business and let me alone!"

"It's early yet, honey. Would you like to drive over to Reedyville and see the movies?"

"No," said Myrtle. "I wouldn't think of making you spend that two-bits on me. I wouldn't want to break your heart."

Andrew laughed tolerantly. "That's not treating me very fair, is it, sugar? You know very well I'm not a mean man, and never was." He parked his car under the trees. He took Myrtle's hands in his own, and this time she did not resist him.

She knew what was coming, but she seemed unable to prevent it. Andrew put his arm around her protectively. He raised her chin and looked into her face. He spoke in his broken, whispered voice:

"You're the most beautiful thing that ever walked on this earth."

He bent over and kissed her on the mouth, but she pulled away from him furiously and wiped her lips on her sleeve.

"You! . . . You!" she cried.

There was a confused, uncomprehending look on Andrew's face.

"I'm asking you to marry me."

Myrtle made no effort to hide her disgust. She got out of the automobile and stood on the sidewalk.

Andrew said: "I'm asking you to marry me. I want you to do me the honor of marrying me."

"You! . . . You!" repeated Myrtle. She went to her room and lay stretched on her bed. She cried with a long, gasping noise. Her mother joined her almost at once.

"I wouldn't bother about him any more if I was you, baby. There's plenty more men in the world."

Myrtle would not be comforted. She buried her face in her pillow and kicked the sides of her bed.

"I declare," said Mrs. Bickerstaff helplessly. "I don't know what's come over people these days, the way they act! I wish your Papa had never moved us from Georgia. You can say what you please, but people in Georgia do *not* act this way!"

"Who is Jim Tallon to think he's so fine?" demanded Myrtle in a choked voice which was getting louder. "Who is he to treat me like I was dirt?"

"Now, baby! Now, baby!" said Mrs. Bickerstaff over and over. She sat beside Myrtle and smoothed her hair.

Neil had heard for a long time the noise of quarreling in the room above him. He strained his ears, but he could not catch individual words; there was only a blurred, buzzing noise and the shrill sound of crying. He turned over, sat against the head of the bed and beat his flattened pillow into shape. He lay down again and thought of his problems at the mill, but he could not go to sleep while the maddening noise above him continued. He jumped out of bed, throwing the sheets angrily over the foot-board. He went up the stairs, not quite knowing what he was going to say, opened the door to his daughter's room and entered noisily.

"What's going on in here? Am I the head of this house, by God! or am I not?"

"Go back to bed," said Kate.

Neil stood irresolutely, still yawning at intervals. His red hair lifted high from his forehead and the skin-like, grayish underwear in which he slept wrinkled in folds over the expanse of his corrugated belly.

Myrtle's face was streaked with tears and the penciling of her eyes and brows, done so carefully earlier in the evening, had run and spread into a wide smudge. Her smeared eyes and her tragic, lifted face gave her a sick and helpless beauty.

"If your father was any part of a man, he wouldn't let people insult his daughter like he does."

"Who's been insulting you, Myrtle?"

"It's Jim Tallon," said Kate, "and I must say I don't blame the child for feeling like she does."

Mrs. Bickerstaff spoke through tight lips, the lavender pouches beneath her eyes twitching with outraged spasms. She turned to Myrtle: "I said from the first that those Tallons weren't any good. I begged you not to get messed up with them; but oh, no! You wouldn't listen to me."

"Now, sugar," said Neil placatingly. "Jim wouldn't insult a girl on purpose. He must have been joking. I know Jim too well to believe he'd do a thing like that."

"Just the same, he said I wasn't any better than a nigger wench

100

on pay-night at the commissary; and I didn't give him any cause for talking to me that way, either."

"It's no use telling your papa about it, Myrtle. He's not man enough to do anything about it. The best thing is to just swallow the insult."

Neil got up, the bed rising under his released weight and creaking. His face became redder than usual and he breathed heavily. He began to shout, his fists doubled up: "By God, no God-damned man in the world can insult my God-damned daughter, and I don't give a God damn who knows it!"

Kate came to him at once and touched his arm soothingly.

"Why, what are you thinking of, Neil? Nobody has insulted Myrtle. I'm sure it's just a mistake, like you suggested."

Neil's voice became louder, his gestures more violent. Sweat came on his face and the matted red hair of his chest boiled against the yoke of his union-suit.

Kate sat down, at length, hurt and patient. "Well, I hope you're satisfied, Neil! You've woke up the children with your big mouth and if the Macbeths and the Renshaws haven't heard every word you said, it's because they've moved to Reedyville."

Neil was thoroughly angry at last and it took his wife and daughter a long time to quiet him, to extract a promise from him that he would not shoot Jim Tallon on sight. The baby was crying steadily below and the other children, clad in their nightgowns, peered through the door at their parents without understanding what was occurring, their eyes wide and interested.

CHAPTER XIII

ANDREW came a few nights later, but Myrtle would not see him. Her mother met him instead and blocked the door. She did not ask him in. When she spoke, it was if all her words were set in italics.

"Myrtle's not well and asks to be excused."

Inside the house Andrew caught sight of Neil. He sat in his stocking feet, his head pressed against his newspaper, as if he were ashamed and wanted it known that he had no part in the matter. He saw the younger children gathered about the lamp, their hands resting on the edge of the cleared table, ready to push back their chairs, balanced for flight if he somehow managed to elude their mother and enter.

"Can I get her something to ease her?"

Kate said again, as if her words had a meaning which explained everything: "Myrtle's not feeling so well!"

"I'll come tomorrow night. Maybe she'll be better then."

Kate smiled fixedly and shook her head. "I don't think she'll be feeling better tomorrow night either."

And Andrew understood at last that he was being dismissed. He twisted his hat, unable to think or to speak for a moment. Then, with dignity, he bowed, walked down the steps and out of the gate. He never returned to the Bickerstaff house at the end of Wampum Street and he did not see Myrtle again for a long time.

It was decided that Edna Cleaver should live at the Tallon place after Susan's marriage and keep house for her uncles. She was, in spite of her immaturity, a capable, hard-working girl, very careful and very thrifty. She made few demands on the people about her, as if she understood in advance that a girl as plain as herself might expect nothing, but beneath her early maturity there was a moving and a child-like quality of unworldliness. She was a better housekeeper than Susan and things at the farm ran smoothly under her management.

Edna put down her basket of sewing.

"Uncle Jim, is it hard to learn to dance as well as you?"

Jim said: "Come on! I'll show you how it's done."

He held her long, lath-like arms to her sides. "Don't be so stiff. Give up more." They practiced for a time, Edna's face set and determined. She had been seeing Bessie daily for the past week and she treasured every word of her advice. According to Bessie, the day would come when every scrap of knowledge, every accomplishment which Edna possessed would be of advantage. She must learn everything she could while her mind was receptive. Edna stumbled and righted herself. She was doubtful if her dancing would ever be good enough to serve in the fight for the unshackling of mankind, and she wondered if Bessie meant dancing, too. At any rate she decided to keep on until she had mastered it.

When the lesson was finished Edna sat down and took up her sewing. "Good Lord!" said Jim. "That was harder work than cutting a cord of stove-wood and stacking it."

Edna looked at him quietly and then lowered her head. "Uncle Jim," she began innocently, "why did you have that gold tooth put where it shows so much?"

"What's the matter with it? I haven't had any complaints about it so far."

"It's perfectly all right with me, if it suits you."

"Lord God Almighty," said Jim. "I was always under the impression that it was dressy."

"You're the one to be pleased, Uncle Jim."

Jim touched the tooth with his forefinger, pressing against it as if it might be loose. "What's the matter with it?"

"I'll go turn the beds down now," said Edna.

Andrew laughed and got up. "You ought not to tease her, Jim." He went to his room, lighted his lamp and prepared for bed. Later on Jim came in. He sat in Andrew's chair, his elbows resting on his spread knees, his palms cupping his sensuous face.

"Why don't you forget about her? Why do you let a woman like that keep bothering you?"

"I'll get over it after awhile. It takes a little time."

"What beats me," said Jim, "is what you ever saw in her in the first place."

"I don't know."

"Didn't you have sense enough to know she was playing you for a fish? She figured you'd do to take her around, and to spend money on her, until somebody else came along that she liked better?"

Andrew said: "I don't believe that, and neither do you. She's not that kind."

"She told me so herself; you can believe it or not." Jim was silent for a time. The affair between Andrew and Myrtle was over at last, in spite of what he had done to keep it going. He'd tell Andrew what happened at the Wrenns' party, for it was better to destroy at once the last vestige of love which his brother still had for the girl. Andrew would thank him for it someday, when he realized, as clearly as Jim did at this moment, that he was well out of the mess he had got himself into.

"Oh, so she's not that *kind!*" said Jim mockingly. "Well, here's something about your sweetheart you didn't know! Here's something I'll bet she hasn't told you yet!" He spoke quickly, gesturing with his hands and laughing as if the matter were a rare joke. He said: "I wouldn't have said anything about the Wrenns' party, but you asked for it, and there it is!" . . .

He stopped, surprised at the hate in his brother's face.

Andrew said: "Get to hell out of here! . . . Get to hell out of this room!"

"You'll thank me," said Jim. "Some day you'll see this thing from the right angle and thank me for all I've done!"

When his brother had gone, Andrew unlocked his desk and read the penciled draft of the poem he had written that night:

I am rich in some things, oh ye people of Pearl County,
And yet I have nothing if I do not have my beloved:
For she is like a golden vessel of many shades:
Her body is a sweet vessel to hold herbs
And her legs are colored like gold:
Her knees are caps of the finest gold:
(God's conscious thumb pressed her navel there)
Her belly is of the purest gold and a shining thing for my
eye:
Her thighs are many shades of gold:
(Her breasts are softer than smoke in the air)
Her cheeks are like coral that lie above gold:
(Pigeons live in her breasts and they lift upward as if they
would fly.)

He broke off and tore the paper to small bits. He went to the window and threw out the fragments, watching them scatter and settle downward. He went outside and stood in the yard. Tobey came out of his kennel, his chain clanking, but Andrew held the dog's muzzle with his hand and Tobey crouched obediently on the ground, his tail moving upward and downward. He made no sound nor did he move as Andrew walked toward the gate and beyond the range of his vision.

Andrew came at last to the house he sought, an unpainted, wooden building set back from Thompson's Lane. The shades were up, and in the window there was a small kerosene lamp with a red globe, a sign to the public that the woman within was not engaged. The woman, hearing the sound that her gate made, opened her door and stood silhouetted in it. When she saw who her guest was, she took her hands from her hips and pressed against the wall flatly, letting him precede her into the bed-room. The room was clean and it had recently been painted white, the tang of the paint modifying the mustiness of the place and neutralizing a little the individual smells of sour-skulled people who had slept there.

Andrew stood in the center of the room and looked at the wide bed covered with a quilt made of multicolored scraps. The woman, who had not yet spoken, pulled down the shades and turned the lamp higher, so that the room was completely re-vealed. She was small, child-like and very black; and she waited until her client revealed his temperament.

"Are you expecting anybody else?"

"Nah, suh," said the woman. "Nah, *suh.*"

She put her hand to her head and fluffed out her short, nappy hair. She walked to him with her hips swaying, her eyes rolled back, very roguish, very professional of a sudden; but she could not keep it up. She stopped half way across the room and threw herself on the bed, all her professional tricks forgotten. She said: "Where my dollar at, white folks?"

She began to laugh with unplanned delight, one black arm hanging down from the bed.

"Where my dollar at?" she repeated. "Where my dollar at?"

When Andrew was again in his room, he took off his clothes, filled his basin with water and washed himself all over. He put on the new pajamas which Edna had made for him and lay stretched on his own bed, his head pressed into his pillow, his hands opening and shutting in the unresisting air. He closed his eyes, frightened at the intensity of his own feelings. He had never envied his brother before, nor had he challenged his obvious superiority, but he envied him now, and in his hatred he cursed Jim under his breath slowly and with concentrated earnestness.

Before him were opened windows and curtains lifting and falling in a small breeze; beyond that was a sky in which patterned stars burned close to the horizon. He thought: "There's no sense in blaming Jim so much. . . . There's no sense in putting it all on him." He lay sleepless in his room for a long time, his torn mouth moving a little and shaping words of comfort against his despair. Then he sat up and covered his face with his hands, feeling all at once that the skies were empty of meaning and that they held nothing for mankind.

He thought: "People are born in sorrow and move about the earth in patterns of sorrow without sense and without plan. Why should I take myself so seriously? I am no more important to the Creator than the trees or the vegetation which live with me on His earth. There is no eye to watch over me nor a hand to direct me, and there will be no preferred fate for me at the end, no matter what I am, or what I do with my life."

He lifted his fist and shook it as if he threatened the imperturbability of God, but he stopped at once, shocked at the futility of sacrilege. For a man must accept the facts of his existence whether he liked them or not. A man must accept, sooner or later, his haphazard fate.

Jim called to him through the locked door, but Andrew would not open it, nor would he answer his brother.

Jim said: "I told you what I did not for my sake, but for yours, and I thought you'd appreciate it. You'll thank me for what I done some day."

It was then Andrew noticed that he was crying, the hot tears falling straight down, wetting the bed clothing and the backs of his hands. He thought: "I'm not afraid of a little pain. When I can no longer feel pain I will know that I have died. . . . I want you to know that I'm not afraid of pain; but I didn't know it was going to be like this."

CHAPTER XIV

On the third Sunday of every month the Reverend A. R. Butler left his congregation in Reedyville to shift for itself as best it could and came to Hodgetown to preach in the Interdenominational Church there. He was a small, grayish man and the raveling fringe of hair above his ears made it appear that he had filleted his skull with a horseshoe of knitted laurel. He regarded the people before him with a dispirited, slightly unfriendly air, as if he had long since lost faith in such abstractions as man's innate nobility, the sanctity of his soul or his final redemption from evil. He stood this night in his pulpit whispering with the organist while they made a final selection of hymns. When the organist had gone and the first song commenced, he drank from the tumbler at his side, stared at the church people of Hodgetown and sat beside the electric lamp which lighted his Bible, his fingers playing a slow tune on the buttons of his vest.

Andrew came into the church before the first hymn was finished. He stopped at the back row of seats and looked about him. He saw Myrtle almost at once. She was sitting between the two Macbeth girls. She turned, impelled by the steadfastness of his glance, and looked at him in turn, but her face was without recognition and there was no kindness in it, for she connected him with Jim's coldness toward her, and she blamed him for it. Andrew's eyes wavered and shifted and he lifted the hymn book which had been thrust into his hands. He fumbled the pages. When he looked up again, Myrtle had turned and was whispering with her friends.

The text for that evening was the familiar, "Come unto me all ye that labor," and the Reverend Butler worked it in and out of his sermon like a tireless shuttle moving precisely among his images and linking them into a coherent whole. Sinners, he said, were like those fishermen who cast their nets across the pleasant fields of the world and lust after forbidden pleasures, denying, in their short-sighted arrogance, all things except their own desires; but when the fisherman has pressed the last drop of wine from his catch and has lifted it to his lips for comfort, he finds, at last, the bitterness of wood-ashes in his mouth. It is then that he turns and hears the voice of Jehovah promising: "Come unto me all ye that labor and are heavy laden, and I will give thee rest!" . . .

The church-goers of Hodgetown stirred restively. They accepted Brother Butler as a fashionable preacher and were willing to concede his intellectual godliness, but he was not popular with them and they riffled the pages of their hymn books in boredom. They liked a fiercer man, a more fiery preacher, one with greater threats for their sinfulness and with wider promises of salvation, at the end, to sweeten the direness of prophecy.

Andrew leaned back against the bench and crossed his legs. The words of the preacher cut athwart his own thoughts and blended with them, but he took in their sound only, selecting those thoughts which fitted his need. He was puzzled and disturbed, and he knew that he must find new precepts for his guidance, new rules by which to govern his life. He had, in the past week, tried to do these things, but he had found nothing for his comfort. He knew only that living was strange and mixed up, and that he did not understand it. That was wrong, for living should be a sweet thing. It should not turn bitter as it did inevitably at the end. . . .

He thought of all the people he had known in his life. Their lives should have been as simple as the lives of the birds who tapped on trees for their suppers, or the cattle that lay under the trees at Gentry's Ford, and yet they were never so. The birds and the cattle were doomed, of course, to the same fate that all living creatures shared. Their contentment lay in the fact that they could not anticipate their pain, nor could they recognize defeat when it came at last. . . . At that moment it seemed to him that only mankind had been cursed with knowledge, and only mankind endeavored, if vainly, to avoid its destiny. . . .

Andrew raised his eyes and looked at the two men and the two women who formed the choir; and Willie Oakshot, the tenor, caught his eye, smiled and winked, but Andrew did not see him. He was thinking: "I'm a fool. I'm a fool to think these depressing things. I'm a fool, and they are not true." He brought himself back to his surroundings, hearing again the cadences of Brother Butler's lush phrases. . . .

For a time, when a man was young, he danced on the fleshpots of sin and hungered after strange pleasures; he followed depraved women, seduced by that soft, misleading beauty which the devil had given them originally and which they, themselves, had, in many instances, improved upon. It was to be deplored, but it was true, that man in his youth, with only a few notable exceptions, drank whisky, gambled, lusted in his heart and whored; and he called those earthy things love. But a day of reckoning must come at last, when he had to see himself as the miserable sinner he was, and it was then he knew there was but one love, and that the pure love of God, and he cried aloud in his anguish of soul and sought the aid of Jehovah. . . . And Jehovah would not turn away from the man who sought his help, even though that man had violated and broken every sacred commandment seven times seventy, for he had plainly said: "Come unto me all ye that labor and are heavy laden, and I will give thee rest."

Andrew looked at his hands. There was a strange feeling inside him and he felt close to tears. He thought: "Life should be a sweet thing and yet it becomes confused, in spite of all a man can do." . . . He tried to crush the recurring thoughts which came from within to trouble him, but he could not. He tried to force himself to listen to the words of the preacher, but he could concentrate on him for a few minutes only, and in the end his thoughts turned inwardly, upon himself.

Brother Butler sat down, his sermon finished. He rubbed his lips speculatively, but his face remained slightly mistrustful, slightly supercilious, as if he had no faith in his power to move these literal people. He had preached for them one of his best sermons, a sermon which had often been admired by their betters, and they could take it or they could leave it. He rose and announced that during the next hymn the doors of the church would be opened to any of those present who wanted to confess their sins and abandon the evil of their lives. There was a whispered word with the organist and the hymn began.

The congregation rose to sing, and Andrew stood with them. He glanced about him again, at the familiar faces he knew, and then a strange thing happened to him. Sweat came on his brow and his hands trembled so that he was obliged to lock his fingers together. He stood undecided in the pew, not knowing his own mind; but when the last stanza began he pushed past the people beside him and walked down the aisle, his mouth moving in prayer. He knelt at the altar and pressed his face into the red plush that covered the rail. The soles of his feet were turned upward to his neighbors, and the cheap, badly fitting coat he wore wrinkled across the muscles of his shoulders.

Brother Butler came to him and spoke in a quiet voice:

"Do you renounce the devil and his evil?"

"Yes! Yes!"

"Do you accept Christ Jesus for your personal savior?"

"Yes!" said Andrew. "I accept Him! I accept Him!"

He raised his head toward heaven, his eyes remote and unseeing. He shivered, his folded arms hugging his chest, and his flesh melted and flowed from his body and he was caught in a strange ecstasy; then his spirit lifted upward and floated and against his fainting senses he felt the slow impact of God.

When he returned home that night he did not go inside at once. He sat on the steps with his head resting against the weathered, unpainted post which supported the roof of the porch. He let his hands rest limply beside him, to raise them after a time and press them against his eyes. His eyelids fluttered twice and he nodded his head, as if he must accept with silent gestures of his flesh the course that his new-found faith pointed with relentless clarity; for it seemed to him at that moment that contentment lay with wide renunciations, and that peace was possible only to the spirit that asked nothing, that made no bargain with itself or the flesh that enclosed it.

He thought: "I am nothing. I am less than nothing at all. I will give up everything and will ask nothing in return."

When he heard Jim come home through the back gate, he wanted to go through the house and meet him, to tell him that he had forgiven him, and that there was nothing in this material world of the least importance; but he stopped, unable to do it. He went instead into the thicket and stood screened by the oaks.

He thought: "Tomorrow, perhaps. . . . Tomorrow."

During the days that followed Andrew went about his work in silence. When he talked at all, it was with Edna, and then only at night after Jim had gone and they were alone. He had grown fond of Edna and he found the involved, endless discussions on those subjects which interested her at the moment an unexpected stimulus for his mind. He alone of the people she knew accepted her seriously, for he knew that even now, underlying the terrified eccentricities of her pubescence, her mind burned with shrewd and clear objectivity; that even at fourteen she achieved a maturity of judgment which he, himself, would never have. But occasionally Edna slipped back over the threshold of adolescence and was a little girl again. These changes were so sudden that it was often difficult to know what rôle she played at the moment.

She put down the book she was studying and marked the place with a slip of paper. Before Bessie had returned to New York she had got out her old high school books, many of which she had annotated in her sprawling, heavy backhand, and gave them to Edna. Andrew drove by for the books and brought them to the farm.

Edna wasted no minute of her time. When her work was done, she turned at once to the books, ploughing through subject after subject in the order which Bessie herself had studied them. There was much she found difficult to understand, since she had no teacher, but when a thing particularly baffled her, as the elementary algebra she was studying now baffled her, she would put the book down and go about her other tasks until the matter was entirely out of her mind; then she would hurry to the book again and open it quickly, as if to surprise a meaning from it by the very force of her puzzled impatience.

"I wish I could help you out," said Andrew; "but I didn't get much education either. I went through Professor Drewery's school, but he didn't teach high school subjects."

Since her uncle's conversion, Edna had felt a new tenderness for him, partly protective and partly contemptuous. She had fallen into the habit of putting the best sheets on his bed, and she cooked extra dishes for his pleasure, for she felt that they were joined together by the bond of their unattractiveness, their remoteness from the ordinary life which others might be expected to lead.

"Bessie said something about Uncle Jim before she went away.

I didn't know what she meant at first, but I do now. She said he was the kind of man who'd put cologne water under his arms before he'd take a bath all over with soap."

"How did she happen to say a thing like that?"

"Oh, we were just talking about the family one morning."

"What did she say about me? What sort of a man am I?"

"You'd get mad at Bessie. Anyway, she didn't mean for me to be a tattle-tale."

"I won't get mad. I'll think it over and try to figure out if she's right or not."

"She said you were inclined to be a little too stingy; and besides that, you were so romantic and impractical that you didn't see the ridiculous side of things."

"What of it?" asked Andrew. He smiled apologetically and shrugged. "I suppose it's true enough. I'll not dispute what she said so far."

"I suppose it don't matter, really," said Edna. "She says I haven't got any sense of humor either, only she decided it would be a handicap in my work, so we're both glad I haven't got one. Bessie says you can't hate anything enough to want to destroy it, if you can laugh at it too."

"That wasn't all she said about me, Edna. You're holding something back."

"Oh, all right then! . . . She said you were the sort of man who started sentences with the word life capitalized."

"What in the world did Bessie mean by that?"

"I knew right away," said Edna. "I knew what she meant because you *are*, Uncle Andrew. You even do it out loud sometimes when you explain how you feel about things."

"Like what, for instance?"

"Like: 'Life ought to be sweet and not the way it is!' or: 'Life is senseless and there's no use in struggling against it!'"

"I'll have to admit that you and Bessie have got me down

right. There's not much I can say." He lowered his head sheepishly and blushed.

Edna's pencil scratched as she worked at her problem. She solved it at last and leaned back in triumph.

"I suppose I am too tight with my money," said Andrew thoughtfully; "but I've worked hard all my life for what I got, and I've had so little this far. Maybe I'd be better off if I didn't try to save, but threw my money away like Jim does."

But Edna was not listening; she was concerned with her own thoughts: "After the revolution comes and this country is governed by fair and unprejudiced people who think only of the interest of the workers, we'll all be better off—except maybe the capitalists, but then they won't mind either, because they'll all be dead! Life will be a rational, common-sense thing for the masses, and Bessie and I are going to help make it that way."

"You're doing it yourself, Edna."

"What? What am I doing?"

"Beginning sentences with the word life in capitals."

"I'm not!" replied Edna indignantly. "You know very well I'd never be guilty of such a thing!"

They looked at each other seriously, and then they both laughed.

"Anyway, it's not what Bessie meant," said Edna. "What I said is constructive. It's not the same thing at all."

CHAPTER XV

ANDREW saw Myrtle only once between his conversion and his baptism. She was picking butter-beans from the vines which screened the porch. He passed on the other side of the street and she did not look up. He heard of her occasionally through Edna, who managed somehow to keep posted on the doings of everybody in the county: it was a sort of training which she imposed upon herself in preparation for becoming a spy, should the necessity for such work arise later in her career, and he knew that for a time Myrtle did not go beyond the limits of her front gate; that she was moody and sullen and cried a great deal. When her work was finished, she would generally go into the yard and sit under the catalpa tree that grew there. She was no longer on good terms with her mother.

It was about this time that Myrtle began to visualize scenes in which she met Jim in a wood or on some lonely road away from other people. In such dramatizations Jim would stop before her, amazed at her beauty and her power. The hateful look on his face which she remembered so well had changed to adoration, and he was breathless before her. He would plead then for her favors and try to take her in his arms, but sure of her will, she smiled and shook her head; and she moved away, always a little beyond the reach of his arms. In these daydreams Myrtle saw Jim come back to her, his voice humble and his eyes contrite, until she forgave him and lifted him up from the road, her lips meeting his in tenderness against a background of jetting fountains, silks and rich brocades.

But despite her preoccupation with herself and with Jim, her

117

conscience troubled her at times about Andrew. She was glad when he joined the church in her presence, as if she felt that he thus publicly renounced her and elected the comforts of religion to any comfort that her arms might have given him.

All at once Jim's behavior became explicable to her. It was reasonable to believe that he loved her after all, in spite of his bewildering conduct. He had merely been acting a part, and his sense of honor had prevented his speaking of his love while Andrew was still courting her. It was typical of Jim to do a thing of that sort! The whole affair was simply one of those irritating misunderstandings between men and women which she saw so often in the movies and which were cleared up completely before the end. Furiously she blamed her mother for her difficulties. If her mother had just kept out of it, things would not have reached the impasse they had. She felt that she now understood Jim completely, and all the things which had perplexed her before became simple in this, her wished-for meaning.

She rocked beneath the catalpa tree, content with herself and waiting, for soon Jim would come to her with his explanations, which, now that she understood his conduct so deeply, she would not even permit him to finish. She would not insult him by listening to an explanation! . . . But the weeks went by and he did not come, and at last she could not resist the temptation to take matters into her impatient hands again.

One afternoon she went in the direction of the Tallon farm. She walked idly, as if she had no particular object to accomplish, but she knew that she had timed herself to meet Jim when he returned from work. She stopped when she reached the spot where the Green Point road intersected the Reedyville highway and hid behind the sweet-gum tree. She had already heard the whistle of the sawmill and before long Jim must pass; she could not miss him now, no matter what road he took.

When she had begun to doubt the wisdom of her plan, when the first touch of self-consciousness came to her, she saw Jim pedaling toward her on his bicycle. At that moment the last trace of her self-assurance left her, and she could think of nothing to say. She crowded against the tree and trembled. She let him pass unchallenged, but immediately she ran after him, calling his name. At the sound of her voice, Jim twisted his neck and looked over his shoulder in surprise, hesitated and turned in a wide circle. He came to her slowly, stopped and balanced himself.

"Well, what do you want this time?"

"There's no sense in you and me acting this way, Jim. I don't see why we can't be good friends again."

Jim got off his bicycle and leaned against it. He tilted his hat from his forehead and looked at her coldly.

"*Again!* I didn't know we ever were good friends. You're not mixing me up with my brother Andrew, are you?"

"You know very well what I'm talking about, and I want to tell you that I don't bear you any hard feelings."

"You don't say! Well, now, I'm mighty glad to hear that."

"I know how you've been feeling, Jim, and I admire you for not wanting to stand in your brother's way; but I want to say again that it wasn't necessary for you to feel that way, because I never cared anything about Andrew and he knew where he stood with me from the first."

"That wasn't the opinion of the people of this county, and it wasn't my opinion, either."

"It's the God's own truth, though."

She took a step toward him, mistaking his silence, and spoke softly: "Andrew's joined the church and he's given up any idea of marrying me. There's no reason now, as far as I can see, why you and me can't go on from where we left off."

"So you're the bitch my brother's eating his heart out for?" said Jim. . . . "He's lucky you didn't take him when you had the chance, if you ask me!"

"Jim!" she said in a shocked voice. "Jim! . . . That's no way to talk to me!"

"If you came here to crow over what you done to Andrew, I must say you succeeded, because he hasn't been the same man since you threw him down. He never goes anywhere except church, and he gets up and leaves the house whenever I come in. If I speak to him, he don't even answer me." He laughed bitterly. "You turned him against his whole family, if that's what you were trying to do, and if it's any satisfaction for you to know it."

She was terrified, knowing that her daydreams were false, that she would never have what she wanted. She touched his hand, but he moved it from the handle-bars and placed it behind his back.

"That's all past and done, Jim. What do you care what Andrew thinks?"

"You bitch!" he said. He spat into the dust. "You dog bitch!" He mounted his bicycle and rode away, his back rigid and his eyes straight ahead.

Myrtle walked through the scrub-oaks and the waist-high, second-growth pine, her breast rising and falling. She came to the footbridge that spanned Black Creek. The sun was almost down and slanting light fell in patterns on the water, gilding the flanks of cows which drank there. The unsteady footbridge shook beneath her weight and she clutched the railing. She spoke aloud.

"I'll get even with him! I'll get even with him if it's the last thing I ever do in this world!"

The cattle lifted their muzzles from the water at the sound of her anger and looked at her, their ears pointing forward, their tails lifted upward and curling across their backs to brush at flies. Then they shook their horns and went to stand in the grass by the bank-side, patient and grouped together until they were milked.

Myrtle grasped the railing more firmly and jerked, and a piece of it came away in her hand. She ran from the bridge and turned into the timber that stretched before her. A feeling of shame came over her and she stood still quickly in her tracks. She leaned against one of the trees and cried. Her heels shoved back the cluttering needles and dug angry furrows in the earth beneath. In her rage she broke the segment of railing, which she still held absently in her hand, into pieces of equal length, measuring one fragment against the other for exactness.

"I'll get even with him! I'll pay him back!" she whispered. She was sick with the intensity of her mounting fury. She stretched out on the pine needles and dug her hands and feet into the earth, her lips moving and her head rolling from side to side.

Birdie Calkins was shelling peas in the dim glare from the arc-light on the corner, and her husband, Will, sat rocking behind her. He was in his stocking feet and his fingers were locked across his belly, above his digesting dinner. His work for the day was done and he was rested and at peace. He stopped his chair and peered forward.

"There comes Myrtle Bickerstaff. I guess the old lady will quiet down now."

Birdie put her shallow pan of peas on the steps and went to the gate.

"Why, Myrtle, where in the world have you been? It's past nine o'clock and your mother has been real worried. She's been running all over town asking if anybody had seen you."

"Nobody's got any reason to worry about me," said Myrtle insolently. "I'm old enough to take care of myself."

"I guess that's right," said Will. "I guess you can, all things considered." He joined his wife at the gate, tilted his head to one side and glanced at Myrtle with sly, heavy humor.

"I can't say I was worried about you myself. In fact, I told Birdie I figured you and Andrew had made up and were off together somewhere."

"Don't pay any attention to Will. He never said any such thing. He's making that up and he's trying to tease you."

A feeling of animation came over Myrtle. She straightened her back, her eyes narrowed and her lips turned down. She laughed loudly.

"Me off somewhere with that harelip? . . . *Me?*"

Again she laughed her disbelief and her derision.

Will said: "Well, there was a time—correct me if I'm wrong —when I used to see Andrew's car parked down the block regular. Birdie and I sure thought it was a match for awhile."

"Don't pay any attention to Will; he's only trying to tease you, Myrtle!"

Myrtle spoke lightly: "Oh, I own up to letting him come to see me a time or two, but that was because I felt sorry for the boob. I knew no other girl in town would have him sitting around the place."

Again she threw back her head and again she laughed. She placed her hands on her hips and swayed them. "A girl would have to be deaf as well as blind to have him around. I never could figure out more than half he said; he talked so funny."

To illustrate her meaning she drew down her upper lip and imitated his grunting, tortured speech. She did it with remarkable fidelity, her shoulders held forward, her head lowered, her fingers turning clumsily at an imaginary hat. Both Will and his wife leaned against their fence and opened their mouths in delight.

Old Mrs. Westerlund, Birdie's mother, came out of the house to see what the noise was about. She had a dishcloth in her hand.

She stood by the screen door and pressed the damp cloth against her apron. She lifted her arms, mottled with liver spots, and pressed her hands against her cheeks, her dry body quivering with unexpected merriment.

When Will Calkins was able to control his laughter he wiped his eyes and spoke pleadingly:

"Do that part again about the slab-pit and the moon coming up back of the dam."

"All right, if you want to hear it; but that wasn't the funniest thing he ever said to me by a long shot."

Elmer Berry and the youngest of the Macbeth girls stopped and stood listening. Then Mrs. Tom Watson and Mrs. Renshaw came out of their houses at the same time and down to the sidewalk to join the group. The sense of elation which had come over Myrtle continued to grow as she entertained her audience.

"You better not let Jim hear you mocking his brother," said Mrs. Macbeth cautiously. "Jim cut a man with his pocket-knife one night in the commissary for doing that. I was there buying some groceries at the time, but I didn't look. I can't abide the sight of blood and it made me sick to my stomach for a week. They taken eighteen stitches in the man, I heard later on."

"I hope he does hear it," said Myrtle scornfully. "I'll tell him so to his face, if he wants to know what I think."

"Lord! Lord! What's the world coming to I wonder?" Mrs. Westerlund sat on the steps, threw her apron over her head and rocked back and forth.

Myrtle turned from her audience, shrugged her shoulders and walked away, her hips swaying insolently. She opened her front gate and went up the walk humming a tune. She snapped her fingers at nothing at all.

"I don't care *that* for any man who ever lived!"

Her time of vagueness, and her short period of imaginative uncertainty, had passed forever, for she had found a way to revenge herself on Jim and she knew it. She felt released and in possession of her faculties again. She ran up the steps triumphantly and went into her house.

The Reverend Butler led Andrew into the study where he wrote his sermons, smiled and sat in his particular chair. He held his legs tightly together at the knees, his calves bracing outward and forming a small tent, his feet turned edgewise on the spilling cornucopia of fruits and autumnal flowers which were woven into his rug. There was a strong sun behind him and it turned his fringe of upstanding hair into a ragged aureole. He cleared his throat and began to talk.

He had asked Andrew to visit him this afternoon not only to ascertain his spiritual needs, but to discuss with him as well the details of his baptism and final entry into the church. The confessional was not a part of his faith or the ritual of his church, but if there was anything that Andrew wanted to tell him, or any advice he wanted to ask, Brother Butler would be glad to act not only as his pastor, but as his friend. . . . There was not, so far as Andrew could tell, any further evil left in him to report.

Brother Butler talked then of plans for the baptism, and when they had been decided upon, he rose to signify that the interview was over. But Andrew remained hesitant.

"There's one man who did me a wrong and I haven't forgiven him."

"Who is that man?"

"He's my brother."

Brother Butler straightened up and placed his hands on Andrew's shoulders, looking into his eyes. He smiled with a tender, brotherly contempt, as if he despised men who came so easily to salvation and with such slight justification for the rigors of conversion.

124

"You must forgive your brother, no matter what it was he did. You must forgive him before you sleep tonight."

When he was at home again, Andrew changed to his working clothes and went to the fields to hoe his cotton. He worked for the rest of the afternoon, his heart completely at peace now, his spirit calm. It was near sunset when he returned to the house and put his hoe away in the barn. Jim was on the back porch pouring water into a basin, and Andrew stood while his brother washed his face and neck and dipped his straight, black hair into the bowl. When he had finished, Andrew held out his hand and spoke.

Jim turned quickly, his face alive and delighted. He laughed with relief. He shook his shoulders and caught Andrew's hand in his own.

"I knew you'd look at it in the right way!" he said triumphantly. "I knew if I kept quiet you'd come to your senses sooner or later!"

The brothers walked to the watering trough and sat on its edge. They looked across fields misted in the twilight, and upward to a shadowed sky. From the pecan tree by the barn, a locust burst into sound with one repeated beat, and then, conscious of the conspicuousness of his noise, dropped his note to a milder key, hesitated and was silent. An ox team passed on the road with a creaking of wood and leather, and a man shouted and cracked a rawhide whip. Edna came to the back door to say that supper was ready, but when she saw her uncles sitting together for the first time in weeks, she went back to her kitchen, picked up her book and drew her chair to the stove. She lifted the overfed kitchen cat, curled him into her lap, and thought of her uncles and the complexity of their relationship. She had not known what the quarrel was about, but she had speculated over it a good deal. Her lips pulled down wryly, for in a flash she saw them precisely as they were with the pure, unclouded cynicism of her adolescence.

She called at last from the kitchen window and Jim got up and went toward her; but Andrew hesitated by the trough, slapping the red dust which had collected on his overalls, the sound of his hands making a shallow noise against the cloth, before he followed Jim into the house.

"How do you file saws, Uncle Jim?" asked Edna. "Do you think I could learn to do it?"

Jim shook his head, the wing of black hair falling to his eyebrows. He was in an excellent humor again, now that Andrew had come to his senses and absolved him of his guilt.

"Now, Edna! For Christ sake have a heart."

After Edna had served the supper she sat down with her uncles and began to eat. She opened her book and put it on the table in front of her. It was a history of the French revolution, and she read bits out loud which particularly took her fancy.

"When you come to think of it," said Edna, as if she had been turning the matter of the saws over in her mind while she read, "I can do a lot of things pretty well. I can cook, sew, scour and wash clothes as well as the next one; and I know all about babies and how to mind and feed them. . . . I never shot a pistol, but I know how to use a shotgun and I can bark squirrels with a rifle better than Papa or any of the boys in the family. I can harness a team and drive a car." She stopped, counting carefully. "Oh, yes, I almost forgot: I know how to dance, too."

"I don't like to interrupt you, Miss Cleaver," said Jim, "but there's still some doubt about your dancing."

"I can kill and scald pigs," continued Edna. "I can skin a beef by myself and Miss Sarah is going to teach me my notes on the piano just as soon as her sore finger gets better."

Andrew said: "That seems to me like a lot for a fourteen-year-old girl to know."

126

"Barking squirrels is going to come in handy when you move to New York," said Jim. "I never been there myself, but I've heard those big buildings are run over with wild squirrels."

Edna looked at him gravely, as if debating seriously the authenticity of this scrap of information. She shook her head.

"I think you're mixing squirrels up with *pigeons!*"

"Maybe I am," said Jim. "It's not unlikely. . . . Anyway, you've got to admit that your pig-sticking experience will be a help when you and Bessie Tarleton take over the country to run."

Edna smiled at his ignorance. "You don't think for a minute that Bessie and I would do that sort of thing *ourselves,* do you? It wouldn't be dignified for anybody in our positions. . . . There'll be plenty other people under us for that sort of work."

"Don't tease her, Jim."

"By God, I believe she really means it!" Jim laughed and shoved back his plate. "I think you better ask Edna not to tease me!" he added. "She came out with all the honors."

Edna smiled and lifted her eyebrows, her bulging, academic forehead wrinkling. She made a mental note of the fact that she was also able to handle men of her Uncle Jim's general type. She picked up her book again and read out loud to her uncles. It was a bloody passage about the guillotine, women knitting and heads that rolled counted into baskets. She looked up from the page and regarded Jim with quiet speculation.

Jim took out a cigarette and lit it.

"I'll settle the matter for you, Miss Cleaver," he said. . . . "One whack would do it easy; just one ordinary little chop!"

He got up from the table and stretched.

"You know, Edna, you make me right nervous at times."

He laughed and came over to her. "Come on, I'll give you another dancing lesson. . . . You'll never lure a dirty old capitalist to his doom if you keep stepping on his feet all the time."

When Edna had gone back to the kitchen with the dishes and the brothers were alone, Andrew spoke slowly, as if the effort cost him a great deal: "Why don't you marry Myrtle yourself, Jim? She loves you and has all along."

Jim said: "What's the matter with you? Have you gone crazy all of a sudden? Here, let me feel your pulse!"

CHAPTER XVI

M YRTLE looked at the empty wood-box behind the stove. It was the duty of her younger brothers to keep it filled at all times, but it seemed as if they could never be made to remember it. She went to the back door and called. The boys had gone off to play, and she got no answer. She decided to go to the wood pile and cut the blocks herself. It would get her away from her mother, at least, and the argument which had been going on between them all morning.

Kate was not to be frustrated so easily. She followed Myrtle into the back yard, knelt down and stacked the stove lengths as her daughter cut them. Later she would carry them into the kitchen.

Myrtle said: "I've told you a dozen times already, Mamma, that the job is mine if I want to take it. I talked to Mr. Dolan yesterday and he promised it to me."

"But you don't know anything about clerking in a store. You got to have experience for that kind of work."

"I guess I can learn like anybody else, can't I? I'm tired of sitting at home doing nothing and moping about like an old sick hen. I'm going to have me some fun while I can."

Kate looked up at the sun. It was a clear, hot day and she decided that she would do the weekly washing that afternoon, when the family had been fed, rather than wait for tomorrow. She would ask Myrtle to help her. "I know your father better than you do, baby, and he's often said no daughter of his should ever do any work. Why, it would look like he wasn't able to support us. It would just about kill him for people to see his womenfolks working."

Mrs. Macbeth, their neighbor, seeing Kate and her daughter at work together, came to the dividing fence and peered over. "Your cannas are sure growing well," she said plaintively. "I don't know what in the world is the matter with mine. They just don't seem to do right."

"You coddle them too much," said Kate shortly. "If you'd quit watering your cannas and fussing over them all day, they'd bloom like mine."

Myrtle straightened up for a minute to rest her aching arms. She had made up her mind to clerk in the store, and she was determined to do it. If it shamed her father for people to see her working, he'd just have to get over it as best he could.

Mrs. Macbeth said: "It makes me real envious to see you handle an axe like that, Myrtle! I can't even bend *over* very well; my back's weak." She wanted to continue the conversation, but Myrtle began swinging the axe again and Kate got up, loaded her arms and carried her first turn of wood into the kitchen. When she returned to the pile, Mrs. Macbeth had gone away from the fence and was peering anxiously at her own flowers.

"The trouble with Mrs. Macbeth is she can't make up her mind," said Kate irritably. "Last week she had those cannas covered with sacking for shade, and this week she's took it off, and there they sit in the hot, broiling sun. Next week I guess she'll dig 'em all up and move 'em on the other side of the walk. No wonder they don't do well. . . . I never saw such a wishy-washy woman in my life as Mrs. Macbeth is!"

"I'm going to work in the store, Mamma. Nothing you or Papa can say will stop me."

Kate sighed and gave in suddenly to her daughter's wish, knowing herself defeated; but she suggested that it would be better for her to tell Neil of the plan first, and to reconcile him to it, since she knew better than her daughter how to handle him. These details being finished at last, and the wood cut and carried into the kitchen, Kate spoke of another subject which was troubling her.

"When I was a girl of your age my own mother interfered with everything I did, and I swore to myself at the time that if I ever had a daughter I'd treat her different; but there's one thing I want to say about the way you're carrying on, and it's just this: I don't approve of you mocking poor Andrew Tallon like you do. It's not Christian or kind and it's going to make trouble. The older people are beginning to criticize you for it already."

Myrtle did not bother to answer her mother. She went and built a fire under the iron wash pot in preparation for the boiling of the clothes that afternoon.

Myrtle started work in the women's department of the commissary on the following Monday, just as she had planned from the first. Kate sighed and went about her housework alone. She missed her daughter a great deal. Myrtle had changed a lot in the past week or so, and Kate was not sure that she liked the change. There was no difficulty in getting Myrtle to go out now, and she talked to her mother freely about her conquests. She had lost all the old sullenness and indecisiveness and she seemed very sure of herself. She was popular with the men who worked at the mill and the men who lived in the county and she went everywhere that her work permitted: to dances, parties and picnics. At night, after the commissary had closed, there were generally two or three young men ready to walk home with her, to sit later on her porch and listen to her sharp, second-hand witticisms, for she had lifted from the magazines she read and the movies she saw a small but serviceable supply of expressions. She varied these tags of wit with necessity, and shaped them to fit such situations as arose; she modified them with the inflections of her voice and the expressions of her face, concealing the threadbare poverty of her borrowed cleverness. These slight pegs of conversation were all that she needed for social success. Certainly the men who admired her asked for nothing else. There was, too, in Hodgetown a group of young girls who followed her about like a chorus, admiring but a little envious, and they aped her affectations and her worldliness.

At the weekly dances held that summer in the company hotel, Myrtle would stand during the long intermission by an open window, fanning herself with a paper fan which advertised a patent medicine, and before her would congregate her particular group. Somehow, at some time during the evening, the conversation turned to her now celebrated affair with Andrew.

"That's not the way I heard the story," said Plez Barrascale. "I heard it was Andrew threw you over for religion."

Myrtle was familiar with these leads; they were the cues that launched her into her act and brought her onto the stage for the benefit of her public. She knew that Jim was only a few yards away talking to May MacLean. He was apparently unconscious of her, but Myrtle was certain that he listened to everything she said.

"Him throw me over?" repeated Myrtle in surprise. "That crazy boob? . . . Why, he hasn't got sense enough to throw *salt* over his shoulder!"

The reply seemed a little pointless, judged even by her own uncritical standards, but she tried to give it significance by rolling her eyes in a provocative manner and caressing her slack lips with her outthrust tongue.

Ellie Lou Macbeth said: "After Myrtle finished with him there wasn't anything for Andrew to do except join the church and get his sins washed away."

Myrtle put her hands on her hips and spoke, her voice slow and insinuating in the manner of movie stars.

"All I can say is this: the church ain't as particular who gets in it as I am."

"Tell about the time you and him threw the love-vine and walked down to look at the river," urged Plez Barrascale.

"That's old," said Myrtle. "Everybody knows that by heart now." She fluffed out her black, wire-like hair and smoothed her eyebrows with a dampened finger. "I'll tell you what I'll do: I'll recite the poem he wrote me a day or two afterwards." She stood among her admirers, collected her thoughts and began:

"Why does not my lord come for me? I am sick with waiting:
Am I undesirable among the young virgins of Hodgetown?
Is there a flaw in me, is there a manifest evil that my lord comes not?
I am young and I am ready for love and my lord comes not!"

Myrtle said: "That part, the way I figured it out, is supposed to be me speaking. . . . But wait a minute until you hear what he says!"

Janie Macbeth laughed and shook out her blonde hair. "I thought he came to see you often enough. Mamma used to say she never looked out the front windows at night without seeing his car parked by your gate."

"Wait a minute!" said Myrtle. "Wait till you hear the rest of it!"

She laughed in her triumph and lifted the rope of pearls which she wore, tightening the heavy strand with her fingers, making a noose close about her neck.

May MacLean spoke soothingly: "Now, Jim! Now, Jim! Don't pay any attention to what she says. It's all in fun and everybody takes it for a joke."

They went outside and walked down Hiawatha Street until the music started again. They stopped under the trees which

133

lined the street. Jim took off his hat and twisted it in his hands.

"She'd better shut her mouth! That Georgia slut better shut her mouth!"

"Now, Jim, leave her alone and people will get tired of it in no time. . . . Anyway, it's Andrew's affair, not yours."

"Andrew never did have sense enough to take care of himself," said Jim. "He always did let people run over him when they wanted to, and now, since he's joined the church, he's worse than ever."

His wave of anger had passed. It left him a little depressed and feeling unjustly put upon. He could not explain to May, of course, or to anybody else, for that matter, but he knew quite clearly that Andrew had nothing to do with the matter, that the issue was between himself and Myrtle alone.

Below the Barrascale farm Pearl River bent outward into a semicircle of shallow water, and it was here, on a Sunday afternoon in July, that Andrew was baptised. The sand-bar that lipped the shallow water, and the bluff that hung above it, were lined with the people of the county who had come to watch the ceremony. Andrew entered the water barefooted, robed in the whitish nightgown that Edna had made for him out of unbleached domestic. He took his place between the preacher and his assistant and stood quietly until his body was bent backward into the river and lifted again. There were but four converts in all, and the entire ceremony did not take long. When it was over and he had changed to dry clothing, he walked through the woods to the place where he had parked his automobile. He walked slowly, avoiding people as much as possible. He was surprised and somewhat disappointed that he felt at this moment much as he had felt before his immersion in the water, that no vast and shattering changes had taken place in him, for he knew then that he had looked forward to baptism as something resembling the exorcising trick of a conjuror, and he had expected his despair to cease with his sins.

Edna was waiting for him in the automobile, talking with old Mrs. Holm Barrascale who sat on a cane-bottomed chair and fanned herself in her son's wagon. She was a woman so crippled with toil and old age that she could no longer straighten her back. She went about sloped slightly to the left and bent forward at a perpetual angle like an unprovable problem in mathematics, and she had to be lifted in and out of her son's wagon. When she saw Andrew approaching, she raised her voice, because she had been discussing Myrtle Bickerstaff and himself, and she wanted to demonstrate to Edna that she was not the sort of person who would wound the feelings of others by talking behind their backs; she would say it to their faces just as quickly.

"I don't see how she had the nerve to come to Andrew's baptising," she continued indignantly; "not after the way she's been running him down to everybody in Hodgetown." She turned to Andrew. "It seems to me that Myrtle hasn't had very good raising; either that or folks from Georgia just naturally haven't got no idea of what constitutes manners!"

Andrew said mildly: "It all went off smoothly, didn't it? I had an idea it would take more time."

"I saw her at the baptising, too, Uncle Andrew. She came with Willie Oakshot, but they stood away from the bank, back of a willow tree, and they left early. . . . She's had her hair cut and curled. It stands out like nigger wool from her head. She's got her finger nails enameled red and she had on long green earrings."

"If it was my daughter," said Mrs. Barrascale, "I'd make her read what the Bible says about Jezebel!"

Later, on the road, Andrew spoke to Edna after a long silence: "She didn't come with Willie Oakshot. She came with Linus Calvert. She met Willie by the bank and they only talked for a few minutes while Linus went to see about his team."

135

CHAPTER XVII

ONE Saturday night in August Jim Tallon came into the commissary and stopped just inside the doorway, looking about him. It was very hot and there was no air stirring. He mopped his face and his neck, raised his eyes and caught sight of Myrtle in the full-length mirror which stood to the left. She was surrounded as usual by her admirers, and as she showed dress material to Eloise Batty she entertained her friends with her reminiscences. Their eyes met in the mirror. Myrtle turned to the shelf behind her and took from its hiding place an envelope which she had secreted among the bolts of cloth. She said, her words audible the length of the aisle:

"Oh, he wrote me dozens of 'em. Once he got started, he rained 'em on me. I don't see how he had time to do his farming." She selected one of the poems from the envelope, smoothed it out and read it, imitating precisely Andrew's gasping, labored speech.

"My beloved is like a cloud in the sky, but she drifts not toward me; she is a maiden and she has not thought of love.

She is water in a cup of crêpe-myrtles, she is lipped about with grasses, she is bounded with sand. . . .

Lie with me my lover, your hands against my face: I am weak with my desire!

I am the hawk that lifts above clouds and above water, whose shadow dips on the sides of hills and measures the tops of trees:

Lie with me my lover, your breath sweetening my blood: I am weak with my desire!

136

Make me a motion and I will step across Pearl River:
I will walk through the fields of young cotton; I will walk toward the moon rising at Tarleton's store; I will walk toward you and catch at branches that hang low.

Walk toward me my lover, my strong love. Walk up the steps of my father and into his house, for your muscles are harder than steel, and your eyes flash with fire.

Come to me clad in scarlet and purple: Come to me with bracelets of gold, with buckler of silver and steel:

Come to me in trappings of silver: Come to me wearing rings.

The wish of my beloved is a thing to make me strong:
For her delight I will leap upward and snatch birds out of the sky,
I will pick stars out of the sky and put them in her apron."

Mrs. Dora Percy said: "Please don't read no more of it, Myrtle, because it's too dirty to be read out loud. All that filth makes me sick to my stomach, for a fact."

"I don't see any dirt in it," said Eloise Batty. "I think it's just silly." She sat on the revolving stool anchored to the floor in front of the counter. "I declare, I don't see how you ever learned to mock him so good, Myrtle!" She laughed again. "How does that part about coming up your front steps go again? . . . Is it like this: Hum hoo me hlad hin harled und *ho-o-o-rpul:* Hum hoo me hwit bwacluts hoff hoold?"

"No," said Myrtle critically. "That's not exactly right. It's close but it's not exactly the way he talks. He don't say it that plain: *this* is more the way he says it."

Jim turned and went back to the soft-drink stand. Henry Gillies, the clerk, opened a bottle and placed it on the counter before him.

"It's right hot, ain't it, Jim?"

Henry was a short man who seemed to have no neck at all and whose red, apple-like cheeks rolled upward as if to obscure his bright, greenish eyes. His collar was opened at the neck and a tuft of black hair protruded. His clothes seemed too tight for him, as if he had borrowed them, for the occasion, from a younger and a smaller brother. His belly pressed forward in a hard half-circle, as mathematically rounded as an arc made with a drawing instrument.

Jim said: "I wouldn't want to see it no hotter."

He wiped the neck of his bottle with his palm and raised the drink to his lips, turned slightly and looked at Myrtle again. She had become more animated, and as she rolled the bolts of cloth before her customer, she laughed. Jim strolled across the store to where hardware was sold. He bent above the case with concentrated and absorbed interest. From this place he could hear Myrtle's voice again:

"Here's some more of it. I'll just pick out a few parts for you because it goes on and on." . . .

"My beloved is a desert in which roots lie quiet awaiting the rains of spring:

She is a garden that is guarded by walls with no gates.

(Be not dismayed, wail not thy fruitlessness: thou art the sound of my ear's hearing!)

I am a river whose waters are swollen, whose dams will break with a rushing noise:

I am a river of water and my beloved is a field in which nothing grows.

(Be not dismayed, wail not thy fruitlessness: thou art the sum of my eye's seeing!)

I will pour my waters into you, I will plant rich seeds in you:

(Thou art the smooth thing of my hand's touching!)

138

And your desert will blossom with every color, and you will be fruitful in perfume and color:

(Thou art the smell of spiced pinks in my nose; yea, thou art the shade of my soul's choosing!)"

Eloise Batty wiped her eyes with her handkerchief. She said: "I declare, we ought to be ashamed of ourselves, all of us, to laugh at poor Andrew; but it is funny, say what you please, particularly that part about him being a river."

Jim came back to the soft-drink stand and put his bottle on the counter before him.

"I heard a pretty good story last week, but maybe you've already heard it too."

"Tell it anyway," urged Henry. "Maybe I haven't heard it."

"It's on old man Snellgrove of Reedyville and his wife, Ulrica," said Jim. He raised his voice as Sam Newsom and T. L. Dolan came over to listen. They stood expectantly at Jim's elbow, knowing his reputation as a story-teller, their lips pursed and their heads bent, ready to laugh at the proper moment.

Jim continued: "Well, I'd better tell you in case you don't know that John Snellgrove is just about five feet tall and don't weigh more than ninety pounds wringing wet, and his wife, Ulrica, is said by some people to be the biggest woman in the State."

Sam Newsom nudged Dolan with his elbow and added a note of corroboration to the story: "Jim's right. She's a big woman and that's a fact. She'd make three of John."

"Are you talking about the Snellgrove whose daughter married young Ben Atkins last year?"

Jim said: "That works right into the story, Mr. Dolan! I was just getting around to that. . . . The daughter's name is Ida, and after she married Ben the old lady used to telephone her every morning and get her to tell about herself and how she and Ben were getting along together."

John Everett came to the stand. He started to speak, but Henry stopped him. He served him in silence and Everett stood beside the others listening to the story.

"One morning," Jim continued, "when old lady Snellgrove called up, Ida had a new story for her. It was a game that she and Ben had invented more or less by accident, and they called it The Royal Huntsman. It all came about over washing up the supper dishes. It seems Ida wouldn't wash them unless Ben agreed to dry after her, and Ben was pretty lazy and no-account about work. So they always argued about it and put it off until the last minute before going to bed. Well, on this particular night, it was pretty hot, so they turned off all the lights in the house to make it cooler, since the moon was up anyway. A little later they went in the bathroom and took a cold shower, still fussing about the dishes, and Ida went and lay on the big poster bed which she brought with her from her mother's house. She said she wouldn't wash those dishes or even budge from the bed until Ben promised to do his share and help her."

Jim paused, picked up his bottle and drank.

Across the store, Myrtle had reached the end of the poem. She turned the last page, fluttered her eyelids and read slowly:

"But my loved one comes not toward me, and I may not seek for her among her people;
And I lie alone in this room until the earth lightens at the east, saying:
'Words will not comfort a man like flesh: there is no substance in them, and wise men have lied!'
There are cows passing at Gentry's Ford and I hear the tinkle of belled necks.

140

They drink their fill of the water and lift their throats to the sky: they low plaintively at the sky."

Jim spoke again, putting the bottle on the counter before him, balancing it evenly at the edge:

"Finally, Ida and Ben thought up a way to decide the matter. Ida said if Ben could manage to touch her while she lay on the mattress without first touching the sides of the bed or the covering, or if he was quick enough to get his whole body in the bed before she could get out of it, then she'd wash and dry the dishes both; if he failed, he'd have to do all the work. Then they got to laughing and skylarking and worked out some rules for playing the game: Ida was to lie in the middle of the bed, but she wasn't to know which side Ben was to approach from, ready to roll away from his hand to the other side where he couldn't reach her, if she was quick enough. When they got it all worked out, Ben went in the next room and called, 'The Royal Huntsman is riding tonight and seeks his true love!' and Ida answered, 'The true love of the huntsman awaits his coming!' . . . Well, sir, Ben figured he'd outguess her, and so instead of running to the side of the bed, he ran straight forward and jumped over the footboard, hoping to get in bed with her before she could get out; but Ida was smart too, and she figured on him doing just that, so when Ben landed on his face among the bed clothes, Ida was by the bureau laughing at him; and Ben had to wash and dry the dishes after all."

The men about Jim laughed prematurely, as if this were the point of the story, but he held up his hand for silence. "Wait," he urged. "That's not all of it! . . . When Ida told her mother about the game, the old lady couldn't get it out of her mind. She kept thinking she'd like to try it, but when she looked at poor, shriveled up old John, who didn't have a romantic notion left in his head, she didn't have much hope. Finally, after deviling him for two or three days, she made him give in, and that night the old lady lay stretched out, covering most of the bed, a regular mountain of a woman, and John stood in the hall waiting to run when she gave him the signal. But what old Ulrica Snellgrove didn't know was this: John had talked to his son-in-law the day before, and Ben had told him all about the game too, and why he had lost. He advised John to use the same method of attack that he had tried, because he believed it would work this time. Mrs. Snellgrove wasn't as quick as her daughter, being so big and fat, and she couldn't possible get out of the bed before John landed; anyway, she'd be expecting him to run around to the side."

"Did John play the game with his spectacles on, or did he have to take them off too?" asked Henry.

T. L. Dolan slapped his knee and began to titter. He said: "Shut up, Henry! Let Jim tell the story."

"Well, anyway," said Jim, "after awhile everything was ready and old John piped up timid-like: 'The Royal Huntsman is riding tonight and seeks his true love!' and the old lady roared right back at him the correct answer. . . . So John started running, reached the foot of the bed, closed his eyes and jumped over like Ben had told him." . . .

Eloise Batty looked up from the dress goods she was selecting and said crossly: "What are those men laughing and making such a racket about? I bet they're telling smutty stories."

Rafe Hall moved away from the group about Myrtle and came to the soft-drink counter. He stood between Dolan and Everett.

Jim continued: "Well, that's about all there is to the story except what happened the next morning. After Ben had gone to the bank to work, Ida called up her mother like she always did, but all she could find out was what the nigger cook told her,

142

and that was that they'd taken old Ulrica Snellgrove to the Presbyterian hospital. Ida was almost crazy and she hurried to the hospital to find out what was wrong with her mother. When she got there, she met Dr. Kent coming down the steps. She went up to him: 'Oh, doctor! I'm worried to death!' she said. 'What in the world is the matter with poor Mamma?' "

Jim paused a moment to let the point sink in; he raised his eyes and glanced contemptuously at Myrtle, as if she heard this story too, and finished quickly:

"For a minute Dr. Kent looked down at the sidewalk like he was embarrassed; then he spoke: 'There's nothing much the matter with your mother, Ida. She seems to be okay; the trouble is, we can't find your father!' "

There was silence for a second. Then Henry Gillies' face lifted slowly and contorted as if he were going to sneeze. He put his head on the counter and laughed, his hard, rounded belly jerking up and down.

Rafe Hall said: "I didn't hear all of it. Tell it again."

"Go away!" said T. L. Dolan weak with his laughter. "Go away! I can't stand no more!" He leaned against John Everett and they shouted with laughter until they both turned red and began to cough. Then Jim finished his drink, straightened his tie with elaborate carelessness and walked away. His eyes lifted and they met Myrtle's again, and for an instant they stared at each other with their hatred naked and unveiled.

Myrtle's eyes fell first. She turned with animation to Eloise Batty and said:

"That was the night the poor sap opened the door of his car and asked me to get out, and before I knew what was coming off, he kissed me. Well, sir, I almost jumped out of my skin. . . . When I got indoors, I scoured my mouth out with scouring soap."

CHAPTER XVIII

JIM came out of the commissary and stood on the veranda which fronted it. Behind him he heard his friends still laughing at the story he had told and repeating portions of it to others who had come up. He passed his hands over his face, pressing upward with the tips of his fingers. A sound of faint music and of fainter merriment came from the direction of the Negro quarters, a sound which ended abruptly as if a door had been opened and closed slowly as some guest departed. He turned, then, his mind made up, and moulded the brim of his hat to a rakish angle. He jumped from the high porch to the ground beneath, steadying himself with his hand, and walked toward the cut through which the railroad tracks passed.

Beyond the Negro quarters was a marshy land drained by a creek, and it was here that the property of the Hodge brothers ended; it was here also that Jim found the house he was seeking. The door opened and an obsequious Negro man stood before him. He was George Stratton, the proprietor of the place, and his fat, blown-out cheeks were traced with scars no wider than fine thread. He smiled and bowed, his right hand clutched about his left thumb.

Jim went into the large back room of the establishment. There were tables with cane-bottom chairs drawn up to them, and to the left there was a small bar. To the right was the kitchen, a smaller room, where a cook in a white apron stood behind a counter and fried fish and potatoes for those guests who wanted food.

It was early yet and there were few customers in the place, but Jim saw Willie Oakshot, Plez Barrascale and the two Cornells boys at a table near the bar. They were eating fish sandwiches and drinking George Stratton's home-made beer. When the men saw Jim, they got up and moved their chairs to make room for him. He said: "Don't disturb yourselves. I just come in for a minute or so. I got a date later on."

He sat alone in a corner of the room and George came at once to serve him.

"I was just a-wondering if you was coming in to see us tonight, Mr. Jim?"

He put a pint of whisky on the table along with a glass and a pitcher of water, picked up the glass, held it critically between his eyes and the unshaded light globe, and polished it expertly with the cloth tucked into his belt.

"I guess you can pretty near figure on me for Saturday."

George spoke confidentially: "There's a couple of young white ladies visiting in Mamie Jackson's place on the Green Point road. I expect you'd relish the company of the red-headed one, if you're feeling lonely tonight."

He leaned across the table to speak more softly and Jim caught the smell of his strong, unwashed sweat. He drew back. He put his palm in the bending man's face and shoved him away.

"Don't blow your breath on me, nigger," he said mildly.

George stood transfixed, as if puzzled over something he could not understand, but unresentful.

"Yas, suh."

"If I want you to flush me a woman, I'll tell you."

"Yas, suh," agreed the proprietor. "Yas, suh."

When Jim had finished his pint he bought another and slipped it in his pocket. He got up and walked toward the door, ignoring his friends. Plez Barrascale called out:

"Who's your date with, Jim? Is she a white girl this time?"

145

Jim stared at him gravely, as if debating an important point. He said: "I wouldn't like to go *that* far, Plez. . . . I'd say she was somewhere between your color and white."

Plez wrinkled his brows in surprise. Then he got up and took a step forward. His face flushed angrily. He was conscious in a sudden panic of his dark coloring and his black, tightly curling hair.

"Do you mean to say I'm a nigger?"

The two Cornells boys stepped in front of him and caught his arms. Sam Cornells said: "Sit down, you damned fool. Jim carries a knife and he'll rip your belly open!"

"Jim was just joking," said Harvey. "He was only handing you back what you handed him."

Jim hesitated a moment and then came over. He put his hand on Plez's shoulder and spoke contritely: "Lord God Almighty, Plez, what's come over you anyway? Can't you take a joke?" His voice was pitched in a low, gentle key, but his hands and his eyes betrayed his excitement.

"Gentlemen! Gentlemen white folks!" pleaded George Stratton. "Don't let's have no trouble in this house."

Jim extended his hand and Plez took it. He sat down again feeling a little sick, his lips smiling falsely.

Willie Oakshot lifted his barrel-like chest and laughed with relief, now that matters had settled themselves satisfactorily. He said: "The trouble with a colored girl is she always asks you to kiss her when you can't help doing it!" He laughed explosively at his witticism, his spurious, blue teeth gleaming in the light.

There was complete silence in the room for a moment. From the kitchen there came the monotonous splutter of grease frying and clouds of gray smoke floated like mist from the cook room through the door and across the bar where the men sat.

"Gentlemen! Gentlemen!" repeated George. "Gentlemen white folks! . . . Let's don't have no ruckus in this house."

When Jim came back to Hodgetown it was past nine o'clock and he knew that the commissary would close soon. He stood screened by the trees across the street and watched the door. He pressed his hands against his forehead and licked his dry lips which seemed parched and detached from the rest of his face. He thought: "If she was a man, I'd shut her mouth. If she was just a man I'd stop her pretty quick."

Later he saw Myrtle and Rafe Hall come out of the commissary together. He saw them turn into Calumet Avenue and walk slowly, their arms entwined. He followed them, keeping a distance which would prevent his being recognized.

Myrtle and Rafe stopped at the Bickerstaff gate and stood there arguing some point. They looked up and down the street and kissed quickly. After that Rafe went away reluctantly; but Myrtle did not enter the house at once. She stood by the gate, her arms resting on the fence, as if she awaited somebody. She looked up, her eyes cold and hard, when Jim approached and spoke to her.

"I figured you'd be the sort of man to follow and try to spy on me. Well, I wasn't far wrong, was I?"

She laughed and twisted her fingers through the huge, imitation pearl necklace she wore. "You Tallons think you're better than other folks, don't you?" She snapped her fingers under his nose. "Well, I don't care *that* for the whole passel of you!"

"You're lying," said Jim. "If I said the word, you'd crawl to me on your hands and knees."

Myrtle said: "I wouldn't spit on such dirt. The sight of you turns my stomach nearabout."

Jim came over to her, jerking her across the intervening space so sharply that her head, with its upstanding, wiry hair, snapped backward.

"Turn me loose," said Myrtle, "because I'm not afraid of you. You can scare some folks with your knife, but you can't scare me." She twisted her arms free, opened the gate and came out on the sidewalk where he stood. "Let's go down the road a piece, if you want to talk to me. I don't like the neighbors to see the sort of folks I associate with."

The Bickerstaff house was the last on the street. Five hundred yards away was an untouched pine grove which divided the houses of the whites from the Negro quarters. Myrtle walked toward the grove, hearing Jim's unsteady step behind her. When they reached it, she turned and faced him again.

Jim said: "There's only one thing I want to say and I can say it quick. . . . If I hear you mocking my family again I'll kill you, woman or no woman."

"That harelip," she said contemptuously, "that boob."

She saw that his face was very pale, and she could feel the warmth from his body, could hear his breathing. She said: "Why don't you go ahead and hit me? You're the kind of a man who'd hit a woman, particularly when you're dead drunk."

"I'm telling you once and for all," said Jim. "You've got to shut your big mouth."

She said: "I'll do what I please and you or no other man can stop me."

Then her anger melted and she was helpless again. She made a peculiar noise, indrawn and whimpering, and against her conscious judgment she pressed her body against his, her arms tightly around his waist, her head resting against his shoulder. Jim lifted her head and kissed her furiously, their mouths wide open and their teeth clicking together.

"Wipe that kiss off! Scour that one off with soap!"

Myrtle whispered: "No! No!—Don't say such things. Don't say things like that, Jim!" A strange feeling came over her. She pulled his head down gently and held it against her breasts. She said: "Jim! Jim! What makes you treat me so mean?"

"You bitch!" said Jim as if he were going to cry. "You dog bitch!"

148

Myrtle was silent. She could not have spoken, even if she had wanted to. She stood against him closely and shivered. Far away in Wampum Street she head Will Calkins' automobile come to a stop, and then the sound of his garage door being slammed.

Jim, too, began to tremble. "If I said the word, I could have you again, and any time that I wanted to."

"Yes."

She pulled away from him and fell to her knees, hiding her eyes. "I'm so ashamed," she said. "I'm so ashamed of myself."

Jim spoke uncomfortably, now that matters had taken a turn which he had not anticipated, his voice thick and unsteady:

"There's nothing to be ashamed about, as far as I can see."

"Go away!" said Myrtle. "I'll do what you want. I won't ever mention Andrew's name again as long as I live unless you say I can. I haven't got any pride. . . . Please go away and let me alone, Jim, because I don't want you to remember me like this."

She stretched on the carpet of pine straw and began to cry, her face covered with her hands; and instantly Jim lay beside her. He slipped his arms beneath her and turned her face toward his, his body pressing against her own. He thought: "I didn't mean to go this far." He realized for the first time that he was quite drunk, and his motives for meeting Myrtle at all were so shadowy that his mind could not hold on to them. He thought: "I'm drunk, but I know everything I'm doing." . . . He felt excited all at once and inexpressibly tender, and nothing seemed of any great importance to him.

"Honey! Honey! Don't cry that way. Speak to me, sweetheart."

"I haven't got any pride left," said Myrtle. "Please go away, Jim. I don't want you to pity me. Don't look at me if you have any kindness in your heart at all."

But Jim threw his leg over her body, pulling her more closely to him with his knee. He kissed her again and caressed her wet

149

cheeks and after a time her crying stopped. She sighed and rested in his arms, the strong smell of corn whisky hanging about them like a cloud.

Later that night, to the surprise of the entire county, who had not even connected them together in their speculations, they hired a car and drove over to Reedyville. They were married by a sleepy justice of the peace whom they routed from his bed.

CHAPTER XIX

AFTER his sudden wedding, Jim had taken his bride to the company hotel in Hodgetown and early the next morning Kate and Neil came to call on their daughter and their new son-in-law. "I wasn't surprised," said Kate. "I expected something like this all the time."

She had cried again before leaving the house, to her husband's amazement, and her eyes were still a little red. She, herself, had not entirely understood her tears, nor the sense of depression which had come over her, because the marriage and settling of her daughter for life was the thing she had most desired. And it was not that she objected seriously to her daughter's choice, for she told herself, with the patient, complacent delight of the completely fulfilled wife that all men were alike at last, and that each man became the same unleashed male, once he had succeeded in bedding his bride. The cause of her unhappiness was rooted at deeper levels; it was more the fact that she could now no longer think of herself as a young woman, for she had become, for all eyes to mark, a potential grandmother; and the wedding of her daughter resolved itself, at last, into an obscene publication of her mother's age, which, when you came right down to it, was nobody's business but her own!

She walked over to Jim, who stood grinning by the unmade bed on which he and his bride had recently slept, and kissed him.

"Don't worry, Miss Katie," said Jim. "I'll take good care of her. She's in safe hands."

Kate shook her head and looked steadily out of the window. It was almost midday and below, in the kitchen, there was the

151

rattle of heavy china set heavily and the sound of ice being chipped and dropped into a water-cooler. Kate became brighter after a moment. Since Jim and Myrtle had married so suddenly, and since this was a Sunday with all the stores closed, it had occurred to her that Jim would not have been able to buy his wife a ring, so she had brought one along which had belonged to her sister, a widow, who had discarded it in Kate's care when she married a second time. Kate took the ring from her purse and exhibited it on her palm. It was wide and old-fashioned and thin from years of wearing. She apologized for meddling in their affairs almost before the ink was dry on the marriage certificate, that not being her way of doing things, but nobody would believe they were really married if the bride didn't wear a ring, so she had brought it along. They could suit themselves. It didn't matter to her greatly one way or the other.

Jim took the ring from her and slipped it on his wife's finger.

When Kate and Neil rose to go, they waited for the bridal couple to join them. Kate spoke, her face puckered with astonishment: "Why, ain't you two having dinner with us today?"

Myrtle said: "Jim and I talked that over this morning, and we think we'd better start out for ourselves from the first." She came to the door and kissed her mother, smoothing back her oily hair, afraid that she might have offended her, for already marriage had softened Myrtle, already her old surliness was dimmed in her happiness. She turned the ring on her finger and held it toward the light from the window, very melting and very womanly in the memory of her recent bliss. The ring would do quite well, she thought, until Jim had a chance to get her a narrower and a more modern one.

After Neil and his wife had gone, Jim sat by the window and read the papers while Myrtle made the bed and cleaned the room. Since the time when he woke that morning and found, with a slight distaste, a bride sleeping beside him, he had had increasing doubts as to the wisdom of what he had done. He was jumpy and his head still ached, but it was clear again at last and he was fully aware of the incomprehensibility of his actions. He turned the pages of the paper nervously. It simply didn't make sense, but he had done it. He'd married her and he'd carry it off. He glanced critically at Myrtle. She was pretty; there was no denying that. Any man would be proud of her for a wife and she was a fine woman in many ways. He could have done worse. Anyway, if it turned out that he'd made a foolish mistake, he'd never let people know about it. . . .

He wondered if Andrew had heard of the marriage and what he thought of him now after such complete betrayal. As he rustled the sheets of the newspaper he felt a sense of shame, a self-condemnation alien to his reasoned attitude toward life. He shook his head in despair. Andrew wasn't one to hold a grudge, he told himself; but as the afternoon passed and Andrew did not appear to offer congratulations, the force of his guilt increased to trouble him. His nervousness increased with it and his head began to ache badly again. He knew that he wanted a drink more than anything. He went downstairs and the manager of the hotel gave him what he wanted. He felt better at once. When he returned to his wife, his old manner had almost come back. He thought, with hurt indignation: "Andrew's acting like a baby. He was the one who wanted me to marry Myrtle in the first place. He suggested it before the idea had ever entered my mind. He wouldn't give me any peace until he got his way."

But this was too great an exaggeration for even Jim to accept. He laughed to himself, feeling the warmth of the whisky in his stomach. "Well, anyway," he thought, "he did make the suggestion one night. It was all over between him and Myrtle long ago, so he can't have much kick coming. It's just his hard luck."

He put on his coat and combed his hair with tender attention, for guests were beginning to arrive and Myrtle was calling him from the sitting room. Later, when their last friend had gone, Jim and his wife went to see Russell Hodge, his patron. Russell had got stouter as the years advanced on him, and the expanse of his vest front was wider than it had been when Jim first remembered him, but there hung across it the same gold chain and the same Masonic emblem.

"Well! Well!" cried Russell. "We're glad to hear the news. We figured it was time you married, Jim, but we thought it was going to be May MacLean."

Jim said: "No. No, it turned out not to be *May,* didn't it?"

Mrs. Hodge half rose from her chair and then lay back again. She was an invalid and had been for the greater part of her life. Her shoulders even in this, the heat of summer, were wrapped in a scarf of white wool, and her swathed feet rested on a stool. Her hair, rinsed with bluing water to give it a purer sheen, was a dead, unsparkling white, and her fluted neck, and the minutely crenated skin of her hands, were of the same pallor. From a distance the coloring of her cheeks made it seem that they, at least, were high with health, but it was merely a supposititious glow, for the perpetual, apple-like bloom of her face was, in reality, only a network of fine, thread-like veins lifting to the surface of her skin and rupturing there into individual pools of color.

Mrs. Hodge was very fond of Jim and she looked now critically at his bride. "Well, nobody can deny that you married a healthy girl, Jim. She's better-looking than May, too. A big, strong girl like her should have a baby to show you by next spring." She, herself, was childless and it was a misfortune to which she had never become resigned.

They laughed, and Jim, flushed and excited again, began to talk of his plans. Russell Hodge was of the opinion that the couple should stay on at the hotel for a week or so and then move to a vacant house on Tecumseh Street, which he would have repaired and painted in the meantime; but Jim was silent, since the idea was not particularly attractive to him.

"How big is the house?" he asked thoughtfully.

"It's got three big bedrooms," said Mrs. Hodge. "That ought to be big enough until the children start coming."

Russell said: "Let's have a drink to the bride's health, now that everything's fixed up."

On the way back to the hotel, Myrtle thought for the first time about Andrew, and she discovered that she had a warm feeling of kindliness for him. She wondered what she would say to him at their first, inevitable meeting. She concluded that she would explain nothing. She would start all over as if she had never known him. This, she knew, would be easy for her since her past, in the larger importance of her marriage to Jim, had ceased to exist for her. As she walked contentedly beneath the line of trees, she locked her fingers through the fingers of her husband. She looked into his eyes, her own eyes tender and swimming in light.

"Let's always be as sweet and loving toward each other as we are tonight. Let's promise never to quarrel or say mean things to each other, Jim."

Jim bent and kissed her. He spoke softly: "I'm willing to make that promise if you are, honey."

He was restless again after supper, when they were in their room once more. He tried to finish the Sunday papers, but he could not interest himself in them. He got up and drummed on the table.

"Why don't you run over and see your folks, Myrtle?"

"You'll come too, won't you?"

"No, baby, you go on alone this time. I'll come and get you later on."

Myrtle's jaw dropped and trembled, but she did not speak.

"All right! All right!" said Jim impatiently. "I want to go to the farm to get some clothes and to see Andrew, if you must know. I've got to see him some time, and it may as well be now."

"It does look like Andrew would have consideration enough to come to see *you* and not make you go way out there by yourself!"

"I'll take you to your mother's and leave you," said Jim. "I'll come by and get you just as soon as I can."

When Jim came out of the oak grove he saw Andrew sitting on the bench beside the barn, his bulk picked out in moonlight. He stopped at the gate and called, and Andrew came to meet him. They stood looking at each other with the gate between them. Jim took off his hat and brushed the wing of hair from his forehead. He smiled ingratiatingly and released the full force of his conscious charm, feeling at once the depth of Andrew's hostility.

His wedding had been sudden, and he'd admit it freely. It must have come as a kind of shock to Andrew. Possibly his conduct seemed puzzling in some ways; anyway, Andrew could be sure that he wasn't trying to minimize the situation or to offer excuses for himself. In fact, he himself did not understand all the cross motives back of the affair and would admit it frankly. It was true that he had been drinking quite a lot at George Stratton's place, but that did not account for everything. It was more that he and Myrtle had both realized in a flash that they loved each other and had all along, and that they might as well get married without any fuss, since they were both of the same mind.

Andrew said: "I wish you both happiness. I can say that truthfully."

Jim leaned across the fence earnestly. He knew now that he had loved Myrtle from the start and that she would always be the one girl in the world for him. It wasn't as if the wedding would really break things up. He and Myrtle were going to live in a nice house on Tecumseh Street, right back of the commis-

156

sary, and there was plenty of room for Andrew there as well. The farm, as Andrew had himself said on many occasions, hardly paid for itself any more, with cotton selling below the price of fertilizing and picking. The sensible thing to do was to send Edna back to Effie and Asa, close the old place and come to Hodgetown to live. He could get a job at the mill where the work was easier than farming, and he would have a steady income.

Andrew said: "My God, Jim! I'm a man too. I'm made out of the same flesh and blood that you are. Don't you think I've got any feelings?"

"The trouble with you," said Jim, "is that you won't face anything out. The best cure for you is to see Myrtle all the time. You'll get over it quicker then and you'll fall in love with somebody else and maybe marry."

"I'm staying where I am," said Andrew.

Jim shook his head with amazed incredulousness. "There's no figuring you out! You were the one who insisted on me marrying Myrtle in the first place and made my life miserable until I did. . . . You got what you wanted, and now, by God, you want to blame me for that, too!"

Andrew said: "How about May? Who was it persuaded you to throw her over after you were engaged to her?"

"You hate me," said Jim, as if unwilling to believe his own words. "After what I've done for you all your life, defending you and taking care of you, you really hate me at last, don't you?"

"I don't hate anybody," said Andrew. "I wish you both a long life and much happiness."

"That's gratitude," said Jim bitterly. "That's gratitude for you!"

But Andrew had turned and was walking back to the bench by the barn.

Jim did not return direct to Hodgetown and his wife. He cut across fields, down Thompson's Lane and over the bridge that

157

spanned the creek. He stopped at the Cornells' place to talk for a minute with Harvey and Sam. They were going to Morgantown and they asked him to go with them; he argued for a minute and then gave in.

Harvey said: "Myrtle will give you unshirted hell when you get back for running out on her like this."

"She won't care," said Jim. "It's not like she was all alone. She's over with her folks tonight and I'll be back before she even misses me."

Jim unlocked the door to his room and went in. He stood in the darkness swaying, holding on to the bedpost for support. When he switched on the lights, he saw Myrtle lying on the bed. She was fully dressed and she was wide awake and she had been crying. He came to her and sat beside her, but Myrtle pulled away and turned her face to the wall. Jim got up and undressed, lurching unsteadily in the room under the momentum of his own drunkenness. He lost his balance at last and tripped, falling forward in the tangle of his trousers.

When he lay again beside his wife he put his arms under her and pulled her toward him.

"Mamma fixed up some wine and fruitcake for you. The Macbeths, the Renshaws and Will Calkins' family all came over to meet you. They fixed up a surprise, but you didn't show up. I never was so ashamed in all my life. I didn't even know where you'd gone to."

"Now, sugar," said Jim soothingly. "Now, sugar."

"How do you think I felt, not even knowing where you were?"

Jim rested on his elbow and looked at her. He bent down and rubbed her cheek with his own. "I couldn't help it this time," he said. "I met the Cornells boys on the way back to the hotel and they rode me over to Morgantown. We had a drink or two to celebrate the wedding. A man can't help that sort of thing after he's just married. Folks all expect it. . . . Now, you wouldn't want people to think I was tied to your apron, would you?"

"How do you think I felt having people feel sorry for me and say I was neglected on the first night after I married?"

"I'm sorry, sweetheart," he said softly. "I won't ever treat you so mean again. I didn't know how it would look, and I didn't realize how late it was getting to be."

Myrtle turned then and lay in his arms. She lifted her hand and shoved back into place the wing of hair which lay fallen across his forehead.

CHAPTER XX

THE waiter at the hotel fixed a special table for Jim and his bride and set it in an alcove screened from the other diners, as if a man and his new wife pursued their marital researches even at meal times, or carried through a secret ritual with the eating of their food. Myrtle came down first and took her place behind the screen. She had fixed her hair a new way and had smoothed it more closely to her head, since she was now a married woman and must behave more conservatively. She had a colored ribbon tied to her skull with a small bow in the front, and her lips and cheeks were rouged very slightly. When Jim had finished washing and had changed from his work clothes, he joined her at the table, his hair perfumed and gleaming with pomade, his freshly shaved cheeks smelling of lilac water. Myrtle began to talk at once. She and her mother had inspected the house on Tecumseh Street that day and they thought it would suit very well after the painting and the papering had been done.

Behind the private alcove, in the main dining room where the other boarders ate, was a sound of loud, roaring talk and the clattering of spoons against serviceable china as the guests filled their plates. When the clatter had subsided again, Jim spoke thoughtfully.

The more he thought of the idea of living in Hodgetown, the more he disliked it. It had never been his plan, and he had accepted it for a time, merely because he hadn't thought matters through to a conclusion; but now, since the excitement of marriage had worn off a little and left his mind free to occupy itself with more practical affairs, he realized he had never really thought of leaving the farm, where there was plenty of room for them all. He had always had it in the back of his mind that it was there, and there alone, that he and Myrtle would eventually live.

Myrtle stared at her husband with increasing amazement. "Why, Jim!" she said at last. "Have you gone completely crazy? What would people say with Andrew there too, knowing that Andrew and me went together so long? Why, I never heard tell of such a thing!"

"Let them say what they please," said Jim patiently. "What do we care? They'll say what they want to anyway, no matter what we do." He narrowed his eyes and rocked his head from side to side. He smiled winningly. "It seems to me that the folks in this county have already said everything they could by this time."

"No," said Myrtle. "I won't go. It's not even decent."

Jim talked ingratiatingly. There was no sense in paying rent in Hodgetown when there was a more comfortable place for them free of charge. He didn't like to live cooped up and so close to other people, with neighbors, almost in the same room with you, listening to everything you said and prying into your business. He liked the farm. He was used to it and he didn't see any sense in making a change. He dispelled at once her doubts concerning Andrew. Andrew, from his very nature, couldn't hold a grudge against anybody very long, and insofar as the neighbors were concerned, they could all go jump in Pearl River.

They got up from the table and walked into the small, unfurnished lobby. Jim thought: "Andrew would have to have a lot of crust to object to such an arrangement. Who does he think he is, anyway, to tell me what I'm going to do, or where I'm going to live? The farm is as much mine as it is his, and I'll tell him so pretty quick, by God!" He became more indignant the more he considered the matter. He thought, with hurt amusement: "You'd imagine a man who'd just professed religion and joined the church wouldn't be so narrow-minded or selfish. . . . I'll tell him that, too, if I have to do it!" He laughed, shaking his head and shoulders, and his discontent vanished as quickly as it had come. He turned and took Myrtle's arm, satisfied with himself on the whole, for he had no doubt but that he could bend Andrew again to the charm of his relentless will.

On Thursday morning Myrtle moved her possessions and the possessions of her husband to the Tallon place. Jim had gone to the mill that morning as usual, but he would come to the farm at suppertime. It had been arranged that they were to occupy the downstairs rooms and that Myrtle was to take charge of the house and run it for the brothers. Edna, who did not fit into the new arrangement, was to return to her parents, and she did not like it.

She stood on the morning of her departure waiting for Andrew to come from the barn with his car. Her thin, immature arms were held rigidly outward and bent at the elbows, her hands resting on her flat hips.

"I wish you good luck, Myrtle. You're going to have your hands full keeping Uncle Jim straight. He's a problem, as you'll soon find out."

"I'm not worrying any."

Since Jim had got his way he had been very tender to his bride, buying her presents which she had not expected and devising surprises for her pleasure. She was reassured once more and she had become soft and certain of herself in her happiness, as if the surety of having what she wanted was a magic thing to wish away trouble. She glanced at Edna, turned her head slowly and gazed at the road.

"I guess I know Jim inside and out by this time."

Edna went to the mirror and adjusted her hat, pulling it down

162

as far as possible on her high, egg-shaped head. She took a long time at her task, smiling knowingly at the reflection of her adolescent homeliness in the glass. She watched Myrtle out of the corners of her eyes, not turning. She lowered her eyes and went away from the mirror, as if the comparison between Myrtle and herself were too painful to be endured. She thought with sardonic amusement: "Oh, yes, you understand him, you big, slow-witted cow! You understand him, all right. Well, you're going to get your eyes opened!" She smiled slyly and opened her lips to speak, but abandoned her half-formed plan. There was little sense in wasting her subtleties on her new aunt; they would only be lost, and, besides, it was better to keep on good terms with Myrtle, since she expected to visit the Tallon place often in the future.

When she heard Andrew calling from the gate, she picked up her valise and debated whether or not she should kiss Myrtle good-bye. She decided against it, since she was coming back to the farm later in the afternoon to help Myrtle with supper and to show her where things were kept.

Andrew helped her arrange her belongings on the back seat, but Edna would not give up her books. Bessie had sent them to her to read and she wanted to return them undamaged. "Bessie picked out a half dozen silly novels for me to read in one dose, one right after the other," she explained. "She said if I didn't want to go shoot mocking-birds and cut down magnolia trees afterwards, she'd be very surprised."

"I don't know about cutting down magnolias," said Andrew gravely, "but I think there's a fine and maybe a jail sentence for shooting song birds."

"Bessie was just joking, Uncle Andrew, and so was I. I didn't mean for you to take me literally."

"Oh, I knew that," said Andrew. "I knew well enough that you were joking, but I thought I'd tell you anyway."

163

Edna laughed: "How about banjo smashing? Do you think I could get away with that?"

Andrew reached out and pulled her hair. "Now, Edna! Now, Edna!" he said. "I wish you'd quit checking up on every little thing I say."

The land lay burning under the heat of August, with light trembling upward in spirals from fields. Occasionally a stray wind blew for an instant and stopped, as if its force had been expended in bending once the spearheads of the pine saplings, or in dipping once to swirl the dust languidly upward from the red clay of the roadbed, and to powder it finally upon the parched grass that grew by the roadside.

Effie Cleaver was waiting for her daughter. She waddled down the steps, her squirming fry behind her. Her face was red in the heat and she rubbed it at intervals with her apron, the sprayed moles distinct and provocative. Edna said: "Mamma's probably expecting you to stay for dinner, Uncle Andrew. You might as well come in. Myrtle won't have anything ready when you get back; the fire wasn't even started in the kitchen stove when we left."

"If you ask me," said Effie, "it's a funny marriage and I don't see how anything but sorrow can come out of it. I can't understand Jim marrying her after the way she mocked us all and ran down the family in public, *certainly* not after the way he went on about it!"

"She didn't mean any harm," said Andrew. "There's not any real meanness in Myrtle. She's sweet when you get to know her."

Effie put her foot on the running-board of the automobile, her huge bosom lifting upward. She shook her head helplessly, collapsing the piled peak of her hair and tilting it toward her neck. "All I can say is this: men are beyond me, and I never expect to be able to understand one of them. They're just beyond me." Andrew started his car and backed clumsily toward the gate.

164

"The three of you living together under one roof ain't going to work out either," said Effie. "At least you ought to have common sense enough to know that, Andy!"

"Oh, let him alone, Mamma!" said Edna in a bored voice. "Uncle Andrew knows all that as well as you do. He said everything he could to stop it, but Uncle Jim wouldn't listen. He was determined to get his way, like he always is, and he moved in with Myrtle, in spite of what Uncle Andrew said."

Outside the gate, Andrew turned in a wide circle, the young Cleaver children squealing and scattering, and running behind him, like puppies, until he turned again and lurched over the small bridge and into the road.

Effie shouted shrilly: "If things don't work out all right, there's always room for you here with us! You're welcome any time!"

CHAPTER XXI

J IM was in a rare good humor. When he returned from the mill that night, he washed his hands and face on the back porch and called to Myrtle and Edna through the kitchen window. His gaiety continued through supper and he talked a great deal, telling stories and waving his hands back and forth. He spoke directly to Myrtle: "I want to warn you about Edna," he began, "because she'll try to find out if you know anything to teach her. If you've got any special accomplishments, you'd better keep them to yourself, sugar, or be drove crazy."

"Have you, Myrtle? Do you know how to do anything special?"

"I don't know of anything unless it's . . . " She stopped in embarrassment. She had started to say: "Unless it's my knack of taking off people," and had paused just in time.

"Go on, tell it!" pleaded Edna. "Say what it is."

"When I was about your age," said Myrtle slowly, "an old lady back in Georgia—she was one of Papa's cousins, as a matter of fact—showed me how to cut white flowers out of potatoes. You do it with a paring knife, and I got so I was better at it than she was. Her name was Mrs. McIver and she was a widow. The knife has got to be very sharp, though. She showed me how to make almost any white flower except a magnolia, and they're too big."

Edna said: "Show me, Myrtle! Show me how to do it right after supper, won't you?"

"You see!" said Jim laughingly. "You see how Edna is? Well,

I warned you, baby!" He went to the kitchen and returned almost at once with several Irish potatoes and a sharp vegetable knife. Myrtle smiled softly and selected the potato shaped the most closely by nature to her needs. She said: "I think I'll make me a Cape jasmine. Watch close, Edna, and you'll see how it's done. It's not so hard if you make the right cuts at the beginning."

"How do you figure on working potato-carving into your future?" asked Jim. "I expect you figure on poisoning it with something that smells sweet, and all the men that you vamp and lure up to your room will smell it, when you roll your eyes up at them and ask them to do it to show that they love you, and then they'll die and you can go through them for the important papers."

"You tell yours, Uncle Andrew," said Edna. "I'll tell mine after that."

Andrew leaned backward in his chair and stretched himself. "Maybe at some time in the future your sweetheart is in jail, and he's suffering a lot because people have told him that you don't love him any more. You do love him, of course, and you want to get word to him to tell him that people have lied and that you'll wait for him forever. . . . The trouble is, the warden of the prison won't deliver your letters, and you know it. So you write a note and hide it in a Cape jasmine cut out of a potato. Then you send this faked flower with a bunch of real ones and nobody at the jail can tell the difference, it's carved so well, except your sweetheart when they give him the bunch, because he's often seen you do it. So he pulls out the potato Cape jasmine, breaks it open and there's your message which gives him the courage he needs so badly to endure his unjust sentence."

The Cape jasmine, with its petals curling naturally, was finished, and Myrtle exhibited it stolidly on her palm. Jim said: "Wait a minute before you tell your story, Edna. I'll be right back." He went into the yard and cut a shoot from the Cape-jasmine bush that grew beside the chimney. He pulled off the superfluous leaves and sharpened the tip of the branch with the paring knife, impaling the carven flower firmly and putting the whole thing into a vase on the mantel.

"It'd look better bending toward the clock," said Myrtle critically. She got up and adjusted the vase, smiled happily and came to sit close to her husband, her arm about his shoulders.

Edna said: "Here's *my* story about the flower. . . . One day the revolution is just about to start and the signal is for Bessie to appear on the steps of the White House with a Cape jasmine pinned to her blouse. If she comes without one, everything is off, and the workers know that they're defeated and must go back to their homes. So the dirty old capitalists hear about it, and since they've got all the money in the world they have every Cape jasmine bush in the United States pulled up by the roots and burned. Well, Bessie *is* in the middle of a bad fix! You see the capitalists operate in secret with the police and the workers don't know what they've done, but Bessie finds out somehow, through secret influence she has, at the very last minute and tells me. I'm not worried at all, because I remember what Myrtle taught me tonight. So when Bessie walks up on the Capitol steps with all those old gloating senators and representatives leaning out of windows and jeering at her, she waits a full minute to make it more interesting, acting like she was completely defeated. Then she takes off her coat slowly, and there pinned to her shoulder is the Cape jasmine I carved for her that morning, and the revolution starts off and the workingman comes into his inheritance after all."

Jim laughed and slapped his leg. "It all works out fine, don't it?"

"Of course," admitted Edna doubtfully, "you've got to assume, for the sake of the story, that people are pretty feeble-minded."

168

"That wouldn't be hard for you to do, would it, Edna?"

"No, Uncle Jim," said Edna seriously. "It's practically no trouble at all. I think that's the most plausible part of the story." She turned to her new aunt. "Now you tell yours, Myrtle!" she begged. "We'll decide then which one is the best."

"I can't make up stories," said Myrtle. "There's no use in me trying, either."

"Go on, sugar!" said Jim. "It couldn't be any worse than the ones we told."

Myrtle thought a moment, her face puckered with creative effort. She spoke at last: "When the good man Andrew spoke about got out of jail, he and Edna married right away, and settled down. But the man couldn't get work, due to no fault of his own, and in a little while there wasn't anything in the house for the children to eat, and Edna got worried about it, and didn't know what to do, so she just boiled the potato and mashed it and they all had a *little* something for dinner anyway." She drew close to her husband's chair and stroked his knee with her palm.

"But that's not the same thing," said Edna critically. "You got to use a Cape jasmine in it somewhere."

Myrtle laughed, her voluptuous face happy and at peace. "Oh, I'm sorry I said anything about the old Cape jasmine in the first place!" She yawned contentedly and stretched out her arms, her breasts rising upward.

Edna said: "Well, we may as well go clean the kitchen."

Later that night some of the neighbors dropped in to see Jim and his bride, and before nine o'clock the house was full. Jim was in the kitchen with his particular friends, fixing drinks for the other guests. There were occasional bursts of loud laughter and the sound of glasses being touched.

Willie Oakshot came into the kitchen through the back door. "By God, if it ain't the happy bridegroom able to walk about without crutches!" he said. "Well, Jim, you sure put one over on us.

You and Myrtle sure gave the folks a surprise they wasn't expecting!" He ran his hands through his thin, pinkish hair, took
the glass that Jim offered him and raised it upward:

> "Here's to your first boy
> And half a dozen more,
> But if any have red hair
> Don't lay them at my door!"

Jim said: "Don't worry, Willie. Knowing you like I do, you'd
be the last man in Pearl County I'd think of accusing."

Linus Calvert said: "Don't take in so much territory, Willie. . . . You ain't big enough to break up a man's home!"

Rafe Hall doubled up with laughter, falling backward against
the table. In the ecstasy of his mirth he broke wind involuntarily.

Willie Oakshot looked about him innocently. "Who stepped
on that bullfrog?" he asked.

Myrtle came to the kitchen door and opened it a little, and
at once the coughing, hysterical laughter of the men stopped. It
was followed by a shuffling silence broken with slight, abortive
giggles.

"You boys come on out with the rest of us," she begged. "You'll
be sick as dogs tomorrow if you keep on drinking that green,
corn whisky. It hasn't been aged enough, and Jim knows it."

Addie Wrenn's prim, finely wrinkled face screwed up to register
her disapproval. "They're telling dirty stories like they always
are, but what fun they get out of it is what I can't see."

Miss Sarah Tarleton said: "It amuses them, I guess. Anyway,
I'm not the one to object to clean fun."

Jim came into the room followed by his friends. His face was
flushed and his wing-like fall of hair lay across his brow. He
walked to Miss Sarah and put his arms about her, tickling her old
neck with his pursed lips. "What is it you don't object to, Miss

Sarah?" he asked. "I'd like to make a note of it in my studbook for future reference."

"Don't you kiss me, Jim Tallon! Not with liquor on your breath!"

"Why, Miss Sarah! How do you expect to get a man to marry you if you don't give out samples?"

Miss Sarah said: "I never heard of such a thing!" She turned and faced the laughing people, her eyes stretched and distorted behind the thick lenses of her spectacles. She said: "I've lived more than seventy years without giving gentlemen samples, and I guess I can continue to do so." She turned to Addie Wrenn. "Give samples!" she repeated indignantly. "Give samples, indeed!" For a moment they discussed Jim and Myrtle, shaking their heads over the unconventionality of the sudden wedding, and then they both stopped and looked up, for they realized that Jim was making some sort of a speech.

Jim raised his glass. "I want to welcome all you folks here tonight and I want to say Myrtle and I will always welcome you!" He smiled winningly, looking very young and irresponsible. "You folks have just heard the second-best-looking girl in Pearl County turn me down," he went on. "Well, that being the case I'm going to have to content myself with the *very* best-looking one!" He went to Myrtle, put his arms about her and drew her to him. He bent slowly and kissed her lips, conscious of the effectiveness of their pose and of the fact that they made a handsome couple. In his pleasure he held the tableau a minute too long.

"Jim's a sweet boy!" said Sarah. "He's a sweet, dear boy, in spite of his rowdiness, and that's a fact!"

Jim stood in the center of the room, his arms still about his wife, their cheeks still pressed together. "I'm especially glad you people dropped in tonight because I know, as well as you do, that there's been a lot of talk since Myrtle and me married, and I want you all to see with your own eyes that there's no hard feelings between anybody in this house." He looked about him until he saw his brother. He was standing with Edna beside the door and he was grinning unhappily at the guests.

Jim said: "Come on over here, Andy. You haven't kissed the bride yet."

"How do you know so much?" asked Willie Oakshot. "How do you know what Andy's already done when your back was turned?"

Andrew's face turned red and he looked at Jim appealingly. He tried to escape by the door, but Willie Oakshot, Rafe Hall and Linus Calvert blocked his way. They caught him and pinioned his arms. They laughed, put their shoulders to his back and shoved him forward. Myrtle stood with her hands on her rounded hips. She was proud of her husband and very happy at this moment.

"Well, I'll be switched!" she said. "This is the first time I ever had a man take on so over the idea of having to kiss me!" She went to Andrew and stood looking at him with no trace of self-consciousness, her eyes soft and very friendly. "It looks like I'm going to have to kiss *him!*" she said. "He seems so particular about who *he* kisses!" She put her arms about Andrew and kissed him twice on his mutilated mouth.

There was a burst of applause and laughter from the guests.

"Here's another one to grow on," said Myrtle.

Jim said: "Here! Here! That's enough. You married me, sugar-pie, not the whole family!"

"Sweet and dear," said Miss Sarah. "Sweet indeed."

Andrew stood for a moment with his head bowed foolishly, feeling apart from these people and their laughter. He walked across the room and reached the door that led to the porch, his raised hand covering his lips.

"I'm going outside and get a drink of water," he said.

But everybody clapped hands and laughed more than ever at his bashfulness and confusion.

172

"Myrtle sure can burn 'em up," said Willie. "He's got to go outdoors now and put the fire out."

Jim looked quickly at Willie and then glanced at his brother disappearing through the door. Willie had too much to say about things that didn't concern him, and he'd find it out some day to his sorrow. It was foolish to think that there was anything between his brother and Myrtle, and yet what could he be sure of? He himself had been frank and aboveboard in this affair, as he was in all his relationships, but Andrew was notoriously close-mouthed; he was a deep one and he would bear watching. Jim shook his head scornfully at his suspicions, because he didn't believe such foolishness for an instant, and yet the force of Willie Oakshot's implications persisted in his mind to trouble him.

Andrew walked to the barn and stood there with his back to the wall. The moon was full and high in the sky, and it lay lightly on the fields like an even gilding. The oak trees stood black against it, silhouetted in their bulk, but across the road, toward the hollow, the tops of the young bays were as liquid and quivering as a stirred lake, their agitated leaves catching the light and shattering it. They shimmered slightly in the stillest air, but when a breeze came there was a quick lifting and shifting among the young trees and the live, silver leaves were like gleaming mullet that leapt ghost-like at night and fell again into water without sound.

Andrew turned at the sound of Edna's voice behind him and stood quietly while she came and slipped her arm through his. "Bessie always said that Pearl County was the hog-wallow of the world. Well, after tonight, I won't dispute her. . . . Did you ever see such vulgarity? Did you ever come across such stupid people in your life, Uncle Andrew?"

"That's just the way people are. They're no different from anybody else, I suppose."

"Anyway," continued Edna, "nobody asked Myrtle to recite

your poems or to give an impersonation of the way you talk as I expected them to." She pulled her own lips down into a dry grimace. "I hope you're grateful for that much at least."

"I expected it, too," said Andrew. "Thinking about it made me turn cold inside."

"I just suppose nobody thought of it," said Edna. "Mercy me, what a pity!" She clucked her lips in the manner of old Sarah Tarleton. "What a pity! as I just said. . . . What an unmitigated pity!" They began to laugh at the same instant, their arms linked together and their quivering backs resting against the planking of the barn.

They were silent after that and sat on the bench by the barn door and watched the moon. Most of the guests had already gone home when they entered the house again. There remained only Jim's set of particular friends. They were having a last drink together and they were all unsteady on their feet. Jim was standing among them, a glass in his hand. His face was flushed again and animated, and he talked loudly. "You can see for yourselves," he kept repeating, "you can see for yourselves that there's no hard feelings between anybody in this house."

When he saw Andrew he shouted drunkenly across the room. "We were wondering where you'd gone to; the boys were waiting for you to come take them home, because there's not a one of them sober enough to drive. You can take them in Rafe's car and then come back here with it."

"I'll come by tomorrow and pick it up, Andy, so you won't really be put out none," said Rafe apologetically.

"I'm sleepy and I'm going to bed," said Andrew. "The boys can get home anyway they please; it's none of my business." He started up the stairs, but before he had gone many steps he had a picture of Rafe Hall's automobile overturned in a ditch, or smashed to splinters against a tree, the men, who now stood below him in the room, mutilated and covered with blood. He

174

came down the steps again and put on his hat. He lifted his eyes sheepishly and saw Edna laughing at him; he, too, laughed a little, apologetically, as if to say: "I know, I know I'm a damned fool and that people will always take advantage of me, but what can I do about it? . . . Rafe might not only kill himself and Jim's drunken friends, but he could as easily kill others in the road, people who are as innocent as you or I. . . . I couldn't rest tonight, seeing these things so clearly; so the sensible thing to do is to go ahead and take them all home safely."

Jim began to laugh loudly and to pound Willie Oakshot on the back. "I knew it!" he said in delight; "I knew he'd do it if I said so! Come on, Willie. You'd better pay off."

Willie took a coin from his pocket and put it in Jim's extended hand. "All right," he said; "you win. Here's your four bits."

"I know him like a book!" said Jim delightedly. "I know old Andy inside and out by this time!"

CHAPTER XXII

J IM was sick the next morning, but he got out of bed when Myrtle called him and washed his face and his head in cold water; then the room began to spin and he groaned, trembled with nausea, and lay back against his pillow, pressing his sweating hands against his lips, weak in his dizziness. Myrtle came into the room with a cup of hot coffee, but he would not answer her when she spoke. She put down the coffee and tried to lift his head. He pulled away from her weakly and turned on his side. He shivered with his mouth opened and his eyes rolled back, as if his body disintegrated voluptuously under his bride's troubled gaze; and then he got up, staggered across the room and vomited into the slop-jar.

Myrtle sat on the bed beside him, stroking his hair and wiping his face with damp towels. She spoke reassuringly. He'd better not try to go to work that day at all, since one day more or less wouldn't make any difference, and she knew that her father would be glad to do his work for him. Andrew could take the message to Neil, or she would go herself, if necessary. Jim shook his head. He had never missed a day from the mill because of his drinking or carousing and it had become a matter of pride with him. He got up after a time, his hands steadier, and began to dress; but he left the farm with no food in his stomach and Myrtle was worried. She went to the gate with him and stood there anxiously watching until he passed out of sight.

Andrew, too, had been watching, but he had not spoken; and when he saw his brother ride away safely he walked through the yard in the direction of the Delta Field. Before him an Orpington cock and his hens were taking their ease in the path that led to the barn. They flushed their wings outward, holding them spread and limp like broken fans, and with a forward, shifting lift of their bodies they sifted the hot sand behind the barrier of their feathers and onto their skins beneath. They panted in the heat, their beaks half opened and their vibrating tongues exposed, their eyes blinking in sleep. Occasionally the cock would stretch out his flexible neck and peck one of his flock sharply on her comb, and the flattered hen would whirr her spread wings in her delight and press deeper into the red dust. She would snap her spread of tail feathers from side to side and sing "Caw! Caw! Caw!" on one loud, unchanging note.

At Andrew's approach the cock and his hens raised their apathetic eyes, as staring as glass, and gazed with a waiting expression, ready for flight if he advanced farther; but Andrew stopped short in the path.

"Go on and wallow," he said. "Don't mind me, because I don't aim to disturb you."

On both sides of the path there were areas of rankly growing weeds, waist-high and colored the grayish-green of rejected jade, whose stalks bent now with the seeds that they bore and whose thin leaves foamed with the cottony spittle of insects. He grunted, turned from the path and walked through the weeds, pressing a way for himself with his arms; but when he reached the barn he stopped with indecision and looked at the house, for he had known, all along, that Myrtle had been standing on the porch watching him as he walked down the path, and that she wanted to talk to him, now that they were alone together for the first time since her marriage. When she beckoned, he hurried toward her, the Orpington cock and his hens scattering before him in confused, hysterical haste. They met at the gate and stood on either side of the fence, each waiting for the other to begin. It was Andrew who spoke first:

"I want to do the sensible thing, Myrtle, now that we're going to live under the same roof, but I don't know what it is. Maybe we can work it out together somehow. . . . You can be sure I don't want to make things any harder for you than they are."

"It's me who should be worrying and making apologies," said Myrtle. "I'm the one—not you, Andrew! And I'm beginning to see all the trouble I've caused, and all the things I done to hurt your feelings." She touched his shirt cautiously, unable to find words for the things she wanted to say.

"It was foolish for Jim to bring you here to the farm. I tried to persuade him not to, as you know."

"I advised against it, too," said Myrtle helplessly, "but he would have his own way."

She was silent for awhile, tracing a pattern on the fence post with her finger, and then she began to talk rapidly. What she was going to say was difficult to express, or at least it was for her, but in spite of her incomprehensible conduct, she bore Andrew no ill will, and never had, and she hoped that he would believe her. The things that she had done to hurt him seemed unbelievable to her now, and when she remembered how she had ridiculed him, and made him a public laughing stock, she was so ashamed that she wanted to run away where nobody would ever see her again, if it was any comfort for him to know it. If he hated her for what she had done, she could not, in justice, blame him. She would understand his feeling easily enough and say that it was justified. She had never believed it possible that she could apologize to anybody, as it went against her grain, but she was apologizing humbly to him now and asking him to forgive her; and more than that, she'd do anything she could, within reason, to put matters right between them.

"I don't hate you, and you know it very well. I couldn't hate you, no matter what you did. I couldn't hate you even if I was willing to try."

"You won't believe this," continued Myrtle, "but I'm not really a mean woman; leastways I'm no meaner than anybody else; but I was just so crazy in love with Jim I didn't know what I was doing, or care either." She looked directly into his eyes for the first time. "I guess you don't know all of it, Andy; you don't know all the reasons that made me act like I did. You don't know what mean things he said that night to me on the road when I only wanted to talk to him and tell him I understood. You don't know everything that happened by any means, not that I'm trying to use that as an excuse."

"I know enough of what happened to let me piece out the rest. I know about the Wrenns' party, if that's what you mean, and I have all along." He laughed bitterly. "Jim couldn't wait very long before he boasted about the Wrenns' party, you may be sure of that. He told me about it just as soon as he got a chance. His excuse was that he wanted to prove you weren't good enough for me."

Myrtle drew away from the fence and looked at him incredulously, her face flushing angrily in her old manner; but almost at once she began to make excuses for her husband, for these things of which they spoke had happened during the period of their quarrel, before he had realized that he loved her, and his conduct, under those circumstances, was normal and understandable she thought.

"The thing now is this," began Andrew haltingly: "What are we going to do? How are we going to work things out? What's our attitude toward each other going to be?"

"I got no particular right to ask it, but are you still in love with me, Andrew?"

Andrew said: "I've got sense enough to know it's hopeless, and and always will be. So don't bother about my personal feeling. Just remember that I'm willing to be anything you want me to be, and that I won't ask anything in return. . . . It's for you to decide how we're going to live from now on."

"I think I'd like to have you for my good friend, if you're willing to be it," said Myrtle after a moment. "I'd like to have somebody to come to, and depend on, Jim being the way he is."

"I'll be that, if you want it," said Andrew quietly; "I'll be whatever you want me to be."

"Remember that I can be *your* good friend too," said Myrtle, "and without no trouble at all." She laughed with relief, touched his shirt again, and walked from the fence humming a tune in her tiny voice, her mind at rest, now that the scene she had dreaded had passed so smoothly. She went back to the house briskly, for there was much work to be done. She had determined to inspect and air all the bedding that morning and, if she found additional time, to reassort the feathers in the set of pillows which her mother had given her the day before for her new home.

When she had disappeared inside the house, Andrew went again to the barn and took one of the picking-sacks from the pile in the corner, for he had decided to gather the late bolls which had opened in the Delta Field after the first, regular workers had gone through. He could not accomplish a great deal unaided, and the result of his labor would hardly be worth the effort, but he liked the monotonous, rhythmic work which tired his back and prevented his thinking too much. He worked steadily for a few hours until, at length, he found himself on the far side of the field. Before him was the creek that marked the western limit of the Tallon land, and across it was a meadow belonging to the Cornells family. He straightened his back and walked to the fence, gazing at the cropped, yellowing sward of the meadow which stretched before his eyes like a motionless sea. The sun was burning and high in the sky, and under it cows rested on grass and chewed their cuds. They lay half asleep, without visible movement, their forelegs drawn daintily to their bodies; and the black, skimped shadows on which they rested were, under the midday sun, like islands cut thriftily to fit the outlines of their individual, recumbent bodies.

The sight of the drowsy cattle at ease on their own neat shadows touched something within his mind, and he bent forward in his eagerness and leaned more heavily on the fence. He rubbed his cheeks and lifted his eyes to the horizon, for a superimposed picture of the familiar scene was coming to him and he sifted his mind for the words that would give his new, transmuted meaning an existence of its own. . . . But before he had found one line to suit him, he heard Myrtle calling, and he turned guiltily, lifting his hand to his scarred lip and covering it.

He spoke in confusion: "I was resting a minute. I didn't know there was anybody within a quarter of a mile."

"It's noontime," said Myrtle, "and I fixed up something for you to eat. I brought it down here, instead of calling you to the house, because I got my work done earlier than I thought, and I figured I'd help you pick cotton." She handed him the food and removed the picking-sack which she had slung about her shoulders like a scarf. "Good Lord!" she said in delayed amusement. "What made you jump when I spoke to you? You work hard enough. Why shouldn't you take a rest if you're tired?" She went suspiciously to the place where he had been standing and stared at the reclining cows, but she saw nothing. "Get up! Get up, you lazy things!" she said laughingly. She struck her hands smartly together. "Get up, and eat some more grass, all of you, if you expect to have a bagful for old lady Cornells at milking time tonight!"

She went to work when Andrew did, taking the row next to the one where he picked, their bodies bent in opposite directions. They were silent, occupied with their own thoughts, until Myrtle laughed, raised her arm and wiped sweat from her eyes. "I was just thinking about you and Jim," she explained. "I was wishing you and him could be one man instead of two."

"And that the composite man was *Jim*."

"I guess so. I guess that's what I really mean."

Andrew stopped and straightened up. He loosened his suspenders and looked about him. The countryside was parched with the dry heat of early September and in the hollow, through which the creek flowed, the irregular, spade-like leaves of the gum trees were already beginning to crinkle at their edges and crisp.

"There's something I want to ask you, Myrtle," he began hesitantly. "It's for my sake that I want to know it, and it's been constantly in my mind since the night Jim told me about what happened between you and him. Maybe I've got no right to ask it at all."

"You got the right to ask me anything you want."

"This is the thing that has hurt me the most of all," he said desperately; "and not your making fun of me, as people thought." He stopped again, looked at the ground for a time and then continued rapidly: "Jim tried to make me believe that the love affair between you two was merely cheap and common, and that you'd let any man that came along do what he wanted with you. . . . But that's not true, is it, Myrtle? You're not that sort of a woman, are you?"

He had expected her to become angry and to turn on him with her old fury, but instead she stopped picking and crouched in the row on her rocking heels, holding to the stalks lightly for balance. She gazed at him in faint amusement, as if these romantic codes with which men tortured themselves were of relatively slight importance in her known world of nursing and diapered necessity.

"Jim is the only man who ever touched me, if that's what you want to know, and he's the only one I have ever met so far that could touch me. I loved him from the very first, I guess, and if it had been anybody else, I'd have died first." She laughed. "Well, maybe I wouldn't have exactly *died*, but if it had been a fellow I didn't want, who tried to take hold of me—well, he'd have had to call in a couple of his friends to help him turn me *loose.*"

Andrew nodded his head slowly, for he could not trust himself at the moment to speak, bent forward and began stripping the opened bolls again, pressing the cotton more deeply into the long sack. The things that Myrtle had told him, and the affirmations she had made, changed the picture he had built up in his mind of her after his defeat, and he felt that he was now free to love her again, for the important part of his love was still undamaged and would remain forever intact. His lips moved silently: "Thank God! Thank God!" he thought. . . . "You are very merciful to me!" A sense of peace came over him, and the old tensions inside him broke and dissipated at last, for he felt as if some rich thing, imbedded within his body, had yawned deeply and rubbed its hands.

"I'm a respectable woman," repeated Myrtle; "at least you've got to grant me that, no matter what else I may be. You can let your mind be at rest there. It wasn't only *you* that couldn't have me; it was you and all the rest of the world, excepting Jim. All the other fellows I ever met in my life never meant two cents to me."

They were silent after that, and they worked together peacefully, for they understood and accepted each other at last. Later Myrtle went back to the house to start supper. She put on extra pots of water to boil, for Jim would be tired and possibly still sick when he returned, and a hot bath, she concluded, would do him good. She stood humming, in her happiness, wondering what would tempt her husband's appetite and give him the most pleasure for his supper; but before she had made up her mind, she heard Jim's footsteps on the back porch. It was an hour before she expected him. She went to the kitchen door, frightened at his silence, and saw that Jim was drinking water from the wooden bucket; that his face was white and drawn, as if he had lost a great deal of blood. She did not speak immediately, and Jim came into the kitchen in silence and sat in a chair by the stove, nervous and strongly subdued.

"I've turned over a new leaf. I've learned me a lesson today that I'm not likely to forget soon. I'm never going to take another drop of whisky as long as I live."

"That's sensible, Jim. A man of your disposition ought never to take a drink. You don't know when to stop."

"I spoiled a saw today. It's the first time I ever done such a thing in my life. I didn't even do it when I was a beginner, just learning to file. . . . I went to pieces and spoiled one of the saws."

He rested his head on his clenched fist. He opened his mouth to speak but closed it silently, since there was nothing, he felt, which could be said in his defense. "I lost confidence in myself and I was afraid of the machinery and the belts. I don't know what happened to me, but it came on me sudden, and I was afraid of everything. I kept thinking I couldn't do my work and never would be able to do it again, and the first thing I knew the saw was ruined." He leaned backward against the wall and closed his eyes. Myrtle came to him and held his face against her breast, lifting the wing-like fall of his hair from his forehead and pressing it back into place.

"What's an old saw, sweetheart? What difference does it really make?"

"Don't ever leave me," he said weakly. "You're all I got in the world, darling. Don't ever let anybody persuade you to leave me."

"I'll never leave you. That's the *one* thing you won't ever have to worry about." She turned from him and went to her stove. "See," she said gaily. "I fixed hot water for you. You go into the bedroom with the tub and have a good hot bath, and then take a nap. I'll wake you up in time for supper. You'll feel better after supper."

"Even if it turns out that you love some other man better than

184

you do me," insisted Jim; "don't leave me. . . . Don't leave me no matter what I do."

"I *married* you, didn't I?" asked Myrtle cheerfully. . . . "Well, I didn't marry you just to leave you!"

CHAPTER XXIII

It appeared that Jim meant to settle down at last, for during the following weeks he avoided his friends and he seemed content to sit at home in the evening, when he came back from the mill, talking to Myrtle and Andrew. He was strangely chastened and meek during this period, as if he exaggerated the sacrifices demanded of a married man, and restricted his liberties unnecessarily to meet some unreal code of his own. He sat too quietly, he answered too promptly, he was too anxious to please; and to Andrew, watching him, he seemed like some miscast actor doing his best with a rôle for which he had no talent. But if Andrew mistrusted his brother's changed outlook, and was mildly concerned about it, Myrtle had no doubts at all, for her husband was consistently considerate of her and was, it seemed, afraid even to let her out of his sight; and in the fullness of her happiness at having him so completely for herself at last, she joked to her mother concerning his devotion when they visited each other.

"You never saw such a man in all your life as Jim is," she protested with delight. "He simply worries me to death, Mamma. . . . He really does, for a fact. Why I can't even go in the kitchen to clear up without having him there behind me fussing about or worrying because I might scald myself with hot dishwater, or something."

"Then I'd advise you to thank the Lord on your knees when you say your prayers at night, daughter. A good, considerate man is mighty hard to find. He's mighty uncommon."

But Myrtle, in her pleasure, would not agree too quickly with her mother, and she prolonged their talks in order to hear over and over the words of approval that delighted her, taking the opposite side merely for the luxury of being proved mistaken at last, feeling that she had achieved in this, her marital tranquility, her ultimate wish, and that existence could bring her no further happiness.

"I never saw such a man," she said. "I simply never such a man in all my life as Jim!"

She did not know, of course, that his exaggerated fears for her, and his thoughtfulness of others, were spurious qualities, alien to his nature, and that his contentment was a counterfeit thing which rested uneasily on the surface of his mind, with no support, from beneath, to secure it; nor did she know that terror lay back of his gentleness, and that he was fissured throughout with doubt, for as he sat at the supper table smiling in his old manner, but quieter and more self-effacing, glancing mildly from his wife to his brother, he thought eternally of Willie Oakshot's implications, and speculated as to the relationship that existed between them under his own nose, in his own house. Their very placidity, the way in which they took each other for granted, disturbed him. Willie had been joking, and the things at which he had hinted a few weeks ago were manifestly impossible, so there was no reason for his suspicions; and this lost feeling of despair, which seemed to move from his stomach upward to his throat, was not justified by any fact. He thought, over and over, to calm himself: "Willie's a damned fool that talks too much, and he always was. I won't pay him the compliment of taking him seriously." . . . And yet he could not defeat the need for thinking over Willie's words as he sat reading the Reedyville papers, nor could he resist, at last, the temptation to stop at the hotel in Hodgetown one night and settle the matter once and for all.

He found Willie in his room, dressing to go out, and all at once he felt foolish, as if the mere sight of Willie shaving and brushing his teeth was enough to guarantee his harmlessness. He decided that he would not even mention the matter which had dictated his visit, or if he decided to do so later, he would lead up to it obliquely. As he sat chatting, thinking how to shape his questions, Willie solved the matter for him.

"Jesus, Jim," he said, "I'm damned glad to see you again, after so long a time. What have you been doing with yourself, anyway? I sure wish we could go out together somewhere tonight, and have a good time, but the trouble is, I got a date." He stuck out his tongue and outlined his lips, touching his faintly blue teeth as if they were very dear to him. "She loves me, too," he continued, winking at his own reflection in the mirror; "boy, does that woman love me! And she can't say no to anything I ask her to do; the word no just won't roll off her tongue where I'm concerned."

"Who is she?"

"Yeah!" said Willie derisively. "Yeah! I'd be a fine damn fool to tell you that, now wouldn't I? I'd be a fine damn fool to tell you, so you could try to cut me out."

"This is the first time I ever saw you when you wouldn't talk," said Jim lightly; "so don't think it's funny if I seem surprised. . . . What's come over you? Can't you trust an old friend?" He rubbed his lips with the tips of his fingers. "Now is the time," he thought; "now is the time to ask him what he meant by his hints." He got up, stood by the bureau, his chin cupped in his palm. "Well, all I can say is this: You sure have changed, Willie! What's come over you? . . . You certainly didn't mind telling what you knew—or maybe you just suspicioned it—about Myrtle and Andrew." Willie finished his tie and smoothed his sandy hair with a wet brush. He was puzzled, and he didn't have the faintest idea what Jim was talking about; nor did he remember his words when Jim quoted a distorted version of them.

"You're thinking that what you hinted at worried me, and that I came by tonight to ask you what you meant," said Jim gaily after a long silence. "Well, get that idea out of your head. I just thought I'd mention the matter while we're here together, since you brought it up yourself, in a way. I know there isn't anything going on between Myrtle and Andrew now, and that there never was anything between them, but I got to thinking that they're together all day while I'm off working, and I wondered what else you knew, that's all." He went back to his chair and sat down. He crossed his legs and narrowed his eyes cunningly. He would take a different angle of attack.

"You boys think just because I'm a married man I'm out of the running, don't you? Well, you're making a mistake if you do. . . . You were talking about your new girl, a minute ago. Well, one of the reasons I've been so quiet the last few weeks is because I've got a new girl, too, married man or no married man." He laughed and tugged at his wing-like fall of black hair. "Please don't say anything about this, Willie," he pleaded, "because I don't want to get the lady in trouble. She's just started to keep company with another man who might be fool enough to marry her. I don't know the man's name, because she won't tell me, but I wouldn't want what I've told you to get back to him. I wouldn't want him to find out how she's two-timing him."

"I think I know who you're talking about," said Willie falsely. "So you might as well tell me her name."

"It's the *last* person you'd suspect," said Jim. "You'd never guess in a thousand years."

"Is it Sarah Cornells?"

"You know damned well it's not. I said a new one."

"It's not one of the Macbeth girls, is it?"

"Christ, no! . . . Christ, no!"

"Is it that milliner who comes over from Reedyville every Wednesday?"

"No, it's not her, but then I wouldn't tell you even if you did guess right."

A look of pain came over Willie's face, and when he spoke his voice was strained and pleading. "Is it Miss Mabel Carter, Thompson Hodge's new stenographer?" He turned and stared at Jim, waiting anxiously for his answer.

"I already told you I wouldn't admit it, even if you did figure it out," said Jim. "At least I'm a gentleman, I hope." He got up and stood by the door. "Remember I told you all this in confidence, so don't talk so much next time. Try to keep things to yourself in future. I know a few things, myself, I could tell if I wanted to."

"If I made any suggestions of the sort you think," said Willie stiffly, "I don't know what I was thinking of. I certainly didn't mean to create any such impression, I assure you, because I've got nothing but respect for Myrtle, and wouldn't even dream of such a thing as her playing around behind your back."

"I didn't believe it, Willie. Don't think I took your statement seriously for a minute. I just wanted to know for sure, that's all. Just forget about it."

But Willie was not to be stopped so easily. "It was all talk with Myrtle," he said. "Maybe one or two of the boys kissed her before she married you. I'm not denying that because I don't know. And I don't know any more than anybody else does about what went on between her and Andrew when they were keeping company. So I couldn't have said what you quoted me as saying, Jim!"

"Get it off your mind!" said Jim. "Lord God Almighty! I wouldn't have even mentioned it if I had thought you were going to take it so serious. I took it for a joke, and thought you would too. I thought you'd say it was just a joke, and not try to deny it."

Willie was silent a moment and then blurted out quickly: "I'll be fair with you, and I'll admit I tried my luck with Myrtle, the same as the other boys did, but I couldn't get to first base with her." He thought again, remembering just what had happened, trying to be impartial. "I couldn't make any headway at all, Jim; so you're *wrong* in your suspicions." He spoke now with assurance, nodding his head for emphasis, as if the ultimate test of a woman's virtue was her resistance to his particular wooing.

Jim turned the knob of the door and stood looking at Willie, amused at his unending credulity, exhilarated at how easily he had got his secret from him. "Give my regards to the new stenographer when you see her tonight; and tell her she'd better say no a few times, anyway." He laughed quickly, his head thrown back, while Willie stared in astonishment and wondered how Jim had managed to learn his secret. "I know what goes on around here," said Jim; "don't ever try to hide anything from me, because it won't do you any good." He shut the door and passed into the hall, but almost at once he opened it again and stuck his head into the room.

"There's just one more thing I want to say to you as an old friend, and it is this: I don't need you to defend my wife to me. I was asking what you meant as a matter of information. You say I didn't hear you right, and I take your word for it. The matter's closed as far as I'm concerned."

He walked down the long corridor whistling between his teeth, feeling relieved of his fears and immensely satisfied with himself. A sense of his old power came back to him, and for the first time since he had ruined the saw he felt restored and complete in himself, knowing that he needed nobody for his happiness and that he existed uniquely, and completely, in and for himself, alone. Again he thought of his marriage, realizing these things about himself, and again he marveled at the inconsistency of his conduct.

And so September passed happily for Jim and his new wife.

Tarleton's General Store stood where the State road crossed the Reedyville highway. It had been there for many years, long before the Hodge brothers built their sawmill three miles to the south. The people of the county, bound by habit, preferred to trade at Tarleton's rather than at the commissary in Hodgetown, or the larger stores in Reedyville. The proprietor was Frank Tarleton, a widower, but he was so incapacitated that his sister, Sarah, actually ran the establishment. During the week, when the farmers were busy on their land, trade at the store, except for an occasional stranger who stopped to buy gasoline, was almost non-existent; but on Saturdays the place was alive with people. They would commence arriving as early as ten o'clock in the morning, anxious to miss none of the gossip, and sometimes bringing their dinners with them, which they would spread, picnic fashion, on tables built in the plum thicket to the left of the store. But on the day of Edna's music lesson the place was deserted and old Frank Tarleton sat alone on the porch of the store whittling.

It was in the yellow house behind the store, where the Tarleton family lived, that Edna began her music lessons with Miss Sarah early in October. She had no talent whatever and Miss Sarah felt it her duty to tell her so plainly, but Edna was not discouraged; it didn't matter whether she had musical talent or not, she argued. She had other things to compensate her, and, besides that, she would learn to play the piano *without* talent if necessary.

She came on this particular Wednesday afternoon of middle October into Miss Sarah's small, overfurnished parlor and sat at the keyboard. Miss Sarah stood behind her critically, correcting the rigidity of her back, the flexibility of her wrists, the hammer-like fall of her fingers on the keyboard. "Don't go at it so hard, Edna," she said mildly. "Lord-a-mercy! A person would think you are going to tear the strings out by the roots."

"I wouldn't bother about piano-playing at all, except Bessie told me to learn how," said Edna. "If she comes back next summer, like she said, I want her to see how much progress I've made."

"I wouldn't take Bessie so seriously, if I were you. I'm not at all so sure she's a good influence on a young girl like you."

After an hour of hard work they stopped and Edna rested her wrists. She and Miss Sarah sat looking at each other across the room, each a little cautious of the other, as if barriers of irreconcilable widths separated them; but there was little justification for the sense of strangeness they felt toward each other when they were alone, and there was, in reality, no wide difference between them, for they were like those words whose roots remain unalterably the same thing, and differ in application only when joined with a positive or a negative prefix.

Edna, to keep the conversation going, spoke after a short, embarrassed silence. "Myrtle is going over to see her mother, and she asked me to come too. We thought we'd go fishing in the millpond, if Mrs. Bickerstaff is willing."

"I think that will be real nice, Edna."

"Uncle Andrew is going to drive us to Hodgetown," continued Edna vivaciously. "He and Myrtle are going to stop by here and pick me up. Then he's going on to Reedyville to see about selling his cotton to the factor."

"I think it's real sweet the way Andrew acts toward Myrtle these days. I was talking to Addie Wrenn about it not so long ago and we agreed it was most unusual. Nobody expected the situation to work out, me least of all; but if it does, it's due to Andrew's unselfish disposition. As I said to Addie at the time, if there ever was a really good man on this earth it is Andrew Tallon."

Edna squirmed in her chair, annoyed at Miss Sarah's platitudes and restive under the sentimental tone of her voice. She felt that there was nothing Miss Sarah, or anybody else, could tell her about her Uncle Andrew, and she resented, as a matter of principle, the pulpit manner.

"Uncle Andrew's not such a sap, as everybody seems to think," she said coldly. "He's a man like any other." Then, fearing that she had been unnecessarily rude, she began to talk about the purposed trip. She, herself, had little interest in fishing, and the thing she really wanted to do was to go to the dam, stand under it and practice oratory. "I read that in one of Bessie's old textbooks," she said. "Now my voice is weak, as you can see, and it don't carry so far, but if I can learn to talk over the noise that the dam makes, then I'm pretty sure to be able to talk over the noise of a shouting crowd as well."

Miss Sarah adjusted her thick lenses more comfortably to her eyes and shook her head in gentle despair. "Lord have mercy on me!" she laughed. "Whoever put *that* idea in your head? You young people can surely think of the strangest things, it seems to me."

Edna began to talk of her plans for the future, to show how rational, how consonant with reality her wish to develop a strong speaking voice was, but before she had finished she heard Andrew sounding his horn at the gate, and she gathered up her belongings quickly, so as not to keep him waiting. Miss Sarah went with her to the road to speak to Myrtle for a moment. Later she stood by her fence watching the car disappear down the highway. She shook her head humorously, threw her apron over her shoulder and began to laugh. "Why any young girl would want a voice louder than the Hodgetown dam is a mystery to me. . . . It seems she'd want to make it softer and more lady-like, if anything!" She laughed again, smoothing her graying hair. "What a pity!" she said. "What an unmitigated pity!"

They found a likely place to fish where the waters of the creek widened, spread languidly outward and left wet marks on the butts of those small cypresses which the Hodge brothers, in their contempt, had spared. It was undisturbed in this place and dark with the overhanging shadows of trees, with faint ripples only when a leaf fell, or where a sunken tree, with a raised, armlike branch divided the faint current into quivering angles, as if the water there were ridged upward and fluted by the drowned hand of a giant. Beyond, where the pool narrowed and found again the

194

original bed which had been the creek, a water hen, thin and up-turned like a tilted vase, dived downward among the weeds with precise grace, her tiny, triangular tail flipping from side to side like a rudder, before she righted herself and rose to the surface, her oiled, sparse body dry and untouched by water, lifted her long neck and made a harsh, disturbed sound like wood splintering.

Edna reached in the can and took out an earthworm, but she dropped it at once and rubbed her hand against her skirt, and the released worm looped away, propelled by its nervous writhings, but eyeless and unconscious of any wished direction, its moist length shining like rainbow silk in the light. "I guess you'll have to put the bait on for me, Mrs. Bickerstaff," she said. "I couldn't hook a worm on to save me."

Kate laughed indulgently. "Why, Edna, I never saw anybody like you in my life. I never did, for a fact. . . . Don't you know that worms haven't got any feeling?" She grasped the line which Edna held toward her, caught up the insanely looping worm and fastened it securely on the hook three times, a knot of iridescent pain as it writhed and excreted the particles of earth on which it had fed that day, its body prolonged outward and to its full length occasionally, and occasionally collapsing to lesser length like a telescope before the unaccustomed eyes of a man.

"I think I'll go up the creek a ways and fish," said Edna. "You two stay here."

She walked away in the direction of the dam, climbed the embankment of yellow clay, growing lushly with wild okra and a tangle of blackberry vines, and stood looking about her, in the place where the thin water poured over the pilings and fell in a boiling mist to other pilings at her feet. A wind caught the blown spray and she moved backwards, afraid of being wet. The water flowing and falling made a roaring, insistent sound which, inconsistently, seemed more definite away from its source than here, where it began. The day was quiet, with two birds quarreling behind her, but without conviction, and farther away were the shrill sounds of the saws and the hum of the unseen mill.

When she had disappeared, Kate spoke more freely with her daughter. "How are you and Jim getting along? Is everything all right yet? Is he still considerate like he was?"

"There never was a man like Jim," said Myrtle. She laughed with delight. "He worries about me all the time, like I said, and lately he wants me to tell him everything I do during the day, when he's separated from me."

"That's good, daughter. It's a good sign to see a man so interested in his home; but I knew from the first that Jim would turn out to be that sort of man and said so. No man settles down so quick as one who's been a little wild beforehand. You can take my word for it."

"If I wanted to," continued Myrtle happily, "I could have Jim so jealous of me he wouldn't know what end he was standing on half the time! He's jealous-hearted, Mamma. There's no denying that."

She sat beside her mother and threw her line into the water, holding the pole idly, and with her mind's eye she saw through the impinging bank of clay and the driven pilings to her right: First, there was the runway that led upward from the pond to the mill, and beyond that her father's oil-soaked office and the filing-loft where Jim worked. She saw him then, without warning, more clearly than she had ever seen him in reality. He was bending over his work, operating with his foot the small, emergency emery wheel which he sometimes used, while about his head flew the dying sparks from the steel.

She pulled in her line quickly and threw it farther into the water, watching the cork float with the stream until the line was taut and straight against the pole. She closed her eyes, feeling the faint tugging of the current against her wrist, and allowed her mind to wander. It seemed to her that no woman had ever been so happy as she was, or so content with her marriage. She had not expected so much from Jim, and she had been willing to take him as he was, to accept his faults as a part of him; but it seemed to her now that he had no faults. She felt that she had not deserved such happiness, but she would take it thriftily, and ask no questions.

"I guess the reason he worries so much is because he loves me even more than I do him, don't you, Mamma?"

"There ain't any doubt of it in my mind," said Kate positively. "There ain't any doubt now and never was."

CHAPTER XXIV

IT was after five o'clock when the three women came back to the Bickerstaff house and found Andrew parked beneath the china-berry tree, waiting for them. They had expected to return much earlier, and they were somewhat irritable, each blaming the other for the delay. "I only caught an eel, a brim and a couple of little mudcats," said Myrtle; "and Edna didn't do much better, but then she wouldn't fish. She spent her time under the dam hollering at the top of her voice. That's one reason we're late. We couldn't make her come back when we called, and Mamma wouldn't leave without her."

"Edna scared the fish out of their senses and they wouldn't bite our hooks, "said Kate Bickerstaff; "otherwise we'd have had better luck, maybe." She smiled her sad smile and smoothed the bladder-like pouches beneath her eyes. "But even at that, I guess I can't complain. I caught me a half dozen fine, goggle-eye brims and three green trout. I'm satisfied with the trip."

"We'd better get started," said Andrew. "It's almost time for the big whistle to blow, and we got to take Edna home first."

"I learned to fish when I was a little girl back in Georgia," continued Kate deprecatingly, feeling that that fact minimized and made less brazen her triumph. "I always liked fishing, and I generally went with Papa." She opened her gate, waved her hand and entered her house. "Well, good-bye all! I got to get my supper going."

Andrew started his car, and Edna and Myrtle sat with him on the front seat. Before them, to the left of the Macbeth gate, was the remains of a watermelon which had fallen from some farmer's

198

wagon and broken in the street, the red pulp lying shattered from its rind and dulled a little with dust. As they sat there, two pigs ran up and disputed the gritty meal, unexpectedly fallen in front of their eyes; they banged each other with the ferocious impact of their shoulder hams and bared their yellowish tusks, squealing in their rage and rearing upward on their hind-quarters, trampling to dissipated juice the pulp which they both prized.

"Durn those pigs!" said Myrtle in sudden anger. "We're late enough as it is. It looks like the Hodge brothers would make people pen their stock up! . . . Run over them, Andy, if they won't get out of the way! The owner can't have any kick coming."

Jim had been home for at least a quarter of an hour before they finally arrived. He had wheeled his bicycle onto the front porch, where it was screened from sight by vines, making a complex ritual of the act, but he had not taken off his hat, nor had he washed his face. He was frightened at the stillness of the place. He stood now and peered through the cracked door at his wife and Andrew, who had just driven up and who stood talking together by the barn. He began to tremble a little and he spoke aloud: "They think I don't know what's going on; they think they're pulling the wool over my eyes, but one of these days they'll find out different. They'll find out I'm not as big a fool as they think. They'll find out I can be pushed just so far."

When he saw them come up from the barn together he backed cautiously into the kitchen and lowered the shade. He got down on his knees and peered under the shade like a little boy, his mouth half opened and dry with his jealousy; but when he heard the impact of their feet on the porch he got up in sudden alarm, ashamed to be caught in so undignified a pose, and stood waiting coldly for the explanations which he felt to be his due. He, himself, would not bring the matter up, that being an error in tactics; so he would remain quiet, as he had for the past weeks, as if he suspected nothing, for sooner or later they must convict themselves.

Myrtle came into the kitchen and started, seeing him standing so quietly by the stove. "Good Lord, Jim! You sure scared me for a minute, standing there like a ghost with his hat on."

Jim smiled gently, but he did not answer.

"There's nothing wrong, honey," she said placatingly. "I only went over to Mamma's to spend the afternoon; that is, Edna and I both went. We all went fishing together later on, so I'm late."

"I see," said Jim after a long pause. "I see."

"Andrew took us over to Hodgetown in his car, and he picked us up later on and brought us home. We took Edna home first." She became nervous under the fixity of his stare. "There's no harm in that, Jim. There's nothing to get sore about."

"What makes you think I'm sore?" asked Jim quickly. "If your conscience was clear you wouldn't have thought of that."

"We took Edna home first; and one reason we're so late is we couldn't get her away from the dam."

"I see," said Jim. "I see. . . . In fact, you told me that once already." He laughed softly and extended his palms. "Well, I'm glad you told the truth about Andrew, at least, because I saw you when you turned in from the road and came through the gate, although you didn't think I did. You'd probably have been more careful if you'd known I was looking at you all the time and watching what you two did."

"I don't care whether you saw us or not. What difference does that make? I haven't got anything to hide."

"Maybe you'll change your tune when I tell you I watched you two whispering your secrets to each other by the barn. Then I saw you go inside together and stay a long time. I won't ask what you did, but I saw it all, because I've been home at

200

least twenty minutes." He stroked his lips with his damp, chilled fingers. "I realize, of course, that it's none of my business," he went on, "since I'm only your *husband;* but I can't help wondering what you did with the fish. If you were really smart, you two would have bought a couple of fish and brought them home to make your story stick. You ought to pay more attention to these details."

"We gave what fish we caught to Mamma. There wasn't enough to divide three ways." She came to Jim, put her arms about him and kissed his dry lips.

"I see," said Jim. "I see."

Myrtle laughed and held him tightly to her. "Oh, Jim, quit acting like you was a wronged husband in a moving picture." She stroked his face, sure of herself all at once. "If you want to know, the place we went fishing was back of the dam by the log-pond, and I was just a little way from you the whole time. I didn't catch any more fish than I did because I kept thinking about you and how much I loved you. I didn't pay enough attention to fishing."

"I wish I could believe you really love me like you say."

"I love you more than anybody, sugar. I always will, too."

Jim put his arms about his wife's waist and drew her against him roughly. He pressed his lips against her neck. "Don't ever play about with me, even in fun, sugarpie, because I can't stand the thought of your looking at another man; the thought almost kills me. I can't stand it!"

Myrtle smiled with pleasure over his shoulder, for to her these uncontrollable fits of jealousy were the most satisfactory admissions of love that Jim ever made to her. He was, since his marriage, too quick in protesting the depth of his passion and too facile at finding words for his declarations, and his ability to state precisely the minute shadings of the emotions he felt troubled her at times, since she herself had no such gift; but this jealousy was

201

not planned in advance. It was spontaneous, a thing she could understand, and it had nothing to do with thought, which she mistrusted.

"Let me go now, Jim," she said happily. "I got to get supper started."

Later that night, when they lay beside each other in bed, Jim opened the subject again. He put his arms about her, his cheek against her own and talked softly. Myrtle was a very pretty girl, and he was proud of the fact, but he would be as big a fool to blind himself to obvious realities as to deny her charm. Many other men must have felt the same way about her as he did, and that was only natural and to be expected. It was to be expected, as well, that she had also liked some of these men at different times, and had, naturally enough—and he was not criticizing her for that—permitted certain liberties with them. That was all past and done, and the past was dead so far as he was concerned. It was only the present that mattered, and he wanted her to know that.

"There wasn't though, Jim," said Myrtle seriously. "Believe it or not, but there wasn't. You were the only man I ever liked enough to let touch me."

Jim stroked her hair gently. There was no sense in her attempting to conceal her past, for he'd been no lily himself, and if he wasn't broad-minded about such things, he didn't know who was. In fact she could tell him anything about her old love affairs that she pleased, and he'd laugh about them with her. They were of no importance to either of them now, but he thought he ought to know, for it wasn't fair for another man to have information about her which he, her husband, did not have.

"But there never was anybody else, baby. You were the only one."

"What in God's name is it that makes a woman want to tell lies when the truth would serve the purpose better?" he asked humorously. "You haven't forgot so soon that I saw you and Rafe

Hall kissing under the china-berry tree the night we married, have you? Your memory is pretty short if you have forgot that, sweetheart."

"That wasn't anything at all, Jim. I did let one or two of the boys kiss me at times, both here and back in Georgia, but it didn't mean anything."

"Rafe did kiss you though, didn't he, baby? I wasn't just crazy drunk when I saw that, was I?"

"Yes," said Myrtle; "he did kiss me, but I'd forgot all about it. I swear I didn't even remember it." She paused a moment and thought. "Oh, yes! Plez Barrascale kissed me once after a dance, and tried to take hold of my knee, but I shoved him off. I'd forgot that, too."

"I see," said Jim. He laughed disarmingly and pressed his lips against her breast. "I see. . . . Then there was Andrew, of course," he added gaily; "Andrew went with you a long time. He must have been getting something out of it, or he wouldn't have kept coming back for more. But that's all past and done with, and you can tell me anything you please about it now, and I won't care."

"Now, Jim," said Myrtle triumphantly. "You are imagining things, because there was never anything between Andy and me. You know as much about what happened as I do."

"But there *was* something between you and Rafe Hall?"

"Oh, Jim! Oh, Jim!" cried Myrtle in a provoked voice. "What makes you keep going on that way? Let's turn over and get some sleep."

"But there *was* something between you and Rafe Hall," insisted Jim patiently. "You admit that, at least."

"He kissed me once or twice. That's all."

"It's *twice* this time," said Jim. "You only owned up to once before."

"Maybe once, maybe twice, maybe three times. I don't remember now," said Myrtle. "Then there was Plez Barrascale, as I said,

and a timekeeper from the company office named Cartwright."
She stopped and thought. "Oh, yes! Mr. Regis Batty tried too,
but I put him off."

"Thank you, sweetheart, for being so frank. You've put my
mind at rest, because I couldn't stand the thought of your loving
anybody but me. You've cleared everything up." He turned on
his side and pressed his face in his pillow. His body was cold and
he felt that his brain worked with a clarity he had never before
known. He thought over and over: "My wife has had love affairs
with everybody in town, even with Regis Batty, a married man."
He said: "Good night, sugar, sleep well. I love you all the more
for being so frank about your past life."

Myrtle turned drowsily and lay on her back. She yawned and
looked at the ceiling. She thought: "Jim's so jealous of me he
don't know what to do. He's simply crazy jealous over me." The
thought pleased her and she smiled her contentment to the darkness. She went to sleep almost at once, her hand stretched forward
in her tenderness and resting on her husband's shoulder.

Jim lay awake for a long time thinking: "I'll find out tomorrow
if they really went fishing together. I'll get it out of Neil. He'll
know whether his wife went along too, or whether she and Andrew
were alone the whole time. I'll lead up to it gradually."

CHAPTER XXV

J IM felt relieved again the next morning, for the mere stating of his jealousy in words, at last, had somehow made it less terrifying. Again he made an effort to settle down in earnest, as other married men did, but the most he could achieve was an acceptance of marriage, and its repeated sameness, as something inescapable, a grim factor in the inevitable frustration of man. He was silent during these days, as if he brooded deeply on his past, and his manner toward Andrew throughout was slightly hurt, slightly patient, managing in his resignation to create the impression that his brother had wronged him, confessed and had been forgiven. But if his manner to Andrew was forgiving and tolerantly polite, he was even more tender and loving than usual with his wife. He sat at night with his arm about her, their cheeks touching, but they talked rarely; and then, on the fourth night, he got up without explanation from the supper table and went out of the house, in the direction of Hodgetown, slamming the door behind him.

He followed the path which led through the strip of uncut pines that separated the whites of the town from the Negroes, and after awhile he knocked the signal which admitted patrons to George Stratton's place. The door opened and the new doorman looked at him for a moment speculatively, turned and touched a button.

"What the hell? What's the matter with you, nigger? Stratton knows who I am."

The doorman shook his head impassively and stood aside as George himself came up and spoke: "It ain't no use in talking to him, Mr. Jim. It's all wasted. And it ain't no use cursing that nigger, because he can't hear nor speak neither." He took the chain from the door and Jim came into the tiny vestibule. "No wonder the doorman didn't remember you," he continued. "This here's the first time you been to see us since you married."

"I been out of circulation for the past few weeks, George."

"The white gentlemen ask about you all the time," said George happily, "and it's mighty nice to have you amongst us again, Mr. Jim. The white gentlemen was wondering tonight when you'd be coming back." He pulled back the calico curtains that screened the bar from the hall, and at one of the larger tables Jim saw a group of his particular friends. They spied him at the same instant, but Willie Oakshot was the first to get up and come toward him. "By God, if it ain't the happy bridegroom out for an evening of fun. God Almighty damn!" The others crowded about Jim and dragged him to the table.

"The last time I was here—it was the night I married, too— you were sitting in that same chair, Willie. What I want to know is this: Are you here *again,* or do you just make your home with the nigger wenches upstairs?"

"There ain't no girls in this house, Mr. Jim, and there never has been, neither; but I knows where there is plenty."

"Now, George!" said Ham Carter, "that's the very last thing a bridegroom on his night off duty would ask for. Bring him a drink, instead. Bring him something to build him up. He's done been tore down enough."

"You can't tell," said Jim. "You can't tell what I'm looking for tonight."

Ellis Nobles clapped the table with his opened hand, making the glasses rattle. "That's right, Ham. You said it that time. He don't want no woman in his condition."

"Where do you boys get that bridegroom stuff?" asked Jim. "I been married almost three months. My honeymoon's long gone."

Willie Oakshot opened his mouth and touched his spurious,

faintly blue teeth with the tip of his tongue. "I always heard that the honeymoon was over when the bride don't get her loving during the daytime any more. I leave it up to you about yours."

Jim said: "Hello, Rafe. I didn't see you there. How's things with you?"

"Tolerable," said Rafe. "Just tolerable, Jim."

"I think Jim's the only one of us with good sense," said Ellis Nobles. "I guess I'll marry one day, myself. I'm tired of living alone and eating café cooking." He was conductor of the accommodation train which ran from Hodgetown to Reedyville to Morgan Center. There was no schedule on Sundays and so that night he was free.

"Look out!" said Willie warningly. "Look out, now, Ellis!" He winked at his friends. "What I mean is, you'd take a mighty big chance on marrying, you being away from home almost every night."

"If I do marry, I'll get me a shotgun first and I'll fill any man I find hanging around my house full of buckshot."

Rafe Hall laughed his high, cackling laugh. "You wouldn't mind one of your old friends, like me, for instance, coming to keep the old lady company while you was working, would you, Ellis?"

"That's what I'll do," said Ellis. "Buckshot or better."

George Stratton brought a drink and placed it before Jim, wiping the clean, sandpapered wood with a damp cloth. Jim lifted the glass to his mouth, winked at his friends and gulped, while George stood behind them, his scarred face happy and content.

"You're a smart nigger," said Jim. "You're a smart nigger to have a man at the door who's deaf and dumb. He can't tell nothing on you if you get arrested again."

"He can't read or write, neither," said George complacently. "That nigger can't tell nothing."

At eleven o'clock the men were still drinking. They had been telling stories for the past hour, and they were getting noisy. They were the only customers left in the place and George came up and stood behind their table, anxious to get rid of them and go to bed.

"Gentlemen! Gentlemen! I got to close up in a little while."

"Go away!" said Willie Oakshot. "Don't you see we're busy?" He turned to Jim. "Go on! Let's hear what happened then."

"Please, *suh!*" said George. "Please, white gentlemen! I know you don't want to get me in no trouble."

Jim said: "Let's get out of here." He stood unsteadily and looked at his watch. He had not realized that the time had passed so quickly. He went outside and stood beyond George Stratton's gate, surrounded by his friends; and he lifted his thin, twitching face and breathed deeply. The slab-pit lighted the sky with a salmon-colored glare, as if some false and terrifying dawn perpetually impended. He stared at the sky for a time, but not conscious of it, and then the weight of the pyramided wood, under which the fires burned eternally, shifted and sank downward with a low, booming noise, and showers of sparks were thrown upward into the sky like burnished insects frightened to flight.

The men began walking toward Hodgetown, staggering a little, supporting each other and laughing loudly at their clumsiness. Again Jim stopped and stared upward at the unreal sky. The burning sparks had separated themselves from the thrown mass in which they had risen above the horizon, and were drifting outward now, but dimmer, and dying together in falling curves. He rubbed his cupped palm over his face, bringing himself back to the world of reality. His companions had passed a little beyond him, but he walked rapidly toward them, not wanting to be alone. Willie spoke insistently: "You were just starting to tell us about the widow-woman with a face to stop a clock who advertised in the paper for a husband, and about the one-legged soldier who answered it and came to visit her."

208

"What happened after the soldier seen what the widow-woman looked like?" asked Ellis. Jim threw back his arms and yawned deeply. The night was hot, with no breeze blowing, but the strip of pines before them was agitated somehow and made the lost, running sound of water withdrawing from a rocky beach.

"I can tell the rest of the story pretty quick. This young, one-legged soldier was in the middle of a bad mess, as I said before. You see he didn't have any folks left, and no way to make a living, and even if the widow-woman's face did make him want to run away every time he looked at it, the fact remained she had money in the bank and a farm with as good grazing land as there was in the whole State. So all that day, while the widow-woman was feeding him up and treating him pretty, to get him to marry her, the young soldier kept looking at the widow-woman and saying 'no' to himself; then he would look out of the window at her good land, change his mind and say 'yes.' Well, sir, that kept up till nightfall. When the widow-woman showed him to the room where he was going to sleep, the soldier took off his wooden leg that the government had bought him and stood it against a chair, and then he fell in bed all tired out, not having made up his mind, even then. He figured he'd decide in the morning, when he was rested."

The men had come to Minnehaha Street, and they turned into Hodgetown. A dog, seeing them pass, began to bark and run alongside the fence, but when he found that he was not noticed, he stopped his noise and his erect hackles flattened. He pushed his whole head through a hole in the pickets and sniffed, his muzzle twitching with uncertainty, and then he withdrew into the middle of the yard and turned around nervously, caught in unreasoning panic.

"But the widow-woman wanted action right now, and she didn't intend to give the soldier no rest," continued Jim, "for later on in the night he heard a noise and woke up; and there she stood, looking more sickening than ever in a nightgown and a lace cap with pink ribbon sewed on it. Well, sir, the first thing the soldier thought of doing was to jump out of bed and run for his life, but when he thought of that money in the bank, and the fine farm, he lay back in bed and resigned himself. He shut his eyes and told a lie. 'Oh, sweetheart,' he said, 'I was just lying here and wondering how long you were going to keep me waiting for my happiness! Maybe you didn't realize it, but I've learned to love you dearly.'"

Jim's audience laughed again at his impersonation of the soldier's agonized voice, but he held up his hand for silence. "Well, sir, when the young soldier said what he did, the widow-woman got so worked up that she didn't know what she was doing; so she went to the chair where the wooden leg was standing and picked it up. She held it in her arms, close to her, and rubbed it against her cheek. 'Oh, honey,' she said, 'you don't know how happy you make me by just saying that! You don't know how pretty I can treat you.'"

"Wh-e-e!" said Willie. "God Almighty damn!"

"But the wooden leg couldn't lie about the way it felt, like the soldier could, not having any reasoning power of its own," continued Jim. "So when the widow-woman hugged it, saying it belonged to her now, and her alone, the old leg began to turn in her arms and pull away, trying to get free. The widow-woman held on for a minute or so, and then she got scared, too, and dropped it, and the leg cleared the room in three jumps and went through the window pane with a crash of glass."

The men, who had stopped and were standing tense, waiting for the climax of the story, leaned forward against the fence suddenly, holding on to the pickets for support, and laughed drunkenly. The dog, a block farther down the street now, barked again deliriously, turning in circles with his tail erect, the hair in his neck pushed forward stiffly like a frayed rope.

Jim spoke again, weak with laughter at his own story: "The

210

young soldier hopped out of bed and across the room to stop his leg from running away, but he wasn't quick enough. 'Come back!' he begged. 'Come back! She's got a fine farm and she won't hurt us none!' But the leg wouldn't pay no attention to him, and the last time he seen it, it was doing about a mile a minute down the Reedyville road, heading for the barn."

"Heading for the barn!" gasped Willie Oakshot. "Wh-e-e-e! God Almighty damn! Heading for Reedyville."

"Heading for the barn!" repeated Ellis. "Heading for the barn!"

An old woman stuck her head out of a window, her gray, stringy hair plaited and hanging down her back, her face covered with cold cream. "You men better get away from this place, all of you! You better get away right now, before I ring up and call the deputy sheriff . . . I won't have roistering under my window."

The men staggered away still laughing feebly, their arms about each other for support. When they reached the commissary they paused and sat on the steps. Ellis Nobles had parked his car there, and he looked at it now speculatively. This was his one night off in the week, and he had driven to Hodgetown in the expectation of an interesting adventure, but nothing of the sort had happened. He was only excited and a little drunk.

"Well, I guess I'll have to head for the barn too," said Rafe Hall. "I got to go to work tomorrow." He got up from the steps and stretched himself, and Hamilton Carter got up with him. He was going in Rafe's general direction, and he'd walk along with him for company.

"Christ, it's early yet!" said Ellis. "I'll tell you what let's do: Let's all go to Miss Violet's house in Reedyville. I haven't been there in God knows when." He got into his automobile and started the engine. "Come on," he said; "come on, if you boys want to go along too."

Jim stood with his foot on the running-board. He wanted to go, but he felt that he must think above his drunkenness this time, and see the reality of things. He had to work the next day, and besides he didn't have much money to spend; then, too, and this was the most important of all, he wouldn't have any way of getting back home afterwards, since Ellis could hardly be expected to do that. He'd better refuse, after all.

Ellis said: "Well, I didn't think you and Willie would back down on me. If it's a question of getting home again, I'll drive you two home before morning. I don't work until tomorrow night, and I can sleep all day."

Jim opened the door of the automobile and stretched out on the back seat. He had done what he could. He had protested to the best of his ability, but he had been more or less forced into this thing. He would feel like hell tomorrow, but it would not be his fault.

"Are you coming too, Willie?" asked Ellis. "Make up your mind. We're just wasting gas."

"Sure!" said Willie. "Sure I am."

CHAPTER XXVI

I T was almost twelve o'clock, with business quiet even for a Sunday night, and Violet Wynn was taking a final beer in her back parlor. She was thinking of going to bed, counting the evening a complete loss, when Ellis Nobles came onto the veranda and rang her bell with the assurance of one who has visited intimately an establishment before and who has no doubts as to his welcome. Jim and Willie Oakshot stood on the steps below him, adjusting their neckties and their cuffs, settling the collars of their coats. They envied Ellis's superior sophistication, and the fact that he lived in the city, with the opportunities that such residence gave; for they themselves had never been in an establishment as fashionable as this one appeared to be, judging from the glimpses they caught of its interior. Miss Violet got up quickly, the bell still vibrating above her head, and started for the door, but when she heard the step of her maid on the basement stairs she stopped and waited, her hand on the knob. She gulped down the last of her drink and smoothed out her dead-white, bloated skin.

Her hair was tinted a shade not far off the clayey interior of cantaloupes, and a crisscross of wrinkles had bitten deeply into her flesh at her temples. When she drew back her head, as she did at this moment to glance upward at the clock, the loose flesh of her neck folded, like a trick done with paper, into a field of exact, diamond-patched areas. She came into the hall and approached the door as the Negro maid slid back the oiled panel above the lock, and peered out.

"Who is it, Lizzie?"

"*Mill* hands!"

Miss Violet thought a moment, and then brushed her servant aside. She, too, slid back the panel and examined her late guests. It was true these gentlemen were not the sort she was accustomed to, or desired to surround herself with, but this was 1929, and times were difficult in all lines of business; one could not always pick and choose. She lifted her fat arms above her head and shook her bracelets down, her relaxed flesh hanging suspended from her bones like the drippings of wax from cheap candles. "Wait till I get back to my parlor," she whispered; "and then let the gentlemen in, Lizzie." She walked away as quickly as she could, her velvet skirt held to her knees to permit freer movement of her legs.

She found the five young ladies who comprised her establishment waiting for her in the small room, for they, too, had heard the bell and had seen the callers from their windows. Violet looked them over shrewdly, speculatively. "Lizzie says they're mill hands, so there's not much money in the crowd, girls," she said casually. "But they'll spend what they've got and they'll buy drinks. It's better than nothing."

"I'm not working tonight," said Claudine, "and you know it. Don't look at me like you expected me to work."

Lizzie came into the room and spoke softly: "They're in the front parlor, and they done ordered whisky all around."

"Now, Claudine," said Miss Violet placatingly, "nobody's asking you to work on your night off. All I ask is that you go in and play a song or two on the piano, or do one of your dances, to get the ice broke and things started."

"*Mill* hands!" said Lizzie. "We're down to *mill* hands, now!"

"I'm not working tonight," said Claudine stubbornly. She went into the hall and stopped before the parlor door, examining, from her safety point, the three men seated before her. Jim was talking to Ellis, his eyes rolling a little and his hands moving nervously; and as Claudine watched him, he finished the story he was telling

214

and laughed, his wing-like lock of hair falling to his eyes. She went back to the smaller room where Violet was still talking to her girls. "All right. I give up. I don't want to be a kill-joy. Them ploughboys won't last long, anyway."

Violet came at length into the large, front room, whose floor was bare, to permit discreet dancing, and welcomed her guests. She apologized for the slight delay, but the fact of the matter was that she had been caught on the telephone when they arrived, and couldn't very well get away. She had made it a practice all her life never to mention names in places of this sort, that being one of the cardinal rules of her profession, but she *would* say that the gentlemen to whom she had just talked was one high up in Reedyville politics; so they could all be sure that there would be no raids or other disturbances to annoy the gentlemen, if they cared to stay the night; and they were as safe with her as they would be in their own homes. She moved about welcoming her guests, her lard-like, unstable flesh trembling.

The girls came in a moment later, and Claudine went at once and sat at the electric piano. The first round of drinks came and they drank in silence. Claudine did not touch hers at once. She held it in her hand for a moment and stared provocatively over her shoulder at Jim. She raised her eyebrows invitingly, winked, turned back to her piano and began to play, but her mind was not on her music, and she kept looking up, glancing over her shoulder at Jim and smiling. There was that thing about him, she argued, which she found desirable; and it was a shame for a man like him to have to do manual labor. What he needed was some shrewd woman to take care of him, and if you put him in a tuxedo, gave him a manicure and had his hair cut by a first-class barber, he'd be a sweet man, mill hand or *no* mill hand. He'd make the sort of fellow any girl would be proud to look out for, or to exhibit to her friends. She was so busy with her thoughts that she lost touch with the company about her, and she looked up, puzzled, when Miss Violet touched her arm and spoke. Miss Violet was more genial now, for she warmed only with drinks which others bought for her from her own stock, and the three men had, by this time, treated her in turn.

"The boys say that Willie has a nice voice," she said. "He promised to sing a song if you'll play for him, Claudine."

"What's your name, sugar?"

"Miss Violet just called me *Claudine,* but don't you believe her. She done that to put people off."

"Wh-e-e!" said Willie. "God Almighty damn!"

"Willie'll want to know where you come from next," said Ellis. "He'll try to find out everything about you before he gets through."

"Yeah?" said Claudine languidly. "What's he going to use? A can opener?"

"I haven't got a can opener handy," said Willie. "I've only got a new two-dollar bill."

Miss Violet wiped her eyes on a lace handkerchief. "Claudine comes from New Orleans, Willie. She's only been with us a short time."

"Claudine plays by ear," said Sadie. "You say what you want to hear and she can play it, if she ever heard it before or if you can even whistle it."

"I knew it," said Willie. "When I seen the class you got, I thought right away you must be a little French girl."

"Think what you please," said Claudine. "You can't prove it on me." She glanced up at him out of the corners of her eyes, smiled and puffed her lips out good-naturedly. She turned back to the piano and struck a chord.

"Whee-e-!" said Willie. "God Almighty damn!"

Jim laughed and flipped a half dollar to the Negro maid. "Here," he said. "Have one yourself. Don't go about looking so down in the mouth. Things ain't so bad. Take yourself a good one, and you'll feel better."

"What's Willie going to sing?" asked Gloria. "Does he know a song called 'When Old Black Joe Played His First Oboe'?"

"Willie won't sing anything except *classical* songs," said Ellis quickly. "You can't get him to sing trash."

"Do you know a song called: 'Sweet Little Sweetheart of Me'?" asked Willie doubtfully. "I seen it in a theatre performance right here in Reedyville when that tent show was running. The play was about a fellow tempted to become a gangster through drink and fallen women, but who turned back to right living just in the nick of time when he heard an organist in the church across the way playing and singing the song."

"Oh!" said Violet in surprise, "did you see that show too? I went to see it twice and I thought . . ." But she lowered her voice and then stopped, for Claudine had already begun the slow accompaniment; and already Willie had lifted his chest and stood on tiptoes. He began to sing:

"You wonder, I know, little sweetheart of me,
As you dream by the mill all the day,
Is my sweetheart as fine as once he used to be?
As pure as on that day he went away?
Can it be that Broadway, and all the bright lights,
The wine and the laughter that makes up his joy,
Have deadened his dream of home with other delights,
And made him forget the love he knew when just a boy?"

Claudine looked up in surprise, for she had not expected a voice as fine as this one. She played more softly now, feeling the emotion of the song and knowing the effect that Willie's singing and her playing produced on their audience. Lizzie came into the room and picked up the empty glasses, paused for an instant at the door and went back to her kitchen to sit until she was summoned again.

"*Mill* hands," she said in a tragic voice. She lifted the drink which

Jim had bought for her and touched the glass to her lips, shook her head and put it down, for she would not lower her standard. She moved toward the table, to pour the whisky back into the bottle, but upon impulse she threw it into the sink instead, and watched it flow down the drain.

Willie drew in his breath, lifted his chin and sang the chorus in a pianissimo which mounted in soft richness without effort.

> "Oh sweet little sweetheart of me that I adore,
> Let your heart be at rest, now and forevermore,
> For your pure love has been a shrine, like a madonna,
> To save my soul from sin and from dishonor.
> And so I give your photograph this good night kiss
> And pray that God will always keep you like this,
> For you have been a saint like no one else could be,
> And that is why I love you so, sweet little sweetheart of me."

When the song was over at last and Willie's voice had died away, there was a silence for a few seconds, and then, as if he and his audience had sacrificed together at the same altar, and had escaped calamity there in song, they all began to laugh, wave their glasses about and shout obscenities at one another. Miss Violet got up and rang for the maid. "I'll buy a round of drinks for the house this time," she said. "It's not often I hear such sweet singing."

Jim came to Claudine. He began to put loose coins in the piano. "How about dancing with me, sugar, if I promise not to squeeze you as hard as I'd like to?"

"Sure," said Claudine. "Why not?"

They danced a long time, their bodies pressed together, their cheeks touching; and Jim explained at last that he could not stay the night, as Claudine urged. It wasn't possible this time, but he'd come back on Saturday night, when he'd have the next day to sleep in. . . . That was one thing; but besides that, he didn't have much money when he started out with the boys, and the little he had had was all gone now. So it would be better to leave with Willie and Ellis when they went, since that was the only way he had of getting home.

"Has anybody in this house asked you for money so far?"

"No," said Jim. "No."

"Don't tell me anything about the women in this town!" said Violet indignantly to the others. "I know what's going on. The things I see! The things I hear from my lady friends! . . . So-called respectable women, too, married to good men that take care of them, and then their carrying on right under their husband's noses! I sometimes think, when entertaining a gentleman guest: 'What I could tell *you* about the way your wife is running around and indulging in immoral conduct! How I could open *your* eyes, if I was only a trouble-maker!' . . . Don't tell me," she repeated. "Don't tell me about the way the women in *this* town act; I know."

"Nobody will, either," whispered Claudine. "You're not the sort of man a girl wants to take money from, honey." She frowned and shook her head. She wanted to make her remarks more explicit, to explain that it was only natural for their relationship to be on the same moneyless basis that existed between others in allied professions when called in to minister to one another's pains, but she found her vocabulary insufficient for so complex an idea.

"Why don't you get a ride to Hodgetown on the truck that delivers the papers?" she asked at last. "That is, if you think my money won't spend." And Jim, knowing himself defeated again, sighed, pulled her head down and kissed her.

"I'm not narrow-minded," continued Violet; "not me! And my motto is live and let live; but if there's one thing I can't stand, it's a two-timing woman. They burn me up."

When Andrew came down to breakfast the next morning he saw that Myrtle had been crying. She explained that Jim had not come home the night before and that she was worried about him. She began to cry again. "There's nothing so bad in all the world as waiting for somebody and not knowing anything definite. . . . There's nothing I know of as bad as that."

Andrew pushed back the food before him and drummed on the table, for the slowly mounting anger that he felt toward his brother made it impossible for him to eat. He wanted to get up from the table, kick back his chair and hold Myrtle tightly against his body. He wanted to curse Jim for the way he was behaving, but he struggled against his wish, knowing, in reality, that it was impossible for him to do those things. He lowered his head, picked up his unused fork and began writing his name over and over on the table cloth, the faint indentations lasting for a moment and then rising upward to nothingness, and when his anger had died away a little, he said the reassuring things that Myrtle wanted to hear for her comfort.

"You're as good a man as I ever met, Andy. I don't know how I'd ever get along without you."

"I'm not a good man," he said seriously. "You don't know what goes on inside me. If you could see what goes on inside my heart. . . ." He stopped, for the feeling of anger lifted in him again. His face reddened and he got up from the table, suddenly irritated at her stupidity. He wanted to shout: "What makes you want Jim back, you fool? If anything, I'd think you'd be glad to get rid of him for awhile. There's no peace for either of us with him here!"

By noon Myrtle's fears had increased so much that he went to Hodgetown to inquire about Jim; but Neil knew nothing, and on his way back to the farm he stopped at the power house on the off chance that Willie Oakshot would have some information, and after a momen't hesitation Willie told him what he knew: Jim had got very drunk toward the end of the evening, and one of the girls at Miss Violet's had taken a liking for him. He had refused to leave with Ellis Nobles and himself, and when they insisted, he had got excited and cursed them; so they had left him at Miss Violet's house, and no doubt that was where he still was.

On the second morning of his brother's absence, Andrew went to see Russell Hodge and told him everything, and together they went to Reedyville to reclaim Jim. They got a room for him at the Magnolia Hotel and called in a doctor to help sober him up. Andrew went back to the farm to tell Myrtle that Jim was all right, but he returned later in the afternoon and sat with his brother that night. On Thursday morning Andrew drove him back to the farm.

"God Almighty, I can't tell you how ashamed of myself I am," said Jim. "I don't know what made me do it, because it's not like me. You know as well as I do, Andrew, that a thing of that sort is not like me."

"Myrtle don't know all the facts. I told her you went to Reedyville and that you got mixed up with some gamblers. Don't tell her the truth."

"It's Myrtle you're thinking about, not me," said Jim bitterly. "If it hadn't been for Myrtle, you'd have left me in that place till I died and rotted to pieces."

They were passing now across the stretch of mutilated cut-over land which had once belonged to their father, and at their approach three gray, undersized goats took fright, rose from their place beside the road and ran bleating through the scant underbrush, their small tails held high. In unison, with perfect timing, they cleared a fallen log, the hard pellets of their droppings erupting unexpectedly from their bodies like stretched strings of jet beads that broke at the same instant and spilled downward.

"You're still in love with Myrtle. . . . Haven't you got any shame at all to sit there and tell me to my face that you still love my wife? You're going to this trouble for Myrtle, and not for me.

After what I've done for you all your life, protecting you and looking out for you, I must face at the end the fact that you don't consider me at all."

"All right," said Andrew in sudden irritation. "I'll admit it, I'm doing it for Myrtle. And I'll tell you something else. So far as you're concerned, all I expect is that you try to act like a man and not like a baby, because I'm sick of nursing you. I took this trouble because Myrtle was worried and asked me to. If it had been left to me, you could have stayed with that blonde strumpet until you rotted, like you said. . . . All right, we understand each other completely now."

Jim caught his breath and drew back, frightened more deeply than he had ever been before, for he realized that Andrew was at last managing to escape him, that the power which he had held over him all their lives was dissipating itself and disappearing. He had seen this change coming in Andrew since the night he had met Myrtle at prayer-meeting, but he had tried to ignore its existence. Now it was inescapable. Abruptly he changed the tenor of the conversation, going through his amusing tricks, one after the other, like a little boy who thinks to escape the anger of his elders if he can make them smile at his innocence. He caught his breath at the idea of an Andrew entirely free, one who no longer needed his protection, for it seemed to him, with such a severance, that his own body could no longer be justified in its separate existence. He talked gaily of his adventure, belittling the woman with whom he had slept and waving his hands about, but this time Andrew would neither laugh at his jokes nor encourage him to go on.

"We're getting down to the way you really feel about me," said Jim sadly. "Your real feelings toward me are coming out at last." He slumped against the seat, feeling depressed and completely defeated.

222

That night he went to see his patron, Russell Hodge, to explain his conduct as best he could and to make the amends that lay in his power, and as he rode on his bicycle down the highway he decided on the renunciation that he must make, if the evil forces that sought his destruction were to be placated. His enemy was drink; it was there that his trouble lay. He would renounce his drinking forever, and as a binder of his good faith he would sign a pledge. He found Russell Hodge sitting on his front porch smoking his pipe. He got up without comment when Jim opened the gate, and he stood listening as Jim told his story: "I won't try to justify myself, Mr. Russell, because I don't know why I behaved the way I did. It's not like me, and I can't explain it. But I want you to write out a pledge in your own hand and I'll sign it. You keep a copy and I'll keep one. I'll carry mine about with me and read it whenever I get tempted."

When the pledge was written, Jim signed it, and at his suggestion Mrs. Hodge witnessed his signature. He came back with his heart lighter and approached the house through the grove of oaks, and stood by the window peering in. He noted with a quick distaste that Kate Bickerstaff had come to visit her daughter during his absence, and she sat now before his eyes talking with Myrtle and Andrew. He stared at them a long time, his eyes fixed and incurious. Tobey came out of his kennel and barked. Jim said: "God damn you! God damn you! I'll shoot you one of these days you black bastard!" He backed away from the window where he stood and walked toward the gate to make it appear that he had just arrived, but before he could reach it, the back door opened and he turned angrily, facing the group that stood framed there. They drew back into the room and resumed their places as he entered. "Well!" said Kate. "Well now! We were all wondering what could possibly upset Tobey so bad. . . . But it's you, I see."

"This is my place," said Jim, "and I'll do what I please on it. If you don't like it, what makes you come here so much? I'm tired of seeing you every time I come home."

"Now, Jim! Now, Jim! Mamma hasn't said anything to make you mad."

"Well, I like that," said Kate smiling fixedly. "I like that, I must say, coming from you." She drew up her heavy, solidly stuffed body. "But I'll consider the source, and not lower myself by replying. I'll try to recollect that at least I'm a lady."

"If you succeed," said Jim sourly, "let me be the first to congratulate you on your fine memory."

"Come, Andrew," said Kate with dignity, "I'd appreciate it if you took me home, like you promised." She nodded briefly and walked toward the porch, her head erect and regal, her shoulders well back, but in her confusion she turned the wrong knob and found herself all at once in the dark closet under the stairs with her face pressed against Jim's old coats and her feet stumbling over abandoned boxes. She rose to her knees, righted herself and came into the room again, straightening her hat; but this time she strode angrily forward in her old, everyday manner, and stood facing Jim, her face contorted and the pouches beneath her eyes twitching with outrage.

"So you've got the nerve to order me out of my daughter's house, have you? You, of all people, presuming to criticize my conduct when every man, woman and child in Pearl County, except Myrtle, knows where you've been for the last three days. I tried to hide the truth, but I don't mind telling her now that you've been lying up with a common woman out of wedlock! . . . You!" she continued angrily. "You dare criticize *me!*"

"Mamma," said Myrtle quickly. "Mamma, that ain't true!"

"Get your things together, daughter," said Kate. "I'm going to take you back home where you belong. I'm not going to put up with him no longer."

"It's all your fault, Mamma," said Myrtle bitterly. "If I'd been

born into the world a man, all this wouldn't have happened!"
Kate stood for an instant paralyzed with incredulity before this
new evidence of her daughter's unreasonableness, and her tendency
invariably to side against those who had only her interests at
heart. "Well, I never!" she said in amazement. "Never in all my
life!" Then there was an instant's hush before they all began to
talk at once, their voices rising furiously, their bodies taut, their
eyes hard.

CHAPTER XXVII

KATE BICKERSTAFF
stood angrily examining her vines, pulling back the yellowing
leaves to determine if there were enough beans left to make a
meal for dinner. The vines had about played out, she decided, and
she might as well tear them down after she had gathered these,
their last fruits. She jerked the pods off vigorously, as if it were
they, and not her daughter Myrtle, who had offended her. When
the last bean had been gathered she sat on her back porch in the
sunlight and shelled them with the sure, efficient thumb of the
automatic housewife, scraping the late beans into the bowl that
she clutched too tightly between her knees. Mrs. Macbeth came
out of her back door and emptied the dishwater from breakfast.
She wanted to talk, but when she had glanced at Kate's uncompromising body she decided not to call attention to herself after
all. Before she could get back to the sanctuary of her kitchen,
Kate looked up and nodded curtly.

She, too, wanted to talk this morning, to tell her unbelievable
experience to somebody, and while she despised Mrs. Macbeth,
and did not trust her, she decided that she would make a confidante of her after all. Certainly *she* had nothing to be ashamed
of, and if Mrs. Macbeth wanted to repeat what she said, little she
cared, for the conduct of her daughter and Jim toward her reflected shame on themselves, and not on her. She got up heavily
from the steps, her knees cramped with the fierce pressure she had
put on the bowl, and came to the dividing fence shaking out her
skirt. She began to talk at once, while Mrs. Macbeth stood half in,
half out, of her screen door, the emptied dishpan tapping her
knees.

226

"I'll tell you frankly, Mrs. Macbeth, I never expected to see the day come when my own daughter would turn against me and join her husband in ordering me out of the house; I frankly never did."

Mrs. Macbeth stepped out onto her porch, and let the screen door shut behind her with a bang. She came quickly to the picket fence and stood opposite Kate. "Why, whatever in the world! Whatever are you talking about, Mrs. Bickerstaff?"

"She thinks he's made out of gold and could do no wrong, like he was the Prophet Ezekiel or somebody. . . . And then for him to say the things he did to me!"

Mrs. Macbeth rested her dishpan against the pickets, rubbed her timid hands and pressed them against her face. "Why, whatever in the world?" she repeated in a small, shocked voice. "Whatever in the world do you mean, Mrs. Bickerstaff?"

"I simply went to see her like my duty dictated, but I wouldn't have opened my mouth to say one word against him if he hadn't acted the way he did. I won't take talk like that from no man, particularly since Neil actually did his saw-filing for him, out of the kindness of his heart, while he was drunk and lying up with that sporting woman in Reedyville, and I told her that, among other things." Kate half-turned from the fence and raised her face to the thin sunlight of late October. "Oh, this is almost too much for anybody to bear!"

"What did Myrtle say to you, Mrs Bickerstaff? What happened then?"

"He drinks and curses and I've no doubt he actually abuses her, too; and now like a last straw he's took to sleeping with strumpets. I told her for her own good the sort of man that he is, and I told it to his face." She drew away from the fence, the half-slack pouches beneath her eyes twitching indignantly.

"I know how you feel," said Mrs. Macbeth, "and I can imagine what poor Myrtle's been through with him. It looks like she'd be scared to live with a man who cuts people to death with his knife, even if he was kind to her personally. I know I couldn't stand it myself, because I can't even bear to hear men talking loud. It makes my heart flutter."

"She took sides with Jim and told me to go home and mind my own business and to stay there," said Kate, but her voice was less positive now, for her mind was unconsciously concerned with the implication of Mrs. Macbeth's words. If Jim was a murderer, she had not heard of it, and neither had Myrtle. She decided that Mrs. Macbeth was speaking figuratively after all, sighed and continued: "She ordered me off the place, when you come right down to it—me, her own mother! She said she knew what she was doing, and if I'd mind my own affairs she'd be very much obliged. She blames me for everything and she told me to get out and stay out. . . . Well, I guess I can take a hint. She and Jim won't see no more of me until they apologize. May God strike me dead if they do!"

Mrs. Macbeth caught her breath and looked nervously at the heavens, as if Kate's words had released forces of evil to overwhelm the town, and stood with her mouth slightly opened as Kate turned away from the fence with her solid, determined stride. "I can take a hint!" she repeated. "You don't have to knock me down with a wood billet!" But she hesitated and came back to the pickets.

"What are you driving at anyway? What's all this talk about Jim killing a man? I never heard nothing about it before. What are you trying to suggest? Come on and say what it is you know."

Mrs. Macbeth raised her thin, blue veined hands and pressed them against her cheeks. Her heart began to flutter. "Now ain't that just like me?" she began piteously. "Always putting my foot where no harm is intended. I'd have torn my tongue out by the

228

roots before I'd have said anything, but I thought you knew, *too,* Mrs. Bickerstaff!"

"I think you better tell me what you know, unless you're joking!"

"There ain't no *doubt* of it, Mrs. Bickerstaff. I seen it with my own eyes. That is, I didn't see the actual *killing,* but I seen the body afterwards on the platform back at the doctor's office. I was busy putting dinner on the table when the killing took place, but Mrs. Westerlund and I went to see the body afterwards. It was all covered up with a blanket except the legs. I remember it well, because I said to Mrs. Westerlund at the time that I didn't see how it was I managed to miss the actual *cutting,* but I suppose I'd just have to thank the Lord for letting me off this time." She laughed nervously. "I don't know why it is, but if there's any trouble going on, or blood spilt, I always get mixed up in it somehow. It just looks like I'm never spared anything."

Kate wanted to press for more details, but she decided against it. She nodded, turned abruptly and went into her house while Mrs. Macbeth stood by their joint fence and thought of the disagreeable things which had been forced upon her in her lifetime, absently polishing the dishpan with her soiled cooking-apron.

On Sunday, after he had returned from church and had eaten his dinner, Andrew went to his room and shut the door behind him, but he could not shut out the sound of Jim's voice quarreling below. He tried to read, but he could not concentrate his mind on the words before him, and he stood at last by his window looking out at the November sky, gray and unfriendly against the low horizon. On the wall, to the left of where he stood, was the picture that the French government had sent to the Tallons after Bradford's death. It was a colored print, and above a background of marching soldiers, picked out and open-mouthed against a burning town, an angel of war, her face angry and distorted, beckoned over her shoulder with a broken sword. Below the print were the words that recited Bradford's particular bravery, but these words, written in slanting, microscopic French, had never been read. Andrew would often puzzle before them, trying to guess their meaning, wondering what fine thing it was Bradford had done; or he would twist his head sidewise in an effort to decipher the name of the general who had signed the citation, but his eyes became puzzled in a maze of scrolls, dots and wavering lines.

He turned away from the citation and stood undecided in the room, still hearing the blurred sound of quarreling voices beneath him. He decided at last, despite the fact that it was a Sunday, to go to the barn where he had a work bench fitted up and plane cedar boards. He was making a linen-chest as a Christmas present for Myrtle, and he wanted his work to be as perfect as possible. He hummed again the hymns which he had recently heard, and sandpapered the cedar wood with slow, delicate movements of his wrists, holding the boards against the dull, afternoon light and squinting his eyes as he examined their surfaces for flaws.

The small rains of November had begun, although the weather was still hot, and ricebirds sat unsteadily on the tops of the withering weeds that grew unchecked between the barn and the back yard of the house. They grasped the weeds with thin and unfleshed claws, their ruffed neck feathers blowing forward in the dismal wind, their puffed-out bodies swaying backward and forward, for balance, like perturbed wire walkers the instant before they fall. There were enough weeds, and to spare, for each bird to have one individually for himself, but when one of the flock had adjusted himself nicely, his neighbors flew from their perches on the barn and crowded behind him until the overburdened plant bent to the earth, and at such times the flock fluttered their

230

balancing wings in a whirring chorus, and cried plaintively, or flew diagonally against the rain, like curling leaves uplifted at an angle by wind.

Andrew paused in his work and stared at the shivering birds through the window beside him. He had seen them, at this season, each year of his life, but it seemed to him that they were earlier than usual this year, and that they had fled prematurely from bitter weather in colder parts of the earth. As he stared through the window that faced him, he saw Edna come past the house, through the yard, and walk in the direction of the barn. She reached the door and called him, and when Andrew answered she came quickly and sat beside him on the bench. Her thin coat was wet through and her feet were sodden, but she seemed impervious to unimportant things. She picked up a handful of the cedar shavings and crushed them. She began to talk rapidly, and Andrew listened in patience, unable at first to follow her, but at length he pieced the news together: It seemed that Effie had received a letter from Bessie Tarleton the night before and in it Bessie had volunteered to send Edna through the Reedyville high school. She wanted her to start at the new term, right after the first of the year, if Effie and Asa consented. She felt that Edna had so much natural ability that it was a shame for her to have stopped school when she did. Bessie had arranged for her to live with a friend of hers, a woman named Ella Doremus, who was an assistant at the Reedyville library.

Edna smiled her tortured, saint-like smile, her damp hands pressed together. "Now, isn't it just like Bessie to think of a thing like that? It's the one thing I wanted most, but I didn't dare expect it to ever come true."

"You'd better take off your coat and shoes. . . . Here, let me wrap this horse blanket around you. I been wrapping old Babe in it at night, now that it's getting colder."

"Bessie says she's got a new job, a good one this time, and

she's going to make me an allowance for clothes and spending money."

"What do Effie and Asa have to say about it?"

"Oh, you know how Mamma is, Uncle Andrew. She says she can't see why I need any more learning. She says *she* didn't go any higher in school than I did, but *she* managed to marry all right, like everybody else, and to have seven children besides." Edna began to laugh. She got up and went to Babe's stall. "I got your blanket, Babe," she said. "I hope you don't mind." The old mare lifted her graying neck and stretched her nose cautiously toward the sound of Edna's voice, but at her unfamiliar touch she drew back and turned quickly in her stall. "Don't worry about what Mamma thinks," continued Edna. "I know how to handle her, and Papa too, by this time. I can scare either one of them out of their wits whenever I want to."

They were still talking of Edna's plans when Myrtle came to the barn and joined them. She had baked a pan of oatmeal cakes, rich with pecan meat, and she carried them wrapped in a towel to preserve their heat. Jim had quieted down, she explained, and was taking a nap, so she thought she'd come down to the barn to see how the work on the cedar chest was progressing, since she was bored, and since she knew Edna was also there as a chaperon. When she saw Edna's wet coat, and the damp edges of her dress, she put down the cakes and shrugged.

"You two may be well up in book-learning, and all that, but you haven't got a teaspoonful of common sense between you. . . . Why didn't you light that charcoal burner? I put it there this morning, while Andrew was at church, for him to light if he got cold." She laughed her small, faint laugh, lighted the paper and kindling beneath the charcoal and stood watching it blaze up. She took Edna's damp clothing and held it before the fire. "Oh, no, neither one of you would think of lighting it. . . . You rather just sit and talk about what ails the world."

232

The three of them huddled about the brazier, eating the pecan cakes and holding Edna's wet garments toward the coals. Edna told again of the letter from Bessie, of her mother's reaction to it and of her own plans for the future. They were in a good humor, and they laughed a great deal. They sat talking together for a long time. It grew darker gradually.

Jim woke after awhile and missed his wife. He got up and walked to the barn and stood outside, listening to the talk. Then he entered and stooped under the bar of Babe's stall, his steps soundless on the straw. From where he stood, in the darkness away from the window, he could plainly see his wife, Andrew and Edna across the aisle; he could hear each word that they said. Andrew laughed his slow, cloudy laugh and began to speak, and at once Jim eased his body past old Babe's outthrust rump and pressed his eyes to a chink between the boards of the stall. As he bent and watched the moving, mutilated mouth of his brother shaping words, a peculiar thought came to him, a thought which he believed he had long since forgotten, but one which had had a terrifying power over him in his childhood, for it had seemed to him, in those days, that the mutilation, on which his eyes were fixed at this moment, had been meant for him. He had been spared only because his brother had been born a year before himself. Nature had become mixed in her victims, and so Andrew, by accident, had been condemned to carry the burden of his, Jim's own, unforgivable sins. He had not thought of this for many years, and he knew, in his maturity, the falsity of his infantile reasoning, but the idea returned to him at this instant with all the force of a fresh discovery. He stood in the darkness of the stall watching his brother's mouth, comforted by the mutilation that he had managed by trickery to escape. He had always escaped, and he wondered, with satisfaction, why it was that his lot had invariably been so much more satisfying than Andrew's, whether or not his good luck would hold out to the end, and what force it was that protected him from harm; but he was thinking only for his own pleasure, and he knew quite well the answers to all his speculations. His unique imperviousness lay inside himself, for his cleverness, and his super-will, were stronger than anything that a furious Fate could devise for his destruction.

At last Edna's clothes were dry and she put on her shoes and stockings. She decided that she should be going home, now that the rain had stopped again. She took the old blanket from her shoulders and walked to the stall. "Here, Babe," she said. "Here, you can have your stinking old blanket back now, because I'm all dry." Then she dropped the blanket in the aisle of the barn and started backward. "Why, Uncle Jim! You scared the life out of me! What are you doing standing there? You scared me out of seven years' growth."

Jim stepped out of the stall and stood before them. "Don't let me break up the fun. Go ahead and talk, and have your good time. I don't mind what you say about me. I'm used to having you three standing together against me, and criticizing me behind my back."

"Now, Jim!" said Myrtle laughingly. "Don't start that all over again. We settled all that after dinner. Don't start all over."

He began to shout. "Get to hell out of here! . . . Get to hell up to the house like I told you! I'm going to have this thing out with Andrew once and for all, and we don't need you here putting in your big mouth."

"Happy married life," said Edna smiling wryly. "Happy married life among the wage slaves of 1929."

"Come on, Edna!" said Myrtle. "I'll go up to the house with you. I'll walk a pieceways with you." She was startled at the violence of Jim's anger, and puzzled before it, for she realized that this time, at least, it was entirely unprovoked.

"You keep away from here," said Jim. "If you come on the

234

place again I'll throw you off! And that goes for Effie and Asa and the whole passel of you sorry Cleavers! You can tell them that with my compliments."

"Come on, Edna," repeated Myrtle nervously. "Come on, let's go up to the house. Don't talk back to him when he's like that. You know by this time how jealous-hearted he is." But there was the usual overtone of pride in her voice, despite her fears in reality, as if this unreasonable concern over her most innocent relationships with others was a thing to be expected, a feeling commensurate with her beauty, an emotion that measured her unalterable hold on him.

"I'll be glad to tell the family what you said, Uncle Jim. Mamma, in particular, will *love* to hear it."

The two women went out of the barn and into the darkening afternoon, looking backward over their shoulders. When they were out of earshot Jim began his grievance again. He walked up and down nervously, his nostrils expanding and contracting. He tried to keep his voice steady and in a low, impersonal key, but it sounded strained even to himself. Andrew had neither moved nor spoken, and he sat now before his brother and listened patiently to what he had to say. Jim wanted to be reasonable about the matter, for he knew very well what was going on under his nose at the moment, and what must have gone on before he fell in so innocently with Andrew's scheme, and married Myrtle. He was not being unreasonable, and he realized that such things did exist and were, in fact, commonplace; but there was no sense in Andrew continuing his denials, since denials were an insult to both their intelligences. If Andrew would only confess what he had done and was, no doubt, continuing to do, he would freely forgive him. There was no reason to be afraid of such a confession.

Andrew shook his head dumbly, got down on his knees and began to gather up the shavings on the floor, stuffing them methodically into a sack. They would do to start the fire with in the morning, and there was no sense in wasting them. Possibly Myrtle would want to put them in the closets against moths. When Jim paused, Andrew shook his head and spoke for the first time: "I've already said all that I mean to say, but I'll say it again: There never was anything between Myrtle and me that you don't know about, and there never will be."

Again Jim began to shout: "You liar! You double-crossing liar! . . . You, a man that holds himself out to be religious! . . . You lying hypocrite, to stand there and say that to my face!"

Andrew got up slowly, upsetting the sack. He walked toward his brother with his fists clenched. He, too, began to shout: "Shut your mouth! Shut your God-damned mouth, because I've got a bellyful of your filth! I'm not standing any more from you. I'm not going to stay here any longer and listen to you. You've ruined your own life, and maybe Myrtle's willing to let you ruin hers, but by God I'm not letting you ruin mine." He talked for a long time, while Jim stared at him in wonder, but behind his words was the thought: "I'm talking louder than Jim. I'm doing everything that I condemned in him!" When he stopped at last and began again to fill the sack with the shavings he had scattered in his anger, Jim spoke softly, his voice mild and placating:

"I don't blame you for turning against me. I can see that I'm to blame for everything. I'll try to do better from now on."

That night Andrew went into the kitchen with Myrtle to help her with the supper dishes, and as they worked they had a long, whispered conversation together. It seemed to him that his continued presence at the farm served only to irritate Jim, and to feed his suspicions. He thought it would be better for them all if he moved over to Effie's place for the winter and left them alone. Myrtle did not agree with him. It seemed to her that Jim was merely like all other men, but he was having more difficulty than most husbands did in adjusting himself to his new situation. If anything, she thought that he would be worse with Andrew away. She hummed a tune, glancing coyly upward at Andrew with her brilliant, deeply black eyes. "I don't see how I could get along without you, Andy. I've got so used to having you around the place; and I thought you liked me a little, too. . . . But of course if you'd rather be with Edna than me, why I won't try to stand in your way."

Andrew looked down at the stack of plates before him. "Edna's right," he thought. "She is stupid. She hasn't the least idea about Jim or what's going on inside him." But she seemed very precious to him, in her impervious unimaginativeness, for to him these qualities, which he saw clearly enough, gave her an appeal that he found plaintive and irresistible.

CHAPTER XXVIII

During the middle of the week, Jim received a postal card which he read and passed on to Andrew. At first he could not identify the signature nor connect it with any face in his experience, but after a moment he remembered, recalling the man and the incident of their meeting. It was Tom Ostermann, the drummer who sold feed, the man who had looked too intimately at May MacLean, and with whom he had fought.

"That *must* be who it is," he repeated, "because I remember now I did ask him to go hunting with me the next time he was through this county, since he liked it so much, but I didn't think he'd remember it. I'd forgot it myself. He says he planned his trip this time so as to be in Reedyville over a Sunday, when I wouldn't be working at the mill." He laughed quickly, the wing of black hair falling to his eyes. "Tom's a fine fellow when you get to know him, and he's good company."

Andrew handed the card back to his brother without comment, for his experience of the past weeks had taught him to be suspicious of Jim's disarming, preliminary bursts of good humor.

Jim said: "There's something I'd like for you to do. Ask Harvey Cornells to lend you his dogs for the day. He likes you, and he'll lend them to you where he'd turn me down."

"Does he say whether he's figuring on shooting doves, or squirrels?" asked Myrtle.

"He don't say what he figures on shooting. He just says he wants to go hunting. It probably don't make much difference one way or the other."

238

They were still undecided on the point when Tom Ostermann arrived early on the appointed morning. He was tall and blond and he moved about briskly. He had a habit of touching the person to whom he talked, to emphasize his words; and when he said anything that he considered particularly effective, he would jab his companion with his elbow as well, as if putting so appropriate, and so final a period behind his remark that he made it indisputable. He arrived at breakfast time, and parked his car outside the gate under the oak trees.

It was a small car, painted white, and it was built to resemble an egg mounted on wheels. There was room on the front seat for two people, and behind that there was a cavern for orderbooks and samples. On one side of the oval were pictures of baby chickens, whose giant, idiotic heads emerged from the car's enameled surface as if they had just broken through their shells. Their mouths were caught wide open in wonder and they stared now at the oak grove, and the cotton fields beyond, with unblinking, vacuous eyes. On the back of the car, above its license plate, were neatly bending words:

C H I C - O - L I C   F E E D
Best for
Baby Chics and Turks.

Jim saw his friend and went to the gate to meet him. They came to the house together and Myrtle set another plate at the breakfast table. "Say, fellow," said Tom genially, "this can't be the same little lady you were with the night I met you. Say, this is a surprise. When you told me a few minutes ago that you were a married man now, I thought it would be the little blonde lady I met in Reedyville."

"Can't a man change his mind? I didn't even know Myrtle in those days."

"Well," said Tom, "you sure married a good-looking little lady, who is also a good cook. You knew what you were doing, and I'll give you credit. That's a combination hard to beat."

"I wish somebody would admire something about me except my *cooking*. I've heard that so much I'm tired of it."

"That's handing it right back, lady. That's the stuff."

Jim got up, went to his wife and put his arms about her. "Don't you worry, because your cooking might come in handy someday. If the worst comes to the worst, and the Hodges shut down the mill like they threaten to do, I'm going to take you over to Reedyville and hire you out to the white folks." He rocked her back and forth in his arms, the chair tilting with her.

"I like that," cried Myrtle in delight; "well, I sure like that! My own husband talking about me like I was just a nigger cook."

Andrew got up from the table. "I'll go over and get the dogs from Harvey. He's fixed it up for us to shoot in his Uncle Edward's peafield." He passed through the door, his head bent forward a little.

"Is your brother married too?"

"*Him?*" cried Jim in surprise. "Oh, no! He's too smart for that. He's too quick to be caught in a trap."

"I like *that!*" said Myrtle. "Well, I must say I like that!"

Andrew walked leisurely through the fields, past the branch and through the Cornells' meadows. There was no particular point in hurrying, as he was sure that Harvey would neither be ready nor expecting him so early. When he returned to the house, Jim had gone into his room to see about his shotgun and Tom was sitting in the kitchen talking to Myrtle. They were getting along well together, and Tom was showing her pictures of his wife and his three children, but when Andrew called, he stuffed the photographs back into his wallet and came into the yard.

"I'm going along, too, if you don't mind," said Andrew. "Harvey lent me his new gun. I said I'd try it out for him."

The three men returned at dusk, satisfied with themselves and the result of their hunt. They divided the birds and Myrtle took Andrew's and Jim's share and prepared them for supper while Jim returned the dogs and the borrowed gun to their owner. Tom said: "I've got a bottle of good rye whisky in the car. I'll fix a drink for just us three if you want to join me, or do you think we ought to wait until Jim gets back?"

"I'd like a drink myself," said Myrtle, "but don't offer Jim one." She explained then that Jim had signed the pledge, for drink was his one weakness, and he was the sort of man who should never touch it. Tom nodded slowly and raised the drink to his lips, drew it away quickly, apologized, and touched Andrew's glass. Jim had not returned when they had finished their drinks, and Tom went into Andrew's room to wash up and to take a nap before supper. Andrew remained in the kitchen with Myrtle and talked of the events of the day as she fixed their supper. He sat on the bench by the stove and plucked the birds, dropping the damp, gray feathers into a bucket at his feet. She turned from the stove and their eyes met, and they both laughed for no reason at all.

It was time for Jim to return, and Myrtle went to the window and peered out in the direction of the creek, following the path that Jim had taken with the dogs. A moment later she saw her husband's head appear above the knoll.

She waited awhile, shaking the stove's damper, and then, as if she had timed everything perfectly, she came to Andrew and put her arm around his neck. "Good Lord! Haven't you got those doves picked yet? I never saw such a slow man in all my life, unless it's Papa." She laughed gaily and rumpled his wiry, tightly kinking hair. "You sure are a help around the house," she added. "Maybe I'd been better off if I'd married *you* instead of Jim."

"It's hard to tell sometimes," said Andrew. "I only want you to be happy. Maybe things are better the way they are."

241

And then, as if moved by an identical impulse, they both turned and saw Jim standing in the doorway. His face was white and impassive, as if he were sick, and his lean fingers plucked at the lapel of his coat. Myrtle took her arm from Andrew's neck and went to him at once. "Why, what's the matter, Jim? You look sick!" She held his inert hand, chafing it with her own, but Jim pulled it away from her wearily. "Jim!" she said. "Jim! How long have you been standing there outside the door, watching?"

When Jim spoke, his voice was very tired. "I've been here long enough to see for myself what I've been suspicioning for a long time." He came into the kitchen and picked up the empty glasses, smelling them. "You've been drinking too, behind my back. You don't want me to drink or have any pleasure, but the minute my back is turned, and you think I'm out of the way, you start getting drunk with my own brother."

"Now, Jim," said Myrtle laughingly. "Tom and Andrew and I had one little drink together. There certainly wasn't any harm in that. There's nothing to get upset about, baby. I saw you through the window, coming toward the house. I was just trying to tease you a little. If I'd had anything to hide, I wouldn't have let you *catch* me with my arm around Andrew, you can be sure of that." She laughed again. "I wouldn't have done that if I'd had a guilty conscience, now would I?"

Suddenly Jim hurled the glass against the wall, and began to shout, no longer able to keep the force of his passion in check: "I see it all now! I see the whole thing! . . . Andrew was pretty smart when he tricked me into marrying his cast-off woman! I've been the goat all along in this thing, but by God! my eyes are wide open now!"

"Jim! Jim! Don't talk like that, baby? Tom can hear every work you say."

"I've been a fool, working hard all day at the mill to make a

242

living for you, so you can stay at home alone with your pimp and laugh at me."

Andrew got up and put down the birds, his face worried at Jim's words, but he did not speak. He thought: "He's worse this time than he was that day in the barn, but I'm going to keep my temper. I'm not going to say anything to him." He had a quick sense of anger against Myrtle, for it seemed incontestable to him now that she somehow managed to precipitate these scenes.

"I come home feeling happy and at peace for once," shouted Jim, "and what do I find? . . . All right I'll tell you what I find: I find my wife lying in the arms of my brother. I find them gloating together behind my back over how they fooled me."

"Jim! Jim! You're making that all up. There's not a word of truth in it, and you know it, honey!"

Jim turned furiously to his brother. "So you think things are better the way they are? . . . I'll say they're better this way, at least for your strumpet and for you. I'll agree with you there!" His voice was getting louder, his gestures more violent. He kicked the chair across the room and stood in the middle of the big kitchen with his legs spread wide, the wing-like fall of black hair lying across his forehead.

Andrew came to him and took him by the arms. Jim began struggling in his brother's grasp. His face was red and his tongue protruded a little, but he was powerless against Andrew's strength. "You're still in love with her though," he panted. "You can't deny that."

Andrew said: "That's not true and you know it. We've been over all that a good many times." Jim tore away from his brother's grasp at last and backed against the wall. He picked up the whisky bottle and held it by the neck, ready to strike if Andrew advanced farther.

"You can say what you please, now, to get out of it, but I know

243

what I saw. I see a dozen different things every day that passes to convince me I'm right. . . . Did you think I didn't notice the way you two whisper together when you think I'm not listening? You think I'm a damn fool, don't you? Well, I've had enough of being the goat. It's my turn now."

"Leave him alone, Andrew. Go outside and leave him alone with me. I'll talk him out of this. For God's sake, get away and leave us two alone together."

Andrew went out of the kitchen and walked down to the barn. When he reached it, he sat on the bench beside the door and looked at his hands, turning them over speculatively, smoothing the skin of his fingers. There was a lull for a moment, as if Myrtle had reassured her husband on some important point, and then Jim started the quarrel again. From where he sat Andrew could hear his brother's voice plainly, although he could not distinguish individual words. He thought: "I don't know what to do. I don't know what's the right thing for me to do from now on. I've tried to do my best, but everything has failed." He sighed unhappily and rubbed his eyes. When he looked up again he saw that Tom Ostermann had come stealthily out of the house and was walking through the yard in the direction of the Delta Field. He got up from the bench, called out in his blurred, gasping voice and Tom came to him. Tom shrugged his shoulders and laughed.

"They're having a little disagreement," said Andrew. "Jim's got a quick temper and a suspicious nature. He's always been like that, but he generally burns himself out quickly." He lowered his eyes apologetically and rubbed his nails against his overalls. "It looks like he could have picked a better time than this, with a visitor in the house, don't it?"

"The noise woke me up out of a sound sleep," said Tom. "I thought at first somebody was being murdered."

"I never saw Jim this bad before," continued Andrew, "but I

244

expect he'll run down in a few minutes. He'll quiet down, and he'll eat a better supper than any of us." They walked together in the direction of the branch, talking of the hunt they had had that day, of the opportunities they had missed. When they returned to the house after an hour, everything was peaceful again. The birds were cooked and Myrtle was putting them on the table. Jim came out of his bedroom. He had washed his face and combed his hair carefully, slicking it down evenly with pomade, and he acted as if nothing whatever had happened. He was gay at dinner, and told jokes with Tom, but when the meal was finished Myrtle got up and went to the kitchen, for the stories that Jim was telling were raw, even for him, and she felt humiliated before their guest. Andrew, too, got up at the first opportunity. He had not spoken once during the meal, but he explained, now, that he wanted to fill the wood-box. It was his last duty at night to see that it was full for the morning, and he had neglected his duty. He went out of the back door self-consciously, his shoulders hunched forward a little, knowing that Jim's eyes were fixed like a dagger between his shoulder blades. When the door had shut behind him, Jim came back to reality. He narrowed his eyes, reached upward and tugged at his lock of black hair.

"Well, Tom, you're seeing the home life of the Tallon family as it really is. An outsider wouldn't have any idea of what goes on here under the surface."

"My wife and I have our quarrels too. I guess every married couple does, but it seems to me that you went a little too far, Jim."

"You say that because you don't know all the facts," said Jim. He lowered his voice and spoke confidentially. "You don't know what's been going on in this house, and you don't know what a position I'm in. If you knew that, you'd think differently."

"Well, maybe I don't. Maybe not."

"For instance, did you believe that story about Andrew wanting to fill the wood-box? Were you sap enough to fall for that too?"

"Sure. Why not?"

"It just shows you don't know, that's all." Jim spoke briskly, logically. "I'll tell you a few things to open your eyes: Andrew didn't give a hoot about the wood-box. It was three-quarters full at supper time and there's enough wood in it right now for two days. All he wanted was an excuse to get in the kitchen with my wife, so that the two of them could laugh and make their plans behind my back."

"Horse feathers!" said Tom sharply.

"You think I'm imagining it?" asked Jim. "Well, I can see how an outsider might think that!" He shook his head sadly and raised his palms in despair of being understood, for it seemed to him that he was thinking at this moment with complete and unclouded lucidity for the first time in his life, and that the things he was going to say should, from the logical deduction of known facts, be true, even if he, himself, still perversely repudiated them with some illogical mechanism of his own mind. He talked then of his suspicions, marshaling all his facts into an overwhelming and orderly niceness of detail. He told of Andrew's courtship of Myrtle and how she had later transferred her affections to him, until he, in turn, had learned to love her, and the implications of such scheming conduct. . . . At that moment they heard the sound of wood falling into the box and Andrew's blurred voice speaking.

"You see!" concluded Jim. "You see what I said is true! They framed me for some reason I don't understand yet. I'm not being as foolish as I sound."

Tom whistled slowly and shook his head. "If all you say is true, I'd clear out of here pretty quick. I wouldn't live like you do, and make myself unhappy, if what you say is true."

"I been thinking of that, but what can I do? I don't know any work except sawmilling, and times are hard all over the county."

246

"Why don't you come down to Mobile and see if you can get a job on a steamer?" suggested Tom. "That's what *I'd* do in your place. I'd take a voyage on a ship and see new countries and people. . . . Come down to Mobile and see Captain Nicolson, of the Waterman Line. I know him personally, and I'll write him a letter if you want me to. Maybe he'll be able to give you a job. . . . Anyway, I wouldn't live like this, if what you say is true, but I still think you're all wet, Jim, no matter what you say."

They both stopped speaking as Andrew came into the room. He went to Tom and shook hands. "I'm going to church in Hodgetown tonight and I've got to hurry, so I'd better tell you good-bye now, as you may be gone when I get back." He went upstairs to dress, and Tom watched him speculatively. When he was out of earshot, he spoke: "You know, Jim, it's hard to believe the things you say about your brother. I was with him all day long, and I must say it's hard to believe."

"That's what everybody thinks," said Jim. "He's a sly one, and has everybody fooled. That's why I wouldn't dare tell anybody around here what I've told you tonight. They'd think I was crazy." He laughed nervously. "And don't believe that religious part either; it's all a blind. It's all a part of the game he's playing."

"How about your wife?" asked Tom, after a long pause. "Just where does she come in? How much does she know?"

"She's an angel," said Jim. "She don't understand the danger she's in. He's got her under his thumb so bad she hasn't got any mind of her own!"

When Andrew returned from church the men were still talking together. He came upon the back porch, his shoes creaking faintly, and looked into the room, unwilling to enter. It was not cold, even though it was so late in the year, but Jim had built a fire in the fireplace and sat sprawled out on two chairs. He had

247

opened his shirt, exposing his peach-colored, slightly soiled under-wear, and his lock of black hair hung down to his eyes. Tom ap-peared somewhat bored, and he kept yawning and glancing about the room. As Andrew watched them, and planned a course of conduct for the future, Jim got up and kicked at a log that burned in the fireplace, sending clouds of sparks up the chimney and onto the bricked hearth. "I'm not going to stand for this much longer. I'm getting out of here like you suggested, Tom. By God, I'm going to ship out as a seaman if Captain Nicolson will give me a job."

"You said that a minute ago," answered Tom wearily. He put his feet against the wall and shoved his chair back, his soles leaving an imprint against the scoured boards. "You said that at least twice in the last five minutes. . . . All right, I believe you! You're going to ship as a seaman if Captain Nicolson will give you a job! . . . You don't have to say everything twice. I'm not deaf."

Jim looked at him steadily, his eyes hard and critical. "I've found out that when I talk to a Yankee it's better to say every-thing at least twice."

"Yeah?" said Tom.

"Everything at *least* twice," repeated Jim; "and one time very slow."

"Yeah?" said Tom. "Yeah, wise guy?"

Jim pulled his lips down and laughed. "I wonder if it could be my Southern *accent?* I guess that's the trouble."

"Yeah?" said Tom. "Yeah?"

"Yeah," said Jim. He laughed again and imitated the bland, high-pitched voice of George Stratton. "You ain't got such a big *talking* vocabulary, is you white folks?"

Andrew turned from the door and walked to the oak grove. He thought: "At least one thing is certain: I can't go on living like this." Later he heard the voices of both men raised angrily,

248

and he saw Tom Ostermann come out of the house, only a few steps ahead of Jim. They stood shouting angrily at each other for a moment, and then Tom shrugged his shoulders, went to the huge, enameled egg which served him as an automobile, and drove off down the road, the cretinous eyes of the new-born chicks examining telephone poles, trees and wire fences with equal and unprejudiced vacuity.

Jim disappeared into the house but returned to the door at once, the string of birds which was Tom's share of the hunt in his hands. When he saw that Tom had already driven away, he hurled the birds into the clump of Cape jasmine bushes that grew by the fence. He stood in the open door, his eyes fixed in the direction which Tom had taken, his face drawn and anxious, as if terrifying impulses struggled within him. He decided that he would stop by the office the next evening when he came from work and ask his friend, Johnny Everett, to hold out a part of his wages each week, to keep the money for him in the office safe until he needed it. When he had enough, he'd clear out forever. He would escape again; he would outwit his destiny. . . . Thinking himself unobserved, he leaned against the door and began to tremble. "Oh, my God!" he whispered to himself. "Oh, my God! . . . What's to become of me? What's going to happen?"

CHAPTER XXIX

ANDREW was up early the next morning, before his brother had come down. He got his automobile from the barn and parked it just outside the gate, beneath the liveoaks. When he returned to the house Myrtle was starting a fire in the stove. She saw him and dropped the stove-lid with a clatter, staring fearfully over her shoulder. "Go outside, Andy!" she pleaded. "Don't let him catch you here talking to me. He's crazy-jealous over us and he went on something terrible to Tom after you went to church. I listened to what he was saying and it made my blood run cold."

Andrew said: "I lay awake all night thinking of the best thing to do, Myrtle. It might be better if I left the farm for awhile. It might be best for all of us."

"Go away, quick," said Myrtle. "He might come down any minute now. Don't let him catch us together again. Go away, Andrew!"

"I'm going to stay with Effie and Asa. If you need me, send me word." He stowed his belongings in the car, but before he had finished he met Jim coming down the stairs. Jim looked at him in surprise, and Andrew explained what he intended to do. He walked to the parked car, his brother behind him. "I expected that of you," said Jim. "You never would face anything out. You'll cause trouble, and try to break up my home, and then you run away and hide."

"I'm not going over that with you again," said Andrew.

"You're running away to hide," said Jim, but his voice was more placating now and his manner less assured. "After all I've

250

done for you all your life, this is the thanks I get for my pains."

"That's right. This is the thanks you get."

"That's gratitude!" said Jim bitterly. "That's gratitude for you! You'd leave me without a word, after all I've done."

Andrew spoke slowly weighing his words. "Here's something else for you to think over: If I never see you again, it will be soon enough for me." He went into the kitchen to tell Myrtle good-bye while Jim stood in the open door, a look of disbelief in his face, not realizing, even now, that such a thing as this could happen to him.

They crowded about him excitedly at the Cleavers', but he avoided the intimacy of their questions. Jim and Myrtle were not getting along very well together, as they already knew, and he had thought it wise to move away for a time until they settled down together to married life. "Just the same, it's a funny marriage," repeated Effie in a provoked voice. "It's a funny marriage, and they've been acting funny." She turned petulantly. "I never seen such a closed-mouthed man in my life as you are, Andrew! You know more than you let on, anybody can see that; and you act like I'm not to be trusted, or even a member of the family."

"There's nothing to tell. I don't know what's wrong with Jim and Myrtle any more than you do."

"It's a funny marriage, just the same," repeated Effie positively, "and no good can come out of it. . . . You can bear me out that I predicted it from the very first."

Asa Cleaver came up from the fields, seeing Andrew's car at the gate. He was a small man with hands and back stiff from years of toil. His bones seemed improperly articulated and of inappropriate lengths, as if assembled by unskilled hands. He had become bald early in life, but as if to compensate for this loss, his brows were two irregular, jutting bushes, whose hairs met above his nose like the interlocking antennae of insects. His nose curved with ascetic harshness, but the lower part of his face was inoffensive and rather pathetic.

"Well," he said. "Well, what's all this howdy-do about?"

Back of the house, and a quarter of a mile away, was the old Cleaver homestead, abandoned in Asa's time when the new home was built. It was in good repair, and the roof was sound, and it was there that Andrew was to live for as long as he chose. After supper that night he talked more frankly with Effie and Asa. They decided that the stories they were to tell the public must, at least, be consistent, and it was Asa who made the most sensible suggestion. He had been thinking a long time about clearing another forty acres, which he owned, and planting it in peanuts, but the work was too much for him to do unaided, and he'd been unable, in his present poverty, to hire help. If Andrew was willing, he could help with the work, and everybody would take it for granted that that was the reason for the move. Afterwards Edna walked with her uncle to the cabin with quilts and sheets for the dismantled bed, and they talked as they put things in readiness.

"If that big, feeble-minded cow had a teaspoonful of brains," said Edna, "half of this would be avoided. I'm not trying to excuse Uncle Jim, he's unreasonable enough without any outside help, but Myrtle eggs him on and makes him worse. I told her that when we walked up from the barn that time, but she denied it. . . . Maybe you're so much in love with her that you can't see it either."

"I see it plainly enough and have for a long time."

"What you find in her will always be a mystery to me, Uncle Andrew. Oh, I'll admit she's pretty, if you like that type, but for a man with as much sense as you've got to let her twist you around her finger for her own ends is simply beyond me."

"Myrtle's sweet when you get to know her," said Andrew mildly. "She can be very sweet when she wants to be."

The next morning Andrew and Asa began clearing the cut-over land of its stumps and underbrush. The work was hard and uninteresting, but he found pleasure in it, for his mind tired with the tiring of his back, and so long as he worked he found peace; but when he had got into bed, his brain awoke, as if it functioned apart from his body and had taken its necessary rest while he was physically occupied. Often he could not sleep at all, and he would sit by his window, a bright fire of pine knots in the fireplace, and look at the bleak December landscape. He was troubled with vague things that he could not define, for he felt within himself, an irrational sense of evil, and he knew only that he was unhappy; that he could not struggle much longer. He examined his conduct step by step in an effort to deduce, by logic, the consequences of the things he had done, to see how and where he had failed, but there was nothing, in reality, that he could fix upon. It seemed to him, then, that it would be easier for him if there were actual guilts that he could take to himself, that he could say definitely: "I am responsible for this and I must accept the consequences"; or, "I went astray at this place, and am accountable for much which has happened since." Edna managed, at his request, to see Myrtle at least twice a week, and to report on conditions at the farm, but from the very first her reports were disquieting. There had been no improvement in Jim; indeed he had got rapidly worse after Andrew's departure, if Myrtle's diagnoses could be trusted.

Edna returned from the farm one afternoon earlier than Andrew had expected her and came hurriedly to the field where he worked. It seemed, this time, that Myrtle had met her at the gate, but had asked her not to come in. She appeared to be frightened of Jim and of the fact that he might return home and catch the two of them talking together. Myrtle had confessed her fears this time; she wasn't afraid of Jim when he was drinking, for he seemed harmless then, and the things he said and the threats he made could be accounted for by the alcohol he had drunk, but now he was not drinking at all, and he was more menacing that way. She was sorry that Andrew had gone away. She missed him a a great deal and thought about him, and cried over the way she had treated him in the past.

Andrew rested his foot on the charred stump that he was uprooting and wiped his face with the sleeve of his jumper. "What are we going to do, Edna? What are we going to do?"

"I don't see how we can do anything. He's her husband, and if she hasn't got sense enough to leave him, that's her affair, isn't it? I don't see how you can help it." Andrew shook his head helplessly, for the vagueness of impending tragedy haunted him, and his own undetermined responsibility for what he knew now must occur remained in his mind to trouble him.

"There's no use trying to hide things any longer," said Edna, "and that's a comfort, because everybody knows what's going on. If they don't, all they've got to do is to go stand in the road any night and listen."

When Neil Bickerstaff returned home that night he found his household disrupted. Hilda, his second daughter, was cooking supper, but the younger children, finding the iron discipline of their mother unaccountably relaxed, sprawled in a wide circle on the parlor floor and cut photographs from old moving-picture magazines, squabbling and bickering among themselves, littering the rug with scraps, and staining it with the paste of flour and water which they had mixed earlier in the kitchen. Even before Neil entered the front door, and even before he heard the quarreling, unchecked noise that his younger children made, he knew

254

that something was wrong, that the ordered routine of his family life was disturbed, so he went at once to the kitchen, feeling by instinct that all solutions of his married life were to be found there, and Hilda, from behind the untidy pile of soiled pots and pans, told him the news.

"Mamma's in her room lying down, and she said you were to come in to see her as soon as you got here. She had the company doctor after she got home from visiting Myrtle, but he said there wasn't nothing very much the matter with her." She opened the oven door and took out a pan of biscuits which had baked too long. "Ph-o-o—!" she cried in a disgusted voice. "It looks like I done ruined that panful too!"

"What's the matter with her, Hildy?" Neil tried to make his voice casual, but he could not hide his alarm. "What's the matter with your Mamma? . . . She was well enough when I left for the mill this morning."

"She went to see Myrtle again, although she'd sworn she'd never do it until Myrtle apologized for the way she treated her *last* time," said Hilda, as if quoting Kate's own words. "I don't know what's the matter, Papa, and she wouldn't say; but I do know she was talking to Mrs. Westerlund and Mrs. Renshaw this morning and they scared her again, and when I got home from school there she was piled up in bed, taking-on with the doctor treating her."

Neil went into his bedroom and closed the door. It was so dark that he could not see his wife at first, but he heard her, for she was still crying faintly. "Who is it?" asked Kate through her sobs. "Who is come to pester me now?" Neil sat beside her on the bed and took her hand. "Honey," he pleaded softly. "Sugarpie! What's wrong with you? When did you take sick?"

"I'm not sick, Neil, I'm just crushed," she answered. "I'm crushed to the ground and stomped on!" She began to weep afresh, with a vigor that surprised her and which interested her as phenomena, in spite of her pain, since she had concluded hours ago that she had cried herself dry and that there were no tears left. When she was calmer, she explained the situation to her husband. It was true that she had sworn not to meddle in Myrtle's affairs again, but she had been hearing so many rumors about Jim, and the way he was behaving lately, that she couldn't resist. She hadn't been able to stand it any longer, for Myrtle was still her baby, in a way, and she had always been so weak and lacking in will power. She had always been so helpless when it came to handling her own affairs, or to taking care of herself.

"Now, Katie!" said Neil soothingly. He put his arm behind her back and supported her against his chest. "Now, Katie!"

"I wasn't so worried as long as *Andrew* was there too," continued Kate after a moment. "I knew he'd look out for her the same that I would, but with him gone away there's no telling what might happen; so I figured I'd swallow my pride and go plead with her to leave Jim and come back home to us where she belongs."

"Now, Katie! . . . Now, sugarpie!"

"I told her, after awhile, that if she didn't leave him I was going to notify the sheriff and have him arrested as a dangerous character." Kate shuddered and put her hands over her face. "The things she said to me, Neil! Her own mother. . . . She blames me for everything that's gone wrong with her and Jim. She said things that I thought no girl would ever say to her mother."

"Now, Katie!" said Neil. "Now, Katie!"

"He's bewitched her," said Kate. "He's got her under a spell. No girl in her right mind would put up with what she does." Her tears broke through again and she beat against the bed clothing with her clenched fists, the slack half-moons beneath her eyes twitching.

"You'd better leave things the way they are, Katie, and quit interfering. You turn her against you more each time."

"Then *you* go see her and ask her to come home," said Kate

piteously. "Maybe she'll listen to you." She smoothed back her black hair, loosened and untidy with the force of her grief. "Maybe she'll listen to you," she repeated bitterly, "because you ain't a mother who's labored all her life for her happiness, and acted unselfishly where she was concerned, sacrificing and giving up for her pleasure."

"Now, Katie! Now, Katie! Don't get your bowels in an uproar, sweetness."

"*You* ain't her loving, unselfish mother, so there's no reason why she should turn on you. There ain't any reason why she would prefer living on with that *murderer* than with you!" Her secret was out at last, and she had exposed the ultimate basis of her illness, for since her talk with Mrs. Macbeth at the fence she had thought of little else. She had determined to say nothing about it, but she was glad, now, that chance had given her this opportunity to tell her fears to Neil, and she repeated, under his insistence, all that Mrs. Macbeth had said.

"Why, I know all about that," said Neil cheerfully, "and have all along. There ain't nothing in it at all. I heard that story when I first come to Hodgetown, so I asked Jim about it one day, and he told me the straight of it. It happened some years ago, and he wasn't more than an irresponsible boy at the time. Nobody tried to arrest him afterwards because everybody agreed he was justified in killing that bigetty nigger."

"A *nigger?*" repeated Kate in amazement. She sat up in bed, feeling stronger all at once. "Was it a *nigger* he killed?"

"Sure," said Neil in surprise. "I thought you said Mrs. Macbeth told you all about it."

"She didn't say it was a *nigger!*" said Kate indignantly. "She deliberately let me think that Jim was a murderer." She threw back the cover, her heels hitting the floor solidly. "Get out of my way, Neil," she said, "I got my work to do. I got to see about supper." She switched on the light and began to comb her hair.

It was typical of Mrs. Macbeth and her sweet, deceitful ways to mislead her about a thing of that sort, to frighten her into believing that her daughter was married to a common criminal, but it served her right for making a confidante of such people. She had learned her lesson well, and she'd know better next time. She'd have sense enough to keep her own counsel in future.

"What made Jim kill the nigger?" she asked briskly. "Did you ask him that?"

Neil said: "I don't rightly remember now. Jim did tell me at the time, but I forgot. I think, though, he said the man shoved him off the sidewalk and then sassed him."

CHAPTER XXX

Effie had found it difficult to make up her mind about Bessie's offer. She looked critically at her daughter, her fingers drumming thoughtfully on the table. "I for one wish you'd never met up with Bessie, and I'm sure your Uncle Andrew will bear me out. Bessie always was a trouble-maker and always will be. I wish she'd mind her own business and leave you alone. Why, you haven't been the same girl, Edna, since she started putting those notions in your head." She turned to Andrew and sighed: "I'd like to have my daughters all sweet and womanly, and not like Bessie Tarleton. I'd almost rather see Edna living . . ." She stopped suddenly, for she had started to say that she'd rather see Edna loaded with jewels and leading the carefree life of a rich man's concubine, but the idea of Edna's plain angularity in such a setting was too much for her imagination to encompass, and she changed her thought, contenting herself with a lesser evil for her daughter. . . . "Why, I'd almost rather see Edna dead and laid out in her coffin," she continued, "than to have her going around saying all the people in this county are as good as I am. At least there ain't any shame attached to respectable death."

"I wouldn't be so sure about Bessie's influence being bad," said Andrew tactfully. "It seems to me that one day we're all going to be proud of Edna, and I for one believe she's going to be a great force for good in the world. I wouldn't be so sure, Effie."

"I hope I never live to see that day," said Effie significantly. "I hope I never live to see my daughter making herself cheap and vulgar and mingling with common people that she shouldn't by right spit on."

259

"Those aristocratic Cleavers!" said Edna. "That outstanding Southern family of illiterate serfs!"

"There ain't no sense in your being sarcastic either," said Effie. She flushed angrily, the bird-shot moles standing out with sudden distinctness. "I guess you've forgot that your papa had to take a strap to you not so long ago to cure your impudence. Well, you haven't grown so big since last year that he can't do it again, or me either if I have to."

"He won't do it again, though," said Edna, "and for a very simple reason: I know too much now, and I've been reading up on the practice of magic. I've got so I can do almost all of the spells myself. If he hits me again, or you either for that matter, I'll do something simple at first, like making the mule die. But if he won't let me alone even then . . ." Edna stopped and stared fixedly at her mother with her pale eyes. . . . "Well, I'll have to start a stronger spell of magic in that case and inflict you all with pellagra or something even worse if I think of it."

"Don't you dare to talk to your own mother that way!" said Effie. "I'll slap your face for you, and it don't make no difference to me how grown up you are. . . . And I've made up my mind at last. You can't go to Reedyville. You're going to stay right here with me."

"Try it!" said Edna. She smiled quietly, sure of herself. "Try slapping my face, or keeping me away from Reedyville, and then see what happens to Papa's mule just as a starter. You'll be sorry you did it when you see Diana's head the size of a wash-boiler and working with maggots. . . . Try it, if you don't believe me." She started toward her mother, her cheek held outward, but Effie turned pale and backed toward the door. "I got work to do," she said hurriedly. "I haven't got no time to stand here talking silly, nigger talk with *you*, young lady!"

When her mother had gone, Edna sat down and quietly picked up her book. "You see, Uncle Andrew? . . . That's one of the

260

advantages of education. Ignorant people don't dare disbelieve, because they can never be sure what you know, or what you can do." She laughed in delight, her bulging brow wrinkled, her damp hands pressed together. "Don't worry about me, because I'm going to school in Reedyville after the first of the year. I've already made my plans. There's nothing can stop me now. Mamma will write Bessie tomorrow and tell her so."

By the middle of December Andrew and Asa began to see the result of their work. The underbrush had all been cleared away, the young, second-growth trees cut down, and some of the smaller stumps had been fired and dug out with picks and crowbars. They sat after supper talking of their work and of what remained to be done, and they decided that they would start dynamiting the larger stumps after Christmas.

At nine o'clock Andrew went to his cabin. He undressed, got into bed and pulled the covers about his chin; but before he even had time to blow out his light, he heard Myrtle calling to him from the yard. He opened the door and spoke to her reassuringly, for he knew that she was badly frightened; and when she stood with him in the room, and had taken off her hat and her coat, he saw that one of her eyes was swollen and was rapidly turning purple.

"He hit me," said Myrtle, as if unwilling to believe her own words. "It's come to that now! . . . He never done a thing of that sort before, no matter how much he cursed and went on." She sat on the bench by the fire and began to cry. "Oh, my God!" she said over and over. "Oh, my God, you don't know what I've been through these last few weeks without you, Andrew! When I look back, I don't see how I ever stood it. He blames me now for wrecking his life and for running you off the place. There's no talking to him any more, because I can't make him listen to reason when I try to make him see the truth. He only curses me and says I wrecked his life." She got up from the bench and began to walk up and down in the room, wringing her hands. "Everybody knows what's going on," she said. "Even the people on the road can hear him shouting and God-damning me!"

Andrew stood quietly, determined to remain as impersonal as possible, since it appeared inevitable that he must now step in and solve this situation somehow. He spoke when he was sure that his voice would not tremble. He knew that what he was going to say would not be heeded, but he said it again. "Why don't you give Jim up, and go on back to your people? That seems to me the only thing you can do now."

"I married him for better or for worse," said Myrtle stubbornly, "and I'll stick to that, no matter what happens. I'll never go home again, no matter what he does to me, or how scared I am of him." Her tears broke through, and for a time she was speechless. "You're the only person in the world I'd ever tell these things to. You're the only person I'd come to for help."

"I want to do the best thing for everybody, Myrtle. It will solve everything if you'll leave him."

"He's got an idea in his head that I am going to have a baby, and he believes you are the father. He talks about it all the time and no matter what I say, it don't do any good. He just goes on and on talking until I think I'm going to go crazy if he don't stop."

"I'll do what you think is best," said Andrew at last. "I'll go back with you and stay at the farm if you think that's the thing to do."

"I ran out of the house, finally, because I couldn't stand it any longer after he hit me." She rolled up her sleeves and showed the bruises on her arms. "I'm afraid to be alone with him. I don't know what he might do to me. . . . You're all I got to depend on, Andrew!"

When they were on the road, approaching the Tallon farm, Andrew spoke pleadingly: "It will be terrible for the baby after he's born, if Jim won't believe it's his. It seems to me that you'll have to leave Jim, sooner or later, if only for the sake of the baby."

"There's not going to be any baby," said Myrtle in surprise. "I thought you understood that. I'm not having a baby by anybody." She spoke hesitantly as if the matter were one of great shame. "It's not possible for me to be pregnant, because I haven't lived with Jim as his wife for a long time."

As they drove into the Tallon yard Jim came up from the gate where he awaited them, and in the glare of the headlights Andrew saw his brother for the first time in three weeks. He was shocked at the changes that had taken place in him. His hair was uncombed and neglected, his finger nails were caked with dirt and his face had the gray, unwashed look of fanatics. Jim came to the car and stood with his foot on the running-board, examining them with detached interest. "Well, the family is complete again, I see. We're right back where we started from."

Myrtle said: "Now, Jim! Now, Jim!"

"So my wife had to go get her pimp to protect her at last? Well, that's natural enough, and I can understand it. A strumpet always goes to her sweetman in case of trouble."

Unexpectedly Jim began to cry, his head resting against the automobile door, his hands clutching its edge. "I don't blame you for what you done, Andrew. Don't think that I do. She's so sweet and so beautiful that I couldn't blame any man for wanting her, too. . . . The thing that hurts me the most is that you don't trust me any more, because if you trusted me you'd admit what you done. That's the thing that I can't bear."

Myrtle lifted her swollen, tear-stained face. "Go ahead and tell him what he wants to hear, Andrew! Tell him we've been sleeping together right under his nose, if that's what it takes to quiet him."

"It's not true," said Andrew. "I don't see how lying will help matters now."

That night Jim went to bed early. He fell asleep at once and slept soundly for the first time in weeks.

CHAPTER XXXI

IF you'd just admit it!" begged
Jim over and over. "If you'd just admit it, and ask my pardon for
what you've done, I'd forgive you quick enough. I haven't been
a saint myself, and I know how a man feels. I never said I blamed
you for taking Myrtle behind my back. If you'll think it over
you'll remember that I never once said that." His voice broke
piteously and he began to tremble. "If you'd just *admit* it! . . .
That's little enough to ask."

"But it's not true," said Andrew. "I can't admit something I
never did." He stopped. His face was troubled and he locked
his hands together. "I'll admit I wanted to, and that I thought
about it a good many times, but I crushed the thoughts from
my mind almost before they got through. . . . I thought about it,
and that I'll admit, but nothing happened. I'll swear it to you
again. Nothing happened at all."

Jim raised his voice. "You liar! You double-crossing liar!
Do you think you can pull the wool over my eyes and get away
with it all your life?" He stood in the middle of the room and
began to shout his endless oaths and obscenities. "Hush, Jim!"
said Myrtle. "Please hush, honey. Folks passing on the road can
hear you."

"I want them to hear me!" shouted Jim. "I want the whole
world to know the sort of brother I've got and the sort of woman
I was roped into marrying for his convenience." Myrtle came to
him and tried to put her arms about him, to quiet him with the
nearness of her flesh, but Jim caught her by the arms and shoved
her so violently that she staggered backward and fell against the
stairs.

"Don't, Jim!" said Andrew. "Don't treat her so mean. I can't stand to see you treat her so mean."

Jim began to laugh, tears of self-pity falling down his cheeks. "I understand that well enough. I can see your viewpoint as a father, of course." He turned suddenly, put on his hat and went out of the house. He walked through the oak grove toward the road, his thin, nervous hands moving up and down in his excitement, thinking of his troubles and of the injustices done him. He would not have believed it possible that his own brother could have betrayed him so completely or wrecked his happiness in so callous a manner. He reviewed the events of the past few months with an unwilling insistence that left him weak, knowing now that he could no longer control the direction of his thoughts. "I've been over all that," he said aloud. "I've been over it again and again. I don't want to think any more. I only want peace. I only want quietness." He sat down beside the road with his face in his hands, impervious to the world about him at last, unconscious of the chill of the December night. Far away, across the withered fields, was the sound of the Cornells' penned stallion beating with his hooves against the boards of his small corral, and the shrill sound of his voice cut through the air like the noise of a distant whistle blowing with unreasoning hysteria.

He got up after awhile and walked beside the road, his hands moving up and down. There was only one solution for him. He would go away at once, while he was yet safe. He would not wait, as he had planned, until he had accumulated enough money. Andrew could have Myrtle, if he wanted her so badly, for he would renounce his rights to her and they could be happy, and he was willing, now, to forgive them the wrong they had done him. He had turned from the highway and was walking down a lane beyond the McRae farm, unconscious of the direction that he was taking.

He stopped in surprise, for the small, unused road had ended

266

abruptly and before him was the outskirts of Hodgetown and the home of May MacLean. He had hardly thought of her since his marriage, but he thought of her now with a tragic intensity, seeing at this moment how different his life might have been if he had married her, as he had always intended doing. He had never loved May, nor had he ever loved anybody, but he was convinced now that it was the intemperance of his affections alone which had reduced him to his present position. He felt tender toward May all at once, and he know that he must talk to her again, to apologize for the way he had treated her and to tell her of his troubles.

The yellow shades were down at the front windows, but behind them, in the glare cast by the wood fire on the hearth, he could see silhouetted figures moving about the room. As he watched the moving shadows, it seemed to him that they were not cast by living people of this world, or of any world now in being, but were rather the shadows of the old, unfleshed bones of those who had lived unaccountably on other and dimmer worlds which had frozen and perished long ago. He stood for a long time staring at the unreal shadows against the yellow shade, thinking his thoughts, alarmed at the strange unfamiliarity of the house itself, which he knew as intimately as his own; but when he saw a lamp lit in May's bedroom, he went steathily to her window and rapped against the pane.

"May! May! Don't be scared. It's me, Jim! I want to talk to you. I've got to talk to you now." May raised the window a little and looked into his eyes. She drew back astonished. "What's the matter, Jim? What's the matter with you? Are you feeling sick?" Before he could answer, she added: "Go down to the front gate and stand there until I come. I won't be long. Don't let Mamma see you, or she'll run you off the place."

When she joined him, and touched his arm, Jim drew his eyes away from the yellow shade and its swaying, silhouetted shadows. He was very tired again, and he did not now remember why it was he had wanted to see her so desperately. He began to talk of the things that menaced him, but his voice was calm and steady. He was a marked and a hunted man, and he told again the details of his courtship of Myrtle, and how Andrew had tricked him into marrying her. He had stood it as long as he could, for the sake of the family, but now with Andrew back at the farm and determined to kill him, he knew that he must go away for everybody's sake, and he was determined to do so; but he could not do it until he had come to see her for the last time to tell her good-bye, to let her know that when he had jilted her he had been forced into the path he had taken by powers outside his control. . . . They might have been so happy together, had things been otherwise, if Andrew had been a different sort of man.

May laughed nervously. "I don't believe a word of all that, Jim, and neither do you! Andrew wouldn't hurt a fly, and you know it as well as I do." She buttoned her coat and leaned against the gate. "What's the joke? Come on, tell me the joke and I'll laugh, too."

"There ain't any joke in it this time, May. If you knew the facts, all the things I've seen, you'd realize the danger I'm in, and why I'm running away at last."

"I don't believe it," said May, "and neither will you when you sober up."

Jim said: "I'm not drunk. I gave up drinking for Myrtle's sake. I'm not complaining, for there never was a sweeter or more loving woman than Myrtle, and I want to do her justice. . . . No matter what Andrew does to me in his hatred, now that he's found out I know, Myrtle is in no way responsible, and I want you to remember it. He's got her hypnotized, that's all. She's under his spell. She don't know any more about him than you do."

268

"Just the same I don't believe it," said May positively. "Drunk or sober, I don't believe you. I've known Andrew as long as you have, and I say I don't believe that he plans to kill you, or the proofs you give." She shook her head and looked quickly toward the house. "I might believe it of Myrtle," she continued, "but not Andrew."

"All right," said Jim wearily. "I'll give you a few more facts and maybe you'll believe me then." He began to talk rapidly, his hands fanning the air, his voice cold and logical. He spoke of his suspicions, piecing out this or that partial fact which he had observed and shaping it to his ends, while May stood listening at the gate, impressed against her will.

"I'm sorry you told me all this, Jim. . . . What made you come tell me? If it's true, I don't want to know it, because it can't concern me. Why don't you tell the sheriff?"

"I'm a hunted man," said Jim. "My life's not worth two cents. It wouldn't do any good to tell the sheriff. Andrew would get me anyway."

"Why don't you go away? . . . I don't believe a word you've said about Andy, but if *you* believe it, then why don't you go away?"

Jim said: "I'm going to leave in a few days. This is good-bye."

He looked again at the drawn shade and the flickering, terrifying shadows cast against it, as the people within the house moved about and put the room in order before they went to bed. The door opened and old Mrs. MacLean came outside and stood on the porch. "May!" she called shrilly. "May!" She came down to the fence where they stood, her sweet-gum snuff brush clasped between her teeth. When she saw who the man was, she began to make angry gestures: "Git offen this here place!" she said fiercely; "and don't you ever dare come here again! . . . Do you want to ruin my daughter's reputation?"

Jim smiled, lifted his hands to his wing of black hair, and

moved slowly toward the road. He laughed, for the things which he had put into words for the first time had relieved him and brought him a little peace. "May said she didn't believe me, but she did," he thought triumphantly. "Now the funny thing is this: I was lying when I told her what I did, and I knew I was all the time." The idea amused him and he laughed again. He walked toward home quickly, his depression forgotten. "Maybe I really believed it when I told her," he said, "but I don't any more. . . . I don't have to think of such things any more. I'm free now."

CHAPTER XXXII

Jim began his complaints the next morning at breakfast, and for a week he continued them without respite and without variation, changing only on occasion to moods of grim gaiety, when he would take a string and attempt to measure the circumference of his wife's waist, or speculate, in a burst of merriment, as to whether or not the baby would inherit its father's cloudy speech and cleft palate. Andrew shut himself in his room and sat in the dark, disturbed at the extent of his anger. He would say to himself, for reassurance: "Jim's sick. There's something strange in him, and he's not responsible. I must be patient with him now, and it may be, if God is willing, he'll get well again." He got up from the chair where he sat smoking his pipe, and lay stretched on his bed, his palms covering his ears, but he could not shut out his brother's excited penetrating voice.

"You dogbitch!" shouted Jim. "You sorry whore! You were too good to marry Andrew, but you weren't too good to marry me and then lie up with him afterwards when you two had me hooked, were you?"

"Hush, Jim!" said Myrtle. "Hush, sugar! You don't know how loud you're talking. They can hear you as far as Cornells'."

"What are you wasting your time for?" said Jim. "You're a fine mother, I must say! Why don't you get busy and start making your baby clothes? . . . No matter what you are, you ought to have decency enough to look out for your baby before he's born."

"Hush, Jim!" she pleaded. "Please hush!"

Andrew got up at last and came downstairs in his night shirt, and Jim stopped cursing and laughed sardonically. "Saint Andrew," he said; "well, bless me if it's not Saint Andrew himself dressed in a robe to represent the Angel Gabriel. . . . The Angel Gabriel in person ready to make his announcement to the husband that will bring peace to the suffering world."

Andrew closed his eyes and stood rigidly, trying to control his anger. "I've been thinking, Jim, and I'm willing to do this, if Myrtle is. You won't believe me, but I'll take her over to Reedyville, if she's willing to go, and have Dr. Kent look at her. If she's going to have a baby, like you think, he'll know. I'll get him to sign a certificate one way or the other. . . . Will you be satisfied then?"

Jim sat down, picked up his paper and turned the pages. "I don't see why you ask me," he said. "It's not my baby. You're the one to decide a thing of that sort, if you want to know. You're the father. You're the one who should be interested, not me."

"I'll go with you," said Myrtle; "I'll go with you gladly. I'll do anything if it will give us all a little peace."

Jim spoke suddenly, throwing the paper to the floor: "Oh, my God! Oh, my God! . . . What's going to happen to us all?"

They drove to Reedyville the next morning, after Jim had gone to work, and called on Dr. Kent; but Myrtle, who did the talking, was not willing to expose her husband's suspicions, or all the reasons for her visit. She said as little as possible. She merely wanted a physical examination, and a letter from the doctor giving the result of his findings. She was sullen and uncommunicative, and she answered the doctor's questions as briefly as she could. When he had examined her, Dr. Kent wrote the simple certificate that she requested, and signed it suspiciously.

"You are a married woman, Mrs. Tallon?"

"Yes, I'm married. I been married almost five months."

"Then the man outside waiting for you is your husband?"

"No. He's not my husband."

Dr. Kent waited a moment for a further explanation, but Myrtle walked to the window and looked out at the shops across the street.

"I think I understand," said Dr. Kent in amusement. "Well, you two have got nothing to worry about this time. There's no evidence whatever of pregnancy." Myrtle took the certificate, opened her purse and paid for the visit with the money that Andrew had given her that morning. She turned, without further speech, and went into the waiting room, where Andrew sat nervously. "It's just like I knew it would be," she said casually. "It wasn't possible, and I knew it all the time."

They drove off together, and in a few minutes they were in open country. The day was mild for December, and against the horizon there were long, spear-like clouds which rested lightly on the tops of pines, while above them, in the still sky, a black necklace of buzzards hovered and lifted exactly, as if impelled by identical impulses, stopped and hovered again, and drifted slowly outward in widening circles, black and motionless against blue, as if moored slackly at one invisible mast.

"I wonder what I could have done or said to make Jim think I was going to have a baby?" asked Myrtle in a puzzled voice. "There must have been something, but I can't think for the life of me what it could have been."

"I don't know, but I don't think it's anything you said."

"Well, anyway," continued Myrtle, "there's no sense in us being so down in the mouth about it, is there? Maybe when Jim reads the letter from Dr. Kent he'll get over his foolishness. Maybe it will settle things once and for all."

Andrew wanted to say: "You're wrong. The letter will settle nothing. If he does believe it today, he'll only fix on something else to torture us with tomorrow. . . . It isn't the result of any

273

one thing that you have done, or that I have done. I don't understand it, but it's deeper and more inevitable than that"; but he remained silent and stared outward at the white, lance-like clouds lying so low to the trees. A strange despair, dream-like in its vagueness, in which Myrtle, Jim and himself were inextricably linked together gnawed at his mind. He understood it but dimly, but he knew with certainty that the roots of their misery lay deeply grounded in the past; that everything they had done or said or thought had been like frail ravelings, hardly important in themselves, but which had blown out, like the gossamer weaving of a spider, and hung limp and pendulous in the air until a strong wind had caught up the dangling ends and had blown them all together; for then the ravelings had touched each other and clung, and had twisted into the rope that now bound them, a rope which no man could break. . . . He shook his head and spoke in his gasping voice. "I don't know what will happen to us all, Myrtle. I can't see yet what the end is going to be." He sighed. "I wish I knew how it will all end."

They drove for awhile in silence and then Andrew pulled to the side of the road and stopped. "I've got about $234.00, counting interest, in the Reedyville Savings Bank," he said unexpectedly. "Let's go back, draw it out and spend it while there's time."

"You know I wouldn't let you do a thing like that!" said Myrtle laughingly. "Keep that money. You'll need it for your old age, or for your wedding if you fall in love again and want to marry."

"I won't need it," he said. He looked carefully up and down the road and then turned in the direction from which they had just come. "If you're going to spend your money," said Myrtle gaily, "why don't you buy that set of books you saw in the window—I mean the set bound in leather with the gold stampings on it?"

He shook his head. "I won't have time enough to enjoy it."

"The thing I want the most," said Myrtle, "is a black velvet cloak like moving-picture actresses wear at the opera. It won't do me any good, though, except to look at."

"We'll buy that first, if there's money enough for it. I'll have to think over what I want, besides food."

"I'd get the books, Andrew. You'll have lots of time to read them before it comes time to plant. Then there'll be all next winter to read in."

He shook his head. "No," he said. "No. The money would just be wasted."

The certificate from the doctor did not quiet Jim or lessen his suspicions, as Myrtle had hoped. He began to shout and to curse more violently. "You two must think I'm a damned fool to believe a story of that sort. If you're not going to have your bastard after all, it's because Dr. Kent's done taken it from you. That's a fine story to come telling me, expecting me to believe it."

"Let him alone!" said Andrew. "Don't argue with him, Myrtle."

"It don't make any real difference to me one way or the other," said Jim, "because I'm clearing out. I'm leaving for good. I'm not living this way any longer."

"Then leave," said Andrew. "We'll be better off when you do go. You've been talking about it long enough. . . . Leave and be God damned to you." His voice became louder and then he, too, began to shout. He walked menacingly toward Jim, but his brother retreated before him, showing in his face the unending terror that he felt.

"I'm telling you not to hit her again," said Andrew. "I can't stand that, and if you hit her again I don't know what I'll do." He stopped, lowered his head and stood by the table. He went out of the door abruptly and walked to the road, and as he stood there he heard Jim's voice raised again. "Edna was right," he said aloud. "Anybody passing on the road can stop and hear what's going on." He felt a deep sense of shame. He came back after a long time, entered the house silently and went to bed. He thought: "We're cheap people. We're cheap and common, and there's no dignity in us."

Myrtle wanted a Christmas tree to decorate and put in the window, for she felt that the day could not be appropriately spent without this emblem of the seasonal good will of men toward each other, and, after she had persuaded him, Andrew cut a small cedar for her and set it up. They were decorating it together, their heads close, when Jim came back from work. He stood regarding them for a full minute before he spoke. They paid no attention to him and he began his unending jokes and obscenities. He spoke of the Holy Family and the appropriateness of the tree, but he thought they were a little premature, unless Myrtle had managed to conceive again since her visit to Dr. Kent. He went on and on in his coldly excited voice, the fall of hair lying across his forehead, obscuring his eye. Myrtle got up without comment and went about preparing supper, but Andrew remained on his knees, securing the ornaments to the small tree.

"All we need, now," said Jim, "is a manger and some hay for Myrtle to litter on." He laughed nervously. "I never figured out just what a manger is, but I guess it's some sort of a stall. . . . We'll move old Babe out, when the time comes, and put Myrtle in."

He came to Andrew, to watch him more closely, and bent above him, his breath beating on Andrew's neck. "We'll have a party, too, after your bastard is born. We'll do the thing up respectable, and get in some of the church folks to stand outside the barn and sing hymns."

"God's going to punish you for your sacrilege," said Andrew

276

in a shocked voice. "You'll be punished for what you're saying now."

"Punish me then!" said Jim. He straightened, lifted his head and laughed gaily. "I defy you, God! Punish me if you dare! Strike me dead if you can!"

Andrew got up quickly, the abandoned ornaments lying at the foot of the tree. He shook his head and went to the door, but he met Myrtle coming into the room, a platter of food in her hands. "You're not going out now?" she asked in surprise. "I'm just putting supper on the table."

"I don't want anything to eat."

"He's going out to pray for me," said Jim. "He's going out to pray for the repose of my soul."

"You ought to eat something," said Myrtle. "You ought not to go so long with nothing inside your stomach."

"I can't eat now," said Andrew. "I've lost all taste for food."

He walked away from the house and stood with his arms resting on the rails of the fence. Before him were the dry, withered cotton stalks standing in exact and barren rows, and beyond, toward the Cornells' land, the dome of heaven stretched high. He was cold without his coat, and he folded his arms across his chest for warmth. He bent his head suddenly and listened, and far away, across the branch, the fields and the meadow land, he heard again the Cornells' penned stallion crying shrilly and beating a drum-like tune with his hooves against the sides of his small corral. Andrew stood in silence, listening, and then he fell to his knees beside the fence and began to pray: "Oh, my God! Oh, my heavenly Father! Show me the way to go, show me the thing to do, for I no longer know. I implore You to cleanse this anger from out my heart and to give me again the resignation that I have lost. Teach me again to accept what is asked of me with patience. Wipe this evil out of me, oh, my God! Wipe this rage from my mind. He is my brother, and I am afraid of my anger, and of the things that are happening in my soul. . . ."

He paused and lifted his head. He heard Jim's cursing voice again, and Myrtle's voice rising with it in fear. He swayed his body from side to side by the fence. "He is my brother. . . . He is my brother, oh, my God, and I would not be guilty of his blood." Then he saw Myrtle come out of the back door and run into the yard. Jim stopped at the door and stood cursing and calling to her, but she would not answer him. She ran toward the barn, but not finding Andrew there, she stood still and called: "Andrew! . . . Andrew!" her voice frightened and pleading.

"This is the time to run to your sweetman!" said Jim. "This is the time, because you need him now!"

Andrew came up to her, and she put her arms about him tightly, her face against his chest. "Don't let him hit me again," she pleaded. "I'm afraid of him! . . . Don't let him hit me again."

"You must go back to your folks," said Andrew gently. "That's the only way out of it. You must go back to Hodgetown tonight. . . . I'll get out the car and take you now. Don't wait to pack your things. I can bring them to you tomorrow. . . . Just stay here as you are, and wait for me."

"No!" said Myrtle stubbornly. "I'll never do that. I got myself into this, and I'm not going back home so Mamma can crow over me."

"You ought to go," said Andrew mildly. "You really ought!" He raised his hand and wiped his face helplessely. "It would be better if you'd give Jim up and go back home. If you don't go, there's no telling what might happen."

"And have Mamma saying 'I told you so' to me for the rest of my life? I'm staying right here," she repeated, "no matter what happens."

Andrew sighed twice and closed his eyes.

CHAPTER XXXIII

ANDREW went to his room, lit his lamp and stood before the mirror that hung above his washstand. He raised the lamp high in his hand and examined himself anxiously, turning his head this way and that, looking at it from every possible angle. There was a sick, uncomprehending expression on his face, and he resembled a man condemned to death for reasons which he can neither remedy nor understand. He heard Jim moving nervously about in the bedroom below; the door slammed as he entered the living room and the blended sound of Jim's shrill anger and Myrtle's pleading voice rose upward. Andrew closed his eyes and his hand raised automatically with a defensive motion and covered his twisted, puckered lips. He turned away from the mirror and opened the door. He stood with his eyebrows drawn together, listening.

"I'm through with you two for good!" shouted Jim. "There's nothing you can say now to stop me. Have your bastard if you want to, but don't put none of my name onto it."

"Jim!" she said. "Jim! You don't know what you're saying. Go unpack that suitcase and get undressed. You'll feel better in the morning."

Andrew stood again by the mirror, but he felt hot and his throat choked him. He opened his window and propped it with a stick, letting the cool, December breeze beat on his face and neck, and with the window opened he heard again the distant screaming of the penned stallion, and the thud of his hooves beating against wood. He thought: "The Cornells ought to stop that stallion. The noise has been going on for a long time. I don't see how Harvey and Sam manage to get any sleep."

"I'm going this time," shouted Jim. "You nor anybody else can stop me. I'm clearing out for good."

Andrew shut his window and closed the door. He sat on the side of his bed, his fingers laced together. "Jim was a man with many good qualities, in spite of his faults," he thought. "He always kept his word; he wasn't stingy with his money the way I am; he was honest, and he never told a lie about anything of any importance. . . . The only time he lied was to make a story better, and he'd admit he was lying if you pinned him down to it. . . . Jim had as many good qualities as bad ones." He wiped his forehead with his hands, as if erasing the unwelcome necessity that struggled within him.

"Get out of my way," shouted Jim. "I've told you for the last time to quit interfering with me! I'm leaving you this time to your pimp, and I wish you both happiness; that I can truthfully say." He laughed bitterly. "That's what your pimp said to me when I told him I was married to you. Those were his words."

"Jim always tried to be thoughtful and considerate of me," said Andrew, "but at the end I couldn't stand it any longer." He lifted his bowed head and stared at the wall where Bradford's citation was hung, and it was then he realized that he no longer thought of Jim as a living man; already he was someone like Bradford, who existed only as a part of a remembered past.

"Get out of my way!" said Jim. "Get away from that door and let me pass! . . . Tell your pimp good-bye for me, because I'm leaving now." There was a moment's silence, and then he heard the impact of Jim's fist and Myrtle's cries at the same time. "Andrew!" she screamed. . . . "Andrew! Andrew! Come quick!" He got up calmly from the bed, as if he had been awaiting this all the time, and walked down the stairs as if nothing had happened. "Getting excited won't help matters any," he thought. "I, at least, have got to keep calm and straighten things out."

280

"Andrew! Andrew!" she wailed. "Andrew, hurry for God's sake. Hurry! . . . Hurry!"

He stood at the foot of the stairs, and looked into the room. Myrtle lay where she had fallen, her head resting against the back of the upset chair, her mouth cut and bleeding. Jim stood behind her with his legs spread apart. He was dressed in his best, ready to go away, and resting beside the door was the yellow, brightly polished suitcase that he had bought a few days before at the commissary. He wore his new, fawn-colored hat, and beneath it his black hair gleamed in the light with its coating of pomade. "Maybe you think you can stop me too?" said Jim. "Maybe you want to try to stop my going?" He pulled downward on his coat, belted in the back and cut too snugly to his waist, straightening the pockets with their small, decorative pearl buttons.

"The last thing I'd try to do would be to stop you," said Andrew, "because I never want to see your face again. Go, and quit talking about it so much. Go, and be God damned to you."

"This is the thanks I get," said Jim. "This is the thanks I get after all these years." He laughed disdainfully and picked up the suitcase. "Don't worry; I'm long gone now. You two will never see me again. . . . Have your bastard together, if you want it, but don't tell folks hereabout that it belongs to me. That's all I ask."

Myrtle said: "Don't go! Don't leave me, Jim. We can patch it up somehow. Please don't go!" But Jim shoved her so violently away from him that she fell again to the floor.

"Don't, Jim!" said Andrew gently. . . . "Don't hit her! Don't do it! I'm telling you not to."

"You don't like that, do you?" asked Jim. "I forgot, you don't like to see that!" He took a step toward the place where Myrtle lay weeping, the profile of her large, heavily cushioned rump turned toward him. He drew back his leg and kicked her, losing his balance slightly, the new, fawn-colored hat toppling on his head and falling. Andrew walked into the room and stood before his brother. "I told you not to hit her again," he said reprovingly, "but you wouldn't pay any attention to me. You did it anyway." Jim laughed and turned to the door. "I'm long gone," he said. "I'm long gone now." But Andrew shoved him aside quickly and turned the key in the lock. "I told you not to hit her again," he repeated. "I've told you that over and over." Suddenly he picked his brother up and hurled him across the room. Jim got up, stunned a little and confused. He said: "Good God! Would you hit me? Would you hit me after all I've done for you?" He backed away across the hall and into his bedroom, frightened before the frigidity of Andrew's wrath. He stumbled in his haste across the bed, not seeing it, and the next moment Andrew's thick hands were around his neck, bending his head backward over the wide footboard. Jim twisted and struggled, throwing his legs high into the air; then his movements ceased, his legs contorted and fell. He lay calm and relaxed at last, his broken neck hanging limply.

Andrew picked him up and straightened him, propping the pillows behind his back, easing him gently, as if he were still alive and feeling, against the head of the bed. He looked calmly at his brother, thinking: "I'm free of you now. . . . I'm free at last." He lifted Jim's chin with his forefinger, but when he withdrew it, the lifeless head nodded and fell forward coyly. He walked to the table and extinguished the light, but the flickering fire of pine-knots cast long shadows across the room which touched the ceiling and the walls mysteriously, dappling the pillows with shadows, touching Jim's upturned hands and his face. He pulled a chair to the bed and sat there in the semi-darkness.

Myrtle came into the bedroom at last and stood quietly. "We've got to think now," she said. "We've got to decide what's the best thing to be done." She had become very calm in this

282

emergency, and she stared at the dead face of her husband as if he were someone whom she had never seen before. She began to talk of practical matters of immediate importance, as though she had lived through a lifetime of these experiences. She moved about with perfect assurance, each necessary detail at her finger tips. She locked the door, took the suitcase from its place and burned the clothing that Jim had packed. Then she piled fresh logs in the fireplace and put the suitcase itself on top of them. When everything had been burned, she would sift the ashes herself, and distribute buttons, or metal work which might be identified, over a wide area. Andrew had committed the crime for her; it was her duty now to preserve his secret.

Andrew said: "I still don't know just how it happened. I don't know what made me do it that minute. I'll never be able to understand that." He got up and stood above the bed. The moving firelight flickering irregularly against Jim's face made it appear that he was alive again and that he was smiling like a precocious little boy who had outwitted his elders at last; that at any moment he would raise his coy head, look about him and laugh mischievously at some joke whose point was not yet apparent to his brother's more phlegmatic mind. Andrew drew away from the bed and stood against the wall, rolling his head from side to side, his palms opening and shutting helplessly.

Myrtle came into the room with the black velvet opera cloak on her arm. "This is warm and soft," she said. "We'll put it around him before we wrap him in the blanket. Nobody knows I got one, so it won't be missed. I was careful not to let on you bought it for me." They straightened him out and closed his eyes and Andrew lifted him to his shoulder and carried him through the door. He stopped when he reached the center of the triangle that made the Delta Patch and put his brother down. Myrtle handed him the spade which she had brought, and held the lantern for him. It was very late now, and it was

283

not likely that the light would be seen, but she had draped three sides of the lantern with dark cloth, and the light was focused on the spot where Andrew worked. She said: "Dig up each stalk by the roots, leaving the dirt. . . . Afterwards we can plant them back so nobody can tell that this place was ever disturbed." She went hurriedly to the house as Andrew worked, but returned almost at once, a pair of scissors in her hand. She knelt beside her husband, pulled the black cloak from his face and severed the wing-like lock of his hair. "I wanted something of his to remember him by," she said desperately. "I wanted something of Jim's that I could put in my Bible and keep forever. . . ."

The grave was finished at length, and they lowered Jim into it; but when Andrew lifted the first spadeful of the earth with which he would cover his brother from the world forever, he stopped, bent down and turned the dead body over, for he remembered that Jim always slept on his back, and that when he was a little boy, and turned accidentally on his face in the night, he had waked up screaming, his body covered with sweat.

"Hurry," said Myrtle. "Hurry, because there's lots we got to do at the house. We got to think what we're going to say to people and how we're going to act in the future." They went back to the house in silence, their crime concealed, and when they reached it, they sat down and looked at each other.

The next morning Myrtle went to see Russell Hodge. Jim had not come home, she explained, and she had discovered that his clothing and the new suitcase he had bought had disappeared as well. Russell Hodge listened sympathetically, but he knew nothing, and she went across to the company office, asking anxiously for information. She told her distraught story to Eloise Batty, Mabel Dolan and other women of Hodgetown that she met. Later she went to see her mother, feeling somehow that it was now possible for her to be friends with Kate again. But Mrs.

Bickerstaff was not to be placated so easily. She stood in the door, blocking it solidly. "This is a hard thing for me to say," she kept repeating, "but you've showed over and over that you preferred Jim Tallon to us at home. Well, you see the thanks you got for it now, I hope. Don't come back to us as second choice, now that he's run off and left you. You better sit home and wait for him to come back, since you admire him so much." Myrtle glanced to the right and saw Mrs. Macbeth's thin face pressed to the crack of the door, listening raptly to the conversation. "All right, Mamma," she said. "That's a good idea. In fact it's just what I *aimed* to do."

"You made your bed," said Kate. "Lie on it. Don't come to me for sympathy, after the cruel way you've treated me."

When Myrtle came back to the farm, she reported what she had done, the precautions that she had taken. It was inevitable that she and Andrew stick together. Their lives were bound together with their guilt from now on, and they must work out some sort of relationship together. Andrew said: "Yes! Yes!" He examined his big hands, raised them upward and smoothed his brow. "Yes," he said again. "We can never leave each other now as long as we live."

CHAPTER XXXIV

WHEN she had carried out all her plans for their protection and there was no material detail left to engage her mind, Myrtle's impassive calm left her, and she went into her room and lay on her bed with the shades drawn, for it seemed, with the underwriting of their immediate security, that she had lost all interest in the routine duties which, before, had constituted her life. As she lay in the darkness of the room reviewing the ground she had covered, and wondering if she had said too much or too little in her talks with Russell Hodge, her mother and the women of Hodgetown, she tried to bring before her eyes a picture of her husband's face, but she was unable to do this; instead she saw only the faces of casual people who belonged to her childhood, whose names she did not now remember, or had never known; people whom she thought she had forgotten. She lay stolidly, like an animal, and adjusted herself to her widowhood, thinking of the years before her. On occasion she would get up and raise the shades, twist the cord around her fingers, and lie on the bed again as though she began over and over some determined action which she was powerless to complete. Andrew cooked the meals and brought food to her on a tray, but she would not eat it. She shook her head stubbornly and turned her face to the wall, staring at its clean, unpainted surface. She turned her wedding ring over and over on her finger, her slow mind burdened with the effort she put upon it. She stretched out her hand and rested it on the tray which Andrew held patiently before her.

"He didn't even buy me a wedding ring of my own. This

ring I'm wearing now is not even mine, by rights. It's the one Mamma gave us the Sunday morning after we were married. He promised to go to Reedyville twice during the time we were boarding at the hotel and get me one of my own, but he never did. He didn't even think enough of me to buy me a wedding ring."

"Jim was always thoughtless of others, Myrtle. It was just his nature. I wouldn't take a thing of that sort too much to heart." He sat on the bed beside her and they had long talks concerning Jim and his character. Andrew told her about their boyhood together and of his father, mother and Bradford. She listened in silence to these things, which she had not known before, and often he thought that she had not even heard him, but she would later surprise him by quoting whole sections of his talks with a photographic duplication of detail that reproduced not only his words but his pauses and the inflections of his voice as well, for despite her sullen reticence she found much comfort in Andrew's words, and her pride, which had suffered so badly at Jim's hands, was restored partially with a more complete understanding of him. She wanted to believe that the failure of their marriage was due less to her shortcomings as a wife than it was to Jim's inherent qualities as a man. Andrew emphasized this point over and over for her comfort, but it was difficult for her to accept it, for she was a woman, and as such she must, by some complex process of reasoning, negative her feelings of inequality with men by the radical method of emphasizing her importance to them, thus attributing the defeat of those men she loved not to their weaknesses, but to her own irremediable deficiences.

"Maybe Jim did love me as much as he could love anybody. I won't deny that. But it was a selfish love, and not like the love you have for me. The pure love you have for me is rare in this world, and I'm just begining to see what a fine thing it was

287

I throwed away when I turned you down. It don't seem believable to me now."

"There wasn't anything particularly pure or noble about it," said Andrew. "I'm a man like Jim and everybody else."

"I don't see it that way," said Myrtle stubbornly. "It seems to me that no man could love a woman more than you loved me. No man could love a woman more than to kill his own brother that he loved too, just for her sake. Don't try to belittle yourself, Andrew."

"But your feelings for me haven't changed?"

She began to cry suddenly. "I don't know!" she said. "I don't know what I think. Don't press me for a decision now."

He got up, sighed, and went out of the house. He walked through the fields, past the branch and toward the strip of trees beyond the Cornells' land. He paused among the trees and sat down. Above him on the projecting limb of a water-oak a squirrel came out, tricked with the mildness of the weather into thinking it spring. The squirrel stared with curiosity. Its baby-like hands were pressed together in applause, and its eyes twinkled with laughter, as if it knew some obscure joke at the expense of mankind. Andrew picked up a clod of earth and made a throwing motion at the squirrel, but the unfrightened animal regarded him humorously and jerked its brush from side to side with the precise timing of a metronome. Then Andrew got up, dropped the clod of earth and looked at the sky. Something in its impersonal serenity disturbed him and he made a choked, despairing noise; and the squirrel, alarmed at last by such a harsh, distorted sound, turned quickly and ran across the projecting limb with a movement of uncalculated grace, a slow movement which began with the tip of its nose and flowed undulant and unchecked through the whole length of its body. Andrew turned away and went back to the house, disappointed that the squirrel had gone away.

288

When he returned, he found Sarah Tarleton and Addie Wrenn seated on the front porch. They had knocked repeatedly, they said, but they had not been answered, and, judging that the family was away, they had decided to wait. Andrew looked at them helplessly but he did not ask them in; then he turned, lifted his arm and covered his mouth. He explained that Myrtle was not well, that she had not as yet recovered from the effect of Jim's sudden disappearance. It had been a terrible shock to her and she would see nobody, not even himself; but he would tell her through the door that the two ladies had called, and he was sure that she would appreciate it a great deal. Miss Addie said: "Do you mean to say Myrtle has been in the house all the time while we were knocking and hollering and didn't even answer us?"

"I just come up from the creek," said Andrew cautiously; "but she was in the house when I left. She generally stays in her room, lying on her bed. I guess it's just got to wear off." After a moment the two old women, feeling put out and angry over the frustration of their good intentions, turned from the door and walked away.

"We certainly don't want to disturb Myrtle, if she's feeling so bad," said Addie Wrenn. "Please assure her of that; but Sarah and I figured now was the time that she needed the comfort of older women, particularly since her mother has publicly turned against her. . . . But of course if she'd rather just be alone. . . ."

"I think she'd rather be alone," said Andrew. He turned back into the house, closing the door slowly against the curious world. "Thanks for coming. It was mighty kind, and we both appreciate it. I'll tell her you were here."

"Don't bother," said Miss Sarah. "It's really not worth mentioning."

He came back into the kitchen and made a fire in the stove,

and Myrtle called to him from the bedroom, her voice hoarse with tears. "Who was it, Andrew? It sounded like Miss Sarah and Addie Wrenn."

"They came by to see you. Maybe it would be better if you got up and talked to people. You can't avoid people forever."

"I don't want to see them," said Myrtle; "I don't want to see anybody except you, Andrew. You're the only person in this world I can depend on. You're the only one I can trust." She began to cry again.

At night, after he had gone to bed, he could hear her still crying. He turned restlessly on his bed, not knowing what to do for her comfort. On the third night she came upstairs and went into the room that adjoined his own, the room that Jim had occupied before his marriage. She opened the door between them and talked as she put sheets on the bed. She was lonely and frightened at night downstairs, she explained, and she wanted to be near somebody. She had wanted to move upstairs with him since the time of Jim's death, but she had held out against her cowardice until this moment. They lay with the door opened between them and talked, going over again the details of the crime, discussing again their attitude toward the world, and their relationship to each other. She regretted again what Andrew had done, and she would, she felt, mourn for Jim as long as she lived, but she understood why he had done this thing for her, and she did not blame him. When she began to sob, Andrew got up and went to her, and she moved to make room for him on the bed as if she had been expecting this for a long time. She took his hand in her own and stroked his fingers. She understood his misery and his love for her at last, and when she compared him with the other men she had known in her life, or contrasted him with herself, she was ashamed, seeing so deeply her own limitations. Andrew lay beside her in the bed. He smoothed her hair and spoke softly. "Don't think such things, Myrtle. There's no reason to think such things."

"You understand me," she said; "you understand all I'm going through."

"Don't cry, Myrtle. Please don't cry. I can't stand to see you so unhappy."

Myrtle said: "We're tied together now, and we might as well make the most of it. I don't ever expect to love another man, but I respect you. You've proved your love for me like few men ever do. I'll devote my life from now on to just making you happy."

"You can make me very happy any time you want to," he said. "You can make me happy if you will. I know how you feel about me, but you can get used to me in time, if you'll try."

"I'll try," she said. "I'll do whatever you say."

He bent above her and kissed her lips. He began to tremble. Myrtle lay helplessly. "Don't!" she begged. "Don't take advantage of me." He put his arms about her and she lay close against his body. "There's no reason to be afraid of me, darling," he said. "You know that by now."

The next morning she moved her belongings to her old room again, but she went about her housework as usual, and when Andrew came downstairs she had cooked breakfast and it was waiting for him on the table. She avoided his eyes, and when he came to her and put his arms about her, she flinched and shoved him away in her old manner. "I thought you were very fine and noble," she said; "but you took advantage of me. I see you this morning for what you really are. . . . You killed Jim so you could have me. It's not hard to see now. You couldn't get me any other way, so you had to kill Jim at last."

He shook his head. "No! . . . No, that's not true!"

She would not listen to him. She went into the kitchen and looked first at the calendar that hung above the table. She discovered that it was Christmas Day, but that fact meant little to her now, and she piled the soiled pots into the dishpan and rolled up her sleeves. She went into the living room and took out the decorated tree which had never been lit, while Andrew walked behind her trying to reassure her, to reconcile her to the new relationship between them, the relationship she had entered into so willingly the night before. She went about her housework sullenly, not answering him, and at last he was silent in his helplessness. It seemed to him then that during the months he had known her she had journeyed around, and completed at last, the small circle of her emotions; that she had reached once more her point of sullen, impervious departure; for she was cautious and stolid again, and she spoke rarely. She was suspicious of others and she avoided Andrew himself as much as possible. He waited patiently, hoping that the mood would pass, but after awhile she even stopped speaking to him at all unless she had some practical, unavoidable thing to communicate. The neighbors who came to see her during these weeks were received with her old, unbending sulkiness and they generally left after a short visit. . . . And then, after awhile, they lived entirely to themselves, for nobody came to disturb them.

For many days the people of the county discussed the strangeness and the suddenness of Jim's disappearance with the whispering, excited interest of country folk, but they could make nothing of it, and they gave up at last in amused despair, grateful at heart that the Tallons, with their drunkenness and eccentricities, had again furnished material for conversation. They had not been at all surprised at the way things had worked out, and they had predicted this obvious conclusion from the first; in fact, they were, in reality, pleased at Jim's conduct, and immensely reassured, as

292

if the inevitableness of his actions demonstrated the existence of God still operating in His orderly world. The people at Tarleton's store, gossiping, agreed that they had from the beginning expected things to turn out this way. Jim Tallon could never be tied down to any one woman, they said, especially to one as practical as Myrtle had proven to be. Jim was not a family man, say what you please, for he had been spoiled by everybody all his life, by women most of all, and he was just the sort to find a good, faithful wife irksome.

It was odd that the more substantial women of the county did not immediately lay Jim's downfall at his wife's door, for they had never liked her, and they had always been suspicious of her. There was nothing very definite on which to base their vague disapproval, aside from the way she had ridiculed Andrew, and they admitted that she had settled down with marriage as respectably as anybody could wish, and that she had made Jim a capable wife, a much better one than he deserved. Nor did they question, at this time, any impropriety in the fact that, as she waited her husband's return, she kept house for the defeated Andrew. The plain, good women of the county, talking of her life and character, felt that possibly men had always hung around her too much for complete respectability, but that she could not rightly be blamed for the shortcomings of her admirers, since men were by nature fools attracted to the first pretty face, having little appreciation of those imponderable, finer qualities which women attribute to, and find inherent in themselves, and with even less perception of the inescapable tribulations which were a woman's destiny. Myrtle had never been man-crazy, they said, and that was certain. They would be fair and just to her; they would give her her due, but they would not forgive her.

But if the people of Pearl County were not surprised at Jim's behavior, Andrew's conduct left them puzzled, there being nothing in the Tallon tradition to account for moroseness, for it

293

seemed to them that he had, at last, made his deformity into a barrier to separate him from people. He left his farm rarely, coming to Tarleton's store or driving into Hodgetown only when it was necessary to buy supplies for himself and Myrtle or to have a wagon mended or a mule shod. They remembered the time when he had held his affliction lightly, or had at least accepted it as a thing that could not be remedied. In those days he had not minded the jokes at his expense; indeed, he had once taken a contemptuous pride in his split lip, exaggerating for the benefit of his friends the grunting sounds which served him as words, but now he spoke rarely, only when his necessities compelled speech, and when he did, he turned the scarred side of his mouth away from his listener, and covered his lips with his hand in the gesture which they found at first amusing and, later on, disconcerting, so that they themselves felt guilty and ill at ease in his presence.

It was at this time that Myrtle, looking at him with her old, sulky expression and seeking a reason to justify in one omnibus criticism not only her physical repugnance to him, but his unhappy, measureless love for herself as well, began to blame him for his lack of emotion, his apparent freedom from remorse since his brother's murder. She was willing, with one small part of her mind, to grant his justification in killing Jim, and she did not, from his viewpoint, at least, blame him for the deed, since he had committed it for her sake, and not for his own, and in these circumstances it was unselfish and justifiable; but he was not, she felt, acting now as a murderer should. He was too quiet, too self-contained and he would not even discuss the affair with her. She herself had, on the contrary, been prostrated with Jim's death, and she had not eaten for four days, while Andrew had gone about his ordinary routine of work and sleep as if nothing at all had happened. . . . If his passion for her had really been such an overwhelming thing, she argued to herself, then his grief now should

294

be an emotion commensurate in its effect with the love which had occasioned his crime. She thought of these things a great deal, balancing and arranging her thoughts in different sequences, as if she sought to find a mathematical formula which would include, within its compact symbols, all her mixed and contradictory reasoning.

She glanced at Andrew with new distaste as she thought of these things, her eyes narrowed and pitiless, her lips puffed out sourly. Her own idea of a murderer was a man with a haggard face and deeply circled eyes who trembled at the approach of strangers and who came, in his weakness, to the lap of his mother or the breast of his sweetheart, relieving himself in a flood of tears. At first her criticism was silent, and she strove to suppress it; later she spoke her thoughts openly, accusing him of his innate hardness and lack of human feelings.

"No other man will ever fool me the way you did," she said bitterly. "I thought you were tender-hearted and thoughtful of others. I thought you were high-minded and noble, but I see my mistake, now that it's too late. . . . Haven't you even got a conscience? Don't you grieve at all about Jim? I don't believe you've thought of him one time."

"How do you know what I think, or what I feel? If I haven't talked to you about Jim, it's because I knew it wouldn't be of any use. You wouldn't have the least idea of what I was trying to tell you. . . . I wish I could cry for four days, and not eat, and get the matter settled like you did. I wish to God that I could do it that easily. . . ."

He turned away, wondering why it was that he persisted in loving her. He saw her so completely, her unbending respectability, her intolerance, the obviousness of her evasions. He felt that compared with her dramatized, shallow sorrow, his own grief was an overpowering thing, and that she had perverted her emotions with the romances she had read, and the movies she had seen, that she could no longer understand such simple things as dignity or courage. He walked to the Delta Field and leaned against the fence, staring at the place where Jim was buried. He sighed, knowing the unalterable hold that Myrtle still had on him. "She's sweet," he thought in despair. "In spite of everything, she can be very sweet when she wants to be."

CHAPTER XXXV

THE days passed monotonously for Andrew, since he saw none of his old friends and since Myrtle avoided him so methodically. He would walk behind her, trying to reason with her, to make her see the inconsistencies in her behavior, but she would not even answer him; she would only stop occasionally, turn and stare and shrug her shoulders. He would shake his head and go away baffled. He lived entirely to himself during these weeks, and it was at this time that he began to write his poems again, as if, at last, he too distrusted the spoken word and its power to convince. He missed Edna a great deal, and he regretted, for his own sake, that she had gone to the Reedyville high school. She wrote to him occasionally, telling him of her plans, her progress and her new surroundings, and he answered at once, but his letters were concerned mostly with the routine matters of the farm, and were pieced out with small, chance bits of news that drifted his way. . . . Then he knew that it was spring once more, for beside the creek the spread, fan-like willows stood out again, breathless and withdrawn, and again the untrimmed, skeletal poplars lifted beyond the Cornells' fences, thin and brittle, like the upstanding bones of ancient fish around which mists of green and mauve settled with an infinite delicacy.

It was the anniversary of the day on which he had first met Myrtle, and he wanted to talk to her about it, and of the things which had happened to them since; but she gave him his breakfast silently, her hard, contemptuous eyes refusing to meet his own, and he could not say the things he wanted to, after all. He went to the barn and sat on the bench beside the door, thinking his depressed thoughts. It seemed to him that not twelve months, but an infinity of time, stretched between this moment and the moment when Addie Wrenn had introduced him to Myrtle; that all the things he had known before that meeting had been blotted from his life as of no importance. He closed his eyes, lowered his head and shuddered, for, as if to negative his thoughts, he saw again Jim's limp and swaying neck, his coy, half-closed eyes and the falling lock of his black hair. This unvarying sight was fixed forever before his eyes, and he knew that it would be there until the day that he died.

Myrtle spoke at his elbow: "You better start your ploughing. Old man McRae started a week ago and Harvey and Sam Cornells are already at work. If you don't start right away, people will begin to think that there's something funny going on." Her voice was short and impersonal, and when she finished she walked away, not waiting for his answer.

He shook his head, got up and went in the direction of the creek; but before he had gone far he turned and came back to the barn. He got out his plough, hitched his mule to it and began to work at the edges of the field; then he stopped and leaned against the fence, knowing at that moment the reason for his indolence and his delay. He dreaded the thought of ploughing over his dead brother's grave. It would be difficult for him even to approach the spot, and he had known that all along. He mopped his face and neck nervously with his handkerchief and resumed his work, his hands trembling a little; but he ploughed steadily all that day, and at dusk he went back to the house, heated water in the tank behind the stove and took a bath. When he had finished, emptied the water, and had put the tub back in its place, Myrtle came to his door and spoke, her voice unbelieving and furious.

"I just been down to the Delta Field and I saw what you've done. Are you crazy, Andrew? Have you taken leave of your senses? You better go back tomorrow and plough all of that field.

If you leave that patch in the middle, you might as well go tell everybody you killed Jim right now, and get it over with."

"That's what I might do any day," said Andrew. "I've thought about it for a long time now. I'd like to do it tonight, and clear my conscience."

"What's done is done," said Myrtle. "Giving yourself up won't help matters any." She went back to her kitchen and put supper on the table, and a few minutes later she came to the foot of the steps and called him. They ate in complete silence, avoiding each other's eyes, and after they had finished, and Myrtle was clearing the dishes away, Andrew went back to his room and sat at his desk. He took paper and pencil and began to write, hoping in that way to ease the pain that he felt, to banish Jim's face from his eyes. He worked for a long time, writing, erasing and writing again, but finally he copied what he had done on a sheet of paper. When he had polished it further, he would put the poem into the ledger that he kept locked in a drawer. His lips moved slowly as he read his own words:

This is my prayer, O my God, and it is a song for harps.

Hear it, Jehovah, and give me my beloved, for I cannot live without her:

I am caught in snares that I set for myself, and love gnaws continuously at my flesh.

There is no need, O Lord, to put out snares for Thy people:

We will snare our feet in a finer net, a net of our own weaving;

Nor is there need to condemn us, the guilty ones, nor to devise evil for the ending of our days:

We are our own judges and we are pitiless: we will damn ourselves unaided, and jealously perform our office,

We will pluck at the strings of our beings with fingers frozen against adversity.

This is my prayer, O my God, and it is a song for strings.

I charge Thee to give her to me, or to crush me with Thy foot.

Put the heel of Thy foot upon me, and press me again into the impersonal earth,

For then will my dust fly to her and blow about her head like a web of gnats;

My dust will circle her head like gnats that make a muted sound;

It will lift and settle against her breast, against the perfection of her flesh,

And though she turns from me, she will take me into her bosom with the air that she breathes. . . .

How can a man be saved, O God, when he is not alone himself;

When he is become, as well, all those who have touched him, the ones he has loved and hated?

For desire flows for a season toward Thy known world, and returns to the place of its birth,

And blocks its original springs: it is thus a man dies.

Then where shall we turn for our comfort, to whom shall we pray? Show us these things!

Where shall we find our lasting peace, at what altar? . . .

We are fleshed throughout with the flesh of others, the fibres of other loves are now ourselves;

We are shaped on the rooted bones of undiscoverable hate,

The trumpets of borrowed lusts blow continuously through us.

I am a trumpet shaped to the lips of my beloved:

Touch me with your lips and I will make my sound:

Blow your breath upon me and I will make a deep sound:

I will rise upward and shout: I will fill the sweet sky with my love;

I will reverberate in valleys and against hills with the clangor of iron!

We have taken the iron from Thy hills, the flint from Thy loveliest valley,

And shaped of it coffins for flesh, fitting our flesh to harsh coffins

Which we never designed for repose: we have lined them with nettles.

We are scored with the bruises of our narrow living; our knees are tattered with fury:

Our raiment is faded with our tears: It is thus that we live. . . .

Then give me my beloved, O my God, for I cannot live without her!

I hunger and I thirst for her: it is she alone that my soul seeketh!

Only she can quiet me, O my God! . . . Only she can ease me!

He went downstairs and stood outside Myrtle's locked door, tapping on the panel. "Myrtle," he pleaded. "Myrtle, let me in! . . . There's no sense in punishing me this way. It's useless. I'll take the blame for everything that's happened, but let me come in now. . . . We can talk things out together some way. Please, please try to be reasonable, my darling."

But she would only answer: "Go away! Go away! Haven't you got any shame left at all?" She turned on her back and stared into the darkness and thought of the way he had betrayed her, when, in her grief, she had in all innocence gone to him for comfort. She had trusted him. She had thought him finer than other men only to find with physical union that he was in reality as he had maintained, merely a man like any other, and on that basis he was intolerable to her. When he had left the door, she smoothed her pillow and went to sleep, for her own gnawing guilts became lighter in proportion to her ability to blame him and to convince herself of the justification of her condemnations. . . . She had known quite well what must occur between them when she went upstairs that night and she had wanted it; and she found it impossible now to forgive him for her own unworthy desire.

Later in the spring the people of Pearl County began again to be interested in the Tallon family, and Jim and his disappearance emerged once more as a topic of their conversation. Nobody could say definitely just who began the speculations once more, after the people themselves had considered the whole subject settled and exhausted of its interest, and there was no new material for them to work on, but it cropped up in a dozen different places at once, as if doubt had lain in their minds without their knowledge and had incubated, at last, after a required interval of time. They began to question this thing and that, piecing the story together, but nobody as yet believed that Jim was dead, and the total result of all the talk was merely that the relationship between Andrew and Myrtle was not so innocent, possibly, as they had at first surmised. . . . But Andrew and Myrtle, living their isolated lives, were not disturbed by this fresh harvest of rumors, because they did not even know of them.

In the late afternoon, when his work was finished, Andrew would go to the Delta Field, and stand with his arms resting on the fence, staring at the withered, last year's stalks and at the new green cotton that surrounded it. He watched fearfully the growth of the young cotton, speculating over his irrational conduct, and wondering why, after he and Myrtle had been at such pains to conceal the crime, that he now endeavored obliquely to disclose it. At last, in his perturbation, he began to doubt everything, to challenge each reason that came to his mind. He thought, then, of the minds of men and what strange inconsistent things they were. It seemed to him that his trouble lay in the fact that his life was now governed too completely by negative qualities, his emotions dammed with too many prohibitions, for he had, during the last weeks, discarded one by one the unifying parts of himself which had held him together and made him a human being. He turned away from the patch resolutely, thinking: "I feel as though I am lying in a ruin at my own feet, like Joe McIver's brick farmhouse after the tornado hit it. . . . I must start putting myself together again." He slapped his big hands against his overalls, wondering what the coming years held for him. His depression deepened, for the writing of his poems, which had brought him relief for a time, had come to an end; he had discarded such things, at last, as childish and of no importance in a world of reality.

CHAPTER XXXVI

Edna came home at Easter
to spend a few days of her vacation with her parents, and Andrew
went at once to see her. As he drove into the Cleaver yard, the
younger children, at the sound of his horn, came from behind
the house where they had been playing, ran to their uncle and
threw their arms about him, clinging to his legs and his waist.
He forgot for an instant his unending depression and began to
laugh.

"I suppose you come over to talk to Edna," said Effie. "It's the
only reason I can think of to make you come. . . . Well, she's
went down toward the gum thicket this morning right after
breakfast; but come in and sit down. She ought to be back any
minute." She turned crossly to her favorite: "Diana! Don't jump
up on your Uncle Andrew thataway. You'll muss his Sunday suit
all up. I'm ashamed of you for acting so boisterous—a big girl like
you, going on nine years old."

Andrew had caught up the baby, Lessie May, and raised her
high above his head. He relaxed his arms, as if he were going
to let her fall, staggered backwards a step or two and pretended
to catch her. Lessie May screamed with delight and clung to his
neck. "Swing me!" demanded Diana. "Swing me, too, Uncle
Andrew."

Andrew shook his head and laughed. "You're too big. You're
too heavy for me."

Diana stood looking sulkily at her uncle, scraping her foot in
the dust and watching her younger sister's pleasure. Suddenly
she lifted her lip with her thumb and forefinger and folded it

backward into a grotesque pucker. "Hoo hoo hig!" she grunted. "Hoo hoo hig!"

Effie and Asa both laughed outright. They had expected Andrew to laugh too, for, after all, Diana was just an unthinking child and she couldn't realize that she was being unkind; but Andrew, to their surprise, did not laugh. His muscles tightened and he braced himself as if he had been struck. His hand jerked upward automatically and covered his scarred lip in fear.

"Hoo hoo hig!" screamed Diana, elated at her success. "Hoo hoo hig!"

Andrew put Lessie May down and walked toward Asa. He sat on the steps, staring at his hands. Effie turned to her daughter. "I'll take care of you, miss, when I get you alone. You ought to be ashamed to mock your Uncle Andrew. . . . Do you think he can help talking that way?" She brought chairs from the house and presently they were seated on the porch. Effie had started talking to Andrew immediately of the thing that impinged the most on her mind.

"Jim's not acting right, and I'll be the first to say it! I was over at Mrs. Russ Dixey's house to a missionary social last week. They were all talking about Jim and Myrtle, and you too, for that matter, when I came in. Of course they changed the subject quick enough, but I wasn't fooled. After awhile Ellen Waters said to me as innocent as you please: 'It's funny the way Myrtle and Andrew go on living at the farm together, not seeing anybody and keeping away from the folks of the county, now ain't it?' And I said right back to her: 'I'd say that came under the general heading of *their* business!' Everybody laughed and then somebody else said, like the matter had come up for the first time: 'Oh, by the way! Have you heard from Jim since he quit his wife and run off to be a sailor?' and I said: 'Well, I haven't heard from him personally, but I'm sure his wife or Andrew has heard.'"

"I haven't heard from him," said Andrew. "Neither has Myrtle."

305

Asa spat into a flower bed patterned like a star in which spiced pinks were blooming. "Jim ought not to do the way he does, causing people to talk." He shrugged his thin shoulders. "Well, if they didn't have Jim and Myrtle to talk about, they'd talk about somebody else. I could never figure out why it is people can't mind their own business. . . . Why, just a day or so ago Mr. Johnny Everett and I were talking about the way people are talking about Jim and Myrtle, and their private business, and how it didn't concern them. I found out from Mr. Johnny a lot of things that I hadn't heard. It seems, for one thing, that the mill still owes Jim some pay. Jim hadn't been taking all his money when the rest of the hands got paid off, because he'd asked Mr. Everett to hold some of it out each week; so Mr. Johnny done what he asked him to do, but Jim never came back for his wages."

"Well, now," said Effie; "that *does* seem right funny, don't it?"

"There were two or three people around when Mr. Johnny was talking to me, and they heard what all he said. Mr. Dolan said it looked like Jim had made up his mind to run away a long time before he done it, and was caching his money until he got ready to go. Mr. Johnny said, yes, he figured that too; but after going to all that trouble, why would Jim up and leave his savings at the last minute? He said that Mr. Russell Hodge couldn't quit worrying about Jim, and if he wanted his old job back he could have it for the taking. He said to tell him that, if we knew where to write him at. He said tell Jim about the money, too, and where should they send it."

"It does seem funny about Jim going away and leaving his money behind," said Effie, as if emerging from deep thought. "That does seem right funny to me. . . . What do you think, Andrew?"

Andrew said: "I don't know. I haven't got any opinion one way or the other, because nobody could ever figure out what Jim was going to do at any one time." He got up from the steps. "I think

306

I'll go down toward the thicket and look for Edna. I got some things I want to talk to her about."

"Go right ahead!" said Effie. "Don't let Asa and me keep you." When he had passed out of earshot she spoke cautiously to Asa: "I didn't mention it a minute ago, but everybody is talking about the way Andrew has changed, too. He's not the same man he was a year ago. I feel strange with him all the time, like I never knew him before. Look at the way he acted a minute ago when Diana innocently took off his way of talking? You know as well as I do that ordinarily he'd have just laughed, and took it for a joke. Take the way he covers his mouth with his hand all the time. He's not like himself any more. He's got morbid it seems to me. He's changed, Asa."

"Everybody changes from time to time," said Asa mildly, "or at least some of them do, more or less, at longer or shorter intervals."

"It's that woman," said Effie. "She's the one that's done it. She wasn't content to just nag at Jim until he had to leave home, she's determined to ruin Andrew as well."

Asa said: "I think I'll go to the spring and get a bucket of cool water for dinner."

As Andrew turned from the road and set out in the direction of the trees, blue butterflies, as small as the thumbnail of a man rose upward beneath his feet in the dry, clear air like a cloud of lifting paper which fluttered its mass, flattened and fell again to the earth, its frail, individual elements quiet and separate once more. He called Edna's name and she answered at once. She came to the edge of the thicket and stood with her fingers marking her place in the book that she was reading. He went to her hurriedly, thinking how she had changed in the past months, for she was filling out with flesh and her old gawkiness was disappearing. The new clothes, which Ella had selected for her, were becoming,

307

and her limp, fine hair had been waved and arranged more softly about her head. When they were in the grove together, facing each other, sitting with their backs to individual trees, the more subtle changes in her became apparent, and it seemed to him that since the time he had seen her she had shed the last remnant of her childhood and had passed into complete and quiet maturity. She smiled and yawned comfortably and began to talk as if they had parted only the day before.

"I knew you'd come to see me right away, Uncle Andrew, so that's why I came down here and waited. I wanted to see you alone and not up at the house with the others." She did not wait for him to answer, but went on at once: "I've been reading a book on natural history, which Ella got for me from the library, while I was waiting for you, and I didn't know how time was passing." She held up the book so that he could verify its title, and laughed at some secret thought of her own, her locked hands pressed between her knees in her old manner. "Are you as crazy about Myrtle as ever, Uncle Andrew?"

"I suppose so. . . . Yes, I suppose so."

"Then you ought to read my book!" She laughed again and continued, in explanation: "My book is mostly about an insect called the mason-wasp. I thought at first that it must be something very rare, but from the pictures of it, it seems to be just a common, Alabama dirt-dauber after all. Anyway, in the spring, when the female gets ready to lay her eggs, she builds herself a house out of mud; but she's got to go through every action automatically from beginning to end, and if you divert her attention after she's once started work, or if you even move the nest she's building a foot or so to the right or left she can't pick up again where she left off. . . . Oh, no, she can't do that! She's got to start all over from the very beginning. When I read it, I kept being reminded of somebody, but I couldn't think who; then finally it dawned on me and I said to myself: 'That's Myrtle all over! That's the way Myrtle is!' "

Andrew raised his hand and covered his lips. "You never were fair to Myrtle, were you? She can be very sweet, when she wants to be. It's a side of her you don't know."

"That's what *you* think, Uncle Andrew," she said gaily; "but then *your* views on the subject are as prejudiced as mine! . . . From now on she'll always be just a respectable dirt-dauber to me, a lady dirt-dauber trying to get her house built in the one way that she knows to make it." She stopped and looked quickly into his pained, serious eyes. She had not examined him carefully before, her mind being still occupied with her book, but now that she saw him more closely, she, in turn, was surprised at the changes a few months could make in people. "I didn't mean to hurt your feelings," she said. "You know I'd be the last person in the world to do that." He shook his head helplessly and turned his face away.

"You're in trouble of some sort," said Edna at last. "I won't ask you any questions, but you know you have my support, no matter what it is. If you want to tell me anything, please do it."

He shook his head again, but he would not answer.

"You can trust me, of course. But you knew that, anyway."

He said: "Yes. Yes, I knew that." For a moment he was tempted to tell her everything, to relieve the guilty pressure that he felt so constantly, but he would not. . . . She was young, and she had troubles enough of her own, he thought; he would not burden her with his. "I'm just nervous and upset," he said finally. "I'm upset about Jim, particularly since Myrtle has turned against me now, and blames me for everything that's happened. . . . I've just about reached the end of my rope." She got up and came to him, knelt down and kissed his cheek, in one of her rare demonstrations of affection. He rose to his knees and put his arms about her, his head resting on her shoulder. He began to tremble.

"It's not hard to understand your feelings, Uncle Andrew. I know exactly how you feel. In fact everybody in the county seems to be taking an interest in Uncle Jim's running away. . . . Well, they've got very little on their minds, it seems to me! It's all I've heard since I got back. Nobody seems to know what happened, and I suppose you don't either, or you would have told me before I went away to school—not that I'm especially interested in Uncle Jim or what he does—but they're trying to turn it into some sort of a mystery now. . . . Mamma keeps going over and over the little she knows."

Then, before she realized what had happened, Andrew was stretched on the ground at her feet, crying with a gasping sound, his body shaken with grief. She lay beside him, her arms about his neck. She, too, began to cry, although she did not know for what reason. Andrew said: "I killed Jim. I murdered him. . . . I've wanted to tell somebody for a long time. I came to see you this morning hoping that I'd be able to tell you, but decided against it." He began to talk rapidly, sketching the events at the farm during the weeks preceding Christmas with the parrot-like precision of a man who has rehearsed events for a long time and sifted them down to their ultimate meanings. He told of the trip to Dr. Kent, of the velvet coat and the Christmas tree. He spoke of the Cornells' stallion and of Jim's brutality to Myrtle. . . . And Edna listened in silence, her cheek pressed against his own, but weaving above his words, and mixing with them, were her own thoughts: "This is the first real test that has ever been put on my character. I wonder what I'm going to do? I wonder if I'll faint, or anything like that, before he finishes telling about how he and Myrtle buried him. . . . When he has finished I'll know how I behave in emergencies. . . ."

Andrew was silent at last and waited for her condemnation,

310

but she only said: "I understand it, Uncle Andrew. I can see clearly enough why you did it. . . . You can depend on me to stand by you, no matter what happens."

"I've been over and over it, until I'm almost crazy, trying to find excuses for myself; but I haven't succeeded very well. . . . I tell myself that it isn't like I really meant to kill Jim; it's more like an accident, because I was so worn out I didn't know what I was doing at the time." He sat up against the tree and wiped his face with his sleeve. "I've thought a lot about that doctor in Morgantown who was up three nights with a patient trying to save his life, but at last he was so tired and confused that he gave the man the wrong medicine and he died. . . . Nobody thought the doctor was guilty of murder; they only said he'd been careless. He was convicted in court of being careless, but that's the worst they could say about him. . . ."

"I'll stick by you," said Edna. "You can rely on me." She had taken the first shock of his confession, and already its impact was beginning to go away, already she was accepting the situation without further comment or questioning. They were both silent for a long time. Edna said: "I suppose you know that I love you more than anybody in the world, even more than I do Bessie, and I always will. I don't blame you for what you did. I think you were justified, but even if I did blame you, it wouldn't make any difference. . . . I think I know what's on your mind now. You want to give yourself up."

"Yes. Yes. That's what I think about all the time."

"Don't do it! You've been punished enough already; there's no sense in suffering more. . . . We'll think up something together. We'll find a way out. You've got me now to talk things over with." She stopped and sighed, for she feared that what she was asking of him was useless.

They heard Effie's shrill voice calling from the field, summoning them to dinner, but Andrew knew that he could not face her again or listen to her questions about Jim. He got up quickly and walked through the grove in the direction of his own farm, and Edna stood watching him, not bothering to answer her mother's shouts. Already she was thinking of what was best to be done and planning a course of action.

CHAPTER XXXVII

F<small>ROM</small> her kitchen window
Myrtle saw him as he turned in at the oak grove and approached
the house. He had not told her where he was going, but, knowing
that Edna was at home, she assumed that he would be with her,
and the thought filled her with resentment, as if she wished to
punish him not only with the ending of her own companionship,
but through the withdrawal of all human contacts as well. She
had eaten her dinner alone, since he was absent, and she stood
washing the dishes she had soiled, and the pots she had used in
cooking. Andrew came into the kitchen and stood behind her,
but he did not speak at once. "I put your dinner in the oven to
keep hot," said Myrtle. "If you want it, that's where it is."

The heat from the stove had brought perspiration on her body.
Her armpits were damp with her sweat, and two irregular islands
of moisture stained her shoulders. Her damp dress adhered to her
skin and followed limply the line of her body. As Andrew stood
watching her, she turned from the dishpan to the table, bending
above it, and as she did so her breasts, as firm and erect as pine
cones, lifted upward and came sharply into relief. Andrew drew
back at the sight of her breasts and stood with his cheek pressed
against the panel of the door. His heart was beating too rapidly
and his throat felt tight and miserable.

"I've been over to see Edna," he said at length. "She's almost
a grown woman now. She's filled out a lot, and high school has
quieted her down. You'd hardly know her."

"Your dinner's in the oven," said Myrtle. "I left a place for you
on the table."

"What makes you treat me the way you do?" asked Andrew

desperately. "I'm a human being too. Don't you think that I've got any feelings? Do you think you're the only person who can suffer?"

She put down the aluminum pot which she had scoured to mirror-like brightness, and which she had partially dried with her cloth, turned for the first time and spoke sullenly: "If you don't like this arrangement, I'm ready to break it up when you are. . . . If you don't like it, just say so."

Andrew said: "I'll eat my dinner now." He went to the table upon impulse and picked up the scoured pot, moving it a little beyond her reach. "Your dinner's in the oven, like I told you," said Myrtle; "you won't find it there on the table." He walked around her to the oven and stood for a moment looking at her damp back, at the firm, beautiful line of her legs. Myrtle shook her head sullenly, picked up the clean pot, put it into the pan and scoured it again. Then she lifted it out of the water, rinsed it, and dried it carefully. When she had finished the operation and had hung the pot on its nail, Andrew began to laugh. "It's something Edna told me," he explained. "It's only one of Edna's jokes. I thought she was exaggerating at first, but I can see her point now, and I think she's right."

When his dinner was on the table, Myrtle came to see that everything was all right and stood at his side. "It's none of my business what you do with yourself, but you're crazy if you see too much of Edna. You know how nosey she is, and how she tries to find out things. Well, the first thing you know she'll be putting two and two together."

"That won't be necessary. She won't have to go to that trouble, because she knows all about it. I told her today."

"You fool!" shouted Myrtle. "You fool! Haven't you got any sense at all? You need a keeper and a straitjacket, that's what you need. . . . Don't you know she'll spread it over the county before night?"

"No," said Andrew. "I don't know that, because it's not true. . . . But even if she did, what difference does it make?" He leaned his arms on the table and bowed his head. "I'd like nothing better than to end this misery that I live in."

"What about me?" asked Myrtle angrily. "Do you think I want everything drug out before the eyes of Pearl County. What about me?"

"Don't, Myrtle," he said. "Please don't. I can't stand very much more."

In May Andrew received a short, noncommittal note from Edna, and he went on the night appointed to Reedyville to see her. She met him at the door and they went into Ella's parlor and sat facing each other. She explained briefly before talking of more serious matters that Ella was away for the evening, this being the night on which her literary club met, and they were alone in the house. He was surprised, again, at how grown up she appeared to be; possibly it was the way that she now wore her hair, or the lengthening of her skirts; but when she began to talk, his slight feeling of unfamiliarity with her disappeared. She came to the point at once. She thought it best to tell him of her reasons for the visit as quickly as possible, and get that behind them. She hoped that he would approve of her actions, for she had been very discreet, and this in substance was what she had done: She had thought of him a great deal since she had seen him in the gum thicket and of the things he had told her, wondering what was the best thing to be done. As a result she had decided to learn something about criminal law and the rules of evidence, at least superficially, and during the weeks since she had seen him, she had ploughed through all the textbooks she could find and had read many decisions. But she was not willing to trust her own conclusions, so she had gone for advice to Milton Overbeck, who was not only considered the best criminal lawyer in the county, but was, fortunately for her plans, an admirer of Ella's as well, and she saw him often when he called. At first she had merely asked general questions, and he had answered them thoroughly, since they were good friends and he took an interest in her. Then later she began clipping newspaper reports of crimes, assembling the facts and submitting them to him to see if he agreed with her own conclusions. "There wasn't any real sense in taking such precautions, Uncle Andrew," she said gravely; "because Milton wouldn't have doubted my motives or been surprised at anything I took up to study. . . . It's one of the advantages of being considered eccentric."

"Yes," said Andrew. "Yes."

"Well, after awhile I submitted the facts that you gave me, changing them as little as possible and disguising them just enough to prevent his remembering them, no matter what happened later on. I decided *against* you in my report and furnished all the arguments I could to see what he'd say. I wanted his decision to be as clearcut as possible."

"What did the lawyer say?" asked Andrew eagerly. "How did he decide it?"

"That's the encouraging part, Uncle Andrew, because Milton said if the facts were the way I read them in the paper, it was ten to one that no grand jury would even indict the man, but if they did indict him, it wouldn't be for first degree murder. He said if he were a prosecuting attorney, he wouldn't take up his time with such a case, particularly if the wife was as pretty as I said her picture showed her to be. If the man was actually brought to trial, he would be acquitted, in his opinion, but if the worst came to the worst, the most the man need expect would be a few years in prison." Edna paused and added seriously: "I'm not in favor of your confessing at all, and I don't see what good can be served by even spending a few years or months for that matter in prison, but I'm telling you this, hoping that it will help you and make you

316

feel more at rest. It's best to know the worst that could happen. You can't go beyond that."

He got up and walked to the window, comforted deeply, for the unending picture of his execution which stood before his eyes had softened. Edna laughed suddenly in her wry, triumphant manner. "So Milton decided against me, and destroyed all my arguments. He warned me of the dangers of too much book knowledge, and said I'd be better off if I could be less academic and more practical."

Andrew sat down after a moment and began to talk slowly: "I'm in sympathy with your ideas, Edna, and I always have been, but I've been thinking that just having plenty to eat and wear and fair working conditions is not the *most* important thing, after all. It seems to me that people's minds are sicker than anything else about them, and if our mental sicknesses could be taken away, then hunger and injustices and the other lesser evils would be taken away without further effort. That's the way it seems to me now."

"I don't know, Uncle Andrew. That's a thing I haven't gone into yet."

"I've been wondering if there are people in the world who understand about such things," he said in his cloudy, gasping voice. "If there are, I want to know about them too. . . . I figure that my life is over, so far as I'm concerned, no matter whether I go to prison or not; and from now on I want to devote myself to mankind. It doesn't matter what happens to me if I can bring peace to others." He stopped self-consciously, afraid that his words sounded romantic and silly to Edna's more practical ears, but she looked at him gravely.

"I don't know," she repeated, "but I'll ask Ella about it. If Ella doesn't know, I'll write Bessie. Bessie will be sure to know."

When he returned and had put up his automobile, he went to the Delta Field and stood with his arms resting on the fence, staring at the place where Jim was buried. "If I confess, maybe I can start my studies in prison right away. I understand prisoners have a lot of privileges these days. I'd confess tonight, and get it over with, if it weren't for Myrtle. I don't want to selfishly drag her into this mess." He stopped and turned to the unploughed patch. "Jim!" he said. "Jim! I'm doing all I can to make it up to you."

He decided that he was living too much to himself, that from now on he would meet his friends once more, for it was his isolation from his fellows that he found the most difficult to bear. He would take up his old life as completely as possible, and his first act would be to resume his visits to Tarleton's store, where the county people congregated on Saturday afternoons. He sighed and wiped his face roughly with his hands. His long talk with Edna had quieted his fears somewhat and had brought him peace.

One Saturday afternoon in June, Andrew shaved and changed his overalls for the suit he wore on special occasions. He put on the shirt that Myrtle had washed and ironed for him that morning and had laid out on his bed. He came cautiously down the stairs at length, buttoning his shirt, and paused at the foot of the stairs. Myrtle was on her hands and knees scrubbing the kitchen floor, and as he stood watching her, she began an old love song which rose thin and clear to the rhythm of her rasping brush. She stopped her song and straightened up, raising her arm and pressing back a strand of black hair which had fallen into her eyes, for she was letting her hair grow again and it had reached a difficult length. When she had arranged the lock in its place and had secured it with a pin, she took up her song again. Andrew came into the high-ceilinged kitchen and listened hopefully, for this was the first time Myrtle had sung since Jim's death, and he considered the singing a good omen.

As if knowing that she was being watched, Myrtle broke off her

318

song and turned, looking at him contemptuously. Instantly he raised his hand and covered his mouth in confusion, an uncertain, pleading look on his face. A wedge of sunlight came strongly into the room through a window set high in the wall. The other windows had all been closed, and the shades drawn, against the heat and the dust from the road, and in the semi-darkness of the kitchen the wedge-like slope of light was distinct and fluid. In it midges drifted or leaped upward, as if under the propulsion of minute springs, hung suspended for an instant and fell again, after their brief vibrations, to their original places. He spoke at last from the shelter of his cupped palm: "I've got to be getting along to Tarleton's now. Would you like me to bring back anything special?"

Myrtle made no reply, no acknowledgment that she had heard him, but she walked across the room and took from the kitchen cupboard the list she had prepared that morning of the groceries and the household necessities for the coming week, and laid it on the table. Andrew took the list without looking at it and folded it to exact squares, his eyes still fixed on his brother's wife; and Myrtle turned back to her work, annoyed at his unvarying slowness, anxious for him to go, but her face was set and without expression. Suddenly her lips puffed outward and twisted in a circular movement, as if the tight muscles of her mouth expressed in pantomine those things which her tongue found too bitter for words. She threw her arms outward in a harsh gesture, walked to the door and seated herself on the steps to scan the road, her eyes as hard and watching as the undecided eyes of a water fowl. Andrew remained in the room for a time looking at her, hoping that she would miraculously relent at last; then he sighed, picked up his hat and walked into the yard.

The noonday heat lay close to the blossoming cotton. Waves of refracted light shimmered upward from the fields toward a horizon that seemed to waver and collapse and reform itself before his eyes. Around him was the garden that Myrtle cultivated, and phlox, larkspur and cockscomb were blooming in beds. The heat lay all about him, and from the Reedyville road to the left clouds of red dust rose upward as people drove past to Tarleton's store. He stood with his eyes half closed in the bright glare and surveyed the familiar scene for a moment before he opened the gate and closed it behind him with a faint clanging of iron, a dull rasp of chains, and went to the barn.

A mixed smell of ammonia, corn fodder and overripe sand-pears reached his nostrils as he stood blinded in the dusk, between the lances of hard light that fell between the chinks in the walls. Old Babe walked stiffly toward him at the sound of his step and rubbed her nose against his sleeve, smelling him. He stroked the flanks of the old mare and talked to her softly.

"You remember Jim, don't you?" he asked. "You still remember Jim?"

He led the old mare into the sunlight and stood adjusting the harness across her graying back. When he had finished, and had guided her between the shafts of the buggy, he raised his eyes and looked again at the road vibrating in the heat, and at the puffs of red dust, like blown smoke, which rose under the hoofs of the teams and settled above the crêpe-myrtle trees, turning their leaves the color of powdered bricks. He saw an automobile, battered and badly in need of paint, drive in from the road and approach the house through the grove of liveoaks; and he knew that Effie and her husband had come to visit them again for the first time in months. Myrtle was still seated on the steps, staring at nothing at all, but when she, too, saw that Effie and Asa were approaching, she got up quickly and put her brush and scrubbing bucket away. Andrew led Babe into the shade and tied her to a ring. He walked to the gate and swung it wide, without raising his eyes, at the exact moment the automobile reached it.

320

"How do, all," said Asa. "Howdy do."

"Don't go to any trouble," said Effie stiffly. "I made Asa bring me over as I only wanted to put flowers on Papa's grave. Maybe you've forgotten it, but today is the anniversary of his death." Her voice was formal and somewhat injured, for she felt that Andrew and Myrtle had slighted her during the past months and that they no longer welcomed her at the farm.

"I hadn't forgotten the anniversary, Effie. I thought of it the first thing when I got up this morning. I've been thinking about it all day."

Effie walked toward the house, her fat legs spread apart and bowed outward against the trickle of her sweat, her children and her husband behind her. When they reached the steps, Myrtle came out to greet her visitors. She had changed her dress and combed out her hair. Effie hesitated a moment, not quite knowing what course to take, and then waddled over to Myrtle and the two women kissed. She felt, at least, that the Tallon family owed Myrtle something in recompense for the shame that Jim had cast upon her, even if she did shut herself away from her friends and from the family. They sat in rocking-chairs on the porch and Effie fanned herself with a palmetto fan. Perspiration rolled down her cheeks and lay undrained between the ridges of her flesh. She wore her hair piled high on her head, and at the nape of her neck tendrils of her damp hair, black with reddish lights in it, curled moistly against her parboiled skin.

The Cleaver children were playing in the oak grove by the gate. They had gathered pieces of broken crockery and tin cans, and Bud was keeping store. Their shrill voices, as they argued, could be plainly heard. Andrew got up from his chair.

"I've got to be getting along to Tarleton's," he said. He unhitched old Babe, got into the buggy and slapped her with the slack reins as she moved stiffly through the gate, in the direction

321

of the Reedyville road. Effie called suddenly to him in her shrill voice:

"Oh, yes, I almost forgot to tell you. Edna's back home for the summer. She said to give you her regards and tell you she'd be over one day before long."

CHAPTER XXXVIII

OLD Babe jogged through the mist-like, settling dust, while the sun beat steadily upon the road and the wheels of the buggy threw geysers of red sand into the air with the soft, kissing noise of wrapping paper rubbed against hemp. Andrew leaned back in his seat, the reins limp in his hands, and looked about him at the old cut-over land which had once belonged to his father, thinking again of the tangled past. He sighed, took out a handkerchief and wiped his neck and face, his eyes lifting to the sky, beyond the mutilation that surrounded him. He was curiously preoccupied with the past this afternoon; he could not shake the power of the past from him, and as he sat in the buggy he thought of many old, vague things that lay in his mind to trouble him, but he thought mostly of his father, this being the anniversary of his death.

He was so preoccupied with his thoughts that he did not realize that Babe, missing his guiding hand, had, in the confusion of her blindness, stopped in her uncertainty and pulled to the left of the road. She kept twitching her hide to the ghost-like, orchestral accompaniment of her bowels and stretching out her stiff, tentative neck toward the roadside, as if she smelled the grass that grew there. Andrew sat up straight and shook his head to dispel the old, unbidden memories which clamored within him, and spoke aloud to the dusty landscape: "Why is everything so mixed up in the simplest life? Why is it that people cannot live together for the shortest time without getting tangled in each other's emotions?"

At his words old Babe hunched her shoulders forward and pulled toward the road, but Andrew touched the reins lightly and she stopped again. He realized all at once that he had been deceiving himself, for he did not want to go to Tarleton's, after all, nor did he want to meet or mix again with the people who would be there buying their supplies and exchanging gossip. After a long time he was aware that somebody was sounding an automobile horn, and that somebody was calling his name over and over in a frail, acid-like voice. He shook himself, and with an effort came back to the present to realize that Ed Wrenn and his wife, Addie, had driven up behind him in the road and had stopped. Addie Wrenn laughed her remote, dead laugh. "I declare, Andrew, your mind must have been about a thousand miles away."

"Yes, ma'am." He lowered his eyes in confusion. He noticed that the old mare had pulled across the road and had blocked it. He straightened her out. "I must have been daydreaming. I wasn't thinking where I was."

Ed Wrenn started his car again, and Addie called out above the sound of the rushing engine: "I wouldn't worry so much, Andrew. Everything will come out all right in time."

The Wrenns drove off with a jerk, clouds of smoke-like dust rising from the roadbed and drifting through the tops of the trees. Andrew watched them until they were out of sight and then slapped old Babe on her haunches with the slack reins. He came to the bend in the road at length and saw before him the familiar scene of Tarleton's store on a Saturday afternoon: Men sat lazily on the steps of the store, yawning in the bright sunlight, coughing, clearing their throats and spitting at intervals, their women standing apart in groups, gossiping, while below them pigs grunted contentedly, imbedded in the hot dust, and plough-horses crossed their forelegs and slumped, saddened at the absence of familiar burdens. To the left, in the Tarleton yard, a flock of penned guinea fowl stuck out their red and white, clown-like heads and made a sound which resembled equally the creaking of a strap and the croaking of a frog.

When Andrew had tied the old mare, he came through the Tarleton yard and approached the store from the rear. Before he could distinguish individual words, he heard a confused babble of talk from within the store, talk so hollow and confused that it seemed to come from excited people in the center of the earth, people who shouted upward together through wells. Finally the tinkling, insistent voice of Addie Wrenn detached itself from the subterranean blur of other voices and he stopped close to the store and listened.

"There he was with old Babe blocking the road, sitting in his buggy like a man asleep. Ed sounded his horn and we both called him a dozen times before he even knew we were there."

Bertha Snowdon, who worked in the store on Saturdays, spoke: "There's something funny about the way Andrew and Myrtle have been acting: the way they've shut themselves up together, avoiding other people. I can't figure it out though. Sometimes I say to myself Andrew's got his head so far in the clouds that he hasn't got enough sense left to know what's going on under his nose."

"I always thought Andrew had plenty of *book* sense," said Addie Wrenn in a diplomatic voice.

"Maybe so, but you can't tell me that a grown man who wrote the dirty foolishness he did when he was going with Myrtle Bickerstaff is all there. You can't tell what's going on between them now."

Miss Sarah Tarleton, who wrote verses herself, bridled a little. "I'm afraid I disagree with you, Bertha. After all, many gentlemen in the past have written verses to their sweethearts and nobody thought the less of them for it."

"I can't understand why Myrtle would grieve so, or pretend to grieve so, over Jim leaving her," said Mrs. Tote Dowling. "It looks to me like she'd be glad to get shut of him; he treated her shameful enough, Lord knows! . . . I even heard he beat her, but

I can't say that of my own knowledge. Anyway, it looks to me like she's finding plenty of consolation in Andrew now, no matter what she thought of him before."

"Well, Mrs. Dowling," began Sarah, "I guess Myrtle really loved her husband; I guess she was always hoping that the better side of his nature would reveal itself one day."

Old Mrs. MacLean, standing alone, chewing her snuff-brush, started to speak, but changed her mind. She could clear up many of these points, she felt, but only at the expense of her daughter's good name. She would remain silent, and she would see that May continued to remain silent. The matter did not concern them. May wasn't going to be mixed up in this if she could avoid it.

"There's some sort of funny arrangement going on just the same," insisted Bertha. "Say what you please! People don't act that way just because a man runs off to sea."

As Andrew stood by the window listening, his face was drawn with pain and his small, blue eyes fluttered and closed slowly. For a moment the conversation became general as Lafe McRae and his family entered the store, and then the Tallons and their eccentricities emerged again as the dominant theme of the afternoon.

"I used to think that old man Lemuel Tallon could do some strange things, and Bradford wasn't no slouch, either, once he got started, but I do believe to my soul that Andrew beats them all for plain foolishness." Russ Dixey cleared his throat. "Guess what he's done with the Delta Patch this year?" Without waiting for an answer he continued: "My brother Ike told me about it, but I wouldn't believe him. So we went back and I seen for myself. Andrew has ploughed and planted the Delta Patch only around the *edges* this year, and right in the middle of the field he left a square of last year's stalks. Don't ask me why he done it, because that's what Ike and me have been asking each other ever since."

326

Andrew, eavesdropping, heard these things and had a sudden wish to run away through the pine woods, not to enter the store at all. A slow, tearing fear started at his heart and spread evenly in waves throughout his body. His clothes seemed oppressive, binding him and his breathing, and he kept flexing his muscles to relieve some inward, urgent pressure. He leaned against the side of the store, his hands clasped together, making his grunting, pig-like sound.

"Jim didn't have any particular enemies at the time he left who wished him harm, did he?" asked Holm Barrascale. "If he did, I never heard of them."

"What puzzles me," said Rafe Hall, "is nobody seen him after he left the mill on Saturday. I was in Reedyville about a week ago and I saw Ellis Nobles, the conductor on the Pearl River Special. Ellis was asking about some of the old boys, amongst them Jim. I told him that Jim had run off and left his wife. 'Where did he go to?' asked Ellis. 'I don't know,' I said; 'but he told some of the boys at the mill beforehand that he was going to Mobile and ship out as a seaman on the steamship *Afoundria* if he could get a job.' "

" 'Well, how did he get to Mobile without riding by train to the junction?' asked Ellis.

" 'I never thought of that,' I said. 'Didn't Jim ride with you that night he left?'

" 'No,' said Ellis. 'I haven't seen Jim Tallon since one night last fall. There was a bunch of us at George Stratton's place that night and we all laughed and told stories.' "

At that point Andrew came into the store, and there was immediately a complete silence. He walked to Bertha with his head lowered, his feet shuffling across the boards. He gave her the list that Myrtle had prepared, turned and smiled feebly at the people who surrounded him. Outside the June sun beat without mercy, and the fields, framed in the doorway, shimmered in heat; but in the store it was dim and cool with the musty tang of calico, axle-grease and apples.

Bertha straightened up and began checking the list, putting each item on the counter. At last the order was filled and Andrew picked up the supplies before him, turned and walked to the door. When he reached it, he faced his audience and tried to smile re-assuringly, but fear came over him again and he shivered. He walked back into the store as if he had lost all sense of direction, turned again in confusion, and in confusion retreated again. When he found the door at last, he lunged into the sunlight as if strug-gling through water; but he stopped when he came once more to the window and stood by it listening.

Bertha Snowdon said: "You see? You see what I mean about Andrew?"

Alice Barrascale spoke: "When I was just a little girl there was a woman named Douglas who lived in the south part of the county. Her husband trapped muskrats in the swamps around Pearl River and when he was drunk, or feeling plain onery, he beat her. Sometimes it was so bad she couldn't move off her pallet for a week. I remember my mother and her sisters talking about it. Well, one day this woman ups and kills her husband with the hatchet he used for cutting hickory poles."

There was a sharp sound of breath and then complete silence.

"People who say such things ought to be ashamed of them-selves!" said Addie Wrenn. "I won't have any part in it, and you all ought to be ashamed even to listen. . . . Myrtle has had enough to put up with as it is. I still consider Myrtle my friend, and I won't listen to such talk."

"Alice hasn't said anything about Myrtle," said Miss Sarah soothingly. "In fact, she didn't once mention Myrtle's name. She was talking about something that happened a long time ago."

328

Mrs. Wrenn said, after a moment: "I apologize to you, Alice. My mind must have been wandering."

Andrew, listening by the window, turned quickly, the roof of his mouth dry, his tongue feeling thick and swollen. He walked to the post where he had tethered the old mare, untied her quickly and began to slap her rump nervously with the slack reins. He was astonished at the things he had heard and seen, at the nearness of the gossiping people to truth, for he had not known, in his isolation, how much talk there had been, nor how far his neighbors had progressed in their speculations. As he turned from the lane and into the road again, it seemed to him that the county arranged and rearranged their known facts as if they played earnestly at anagrams, and that very soon now the proper sequence of events, the unifying and missing parts, would come to them, and his crime would stand inevitably revealed. This knowledge frightened him, for although he had considered confession for a long time, he had not quite accepted it; now it suddenly appeared to be inescapable.

CHAPTER XXXIX

A T four o'clock the heat's force had somewhat abated, but the sun was still high in the sky. Andrew reached the grove of oaks to the left of his home and turned in from the road. Asa Cleaver saw him and hurried down the walk to open the gate, and stood wiping his face with his handkerchief. Andrew drove into the yard and stopped before the barn. He unhitched old Babe and she went through the door obediently, and Andrew followed her. He guided her to her stall. He put his arms about her throat and patterned her straggly mane into a gray loop which hung sidewise on her neck, shaping the tilted loop and letting it fall again. He clung to the old mare tightly, and Babe nuzzled his shoulder with her lips as if she understood his emotion and would quiet him. He said: "You remember Jim? . . . You still remember Jim, don't you?"

The Cleaver children were running through the grove of trees and down the slope that led to the creek, shouting in their sharp voices. Beside them raced Tobey, the mongrel hound, whose bark was baritone and dignified, and Benny, a new fox terrier, who yipped shrilly an inch behind their flying heels. Some distance back of the children, Effie and Myrtle walked with their arms full of the flowers they had gathered. Effie was holding the flowers away from her body and shaking her shoulders at intervals, endeavoring to separate the sodden cloth from her perspiring back. They were going to the Tallon burying ground, a fenced plot shaded by willows, which lay on the knoll overlooking the creek. Andrew, from his post by the barn, stood watching them until they reached the cemetery and opened the whitewashed gate. The racing children stopped, the dogs became silent of a sudden, and there was no sound in the hot, June air except the noise that Babe made as she crunched corn with her worn teeth and the contented, minor cluck of hens immersed in their baths of dust. All about him in the fields the young cotton was grayish-green, one precise, unvarying shade, and it rippled occasionally under the hot breeze that came intermittently from the direction of the creek.

Effie's surprise was genuine when she reached the burial plot and saw that not one weed obtruded on the graves of her people; that the aisles between the mounds had been swept recently with a brush-broom, and that white sand from the creek had been scattered on the walk; that against the fence, phlox and blue larkspur, which Myrtle had planted herself, were blooming together in one narrow bed. She entered the burying ground solemnly and seated herself on a bench. The graves stretched before her, more than a dozen of them, calm and untroubled. She bent forward on the small bench and began to arrange her flowers, her children squirming beside her uncomfortably. Myrtle had not entered the graveyard. She stood at the gate with her face turned toward the creek, as if some inborn delicacy forbade her looking at grief which she could not share. Presently Effie spoke to her, her voice somewhat surprised, as if she had expected the burial plot to be fallen to pieces and grown over with weeds.

"You're a real sweet woman, Myrtle."

"It's nothing more than right for me to take care of the graves of Jim's people."

"I wouldn't say that you owed us Tallons much love, if you asked me," said Effie. Then more indignantly: "I don't know what came over Jim to make him treat you the way he did. He ought to be ashamed of himself for the way he acted, and if I knew where he is now I'd write him a letter and tell him so."

Turning to her bored children she added: "Bud! Diana!" . . . You all go down to the creek and play in the white sand where

Mamma used to play when she was a little girl; but don't get wet. Take Lessie May along too, if she wants to go, but don't leave her go wading." The children, who had been sitting silent and depressed, scurried to the gate and presently they ran down the slope of the hill that led to the creek. There was a silence between the women, after they had gone, until Myrtle spoke, weighing her words carefully as if she were voicing something important for all people to hear: "I want Jim back! It don't make any difference now how mean he treated me!" She opened the gate and walked toward Effie, and Effie got up and took her in her arms.

"Why, honey, don't cry that way. Everything is going to come out all right in the end."

"I want Jim back!" She stood with her face lost in Effie's bosom. "I want him back! I want him back so bad!"

"I know how you feel, Myrtle, and he's coming back to you too. Don't you worry so much. Before the year's out he'll be right here again asking you to forgive him for what he done."

Myrtle said: "I'll never see him again, Effie, and I can't stand the thought of it."

"Now, honey, that's right foolish, and you know it. Jim's coming back to you. I know Jim right well, and you can believe what I say."

"Nobody knows what I went through, Effie. I never told a soul. I said I'd never tell anybody, and I didn't either."

At that moment the women heard Asa Cleaver's voice and the grunting, pig-like voice of Andrew. Myrtle wiped her eyes and sat upright quickly. Her mood of abasement had passed. Her eyes became hard again and watching. Effie spoke to Andrew with mild indignation. "It's a shame you haven't told Myrtle more about your own kin. It really is!"

The graves of the Tallons, mathematically precise, were lying before them. Grass grew thick and green over each of them, unhindered by marble, as grass should grow over every grave. At the

332

head of each mound, a wooden slab recited briefly the biography of the particular bones that it shadowed, and around the margins of the plots, there were lavender and pink seashells which had been carried inland from the Gulf. Effie got up, pulling her damp dress outward from her body and began to arrange the flowers on her father's grave, talking all the while of him and of the others who lay beside him. Her husband yawned and stretched himself, wearied with family matters which he knew by heart.

"That's Bradford's grave," continued Effie. "When they brought him back from France, Mamma wanted to have just a simple funeral, a short sermon and a prayer, and maybe Willie Oakshot to sing a song, but Papa wanted a band from Reedyville and guns fired. Papa almost died himself when the men brought Bradford's casket through the gate. He cried steady for a day and a night and wouldn't talk or answer questions. Finally he told Mamma to do whatever she wanted to. So Mamma had a few people come over who had loved Bradford when he was alive, and Preacher Boutwell spoke and said a prayer. But Papa wouldn't come to the graveside after all. Papa was a happy-natured man who liked to joke and laugh; he couldn't stand sadness of any sort; it tore him all to pieces. . . . That morning when folks started to come to the service, Papa got drunk, and while the Reverend Boutwell was speaking over Bradford's coffin, we could all hear Papa in the house crying and smashing dishes."

Myrtle sat quietly on the bench and rested her face in her palms, but she did not listen to her sister-in-law. A hot wind had risen from the creek and the blossoming cotton, quick and exact, bent beneath it in one direction. Across the creek, in the direction of the Cornells' farm, cows with tinkling bells were crossing at Gentry's ford. Then a Negro woman passing down the lane laughed in a voice as deep and as rich as the earth; and in the swamp, a long way off, two hounds bayed in different keys. . . . These sounds, blended and yet separate, came through the still afternoon and reached Myrtle's ears across the drone of Effie's endless recollections. They came blurred and sweetened with their remoteness, as if they had been filtered through gauze. But Myrtle was hardly aware of the sounds about her. She rested her head against the crêpe-myrtle tree and looked at the bland, unvexed sky, thinking of nothing but her own unending trouble.

At last Effie rose from her haunches. She raised her eyes and squinted at the sky. "Laws sake! It must be almost five-thirty. I got to hurry home and fix supper for the family." She turned toward the creek and called shrilly to her husband and children. The exertion flushed her cheeks more than usual. The veins in her neck stood out and the bird-shot moles emerged with gradual distinctness.

CHAPTER XL

WHEN the Cleavers had gone Andrew went to his room and changed again to the overalls which he wore about the farm. Below, in her kitchen, Myrtle was building a fire in the stove. She too had changed her clothes, her finery put away, and as he listened Andrew heard the door of the fire box open and close with a metallic clatter. All at once he had a sense of unbearable weariness. His clothes felt oppressive in the heat and damp with his sweat, and his flesh twitched nervously. . . . He would go to the pool and bathe, or he would lie upon the sand in the late rays of the sun. He came through the kitchen where she was, but Myrtle did not look up from her work, nor did she make any sign of recognition.

The sun was far in the west now and there was promise of a fine sky later. The strong, slanting rays of the sun sifted through the leaves of the trees that lipped the pool, and spread on the marsh beneath them, wavering, unexpected designs so transient and so inexplicable that they seemed flashed against the land by a distant mirror grasped in a petulant hand. Mosquito hawks drifted above the pool or skimmed the surface, and to the right a cock yellow hammer sat high in a cypress tree, near his secret nest, and tapped patiently, seeking food.

Andrew stood looking about him for a moment and then he lay upon the bar, his face pressed into his hands. He lay that way, without movement, for a long time. Many things were crowding into his mind from the dark places where he had willed them. He struggled against the compulsion of these things that he wanted to forget, but he was impotent against their power. Before him the pool was tranquil with the first, unwavering shadows of trees. He got up, upon impulse, and took off his clothes. He ran forward and dived into the water, came to the surface again and shook his head, grunting like a porpoise. He swam strongly for awhile, splashing the water with his arms and turning about. Finally he rolled on his back and floated. The hot wind which had blown intermittently all that day began again, and the bay trees lining the bank lifted upward under its insistence and broke into patterns of running silver. He looked at the young, agitated trees above him, aware dimly of their beauty, but not caring, until the gust subsided and they were lifeless and limp again. He stood upright in the shallow water near the sand bar and raised his eyes to heaven, questioning it as if he wanted to find guidance there, but all he could tell surely was that the sky was blue, all one color.

Above him on the knoll Myrtle was preparing supper. Two threads of smoke rose from the chimney, one pale gray and one pale blue. These threads touched each other for an instant, clung, drew away and touched again, and wrinkled imperceptibly into nothingness. As Andrew stood watching the unmixed, entwined smoke and thinking his thoughts, a feeling of terror at things unblended, and yet joined together, a sense of the inherent evil that lay in himself and in all men, lifted upward from the dark places of his being and he trembled. Chill came over him. He came out of the water, put on his clothes and beat his arms against his chest, but the faint iciness persisted. He began to move about aimlessly, without direction, trying to bring warmth to his blood again, but not succeeding.

He stopped suddenly and touched his mutilated mouth. He spoke aloud: "I see his face the last thing before I go to sleep at night; I see it the first thing when I wake up in the morning. There's no sense in condemning myself so completely. . . . There was a foreman in the planer mill one time who was supposed to inspect the machinery to see that everything was as safe as possible for the workmen. He got careless after awhile, and when he thought nothing would ever happen a belt broke and killed one of the feeders. Nobody said the foreman was a murderer; they couldn't even say for sure that it wasn't an accident that couldn't have been helped, no matter what he did, or how often he inspected the belt. Afterwards the foreman went on just like he had before, joking and laughing like other people." He walked up the slope, past the burying ground and through the trees, a sense of relief in his heart, for he knew now that he was going to tell people what he had done. When he reached the house, Myrtle was setting the table for supper. She turned and looked at him, and then went on with her work, and Andrew drew back, helpless before her unending contempt.

"Folks at Tarleton's were all talking about Jim. There's no use in trying to hide it any longer."

Myrtle did not answer at once. She stood by the kitchen table, a pitcher of water held thoughtfully in her hand. She felt, then, how little she knew about him, and how foreign his reactions and motives were to her own; that he belonged to the incomprehensible older generation which included her father and her mother, and which she never expected to understand.

"They're talking about the Delta Field most of all. They're all wondering why I left that unploughed patch in the middle." She walked to the stove, lifted the lid and threw in a piece of wood. She set the kettle on to boil. "I told you to plough all that field, but you wouldn't listen to the common sense I tried to tell you."

"People are hinting that we know more about Jim than we let on. . . . What they are hinting at today, they'll be saying for a fact tomorrow. I'm going down to the road now and tell the straight of it."

Myrtle turned her back and went on with her cooking. "I told you to plough that whole field, and to plant it too. I told you the first thing folks would spot would be them dry stalks, but you wouldn't listen to me. You wanted everybody to know about Jim and to drag me through all that mud."

Andrew sat down on a chair and looked at the uneven, pine floor which Myrtle had so recently scrubbed white. "I tried to plough it, but I couldn't do it. I couldn't plough over Jim; not with him buried face upward. I shouldn't have buried him face upward." He got up and went to the door, leaning against it.

"Little good telling will do now. We'll have to think of something else." She went to the table where he had piled the supplies he had bought that afternoon at Tarleton's and unwrapped the separate parcels, dropping string and paper onto the floor. He bent down at once, smoothed out the paper with his trembling hands, and folded it neatly for some further use, winding the loose string about his thumb and index finger and securing it in a precise loop. "I'm going to do it now," he said. "I won't bring you into it. There's no reason why you should be affected; I'll swear you didn't know that I was going to kill Jim, which will be true enough."

"Drink some coffee," said Myrtle. "I'll have it ready in a minute. You've got some sort of a rigor."

Andrew shook his head. He walked out of the kitchen and into the yard. On the road puffs of red smoke still rose above the crêpe-myrtle trees, but less frequently now, as the last people returned from Tarleton's store to their homes. He watched the puffs for a moment and then walked through the oak grove, and stood by the roadside. In the distance two brown mules drawing a green wagon were approaching. When the wagon was almost abreast of him he straddled the middle of the road and held up his hand. Holm Barrascale pulled up his team in surprise, but he did not speak, while his wife, Alice, turned her whole bent body with one motion to stare at the figure before them.

"What's the matter, Andrew?" she asked. "Have you took a chill?"

338

Andrew held onto the side of the wagon and clamped his jaws to end the chattering of his teeth. "Listen to what I say. Listen carefully, and tell the sheriff: Jim didn't run off to Mobile that Saturday night, because I killed him. I buried him in the middle of the Delta Field. I'll wait until the sheriff comes for me."

Holm Barrascale jumped out of his wagon and came to Andrew, and the Barrascale grandchildren stared with their mouths open, unable to take in the meaning of the words they heard. Andrew said: "I don't know why I'm trembling so, but it's not because I'm afraid. I'm willing now to take my punishment."

An automobile had driven up during that time and Andrew repeated his story to Addie Wrenn and her husband Ed. Addie's tiny mouth drew tight, and the fine, radiating lines that surrounded it stood out distinctly.

"Myrtle didn't have anything to do with the killing," said Andrew. "She didn't know what was in my thoughts when she called me that night. She is in no way to blame, and I want that understood."

Addie said: "Andrew! Andrew! You're out of your mind. You don't know what you are saying!" She, too, got out and came to him, putting her frail arm about him. She turned to Russ Dixey and his family, who had driven up at the same time, and stood listening. "I for one don't believe a word of what he says!" she repeated. "It's not possible. Why, I was in the room when Andrew was born, and I helped nurse him when he was a baby. . . . I don't believe a baby like that could do such a thing. I don't believe one word of it!"

"I did it, all right, and I did it alone. There's no doubt there." He walked away, went back to the gate beside the barn and stood there. He had nothing further to tell these people. When he looked at the road again he saw that Lafe Cornells had driven up and that Holm Barrascale and Russ Dixey were talking to him excitedly. In an hour everybody in the county would know the story.

Later that night they would come to take him. He rested his trembling body against the fence. . . . Let them come quickly! They couldn't come too soon!

Myrtle met him at the steps, a dishcloth in her hand. "What's done is done," she said. "You didn't do anybody any good by telling." She went back into her kitchen and began setting the table. "Come inside and eat your supper," she said. "You'll need a hot supper!"

He shook his head and stood looking at her in surprise, realizing, all at once, that she was no longer of the least importance to him, as if her small and personal condemnation was already swallowed up and lost in the larger contempt that the whole county must soon feel for him. His trembling stopped and he felt very calm, very sure of himself for the first time since Jim's death.

"You needn't try to let me out of it," said Myrtle, "because I aim to take my full share of blame. I promised to stick by you and I'll do it. I'll go on the stand for you and I'll tell everything that happened between me and Jim from the very first. I'd almost ruther die than to do anything so shameful, but that's what I'm going to do if they bring you to trial."

Andrew turned away from the stove, and walked to the barn, no clear purpose in his mind. When he reached it, old Babe came out of her stall and sniffed him, and Andrew put his arms about her neck, rubbing her ageing withers. The sun was well down now, and the colors of the sky had faded to grays and pinks, like a diminished flame seen through new wood ashes, but in the barn it was so dusky that the stalls and the cribs melted and flowed together. He walked out of the barn at length, closed the door behind him and sat on the bench beside the wall. He smiled to himself and rubbed his hands together, for he felt whole again, and it seemed to him that he was starting his life once more on a firmer basis. He was, he thought, like those dry Jerusalem plants which peddlers sold at fairs, which, when placed in a glass of

—

water, unfold their leaves and come miraculously to life before a man's unbelieving gaze.

Myrtle came out of the house and walked through the yard, her large hips vibrating, her breasts lifting upward like pine cones under the flimsy covering of her dress. Her hair had become loosened of its pins and hung about her shoulders, and her full, humid lips were half opened. She reached the fence and stopped there, and looked at him with her hard, undecided eyes for a moment before she turned her head and stared in the direction of the Reedyville road.

To the east, behind the trees that marked the limits of the Cornells' land, a moon colored like an orange was rising. The moon seemed caught in the web of the trees and unable to escape them, until, imperceptibly, it lifted clear of the entangling branches and swung upward, washing the woodland and the quiet fields evenly with a yellow light.

CHAPTER XLI

THERE were people running toward the patch from all directions: through the oak grove, from behind the house, over the footbridge that spanned the creek, across the blossoming cotton. Three men came up to Myrtle. they carried lanterns in their hands, but the brightness of the moon made it unnecessary to light them. Myrtle turned her head slowly and recognized Lister Wentworth, sheriff of Pearl County, with two of his deputies.

"I came to arrest Andrew Tallon for the confessed murder of his brother," said Lister. "It'll be better for everybody if he don't make any trouble."

People were crowding behind Lister, a multitude of people, their faces eager with their excitement, their breathing quick and audible. Myrtle lifted her arm and brushed back her dangling hair. "There he is," she said, pointing to the bench by the barn. "Go take him, if you want him so bad!" She puffed out her lips and stood insolently, her hands on her hips. "He killed Jim protecting me. He did it in self-defense, and I'll testify to that in court. . . . Arrest him, if you want to go to that trouble, but you'll only have to turn him loose before the week is out."

"Save it, lady!" said Lister. "You'll have a chance to tell the judge all that later on. Save it. It'll all keep."

"Then you can take me too," said Myrtle. "Wait a minute until I fix my hair and put on my hat." She shrugged and walked through the crowd, looking neither to the right nor the left, until she reached her house and entered it.

Immediately the gaping people began to talk excitedly and to gesticulate, going over this or that bit of half-forgotten evidence, remembering everything now and putting everything in its proper sequence. They were still talking together after Lister had taken his prisoners away, crowded against the rails that fenced the unploughed patch, staring fixedly at the square of dry, last year's stalks as if they expected other and more shocking crimes to reveal themselves to their eyes. Edna Cleaver came past the gate and walked toward the field. When she reached it, she stood on the far side, apart from the crowd. She lifted her egg-like face to the full moon and folded her thin arms across her breasts.

"Poor little Edna," said Miss Sarah sententiously. "She was so fond of her Uncle Andrew, and I know her heart must be torn now with every conflicting emotion."

"I could believe it of *anybody* else," said Addie Wrenn, "of anybody else in the county. . . . But Andrew! I can't take it all in, even now!"

"I'm going over and talk to Edna," said Miss Sarah. "I feel it's my duty. I'm going to tell her that she must *not* become embittered, and that she must resign herself to the bludgeonings of our Merciful Father."

She walked away, her eyes distorted behind their thick lenses, her neck thrust forward as she stepped cautiously. The watching people saw her approach Edna and began to talk. Edna turned after a moment and looked at Miss Sarah with rapt astonishment. She pressed her damp hands together and smiled the agonized smile of a medieval saint taking the impact of his first arrow. Her lips moved wryly, and when she finished her speech she turned from Sarah Tarleton and walked to the road. Sarah went back to her group. Her old face had a twitched, uncertain expression, as if she suppressed a sneeze with the expenditure of too great an effort.

"What did she say to you, Sarah?" asked Addie Wrenn.

"First she laughed in my face when I tried to console her, then

343

she said that in her opinion people weren't fit to eat slops out of the same trough with hogs."

The group of substantial, excited people surrounding Sarah gave a gasp of shocked astonishment.

"What did you say then?" asked Alice Barrascale. "What did you tell her?"

"What did I *say?*" repeated Sarah in surprise. "What did you expect me to say as a God-fearing, Christian woman? . . . I denied her words, of course! I said people *were!*"

The district attorney could make no case against Myrtle, and she was released after a short interval in the Reedyville jail. She testified at Andrew's trial, and when it was over she left Pearl County and has not been seen there since. There were good minor witnesses for the State, each called to establish a single fact in the tangled relationship which had existed between Myrtle Bickerstaff and the Tallon brothers, but the prosecuting attorney, doubtful of his case from the beginning, expected little from them.

The actual circumstances of the crime, and the events which had immediately preceded it, were not disputed, for both the prisoner and Myrtle had recounted them with a completeness of detail which had left the people of Pearl County, who packed the court room, with their mouths opened in shocked excitement. The evidence of other witnesses tallied with unimpeachable exactness and supported minutely the story of the principals in the case, and the prosecuting attorney was less interested now in discovering new facts than he was in reinterpreting, in the interest of justice, the material already on the record. . . . If the State was to sustain its charge of first degree murder, and if the crime was one punishable by death, then the important duty before him was to establish, somehow, the premeditated intent to kill that it claimed. It was May MacLean who obliquely created this inference for him.

344

She had been called to reconstruct the meeting between Myrtle and Jim in the drug store, when to the surprise of the prosecutor a few chance questions drew out the fact that Jim had visited her only a short time before his death, and had spoken of his fears and of his reasons for leaving the county. She had been sitting at the time with her hand resting on the arm of the witness chair, her right leg already extended, for her expected testimony had been given and she was ready to get up at the word of dismissal and resume her seat.

The prosecuting attorney, not quite knowing what next to do, opened one of his law books and stared with complete concentration at the blank piece of paper which his clerk had inserted in the volume as a marker, pursing his lips knowingly. To cover his silence, while he thought, he said at random the first thing that came into his mind:

"Did you ever see Jim Tallon to speak to after he threw you over and married Myrtle Bickerstaff?"

"Yes, sir. I saw him one time after that, to speak to."

"When was that, as nearly as you now remember?"

"It wasn't so long before he got murdered. It was about a week, maybe it was two weeks, before Christmas; anyway, it was on a Thursday night, because Papa had gone to lodge meeting."

The prosecuting attorney rearranged his files and again stared with concentration at the blank sheet of paper before him, nodding his head, as if May's words checked precisely, so far, with information already in his possession. He tapped his teeth with his pencil, undecided whether or not to pursue this slight lead, as profitless, no doubt, as the others.

"Where did this meeting with the murdered man take place?"

"It took place at home, but I talked to him down at the gate. He knocked on my window just when I was about to go to bed, and said he'd come to tell me good-bye, because he had to go away. Mamma came out after a little and run him off the place."

345

"What did Jim Tallon say to you on that night?"

"He acted funny, like he'd been drinking, but he said he hadn't."

"What did he say to you on that occasion?"

"I didn't believe what he said, but it turned out later that Mamma had been listening behind the window to most of it, but she couldn't decide whether it was true or not."

"What did the dead man, James Tallon, say to you that night?"

"I told him at the time that I might believe it of Myrtle, but not Andrew. It wasn't possible to believe such a thing of Andrew, because he wouldn't hurt a fly."

The face of the district attorney became red with exasperation. He raised his voice to a shout and banged on the table with his fist.

"Did Jim Tallon say he feared for his life and that was why he had to leave? . . . Answer yes or no!"

"He said that, yes! . . . That's part of what he said, but I didn't believe him. I didn't take him seriously at the time. I knew Andrew too well."

"Never mind what you thought," said the prosecutor. "Repeat Jim Tallon's words for the jury as nearly as you can!"

"Jim said a lot of things that he didn't really believe. He was like that, and if you'd known Jim too you'd understand what I mean, and not be asking me these questions."

She was a frightened and an unwilling witness, and after a moment she began to cry, twisting her handkerchief in her hands; although once she had started, she repeated Jim's words as nearly as she could remember them; but before she had finished, the attorney for the defense rose to object to the admission of such hearsay evidence, and the judge sustained the motion, ordering what Jim had told May MacLean of his fears stricken from the record, and expunged from the brains of both the jury and the people of the crowded court room as well.

The trial had taken on a new interest with the beginning of

346

May's unanticipated testimony and her audience leaned forward in their eagerness to listen, nudging each other significantly with their elbows, for she had cleared up several points which had lain unsolved in their minds, and they nodded their head significantly. May was a truthful, respectable girl, as they all knew, and there was no reason why she should lie, or testify unfairly against Andrew. On the contrary, she had every reason to dislike Jim after the way he had treated her and to hate Myrtle, who had supplanted her in his affections. If she wanted to lie, it would be the other way around. . . .

Andrew sat with his head bowed, his hands pressed together with fingers interlocked, hearing these damaging things from his brother's lips. After awhile the actual words no longer registered on his brain and he saw only Jim's body pressed against the pillows of his bed, the lock of black hair falling wing-like with his broken neck, the firelight flickering across his coy, lowered face and giving it a semblance of life. He leaned back in his chair and closed his eyes, understanding the expression in Jim's face at last, for it seemed to him at that moment that his brother smiled triumphantly in death and that he was saying: "You thought you could kill me and then go free, didn't you, but I have anticipated everything, as you see. I haven't yet lost the power to get what I want from you or to bend you to my will. . . . You were a fool to think you could escape me."

When the evidence had all been given, the district attorney began his summary to the jury. This was, he said, a simple case of simple people and one so uncomplex in motivation that it hardly justified the expense the State had gone to in examining so many witnesses. He had, as they knew, served the public conscientiously for many years, but in all his time of office, nothing quite so obvious, so open-and-shut, had ever been brought before him. The prisoner had confessed, and the actual details of the murder were not disputed: the jury's duty in this instance was merely to determine the *degree* of guilt; but the learned judge, in his charge later on, would undoubtedly give them explicit instructions in that respect, informing them of the several alternative verdicts that were possible in the circumstances. But there was one thing that he, in his distasteful duty as a prosecutor wanted to emphasize: they were to disregard the evidence of the witness MacLean, for the learned judge had excluded it from the record as hearsay and inadmissible; they were to disregard that damning piece of evidence, no matter how true it was, or how greatly it had impressed them.

He went to his table and riffled the pages of his books. He adjusted the black, flowing tie that he wore and touched his pudgy forefinger to the deep cleft in his chin. He felt, he said, from a close study of the case in hand, that the murdered man had known for some time before his death of his brother's evil intentions toward him and faced with this dilemma he had thought it better to give up his wife, the undoubted object of his brother's lust— as amply proven by the obscene poems he had written to her— and leave the county, rather than report the guilty man to the police. He, the prosecuting attorney, was not satisfied with the part Myrtle Tallon had played, but there was no evidence to show that she actually participated in the crime. The most that could be proven against her was that she had become the mistress of the prisoner after her husband's murder. Whether or not she had been the prisoner's mistress all the time was one of the points which had not been entirely cleared up; at any rate, the witness Myrtle Tallon had denied such a thing, but they, the jury, as men of the world, would know how to value the evidence of a wanton woman who had confessed adultery on at least one occasion. . . . In his own opinion, much of the testimony of both the prisoner and his odalisque regarding their intimate relationship had been a tissue of cleverly woven lies.

The people of Pearl County turned at this moment and stared fixedly at Myrtle. They did not know what an odalisque was, nor with which foreign and shocking perversion it was bracketed, but they hoped to discover the meaning of the word in her stolid face.

A moment later a more personal note came into the district attorney's summary, and he spoke huskily, his voice pleading: "I am a humane man like yourselves," he said, "with a wife and family of my own, but I must do my duty to the State and to the high office I hold. This duty is at times a distasteful and unpalatable one, and it carries with it serious and weighty responsibilities. I have not shirked these responsibilities of office in the past, nor will I do so now, since I act with a clean and unsoiled conscience. For many years in my work I have made a deep and profound study of felons and I say and affirm to you now, with no fear of contradiction, that I have learned and mastered completely the workings of the criminal mind and that I have every detail of his warped psychology at my finger tips. I am not boasting to you, my friends, nor speaking with braggadocio; it is only natural that a man whose life work is the bringing of malefactors to justice should know every dark and opaque spot of the human heart before condemning it." His voice suddenly took on a more matter-of-fact tone. "Had I been derelict and remiss in my duty, had I neglected to learn from observation these things which you gentlemen in pleasanter and happier professions are not expected to know, I could not make the request that I am about to make of you, for otherwise I would be more criminal and depraved than the insensitive murderer who sits before you waiting judgment." His voice had become rounded and rolling again. He took out a handkerchief and wiped his forehead to the line of his extravagantly roached hair and resumed. "You of the jury as decent citizens can take my word for this, but if you doubt me, you have only to look into the prisoner's guilty face, because there is nothing obscure and hidden about this case; it is a situation as old as the hills. Andrew Tallon wanted his brother's wife and he was not content until he had planned his deed and murdered that affectionate brother in cold blood! I am familiar with these situations and I give you my assurance that is what happened. . . . That, in my opinion, is what all the evidence in this case boils down to at last, and I ask you to do your duty as I am doing mine. I ask for the conviction of Andrew Tallon on the charge of first degree murder, and I ask for his life as a forfeit for his crime." He paused and pressed the tip of his finger against the deep cleft in his chin, well satisfied on the whole at the manner in which he had handled this unpromising case. He turned to the table and shuffled his papers for a moment, refreshing his memory with the lines he had discovered the night before in his dictionary of well-known quotations. He cleared his throat, faced the jury again and concluded: "There's little else for me to say. The matter rests now in the hands of you gentlemen, but I would like to end and conclude my summary with the words of that great, English poet, Lord Albert Tennyson, whose name is so familiar and well known to us all:

"Go now, my friends, and strike, for you are just;
Strike dead those men who like a race of worms
Rise up and kill their brothers in the dust,
They are not worthy to live!"

He smiled with self-depreciation at the jury, raised his hands outward and bowed his head. "I have changed the wording of the quotation a little, as you will recognize at once, to make it fit the present situation," he said apologetically; "but the poet's meaning remains the same."

It did not take the jury long to find Andrew Tallon guilty, nor for them to give the prosecuting attorney the gift that he asked. The judge sentenced him in due course, and he was executed the following October.